Great Tabaihs Sea

Kdyne

Port Regael ★ Navarrian Hills

Havarre

Timaru Desert

Coligny

Beacon's Bluff

Beggar's Bay

Fehrael

Telos Isle

West Agaes Mountains

South Fehrael

Cape Bede

Orhe

Nantes

Brefi

Farne

Ghent

Donegal

Emden

East Agaes Mountains

Breda

Gaspard's Field

Inner Realm

Coragaes Pass

Brazenose

Diachrieno River

Nik ≈ 1.5 centimeters

Rod ≈ 1.5 meters

Span ≈ 1.5 kilometers

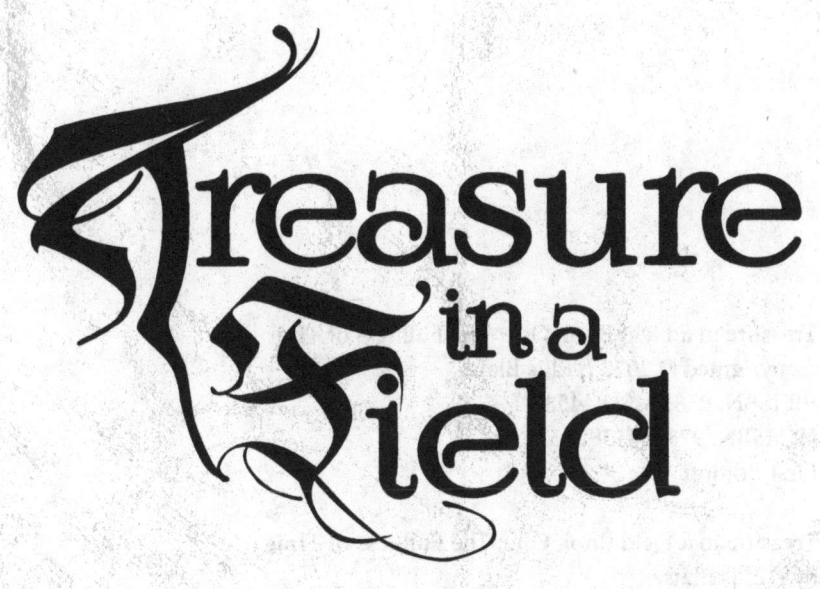

~Book One~

The Fullness of Time

J. Ellis Blaise

Ten|16
PRESS

www.ten16press.com - Waukesha, WI

Treasure in a Field Book One: The Fullness of Time
Copyrighted © 2023 J. Ellis Blaise
PB ISBN: 9781645384458
HC ISBN: 9781645385653
First Edition

Treasure in a Field Book One: The Fullness of Time
by J. Ellis Blaise

For information, please contact:

www.ten16press.com
Waukesha, WI

Editor: Jenna Zerbel
Cover Designer and Illustrator: Draženka Kimpel
Spine & Back Cover Design: Kaeley Dunteman
Interior Designer: Jayden Shambeau

To Denise, Bailey, Holly, Wesley, and Jessi.
"Who is on the Spotify?"

And to Grant Delzer (2000–2022)
"Here's to the adventure!"

Acknowledgments

While this list is far from exhaustive, here are some of the key players: Jenna Zerbel and the Orange Hat team, Drazenka Kimple, Livia Gonzalez, Diana Schramer, Carol Paur, Paula Payton, Patti Hanson, Karyn Sarmann, Fulton Varsity Club, Dan Buschmann, Karen Reed, "the Letterheads", Deb Siri Johannes, Lori Mulsoff, Jean Buchanan, Lisa Petrocilli, Lynna Buck, Lindsey Slater, SCBWI, Mocha Moment, American Printing, and Grimm.

Thank you all!

Table of Contents

The Trouble with Dark Magic

Prologue

ela's body jerked heavily as she caught herself. Dangling by one hand, her right arm twisted and strained. Stifling a scream, she clenched the braided rope, even as it burned into her palm. She peered down over her shoulder. Far below, torches illuminated swirling snow and whirling courtyards. *No! No! I will not fail. The Underground has entrusted me with this task. I cannot fail.* Her long legs flailed, sweeping the rounded stone tower and fighting to recover a foothold. Bela goaded herself, *I will not fall, I will not fail!*

She swung her free arm above her head, got hold of the rope, and pulled hard with both hands. Large flakes of snow bit at her cheeks. Bumping the bossed stone, she found a toehold. She gritted her teeth and vowed, *King Ninian will not capture me too!* Back in control, she released one hand and reached for the end of the rope that dangled below her. In a swiveling movement, she looped and tied it around herself. *If I slip again, at least I'll be caught up in a tangle of rope and not end up a pile of broken bones in the castle gardens.* Confident, she continued her climb.

Bela had begun her ascent at the beginning of the second watch, climbing the southeast side of the northernmost tower. It felt like an hour had passed, but the magic into which she climbed did have a way of confusing the senses. Several more well-placed steps, and she rose above four other towers surrounding her. Her dark, loose-fitting clothing allowed her full extension of her limbs and, she prayed, stealth.

To the north, lanterns dotted the immense stone structure that guarded the bay at Port Regael. The colossal statue of King Gaspard erected above the structure—dauntingly silhouetted against the night sky—fortified her allegiance. King Ninian had recently completed a statue of himself off the coast of Orhe Mireth. He began to overlay his monument in gold to do one better than Gaspard but only completed the head and upper torso before depleting his resources. *Incomplete, like his reign!*

Bela did not fear the heights or that she had almost fallen to her death. She did, however, fear the evil magic—the sorcery that guarded the top of the tower. Climbing into a dormire spell was a lot like climbing high in the Agaes Mountains. With every foothold, she took two breaths, each long and labored. But she continued to climb, pulling against gravity and pushing ahead into thick magic. Like an invisible fog, the spell was dense, and the metallic taste in her mouth only intensified as she drew nearer to the top of the tower—another sure sign of dormire.

Her head drooped forward. She jerked it back, and her sight went into a spin. Closing her eyes, Bela counted to three, inhaled, and shook her head but was unable to clear her foggy senses. Looking up through blurry eyes, she gained some semblance of focus and pressed on.

Reaching the parapet, icy wind slapped her face and stole her breath. She stretched her slender arms taut and pulled herself through a crenel in the battlement. Twisted in her rope, she fell limp into a thin layer of snow atop the tower. With her chest tightening, she struggled for oxygen that was not there.

Sleep it off.

You would do well to rest now.

Voices swelled like mist and floated around her. Or were they her own thoughts?

You never should have come.

A foolish young woman like you will never outlast the spell!

Sophia is already dead, and you will die beside her!

Like a cloak, silence fell over her and a hush pushed against her ears. In that quiet space, Sophia—her mentor and teacher—whispered words that Bela recalled from her tutelage, *"The trouble with dark magic is that it will deceive you. It would have you lie down and rest, only to strangle you in your sleep. Break through, for you must keep moving."*

Her mind, though wrenched, was impelled to resist the spell—a deflection of sorts. *An unexpected gift from Sophia?* Bela felt a sudden shove against her ribs, as if someone were begging her to move. Bela twisted, her joints stiffened, and her body ached. She pushed herself onto hands and knees and crawled from the rope. Straining to lift her head, she fought against the weight of the spell and looked ahead through a flurry of snow.

"Sophia!"

Sophia lay motionless, chained to the top of the tower. Strands of her greying ginger hair whipped and knotted in the wintry wind. The rags of a white gown left much of her skeletal frame exposed to the elements. Bela lunged forward and cradled Sophia's head in her arms. Sophia's face, long and ashen, turned toward Bela, but her eyes remained closed, and she spoke not a word.

"Oh, my dear friend," Bela whispered. "Let's get you out of here."

Tones of Home

1

If your heart is cold, you'll find no hope, young Wesley!" A sturdy voice jostled his attention. With his legs dangling off the back of the wagon, Wesley looked up. He knew that voice; it was Olivetan, a commander in King Ninian's army, riding up on his russet steed. Wesley's heart rallied at the sight of him! He admired the confidence in Olivetan's voice and the gentleness of his character. Olivetan reminded him of a gallant person from his family's past, about whom he had heard many stories and dreamt of often—a person whom he had never met, but he had trusted forever…

The horse nickered, shook her head, and released her breath as she slowed, coming up alongside him.

"Yet hope is a gift, Master Olivetan," Wesley replied. "Many keep it as treasure."

"Listen to our sophomoric brother, Philor," Aarn said and slapped Wesley across the back. Wesley splayed his arms to keep himself from falling off the back of the cart but kept silent. He knew better than to play into his brother's banter.

And of course, Philor, Aarn's twin, could only heighten the snide remarks. "Yes, it seems he's delusional, excavating imaginary treasures again." His brothers laughed together, but Wesley ignored them. Seemingly, Olivetan did too.

"Well spoken, young sage," Olivetan said and stroked the silver stubble on his chin. "Your reply seems beyond your years. Tell me, now, how old are you?"

"Nearly fifteen," Wesley said, lifting his chin and straightening his poor posture.

Two other horsemen trotted by and invited themselves into the conversation. "Sorry, boy. Haven't they been feeding you on this journey?" one jeered.

The other nodded and said, "At least he doesn't have to worry about being eaten by pirate trolls." Then the two trotted on, chuckling.

"No, but they may use him for a toothpick!" Aarn called after the soldiers. And with that, Philor just about burst apart in amusement.

Olivetan leaned in and said, "My father always told me, 'Small potatoes, hard to peel.' Never be ashamed of who you are, son."

Wesley smiled widely as he lifted away henna-colored curls dangling before his eyes.

"Now," Olivetan said as he righted himself, "you may want to clean yourself up a bit. I can't tell if that's hay or hair sticking out all over your head."

Wesley bit his lip, and his face warmed. He set to brushing off his dusty, straw-covered clothing, shook his head, and used his fingers as a comb to separate the pieces of his straw bedding from his hair.

Olivetan pointed and continued, "Look ahead! From the top of that hill, we'll be able to see across Beggar's Bay to Fehrael. It won't be long now."

Olivetan rode on, as shouts from over the hill demanded his immediate attention. He led several scouts on horses, and they followed him ahead on the inclined path. Mighty horses clomped past, obediently stepping, adorned with leather tack and shiny steel attachments. Each man wore a stoic face; none of them bothered to notice Wesley. But Wesley examined them carefully—their long dark blue coats, their rigid felt hats. They were suited properly to represent King Ninian. Not to mention their squared chests and threatening scowls—fearless.

Wesley could not help but stare at the sabres on their belts. The sheaths, made of brilliant silver, were half the height of a soldier and engraved with the kings' insignia—two lines woven together, looping on the ends, stretching up and down diagonally toward the center, crisscrossing and coming together again. Each side was a mirror image of the other—the emblem for the co-regency of Nantes, two kings ruling as one. And Wesley noticed now that the symbol was also burned into the stocks of their rifles.

The imminent threat of pirate trolls pilfered his thoughts. Before these last few days, he had only feared the bears that roamed Nantes. But at least they were indigenous, and for the most part they left people alone. The trolls were unnatural, contrived by a spell. He had heard the other boys tell stories about how trolls can hear a whisper from twenty spans away, and they said that a troll's head could spin completely around!

Traveling south, the wagon Wesley rode on was one of many in the caravan carrying young men and boys who volunteered their service for King Ninian. Wesley shared his rickety ride with five others, two of whom were his coarse and slightly older twin brothers, Philor and Aarn. His oldest brother, Derian, remained at home to care for his sisters and the farm.

Philor and Aarn did not pay Wesley much attention. He knew

that they too were uneasy about what might lie ahead, but they hid it well. The other three boys were about the same age as the twins, but unlike his brothers, their apprehension was evident as they drew back into the corners of the wagon, chins down and hands clenched.

Wesley bumped along and slid sideways to steady himself against a sideboard. To the west towered a stone wall, hanging over them like storm clouds. Comparable to the height of their barn back home, he would have guessed it be about fifteen rods high. It stretched out as far as he could see in front of and behind him.

The ancient wall outlined the kingdom of Nantes. It hid from his sight the Greater Tabaihs Sea. Every so often, they rolled past a guard tower built into the wall. An iron door sealed the entrance to steps that led up to a tower. Some of the doors, almost completely covered in vines, looked as if they hadn't been opened in years. Wesley had been told that two guards worked each tower and that they had a meager living space built in below the lookout. Every three days, men moved from tower to tower upon a path along the top of the wall. Doors were used only in more populated areas, where guards checked in and out.

Since leaving Port Regael, shades of the grey wall had darkened Wesley's western gaze. Now, moods of grey darkened his spirit as the boys began to share their distress.

"My father says the king's armada has failed us. The pirate trolls will bring down Nantes," one boy muttered as he crouched in the cart, not even looking up.

In the opposite corner, Aarn flared, "King Ninian may have failed us—that doesn't surprise me. Since King Ninian I, three generations have passed, and the royal line has been incapable of unearthing Gaspard's treasure."

"Now, the third king in the line of Ninian still seeks but cannot find! And he fails to restore the co-regency." Philor persisted, and his eyes lit up as if he had been struck by some surprising new thought. "If only you and I could reign!"

"Yes!" Aarn beat his fists against his chest. "The pirate trolls, they would never take Nantes!"

Beside Aarn, Philor thrust his arm upward. "Those vile beasts will soon feel the might of our battery!"

"Yes!" Aarn agreed. "The might of Gaspard!"

Pricks of heat dotted Wesley's chest, spreading quickly to his neck and face. *Would Aarn be so quick to sever our pact?* To even mention the name of Gaspard in front of Father was worse than not doing one's chores. Even though the royal line of Ninian had searched for an heir, Father would not have his children speak the name of Gaspard and risk any identification with that name. Wesley had never understood why.

The three other boys stared wide-eyed at Aarn. Wesley could hardly believe that his brothers would be so thoughtless. *You idiot, Aarn! What are you doing? Don't be reckless!*

After the silence, one of the boys finally asked, "The might of *Gaspard?* Do you mean *King Gaspard?*"

"Of course," Aarn replied without hesitation. "Gaspard is my—"

"Hero!" Wesley interrupted. "Our duties for Nantes are in his honor and legacy!" He attempted to sound fierce, but his voice slumped.

Aarn scowled at Wesley. "Yes, that's right, *little* brother. He's my... *hero.*" Then he raised a fist, as if threatening Wesley that he had better shut up. Wesley quickly looked away, and his heart grew somber.

"Well, I've heard whispers of evil magic and sorcery," another boy warned.

"I am afraid, too," Wesley attempted to encourage the others as Olivetan did for him. "But we are peacekeepers! By repairing the breach, we maintain the peace Nantes provides. Our mother often spoke of everlasting peace." His words stirred his own excitement.

"We'll send you to negotiate *peace* with the trolls, Wesley," Aarn said. The twins laughed together, enough to even get fleers out of the sullen boys. "We certainly do not come in peace!"

Wesley said no more. He quickly turned his head to wipe a tear and swallowed the lump building in his throat. He thought that *peacekeeper* was a noble title to embrace. Yet, what did he know of everlasting peace? He doubted his own words. Had he held onto an airy confidence? Could peace really last anywhere?

He pushed himself back to keep from slipping off the wagon and turned to view the path ahead. It curved to the east, crossed a river, and went up a hill. From the top of the hill, he hoped to see beyond the wall and get a glimpse of the Greater Tabaihs Sea, maybe even Telos Isle and light from Beacon's Bluff!

But until then, he was awed with the view to the east—a swift river, a field of wild grasses, and then mountains upon mountains, some reaching beyond the clouds. In the Navarrian Hills near his home, the mountains were enormous. But these mountains dwarfed them. Some of the men spoke about how the mountains grew larger the farther south one traveled. Wesley had not believed it until he saw it for himself—and they had only traveled a couple of days out from Port Regael.

Waterfall after waterfall spanned high, spraying mist across the valleys. Vast forests, thick and deep, surrounded and climbed the mountains. The late afternoon sun lit the rims of slate-colored clouds in fiery pink. The entire landscape had a warm glow. Wesley sat a bit taller knowing that their mission to repair the breach was helping to secure Nantes from a hostile World Over.

Again, he thought of Olivetan's encouragement. In this, he found courage—a courage he had felt before through the stories his mother shared of his great-grandfather, King Francis Gaspard. This was why Wesley was so eager to see Olivetan each day on this journey. Although he never met his great-grandfather, Olivetan reminded Wesley of him, which then led to thoughts of his mother and, of course, home.

Wesley's thoughts took him back to the farm and how he wound up on this journey far from it. Just three days ago, he had been home.

2

ome was in the hill country of Navarre, in the northwestern region of Nantes.

By cart it was about a two-hour journey east of the capital city, Port Regael. Surrounded by clear streams and incredibly high mountains, Wesley lived in a fieldstone cabin with his father, three brothers, and two sisters. Mother was sorely missed. It seemed he needed her now more than ever. *How long does it take to unfeel the ache of losing someone?* Worries and anxieties stirred around dark spaces inside of him, making it difficult to find rest in his questions.

Three years earlier, his mother, Sophia, had died.

When Mother was alive, her love had filled their lives like light on a sunny day. She never seemed to grow tired, her eyes were sharp and inviting, and her words always timely, sensible, and bold. It was never clear in Wesley's mind how she had died. His father refused to talk about it, and he did not permit the children to talk about it either. It seemed that it pained him too much. In the evenings, Father would sit and stare with muddled eyes, watching the rocker where Mother used to knit. Wesley felt that he understood his father's pain. For years, he winced as he recalled Mother brushing the long, red hair of his youngest sister, Jess.

When Mother passed, his family had been living somewhere just north of Brazenose. Only a day or two after her death, they moved north. Taking only what they could carry, they left hours after the sun had set. Father explained that they could not risk being seen but did not say why.

It took at least four nights of traveling through the dark to reach Breda. Wesley remembered hiding in the foliage as his oldest brother, Derain, pulled on Father's old cloak and lifted the hood to cover his face. On the roadside, seemingly far from any village, Derian purchased bread, cheese, and dried meat from strangers. Immediately after getting the necessary supplies, they pushed back into the dense wood, where they ate and then slept until the sun went down.

Their days had followed this same pattern until they found a home in the Navarrian Hills. After settling in, Wesley discovered a small cemetery only a short walk away from the farm. He set up a cairn for his mother but kept it to himself. It had been a comforting place to go, where Wesley could speak to her as if she were still with him.

"Mother, will you tell me again of your grandfather?" Wesley would ask his mother before bed when he was much younger.

"Yes," he could hear her say. "Your great-grandfather, King Gaspard, was co-regent of Nantes. King Gaspard discovered the treasure in a field, a treasure that will set all things right. And so, he sold all he had and bought that field."

"He sold *everything*?" Wesley would say.

"All but his braies," Mother replied, and together they would laugh.

"But he never returned?"

"No, son. King Gaspard disappeared, and the royal line of King Ninian still searches for an heir to restore the co-regency."

"And the treasure?"

"Ninian seeks the treasure, as well."

"But can we not help? With Great-Grandfather's writings, could we not restore the co-regency and lead the way to the treasure? My brothers and I as heirs to the throne…What celebration there would be!"

He had spoken to his mother often about the secrets their family kept.

And Mother would remind him, "It is not to be until the…"

"…the Fullness of Time." Wesley would finish her sentence.

"Until then, we wait in silence."

Wesley dug his knuckle into the corner of his eye. He had not slept well in the cart. Though he kept his ambitions quiet, like his brothers, his own zeal for the kingdom fought against his obligation to secrecy. He dreamed often of finding the treasure himself. Lifted high, he would ride into Port Regael, treasure in tow. Derian would step aside and offer his place on the throne as a reward. His brothers would serve him. *That would be the Fullness of Time!*

With the "royal parchments," as he and his siblings called them, handed down from Great-Grandfather, Wesley's mother had taught him to read. Large, ornate initials began pages of careful, unbroken letters, enclosed in colorful braided borders. Like his mother, Wesley treasured those writings. Often, he could be found reading after everyone else had long been asleep. It was as if the writings had a life of their own.

I wonder if Father secretly looks at the writings after we have all gone to sleep...

After the death of their mother, Father had not been the same. Nothing seemed to move him to joy. Abandoning the old stories, he disconnected himself from the children, and they felt the strain. But it was more than Mother's death alone. William had been working in the mines for seventeen years, and he looked like it—sunken eyes, drooping face, and sagging shoulders. His days were spent in dark caverns, and he returned home long after sunset. Avlae said that Mother had long spoken of Father's despair. Without her, his dark days were even more barren.

Yet, Wesley knew that their father's role as a miner did more than provide for his family; it ensured the security of their land. Under King Ninian III, William mostly worked the copper mines. Copper and iron ore were the main exports of Nantes. And several months ago, gold was found in some secret place that Father called the *Inner Realm*. Wherever that was, his father was not allowed to say. When they had arrived in the Navarrian Hills, William took a position close to home mining saltpeter, the main ingredient in gun powder, found on the northwest side of the Timaru desert.

Wesley thought back a few days, before this mission began, to when he still had a family routine and Avlae's counsel. Chores on their small farm, running through the apple orchards, and jumping into the creek had been replaced with sleepless nights in a wagon. Sure, back home he'd still had to put up with his brothers' banter, but at least things were normal. Or so he thought.

Three days ago, on the morning that he and his siblings had

left home for Port Regael, Father refused to join them. Father's voice repeated itself in Wesley's ears, saying, "Port Regael does not welcome me, son. It pains me even to consider going. Many things I have forgotten, and I do not care to recall. And many of the things I do remember keep me away."

Wesley wondered what could have happened to his father when he was a young man. Did he meet Mother in Port Regael? Had he been abandoned by his parents? He knew his father was stuck in some debilitating state of mind. Wesley wondered how his father took the news about the breach. Certainly, he must have heard by now...

The Eve of Enrichment

3

Three Days Ago…

The siblings had had to leave before sunrise in order to arrive early on the narrow, brick streets of Port Regael. It was a two-hour trip, and like any other week throughout growing season, Wesley and his siblings needed to unpack produce in the square before the market opened.

Yet, it was not just another day to sell their goods, as special as those days were to Wesley. They had also come for the merriment, for it was a ceremonial day in Port Regael. "The Eve of Enrichment!" folks were calling it in the city, throughout Nantes, and beyond.

Buyers and sellers filled the square and lined the streets. Stands with exotic spices, jewelry, an assortment of unguents, and medicines attracted overlapping lines of people. Painters and sculptors displayed and sold their work. There were tricksters with cards, jugglers with axes, and men on stilts with long pants. Musicians strummed and sang, echoed by a chorus of off-tune accompanists who danced and cheered and swirled in rhythm.

Overcrowded tents supplied plenty of food and drink. The aroma of bread and roasted game aroused Wesley's hunger. Men laughed, shook hands, and clanked their mugs, spilling ale in the bond of fellowship.

In the distance, Wesley could hear the calling of an auctioneer, the rifles from a tournament, and the bells at the river locks signaling the outgoing tide. The square was wonderfully raucous.

Across several tables of fruit and vegetables, Derian, his eldest brother, shouted, "Wes! See to your sister!"

Immediately, Wesley weighed the situation. An arm's length away, his five-year-old sister Jess had walked out from under the produce stand and into the path of an oncoming horse and cart. After dropping a crate of apples upon the table in front him, Wesley quickly reached for Jess. His sleeve caught the edge of the crate, pulling it off the table and spilling apples all around him and into the street. Wesley lunged forward to catch himself, boots searching for footing among the rolling apples. With his torso splayed across the capsizing table, he rolled, tucked, and spun—then fell onto his back, landing on the rolling apples.

Giddy at the sight of horses, Jess had not noticed his fall. The apples that rolled into the street stole the horses' attention straightaway. The man driving the cart attempted to steer away, but the horses stopped dead in their tracks to enjoy the fragrant fruit only a step away from Jess's outstretched hand. Cooing, she petted the forelock of one of the horses. Pursing her lips, Jess fluttered her best horse imitation. Despite the stinging on his left elbow, Wesley could not help but laugh.

Avlae ran over and scooped Jess into her arms. Derian apologized to the driver and helped Wesley collect apples.

"You've got a pretty bad scrape on your arm," Derian said, sorting out bruised apples.

"It doesn't hurt," Wesley argued. "When can we go?"

"Have Avlae bandage your arm."

"It's fine. I'm missing the festival!"

"Let's see," Avlae said, clenching his arm. "Hold still!"

Just then, a desperate voice called from across the river. "Breach! Breach in the wall at Beggar's Bay! Breach! Breach!" a man cried.

Over the lively crowd of people who filled Fane River Road, Wesley saw him approaching—a guardian of Nantes—riding with urgency, as if an enemy were coming down upon him. He rode in from the southeast, on the opposite side of the narrow river, forcing his way through the crowd. People in his path ducked into the doorways of storefronts on one side, while others fell or jumped into the river.

Wesley pulled his arm away from Avlae and gaped at the frantic rider. Others around him stopped what they were doing and did the same. The horse bolted left and darted over an arched bridge crossing Fane River.

The man was steering the horse with his legs. Wesley knew then that this was a seasoned horseman. He had read many tales about men of this sort. They rode into battle with both arms free to handle their weapons and moved as if attached to their horses. But this man carried no weapons. With one arm, he cradled his mangled other. He rode slouched over the saddle, and his elegant white shirt was torn and bloodied. He struggled to hold up his head of tousled dark hair.

Coming off the bridge, the horse slammed into a baker's cart and kicked up with its front legs. Bread and pastries were flung about but would not go wasted. Children rushed in, scurrying for a share. The baker managed to keep his cart upright but wound up on his bottom, cussing and cursing all the while. The rider leaned toward Wesley and drove hard.

The clatter of hooves rumbled louder, as did his voice. "Breach!" he called out again. Locking eyes with Wesley, the man shrieked, "Breach!"

Cracked lips squared his pale-yellow teeth. The man's eyes evinced unfathomable terror, and in a whirl of dust, the horse thundered past. The wind whipped particles of dirt and grit, stinging Wesley's eyes. Dark clouds invaded the sky behind the rider, as if attached to him by a rope that stretched to the horizon.

Breach? Invasion! We're under attack!

Wesley studied the crowd. One of the king's footmen—in his black, baggy pants—chased after the rider while those along Fane River Road appeared transfixed. Merchants hovered over their wares. Brass bells from several sheep echoed above muted shuffles. After a few minutes, murmurs grew among the masses.

"Derian!" Wesley shouted while spinning. He then collided with his eldest brother.

"Look to the square," Derian replied grimly, twisting his brother back around.

Now several of the king's footmen pushed through the huddles of people. Flat-fronted oval hats pressed over their royal curls. Wesley and Jess had made their own versions of the hats back home—a playful jest. But he was not laughing today.

One of the footmen stepped upon a platform, his tasseled staff and red sash marking his higher rank. His voice carried over the crowd as he addressed the people, "One man's fret need not be ours! It is, after all, the Eve of Enrichment! Do carry on, back to your business! No need for alarm, now. We are well protected!" The footman stood resolute.

A large man—cumbrous with animal hides draped over his

shoulders—teetered up and wiped his frothy beard with his sleeve. Taking another step, his foot got caught under his robe, tripping him forward. He stepped fast and stayed upright but not before spilling ale down the front of the footman. Repulsed, the footman slapped the fool, attracting spouts of laughter from the crowd. Shaking his head, the drunk seemed to be mostly concerned with finding his balance.

The drunken oaf lifted his drink and with a jolly voice bellowed, "Blah! Who's alarmed, sire?"

With that, he pressed open the lid of his flagon and tipped it back, most of the ale missing his mouth. The crowd hollered and cheered, and the revelry resumed along Fane River Road. The high-ranking footman looked at ease, seemingly pleased with his response and the drunkard's antics, which was enough to tip the scales of the crowd's concern back toward celebration.

Wesley jumped back toward Derian. "Do you think the breach will delay our mission?" For months, Wesley had anticipated the expansion of Nantes. He had seen the drawings in the square. Nantes was to be expanded north and east to include the coastal cities of Tumbrel and Palanquin, south beyond Preeve, and many cities between.

"King Ninian will not turn away the thousands who have come to serve," Derian said and went back to stacking empty crates.

"But I didn't volunteer to be sent off to war against an invading army! I came to celebrate and serve by building and extending the wall, to share—"

"—a coveted culture." Aarn puffed up his chest and canted, "Young men and boys have an essential role in the expansion of Nantes!"

"We've all heard the propaganda, Wesley," Philor said and

reached for a wooden bucket. Bending over, he flipped an empty crate and stepped up onto it, placing the bucket on his head and announcing, "Send us your boys to build!" Aarn tossed a broom, which Philor caught and raised as a scepter. "Nantes will grow! Yes, it will grow from an insignificant island at the tip of a peninsula to include many cities, extending up into the mainland. It is the Eve of Enrichment!"

"You mean, the Eve of *Encroachment!*" Aarn laughed hysterically.

"Shut it! We've customers coming!" Avlae demanded. Her brow straightened, and her eyes threatened.

Angrily, Derian kicked the crate out from under Philor, sending him down hard on the bricks and cracking his bucket crown. "You two disgrace our family name!"

Wesley shrank back. Jess pushed in behind him, cautiously watching.

Derian shook his head, then extended a hand to help Philor to his feet. His voice softened, "King Ninian will not fail us. He has counselors and a mighty army." He took a step toward Wesley. "He will not send you off to war. Tonight, at his address, you will hear his intentions to spread peace. Look around you, brother, and take courage." Derian motioned to the crowd.

"Perhaps this is the 'fullness of time'?" Philor quoted from a poem that Mother often read. He was not going to let up. "'The advent of an heir, a moment sublime, to lead from despair at the Fullness of Time.'" He lifted an eyebrow, gave a sneer, and looked at his twin to bolster his claim.

Clenching his jaw, Derian lashed back, "Not another word!"

"Don't you dare mock our mother!" Avlae yelled.

Philor ignored Avlae, stepped closer to Derian, and pressed,

"This may be the time Mother spoke of, the time to make known our birthright."

"A breach in the wall could certainly cause despair," Aarn added with an intellectual flare.

"Indeed, brother," Philor said, nodding quickly with a crooked smile. "And as brothers, we'd rule Nantes. Ninian would have to confer with us!"

Derian's face grew red. "We have been through this. The prophecy speaks of the time when we would all be of age for the crown…"

"That's what *you* decided it meant," Philor leaned in until his chest pushed against Derian. Though younger, Philor had grown several niks taller than his oldest brother. "And should we trust that you alone can interpret the prophecy?" Philor shoved Derian.

Derian leapt forward and grabbed Philor by the shirt. He raged, "You will not mention this again until you have returned from your service to the king! Wesley will be fifteen by then, making us all of age. We will honor our mother, as she honored King Ninian. We will approach the king together. Is that understood?" Derian looked from brother to brother. "Make this pact with me now; we do not speak of this until you three return!" He released Philor with a thrust.

Jess tightened her arms around Wesley's leg.

Philor poised himself to take a swing at Derian, but Aarn stepped in. "What are mere words, Philor?" Aarn looked back to Derian and gave a sinister smile. "We'll make this pact. But be wary, brother. Did Mother not say to hold all things loosely?"

Derian's eyes turned to Wesley.

Wesley nodded. "You have my word."

"You are so callow." Philor laughed and stepped away.

"Are you coming, Wesley?" Aarn asked carelessly as he disappeared into the crowd with Philor.

"May we leave to take part in the festival now?" Wesley asked timidly. Weary of all that had just happened, Wesley needed to get away and sort things out in his head.

Derian tilted his head as if Wesley were neglecting something. "What?"

"Your arm?"

Beside him Avlae stood, bandage in hand, and tended to his wound.

Derian threw his hand out and dropped his chin. "Go on!"

It took Wesley several attempts to loosen Jess's arms, clutched around his leg. He then ran off behind his twin brothers. Bolting through the crowd, Wesley dodged people as he chased after the twins. It was always like this—he was a step or two behind them.

The face of the guardian who spoke of a breach haunted his mind's eye. Frantic, he tried to calm himself. "Find a way to work with your fear. Use it to teach, use it to teach…"

Finally, up ahead, in a green opening bristling with archers and round targets attached to piles of hay, he spotted Philor. The twins were hard to miss, being a head taller than the others. Wesley slowed his pace, composed himself, and stepped over to his brother.

"Philor?" Wesley asked.

"What is it?" Philor slid an arrow out from a leather quiver, took his stance, and drew his bowstring. He released his shot and missed the bullseye by the width of a finger.

"You only missed by a nik!" Wesley was astonished, though he already knew his brother to be a superb hunter. "Can I try?"

"Must you be here? You have the entire festival to enjoy, and yet you stand behind me, stealing my concentration," Philor snapped.

"Derian said not to wander about alone."

"Please, go wander, brother." Philor rolled his eyes and turned to examine the target.

"But do you not remember what Mother used to say?" Wesley interrupted.

Philor hesitated. "Do I dare ask?" He lifted his bow and curled his lip. With a puff of breath, he blew the hair from his eyes and took a stern sighting down his arrow.

"You remember the stories Mother used to tell? She often spoke of magic. And especially at occasions such as this, she said we would see it, feel it."

Philor held his aim and said, "Did you not see that man with the cards? Or the lady with the rings who could tell your fortune?"

"Yes of course, but those are illusions, a mere sleight of hand. Just a cover-up, a trick. Mother warned against that kind of magic," Wesley said.

"Yes, yes, a quick thrill." Philor remained set on the target. "I don't believe in the magic Mother spoke of. She said it gave life, yet she is dead."

"That is not what she meant—"

Philor let his bow fall to his side and hollered, "What is it then, Wesley?" He now had the attention of other archers. Seeing the glares, Philor lowered his voice. "What are you looking for? Go find your magic and leave me to compete!"

Wesley said nothing more. He knew what his mother had said. Spurious magic pulled people in subtly. Many admirers were caught off guard and wooed down a spiraling path of deceit. Mother had

always said it led to the one who embodied such foolishness—
Aphrosyna. Aphrosyna traveled the wind, looking for simple minds
to steal. Stories of her were few, but Mother taught the children
that as a young woman, Aphrosyna raised a boy who became a
sorcerer. And when she grew old, in a desperate move to save her
life, her son the sorcerer transformed her into a malevolent spirit.

It seemed as if all knew the tale, but most only considered it
a legend. Yet, Wesley's mother had always been clear. "Do not
be deceived, for you'll know deep inside what is true and what is
false." He often wondered *how* he would know. Supposedly, the
magic Mother spoke of was easy to see, yet its source was beyond
knowing. It was not to be manipulated like a trick, but rather used
as a guard to keep one from foolishness. Lately, Wesley found that
he had more and more questions of magic—as if he had to solve a
riddle. Mother's teachings were key to his pursuit.

The magic Mother had spoken of was beautiful and tangible and
existed in truth. It did not pretend to be something else. She had
said it shaped joy and peace. The treasure in the field would release
such magic at the Fullness of Time. Until then, there were only bits
and pieces of a mystery that one may see more and more as the
Fullness of Time grew near.

Strange. Will I be able to perceive the pieces? If so, then how?

When he was young, Wesley had believed that he recognized the
true magic Mother spoke of. It seemed he had seen it all the time.
But try as he might, it eluded him for a long time. This unsettled
him. He needed to figure this out. But without Mother to guide
him, he was left to cast about on his own. His brothers were of
no help. Father refused to talk about it. Avlae would only repeat
Mother's warnings.

Despite his misgivings, he considered the woman with the rings. Wesley reasoned that she was likely the only person left with whom he could talk about magic before he was set to leave for his mission in service of King Ninian. *If Mother said I would know true magic apart from magic that was false, then I must test it. The woman with the rings, perhaps she could help me!*

A Lesson in Magic

4

esley found himself next in line. Two girls who seemed to be about his age giggled at the table ahead of him, blocking his view of the fortune-teller. Colorful balls of smoke—jade, blue, and red—lifted above them and burst, covering them in glitter. The girls gazed wide-eyed at each other. Skipping away, sparkles fell from their hair, leaving a trail behind them.

What harm could come of this?

Wesley watched the girls disappear into the crowd before he turned back to the fortune-teller. The woman—hands folded and elbows on the thick, wooden table—tilted her head and nodded at him. White patterns decorated a transparent scarf that shaped her narrow head. Thin, dark brown eyebrows peaked above her diamond eyes. She placed her hands on the table and straightened her head.

Shoved forward by someone, Wesley tripped ahead and caught himself on the table's edge. He ignored the laughter of the testy bullies behind him. The fortune-teller locked eyes with him and remained silent. It was as if she were waiting…

"Oh, yes," Wesley said and threw his hand deep into his pocket. He had planned to purchase a bag of colorful stones, but he needed answers more. Retrieving two small silvers, he dropped them on the table, and the fortune-teller whisked away the coins.

"Your eyes are deep," the woman said in a low tone.

Wesley was not sure what that meant, and his face must have told her so.

"In other words, you are not a simpleton," the woman explained. Her voice floated, soft and smooth, like smoke from an extinguished candle. "You are curious, yet I sense doubt. What do you seek?"

On the table before him, two thin copper-colored rings were attached to each other, like a figure eight, though one was perpendicular to the other. *Do I dare ask?* He stalled, pretending to consider her question. The woman slid her hands close to the rings. Her wrists were adorned with black beaded bracelets, and her long nails were painted silver.

"Magic!" Wesley blurted. "I am looking for magic..." His voice trailed off, and he avoided the woman's eyes.

"*Yes*...of course," the woman hissed. The shadow of a forked tongue licked across the table. Wesley jerked his head upright, and the woman smiled, lips pursed.

Did I imagine that?

"You've come for magic, now," the woman said, lifting the rings. "Magic is no mere trifle."

Wesley pressed his hands against the table so the woman would not see them shaking. *Am I really going to confide in someone, despite Mother's warnings?*

The twins would only tease him. Derian might shrug it off. But what would Avlae say? What would Father say? Yet, Wesley knew this was his chance for some kind of answer. *Any* answer was better than no answer. Where else could he go? Besides, he had already paid the woman—no turning back. Whatever she offered, he would start there. He quickly searched left, then right, to be sure he had not been seen by someone from his family.

Finally, he leaned over the table and whispered, "My mother spoke of different types of magic."

The woman's eyebrows straightened, as did her posture. "Go on," she said, and she slid an index finger into one of the rings. The skin on her finger paled as it passed through.

"Can you teach me to discern between true and false magic?" Wesley asked. The table grew cool under his palms.

With the empty side of the dual rings dangling from her finger, the woman said, "Stretch out your hand…" Her maroon lips formed her words perfectly. Her voice was hypnotic. "Place your finger into the other side."

Sweet like strawberries, her breath numbed his nostrils. Immediately, his anxiety left him. He lifted a steady hand and extended his index finger, then pushed it forward into the ring. A rush of warm wind threw him across an abyss.

In an instant, he sat beside the woman on what seemed like the top of a temple. Below he saw his father, wedged among other men in the back of a wagon, returning from the mines. Outlined in the moonlight was Wesley's home, far beyond his father. Then…fire.

"Father!" Wesley screamed, jumping to his feet.

Scores of flaming arrows rained from the sky and pierced the ground around the wagon. Father leapt from the wagon as the ground swallowed it up. He ran toward Wesley as another barrage of flaming arrows hailed from the sky, eventually striking him down.

"No!" Wesley looked to the woman, but she was gone. And no longer was he upon the temple, but he stood on what felt like a brick road, like in the square at Port Regael. Enclosed in blackness, he lifted his hand but could not see it.

Flames encircled him, lashing out like lassos to snatch him. Each breath seared his lungs. His skin felt ice cold, but the blood in his veins raced with intense heat. Stiffened knees buckled beneath him, and the fire became like hands, escorting him into red, glowing coals.

Then came Mother's voice, soft as a secret in his ear. "You have neglected my words. Remember the magic you seek. A person can feel it—gentle as a cool wind, comforting as a warm fire. It is something given and shared." Her tone escalated as she spoke. "It makes children laugh and dance. It is never divisive. It is celebrated and breathed. It is gentle and whispery, wild and explosive. It is the smallest seed that grows into the sturdiest tree!"

Two large hands lifted him from the fire and placed him upon tender space. Soft light seemed to emanate from his own arms and hands, illuminating his clothing. Around him, the organic scent reminded him of the bog, and his feet, now bare, sunk slightly in what seemed like peat moss. He could hear low breathing and felt warm breath part his hair from above. Yet, he never saw the giant's face. Enormous hands, palms up, met in front of Wesley. By the light of his own hands, he could see that the giant's hands were rough and calloused, stained with dirt but clean. These were not "idle hands," as his father would say. They were stout and told a story of hard labor. One hand alone could grab hold of Wesley and crush him. Yet, he was not afraid nor worried in the least.

Instinctively, Wesley placed his hands—together, palms up— in the hands of the giant. Just above him, a tiny seed appeared. It floated down and landed in the crease between his hands. The giant reached down with his left hand and pushed into rich soil. He lifted out a handful and then sifted the dirt through his fingers. Small, moist clumps fell apart until Wesley's hands held a heaping amount, and only the tips of his fingers showed. Finally, the giant released the rest of the dirt to the ground and placed his hand back under Wesley's.

In less than a moment, a bud sprouted, quivering as if it were stricken with cold. Dust leapt from the bud like fireflies, dancing around it and flying off into the black. Vines stretched and reached upwards. The larger it grew, the more magical dust it produced— until it was as bright and warm as a torch in his hands. Roots grew between his fingers, then down between the giant's fingers, shooting to the ground. The stem grew thick, bore branches, and sprouted green and silver leaves.

Now a tree, too heavy for Wesley to hold, the giant had to bear the weight. Wesley's hands were stuck, squashed between the tree and the hands of the giant. Pain wrenched his forearms. A cacophony of sound split his ears as azure and indigo flowers burst from the branches one by one like fireworks. Songbirds came screeching but then nested in the branches and quieted, whistling a tune his mother used to sing. Everything flared brighter and brighter...

Wesley was thrown to the ground. A crowd had gathered around him. Frantic stares worried for him. He propped himself up on his elbows. Behind the table, the fortune-teller stood aghast. The ring on her finger had broken from his. He looked at his hand to see the severed ring dripping like wax. With a flick of the wrist, he hurled it from his hand.

The fortune-teller gaped at the ring on her finger—it was blazing and red-hot, but that was not her concern. "This ring is inseparable!" She glared down at Wesley. Her words fell, heavy with threat. "Who…are…you?"

Mother's voice rang in his head, *"Flee!"*

The King's Declamation

esley had no intent to tell his siblings what had happened with the fortune-teller. The twins would jape him, and Derian would scorn him. Tired from a day of work, Avlae would say, "You just won't be told!" Although, after she got some rest, she may seek to understand what had happened. No need to risk that. He did not want any of that now.

His insides were chilled—partly because his clothes were damp from the afternoon rain, but mostly because of the guardian's face and his encounter with the fortune-teller. In this moment, Wesley just wanted some assurance. He longed to hear King Ninian's address.

"Stay close, Jess," Avlae said. She threw a satchel over her shoulder and took Jess by the hand.

Jess reached up with her other hand and offered Wesley what was left of her candied apple. He gave her a half smile, accepted the gift, and as Avlae lifted her away, he slipped it into a rubbish barrel. At a nearby fountain, Avlae wetted a cloth and washed Jess's little fingers and face.

Twilight came early as overcast skies hastened the daylight. Women lit lanterns, merchants closed their shops, and musicians cased their instruments.

Walking narrow cobblestone streets glazed from recent rain, the siblings pushed forward with the masses, plodding their way toward Regael Castle. The castle towers never left their sight. Far above the city, the east and north walls were erected on a promontory cliff—a sentinel to the sea. The west and south walls flowed down and around the hills, making a seamless transition into the seaside city along the bay.

The mass of people stalled at the lower southern entrance. Carts and people crowded the siblings. Wesley stared up at blueish-grey faces pushing in ever closer. Laughter and endless conversation filled his ears, and occasionally a stranger's elbow.

He began to fidget and squirm, searching for some way out of the crowd as his breath quickened. When he reached out and clasped the edge of Derian's cloak, Avlae put a hand on his shoulder, just like Mother would have done. She pointed up, and though Wesley could not see ahead, he could see above. They passed beneath wide stone arches that connected walls on both sides of them—it was like traveling through Merchant's Pass outside of Navarre.

"You know, we will miss you," Avlae said and reached close to cup his chin. "Jess has already asked many times how long you three will be gone."

"I'll miss reading to her. Will you do that for me?"

"Of course." Avlae looked aside and brushed her shoulder across her cheek. "Do take care…"

"What is it?" Wesley asked.

Avlae slowed her pace and allowed others to step in front of her, seemingly trying to get out of earshot of her other brothers. "Something is…off."

"Off?"

"Oh, I don't know." She shook her head. "Something feels wrong—"

Wesley grinned, making sure that Avlae saw him.

Avlae stopped walking, and the evening did not hide the suspicion in her eyes. "What?"

"The young man from the castle. Did he not come to the market like he usually does?"

Abruptly, she pulled Jess in front of her so she would not keep walking, covered her little ears, and bent to meet Wesley eye to eye. "How do you know about him?" Jess squirmed to push away Avlae's hands.

"We all know!"

"Well, Father doesn't know, and you better keep it quiet…He always comes to see me. And when he doesn't—"

"He sends a note."

"Oh, Wesley, you little…" Avlae sighed. "Yes, he sends a note. As of late, he has confided some of his suspicions with me."

Jess finally wrestled away from Avlae's grasp. "Ouch!"

Again, she took Jess's hand, shifted upright, and strutted ahead. "Not a word, Wesley."

In no time, the crowd spilled into the courtyard.

Torches and fires illuminated the castle gardens. The courtyard filled behind them, pushing the siblings closer to where the king would address the crowd. They waited, eyes trained upon the golden drapery of the upper terrace. First, two attendants stepped through—then King Ninian himself. The people greeted their beloved king with uproarious applause and cheers. Wesley pictured himself at the king's side, stepping out to greet his subjects, assuring them of peace and proclaiming the return of Gaspard. *Do my brothers envision the same?*

A simple gold diadem pressed into the king's thick, long, silver hair. His ruffled cravat pushed up below his bearded chin and fanned out over the top of his lavish robes. Wisdom lined his craggy face, yet he stood robust and a head taller than both attendants. Without a smile, his self-assured eyes took in the crowd. Parting his deep purple cape, he lifted his arms, revealing billowy pearl sleeves. Voices fell silent, and all became still.

"Our fathers built Nantes, seeking prosperity for World Over."

When Wesley thought about World Over, he pitied those outside the walls of Nantes. In an ancient dialect, World Over was called Perahzie—*unwalled*. There were few who used that language now. On the maps he had seen, uncharted lands and seas faded off at the edges and included sketches of scary creatures poised insidiously. He shivered just thinking about it. *Perahzie* seemed more fitting a name. Perhaps that is why it was changed to *World Over*.

King Ninian continued, "Now, we take up the torch to carry their vision forward. Our freedom and security, we will share. In providence, I commence forthwith the extension of this great land!"

Wesley's own shouts of excitement were drowned out by those around him.

"To those of you who have come to give your services, on behalf of Nantes, I thank you. Your kingdom thanks you. Generations to come will celebrate your efforts and sacrifice. King Gaspard's dream—my dream, the dream of all Nantes—will come to pass because of you. Others will find a better place. Many more will strive for peace and safety and come to us as we extend our way of life into the uncharted lands!"

The twins began to holler in unison, "Gaspard! Gaspard!" until it caught on in the crowd. Wesley joined right in. He looked at

Derian, who stood silent. The glare Derian shot told him to hush up, so Wesley backed down. The twins ignored him and chanted on.

King Ninian waited several minutes for the crowds to quiet before he continued.

"Friends, know that the search for the lost family of Gaspard remains the priority of the council. Yet, as history teaches us, victories are not gained without trials. Today, a new matter calls for our urgent response. This morning, we were reminded of the evil that threatens our world. We received word concerning a breach in the wall. This bane occurred not far from Fehrael on the south side of Beggar's Bay. As your king and protector, it is my duty to inform you that pirate trolls have entered our realm."

Hushed murmurs rose from the crowd.

"Now, now, you can be confident and assured that we remain in control. Several of the beasts have been captured, and some have been killed. Yet, many more escaped into the West Agaes Mountains." He raised a hand to quiet the rising concern. "Hear me clearly!" In cadence with his words, he threw his fist forward. "I have full confidence in our men. We will respond to the call. It is our duty to protect you. This trespass, this intrusion, this foray—we will overcome for our good land!"

Wesley found himself encouraged with every word.

"World Over has never seen power such as that of Nantes! Our flag will instill fear, a mighty and unrelenting force. Those who dare to oppose us will contend with an invincible foe. Those who are not with us will be made to bow before us. We will prevail at all costs! We will reign supreme—"

One of King Ninian's attendants placed a hand on the king's shoulder.

King Ninian's voice softened, "Friends, we will not let this cowardly attack impede the mission." Then, like an anthem, he called, "We will fight for justice and security, and we will remove those who stand in our way!"

The crowd's response could not be contained, a roar so thunderous that it brought Jess to tears. She raised her arms up to Avlae. Avlae picked her up and pulled her close while Jess put an ear against Avlae's chest and covered the other with her hand. Avlae smiled, seemingly thrilled by the king's speech. She bounced slightly, cradling Jess and assuring her that all was right.

"The expansion of the wall will go forward as planned. For some of you, your services will be needed to repair the breach. As I speak, the council prepares a regiment of soldiers, which on the morrow will be set to leave for Beggar's Bay. And in the days to follow, the rest will set out to extend the wall. Even while we repair, we will expand! Report to your posts immediately, and you will receive further instructions. You are dismissed."

Present Day...

The power of King Ninian's words again obliterated Wesley's doubts, even now. The noise from the cheering crowd in his memory became the rolling of the wagon wheels. It was then that a raspy voice jerked him, as if by a cord, from his thoughts.

"Prepare the way for the Great King! Set a path for him!" a voice cried in the distance.

As Wesley's wagon crested the hill, he witnessed the commotion that held Olivetan's attention—a large, earthy group of men, women, and children...and a bedraggled little man above them, with a voice like rushing waters.

Habormoss Textiles

6

Habs dipped his quill in a nearly empty inkwell. With thick fingers, he struggled to write smoothly, and when he went too slowly, the ink pooled up. His old eyes needed help as well, but he had left his glasses in the back room.

After writing one receipt, he reached for his bergamot tea. The cup had long since gone cold, but as he often said, "I'll drink it hot or cold, or even a day old!" Alas, upon setting the cup back down, he realized he *was* drinking yesterday's tea.

Habs looked up from behind his sturdy oak desk and studied the view through a large section of paned windows. Early morning commerce filled the streets of Port Regael. People had been hustling by, back and forth, for nearly three quarters of an hour. Two days had passed since the Eve of Enrichment, and still many visitors lingered in the city. Like celebrations of old, Habs expected many to carry on into next week.

This can only play well for the Underground. It will keep the king's men busy with other matters and keep them out of mine!

Habs's fingers tapped a staccato rhythm on his desk. Mahre, his assistant, was unusually late. He needed Mahre to finish several receipts for the day's shipments so he could leave for the docks. He prayed that he would not have to contend with Ninian's soldiers along the route.

Finally, the door of the shop swung open. Mahre bounded in with the clamor from the street. Startled, Habs fumbled his pen and splotched the paper.

"Good morning, Habs! Nerves a bit frayed this morning?" Mahre asked. He raised an eyebrow and gave a jaunty smile. Sunlight haloed his brown shoulder-length hair.

"You're late, Mahre." Habs looked down and continued writing.

"Yes, but—"

Habs cut short Mahre's excuses, "I need Jansen up at the castle to locate a cart and driver for these deliveries. Have you seen him?"

"Yes, we spoke last night, and I'm not sure which of you is more irritated."

"You know that working with the couriers at the castle is always problematic." Habs huffed and threw out his arms. "There will be delays in Navarre. My shipments will sit for who knows how long until the next cart comes along! It makes my head ache." Habs set his pen aside, put his elbows on the desk, lowered his head, and rubbed his eyes with the heel of his hands.

"Jansen assured me your packages would ship. Now, I have—"

Habs lifted a hand, again interrupting Mahre.

"What is it?" Mahre asked, plainly irritated.

Habs tilted his head and looked beyond Mahre, double-checked the window, and spoke in a hoarse whisper, "The shipment arrived last night."

"*The* shipment?"

"*Shh, shh,* lower your voice, you clod! I would be on my way to the docks to pick it up right now, but much like you, Gabrell is late with the horse and cart."

Mahre folded his arms. "Hence, your uncommon display of anxiety this morning."

Habs nodded slowly. "And you, Mahre? Are you not masking your own worries today, my friend?"

"Did you think it would be easy to stand against Ninian?"

"You know damn well—" Habs laughed aloud, almost falling for Mahre's surreptitious attempt to set him off.

Habs had no children of his own, but over the years, Mahre had become his son. Below Mahre's right earlobe, a wide scar began, curved to the front of his neck, and disappeared beneath his thin ecru shirt—the only visible evidence of the torture he had gone through five years ago. Habs had helped to save him from a spell that bound him as a pirate troll.

To even attempt such a thing had risked both their lives. Mahre, though he was young, was old enough to weigh the decision, and he knew that death would be far better than living under the curse. Habs had brought in Sophia to reverse the spell of aberration. In his reaction to the antidote, Mahre had brutally tortured himself. Rolling over the ground, his beastly hands had lacerated his neck, torso, and limbs. When he returned to his human form, shreds of skin on his slender frame hung from exposed bone. He had clung to life with trembling breaths, and the reversal lasted an entire afternoon. Habs had wiped off the blood, cleaned and stitched the wounds, and sat by Mahre's side for three days until the fever broke.

Now, Mahre stepped up and slapped his hands on the desk. Leaning in, he spoke just loud enough for Habs to hear, "You've done it! You ol' smuggler."

"One step at a time. I'll find rest when the writings are in our hands and we are far from Port Regael." Habs sat up and slid backward in his chair. His trade from another life had its benefits, but nothing he smuggled in the past had distressed him as much as today's shipment. "These are the parchments we've waited for," Habs continued and raised his fists in victory. "Provided that all is in order, the Underground must move in the next few days. You will need to inform the others tonight. We mustn't delay. Ninian has been too close as of late. The parchments need protection."

Habs did not want more trouble with Ninian. Yet, he needed this shipment—it was essential in finding the treasure. And at all costs, the parchments must be kept from Ninian's vile hands.

"Is this...the Fullness of Time?" Mahre asked.

"I do not dare say for certain. Perhaps Quesnel can answer that. Nevertheless, the Underground must be on its way to Dochart's Glen."

"Ah, a haven in the hills," Mahre added. "Of the havens, I believe you said there are six in total. Is that correct?"

"Yes, yes, but we're not—"

Mahre broke in with mocking skepticism, "Three east and three west of the River Proscl, six total discovered in World Over, each offering refuge for travelers, yet elusive to those who seek to find them? And you would risk the lives of the Underground—men, women, and *children* mind you—to take shelter somewhere you cannot even point out on a map!"

"What would you have me do, Mahre? Do I ignore the words of Gaspard? Do I risk hiding the Underground in, say, Coligny? Where Ninian can track us and butcher us all?" Habs's patience frayed, yet he saw how his words stung Mahre. "Look, we've been through this many times. King Gaspard found shelter, and at one time, even Quesnel found shelter in Dochart's Glen. We'll be safe from Ninian for a time."

Mahre's chin dropped, his feet shifted in place, and he became silent.

Outside the windows, a horse and wagon arrived. "And here is Gabrell."

Habs stood from his desk, and Mahre helped him spread a heavy, dark cloak over his shoulders.

"Thank you, Mahre. I'm going to miss this place. The work has been good to me."

Habs worked with cloth textiles, from rugs to clothing and tapestries. His family established the business even before Nantes became a country. At a time in his life when he had had nothing else, his father entrusted the business to him—Habormoss Textiles. Reminiscing on his many years in the shop, Habs rested a hand on Mahre's shoulder.

"You have done well by your father," Mahre replied.

"My father longed for the day when these writings would be in the hands of the Underground! He would certainly be in all his glory today."

"And nervous as hell," Mahre said, finally flipping his frown.

Habs laughed and said, "Ah yes, we are much alike."

Habs had recently celebrated his sixty-third birthday, but he still remembered when his father turned sixty-three. Each time he looked in the mirror, he saw his father. Though he had passed away eight years ago, Habs often pictured his smile—his burnt-orange mustache with just a touch of white. His father's narrow, bushy beard hung directly below his chin and was completely white.

Shaggy, greying ocher hair, which receded on the left side of his forehead, was combed straight up on top. Reddish-brown bristly eyebrows were a distinguishing mark he had said he receieved from his grandmother. The thought made Habs smile. He missed his father, especially today.

Mahre opened the door for Habs and followed him out to the cobblestone street. An autumn chill straightened the hair on Habs's arms despite his layers. A waft of freshly baked bread warmed his insides. Shades of maroon and orange, gold and brown patterned foothills northeast of the castle. A hint of burning oak from nearby chimneys reminded him of sitting in his favorite chair, reading a book by the fire.

"Good day, Mr. Habormoss," a young stable boy said.

"And you, Gabrell."

Habs stepped onto the tongue of the cart, reached for the seat rail, and pulled himself up. Gabrell handed him the reins and left to go about his business.

"You'll find everything in order, Mahre, in case things don't go as planned."

"Of course. Oh, and here." Mahre reached into the pocket of his drab leather vest. "Before you rudely interrupted me…." Mahre paused, smiling at Habs and handing him a sealed note. "I was going to share this with you. This is why I was late. Bela insisted I get this to you."

Habs broke the seal and read the note to himself:

The Curse awoke, the night her cloak, fast on the devil's winds
—yet its treasure stowed, more worth than gold,
will greet you with a kiss.

Bela always used poetry to code her messages. Habs had tried it once but decided he was not a poet.

"Good news, Habs? You don't look well." Mahre jumped up to get a glimpse. "Need someone to translate?"

"No, no, it's clear, just…" Habs's fingers tightened, crumpling the message. He had only dreamt that a message like this would one day arrive. For so long, only silence. For so long, he carried only hopeless hope. Hope for closure, for news of Sophia's death. But life? Why now? It was so abrupt, so perfect. *Sophia is alive! Is she well? How will we rescue her? How will we get her out of the city? What has she been through? Why did Ninian bring her to Port Regael? My dear cousin, Sophia…*

Habs held the note against his chest and swallowed hard. He could have cried, but not now. Instead, he pushed away his emotions. But then another wave of anxiety overtook him.

Habs had helped to raise Bela—she called him Father. As a young girl, she would visit Habs at his shop. That was when she had met Sophia. That is how she had gotten involved in the Underground. That is why Bela had blamed herself for Sophia's capture. *I must get word to her. Bela would want to be part of the rescue. Maybe she is already planning a rescue…Enough.* Bela could take care of herself, but Habs worried for her often. Now even more so.

Habs quickly reread the note before folding it and slipping it into his pocket.

"This is quite unexpected." Habs waited for those passing by, then lowered his voice. He found himself inaudibly mouthing his words. "It seems that *Calbha's Curse* sailed into the harbor."

Mahre rushed the cart, rose to his tiptoes, and stared at Habs. Mouthing his own words, he asked, "Medici…in Port Regael?"

Habs lifted his hands and signaled for Mahre to step back. He raised a finger to his lips. *This* news was not unexpected. Mahre needed to mind his reaction.

"What are the chances, Mahre? The *Curse* arrives days before our shipment, and now…" His vision spun into a blur, and he steadied himself by taking hold of the rail at his side. Habs spoke gravely, "We'll talk when I return. Ninian may be closer than we thought. Be on guard, watch yourself. If I fail…If Ninian has somehow discovered our shipment, you must find Bela, gather the Underground, and leave Port Regael immediately."

"Do you, at this late hour, doubt your suppliers? You will not fail."

"But you will hold to the plan if I do," Habs ordered. "You and Jansen must not come to my aid, nor will you allow her to amend our tactics."

"Bela?" Mahre laughed. "You appear to be more certain of her subtleties than your own return."

"Are you entertaining your own doubts this morning? When it comes time to leave, you'll go with or without me."

Mahre frowned, his shoulders sank, and he nodded in agreement.

Habs cocked his ear. "Now, there are the bells in the harbor. The lock-gates will soon be in place. Crews will begin unloading ships." Habs raised his voice to say, "Don't forget to finish this morning's receipts."

Habs felt the sting of his own words, but he could not bring himself to look at Mahre. No time for affections. No time to mend his words. This rebellion was just getting started. He snapped the reins and began to make his way to the river docks.

ort Regael had the largest difference between high and low tide that Habs had ever seen in all his travels, at least the height of the highest castle tower—eleven and a half rods! The first set of bells marked the beginning of low tide.

Three rivers flowed from the mountains, through the city, and into the bay. A lock-like system was constructed at the mouth of each of the rivers. When the bells sounded, it alerted the operator to either open or close the gate. A second set of bells also affirmed that the water gates were in place. In several hours, ships in the harbor would be stranded during low tide. On the other hand, ships that docked in the rivers along storefronts and storage buildings were ready for business. Adjustable vents in the gates regulated the water depth in the rivers.

As a child, Habs had played in the bay after the tide had gone out, finding mussels and mischief. The mussels were delicious. The mischief led to whippings when he was caught smearing seaweed and mud across the bottoms of fishing vessels that were recently cleaned. He chuckled to himself, remembering his boyhood. How life had changed.

Habs waved to many friends along the narrow streets of Port

Regael. Most days, he would stop to chat, but not today. Passing them by proved to be difficult, but it was better that he did not stop. Very few local business owners knew of his position in the Underground. It was good they did not know about it, for most were opposed to the rebellion against Ninian. And besides, if his friends were questioned later, they could honestly answer that they knew nothing about it.

His mind lingered upon the letter from Bela. Sophia was alive, but for how long? One never knew with King Ninian. It had been three years since she was captured, and Habs had considered her long dead by now. Oh, how the Underground had grieved. It had taken months to reorganize.

After Sophia had been captured, no evidence surfaced concerning where Ninian had taken her. No spies had reported Ninian moving prisoners, nor was there any word from Alexander and Irene, who watched over the northern slopes.

The aroma of fruit pastries distracted Habs from his rumination. His empty stomach rumbled, and Habs realized that in his haste, he had skipped breakfast that morning. He was not sure if he had the courage to stop for apples at the produce stand of the Delaine children. Seeing little Jess, knowing now that Sophia lives on…it just might overburden him.

For three years, their father, William, had lived with the children of Gaspard right under the nose of Ninian. Given his surname, Delaine, they came and went from Port Regael without the slightest suspicion of the king and his inner circle. Ninian never knew that Sophia had married.

Habs laughed to himself. How long could it last? William's welfare was questionable. The children were getting older, wiser. No matter, in the days ahead, they would discover Ninian's corruption. The Underground would gather the children on the way east—no easy task. The children only understood the Underground as a no-good band of rebels, a mere nuisance in the kingdom.

Habs pictured himself trying to explain to them, "We've come to take you with us on our way east. You can trust us. By the way, King Ninian seeks to kill you. If you still don't believe me, maybe this will help—your mother is alive!" *There is no way this plan can go well...*

The one thing that Habs counted on was that even though, on the outside, the children took their father's surname—*Delaine*—on the inside, the name of Gaspard coursed through their veins.

"Good morning, Mr. Habormoss!" Derian called as Habs was still deciding whether or not he could slip by unnoticed. Derian had picked up a couple of apples and was walking out from behind the tables, toward the cart. He looked just like his father, William.

Habs cleared his throat so that his voice would not crack. "And you, Derian. So, I hear that your brothers are in service of King Ninian?"

"Yes, they were some of the first to leave. In fact, they are on their way to repair the breach as we speak."

"You'll be glad to know they are in good company. My dear friend, Olivetan, leads the mission."

"Thank you, sir."

Jess stepped quickly up behind Derian. "Mr. Habormoss!"

She hadn't been to the market with her siblings in months. *My God, it's Sophia.* Habs pinched the inside corners of his eyes, dabbing tears before they rolled. He used the moment to reach into his purse with his other hand and handed Derian several coins in exchange for the apples. "You keep the extra," he said.

Seemingly perplexed, Derian tipped his head sideways and cleared his throat.

"Is it enough, Derian?"

"Yes, sir. Thank you." Derian again tilted his head and spoke in a smaller voice, "I think Jess would like a hug, sir."

"Of course. Come here, young lady!" Habs reached out from where he sat. Derian lifted Jess, and Habs enfolded her in his arms. "Oh, you've grown so, my dear." Jess said something, but her words were muffled against Habs's cloak. He squeezed his eyes tightly shut while holding her, then he held her out and asked, "Are you missing your brothers?"

"Yes, sir. I love them. They read to me," Jess replied in the gentlest tone. "And Derian says he will miss them while doing chores."

Habs shook as he chuckled. "As would I." He placed Jess back into Derian's reach. "Leaving for Navarre today?" Habs asked Derian as Jess scooted away.

"Yes. Avlae, Jess, and I are traveling home this afternoon."

Habs looked beyond Derian, where Avlae attended to other customers. If she came over, Habs feared that he would collapse, sobbing. This false composure could not last. *How does William keep up the duplicity?* For a moment, Habs pitied William. But the pity did not last long. Habs thought William had it easy, hiding in the mountains of Navarre. Where else could he cushion his fragile mind? Where else could he prop up his feeble fortitude? How many times had Habs wanted to slap William out of his depression…

It was time to go.

Habs placed his right hand on his left shoulder, rested his chin on his wrist, and said, "Very good. May the Great King protect you on your journey home." And Habs was off.

He crossed Fane River, then the Kells. As he neared the River Poddle, his stomach tightened and fluttered. Drawing nearer to the docks, his nerves began to torture him.

Habs pulled back the reins and slowed the horse. Poddle was the widest and deepest of the three rivers that cut through the city. He had thought it might be less suspicious to use a large ship at the most frequented dock on the river farthest from his store to smuggle in his goods. Now, he wondered if it really mattered at all.

Before he could turn his cart onto the road along the river, from behind, a heated voice ordered him, "Stop your cart! By order of the castle guard!"

Habs immediately brought his cart to a halt and remained still. Not wanting to look back, he waited, silently cursing Mahre.

If Mahre had been on time, this would not have happened. As a smuggler, I was always on time. Hell, I was always early. Unacceptable. His fingers bounced in a quick rhythm against his seat. *They most certainly discovered my shipment. Mahre will need to get the Underground out of the city. How will I get a message back to him?*

Habs wiped his brow and took the last bite of his second apple. With the tip of his boot, he repeatedly tapped the footrest on the carriage, while his eyes darted about. Heat crept around his neck until he felt like he was suffocating.

"Well, Habs, it looks like you have the undivided attention of Regael Customs this morning."

The familiar voice pulled him from his angst. Closing his eyes in a prayer of thanks, his tension dispersed like ripples in a pool. He looked back, fighting the urge to throw his apple core, for he could not risk giving away their relationship. Sitting astutely atop his horse, Jansen grinned, seemingly pleased to throw Habs into a fluster. Gold epaulets squared the man's courtly posture.

"Jansen, you—" Habs mumbled to himself.

"Move along, old man. I am to escort you to your shipment."

Jansen had done some smuggling for Habs back in the day, only *he* was never caught. Years went by, and one day Habs spotted Jansen in a crowd of people at the docks. Jansen had just arrived in Port Regael, and the two picked up their friendship right where it had left off. Jansen had been hired by the king as a translator and advisor. Habs had needed someone who worked closely with Ninian, and Jansen was more than willing to join his friend.

Jansen spoke from behind as they turned the corner in front of tall brick buildings that lined the docks. "You can see your welcoming party in the distance."

"Have they opened any of my crates?" Habs asked, not sure if he wanted to know the answer. "And what are you doing here, Jansen? Are you not delayed for your appointment at the castle? If you haven't spoken to Bela—"

"Just listen. Keep your eyes straight ahead. Please, no more questions. I'll have just enough time to bring you up to speed before we are in earshot of the king's men."

"But—"

"Late last night, I heard that they were forming this wonderful greeting for you. I thought it best for me to be here and help you get through customs. None of your crates have been opened yet. I do expect the king's men to open them, and when they do…" His voice slowed. "Stay calm. You assured me that you had nothing to worry about. Now, no more questions." Jansen raised his voice so that the other soldiers might hear him, "We will be the ones asking the questions!"

Jansen rode up to join three of Ninian's sentinels. Habs stopped his cart parallel to several crates, which were already unloaded from the ship and stacked on the dock.

"Good morning, gentlemen!" Habs smiled as he eased himself off the wagon. He walked to the back of his cart, released the latches, and let down the wooden gate. "Would you men mind helping an ol' fella load his packages?"

One of Ninian's men stepped forward. "We have reason to believe there may be some items of the king's interest in the shipment you are receiving today. Therefore, we are detaining the crew and captain of this ship while we search for the items in question."

"I certainly…do not…approve," Habs sputtered. His voice was shaky, as if he *were* smuggling something. He slowed his breathing and spoke again, "I'll have you know that I am a close friend of King Ninian, and he will hear about this delay." Habs made a fist and slapped the back of his hand into the palm of the other. "And, of course you know, I don't choose the riffraff that sails these ships. I will not be held accountable for whatever these miscreants might be smuggling." He threw his arms and took several steps away from the packages.

"Your past would tell us different," a soldier warned.

Habs craned his head back. "There you go, dragging out my past and disregarding twenty-five years of honest work." Once again turning away, Habs pulled out his pipe and tobacco. "Have you checked the ship's log?" he called while packing his pipe.

"The logbook checks out. In fact, they have arrived a day ahead of schedule," the suspicious soldier replied.

"Well, that's why I work with this company," Habs said, and he tramped back toward his cart. "They make wise use of the wind and deliver early."

"We'll see," returned a doubtful voice. "We have men aboard, searching the ship. And we'll be opening these crates, as well."

Ready with crowbars in hand, two other soldiers examined Habs with narrow eyes.

"One…one request," Habs said, then told himself to be calm. "Allow me to help you. This is costly fabric, some of which is for King Ninian himself. It must be handled with care."

The one who seemed to be in command nodded in approval toward the others. Two soldiers worked to pry open the first crate. Habs carefully lifted a folded square of deep maroon brocatelle, its raised golden pattern glimmering in the sunlight. The soldier took an end and walked backward to open it to full length. One by one, draping the fabric over the back of Habs's cart, they emptied the box.

"Satisfied?" Habs asked sarcastically.

He need not say anything else. Instead, he just looked at them as if to question why they were wasting everyone's time that morning. The soldiers hastily moved onto the next crate, leaving Habs to repack. When he finished, two other soldiers loaded the crate into the back of his cart.

"May I ask what you are looking for?"

The men ignored him and continued their search. Habs leaned against a post on the edge of the dock and lit his pipe. Every now and then, he would glance at Jansen, who was now helping to tear into the crates. Yet, Jansen found a way to reassure Habs that all was going well with a slight nod each time another crate passed inspection.

Habs shuffled back and forth, hoping to relay his urgency to get back to work. Each crate was unpacked and packed again, until all five were inspected. It felt like the entire morning had gone by. He cleaned out his pipe and packed it again.

"Well then, are you content?"

The soldiers delayed, mumbling amongst each other. Every now and then, Jansen threw a disdainful look at Habs.

"Thank you, then, I'll be on my way."

"Not so fast, Habormoss," one of the sentinels said as he stepped between Habs and the cart. "You have had an unusually high volume of goods flowing through these docks lately. The law permits us to hold your possessions until your taxes can be reassessed."

Habs released the fire that had grown in his belly. "Enough of your foolishness—"

Jansen cut in, "That *is* true..."

"What?" Habs shouted, but he quickly figured that Jansen was up to something.

"However, I believe this happened several months ago, as well. Didn't King Ninian have your taxes apportioned to cover any extra weight?"

"Indeed, he did," Habs said and almost laughed. "Indeed."

"In that case, you are free to go, but we'll make note of this," Jansen said, and his voice became grim. "Do be careful, Habormoss. The king's men will not be fooled. Now, off with you before I decide differently!"

"Very good, then. I'll be on my way. Thank you, thank you all." Habs scrambled back up into his cart, his pipe clenched between his teeth. Grabbing the reins, he immediately rolled out of the docks. *I just need to get back to the shop!*

The Prophet

8

Before Wesley saw the diminutive stature of the bellowing mountain man, he would have sworn that the voice he heard was the voice of a giant. Again, the little man's roaring voice commanded Wesley to heed his words. "He is not far off! Run a pathway into the desert!"

The cart Wesley rode in circled up and onto a small hill, not far from the crowd that had gathered to listen. The boys crawled over each other to lay their eyes upon the one who could raise such a ruckus. Wesley, being the smallest, was pushed to the bottom of the pile. He managed to twist his way through the maze of arms and legs and poke his head up just above the frame of the cart. He rested his chin on the rough wooden edge and listened eagerly.

"His name will echo across the sea and over the land—from town to town and shore to shore!" the little man yelled, stretching his arms wide.

"I'm not impressed," Aarn said in a quiet voice.

Wesley found the man's voice upsetting, as if sounding an alarm. But his words also offered consolation—words of change and freedom. An odd-looking fellow, he stood just a few niks taller than a dwarf. His long, grey-mottled brown hair and beard were twisted and snarled. Ragged garments, torn and filthy, draped his haggard demeanor. Scars on his wrists and neck portrayed a painful past, and Wesley pitied him. Thick eyebrows met above his nose, and one eye was larger than the other. All this, along with his semi-toothless grin, had Wesley's rapt attention.

Lifting his arms, the man called in a raw voice, "Make ready a level footpath!"

There had to be sixty or seventy men gathered around him, along with women and children. As far as Wesley could tell, most were wanderers and mountain men. And as he would find out later, some families had traveled from as far away as South Fehrael to hear the eccentric fellow. Few eyes seemed troubled by the presence of King Ninian's men. Olivetan's soldiers spread out, keeping a short distance behind the crowd.

"For his enemies will gather before him. They will stagger in silent wonder. They will open their mouths to speak, yet their tongues will become numb! Justice, like an iron rod, will break them like clay pots!"

Wesley found himself drawn in. The man's words flowed like a river from his mouth, and all who listened seemed to drink it in and have their thirst quenched.

His words were clean.

His words were confident.

His words were courageous.

"His throne is established! His reign of peace is everlasting! His storehouses overflow with goodness, as do his vaults with virtue. He offers his hand to the fallen. He raises the weak!"

Even some of the soldiers seemed to be mesmerized, and with their eyes fixed on the little man, they loosely held their positions.

Wesley examined Olivetan. He had climbed down from his horse. Shaking his head and pacing, he looked to be awaiting his turn. Other ranks stood at attention and waited for orders.

Wesley had heard many in the caravan speak of this sect, though until today most had not witnessed a gathering. Yet, here they were—people of the Underground—and even their leader. Now, it seemed that if they captured this strange little man, they would succeed in severely weakening those who opposed King Ninian. Repair the breach, seize the pirate trolls, and disband the Underground—a triple victory!

Fearlessly, the mountain man continued his rant. Wesley had heard plenty of stories about this cryptic crusader from among those in the caravan, and now he fully realized the truth. This leader wasn't one to hide. He had no fear of King Ninian. Should they arrest him, it would not be his first trip to the dungeon at Regael Castle.

Let's detain him and be on our way!

Before this trip, Wesley had only heard whispers of the Underground's movement against King Ninian. Father had said it was a scandal created by discontented citizens. *Why did Father lie? It does not matter. Mother said to honor King Ninian. First the breach, then this. These trespasses go against all that Nantes was created to be. We must defend peace and unity.* "For the kingdom," Wesley heard himself say aloud.

Someone from the crowd helped the man down from the rock, and Wesley lost sight of him. The crowd parted, as his hearers stepped to the side and allowed him to pass. Olivetan walked toward the provoker with his sword drawn. As the mystery man came into view, he extended his arms as if to embrace Olivetan. And it seemed he would have, were it not for the sabre nearly pressing into his chest.

"Why do you concern us with your trifling appearance and your frivolous talk?" Olivetan demanded. "Of whom do you speak, derelict?"

"Sir," the man said. "It is of my king that I speak." He seemed surprised that Olivetan did not know.

"We do not lead his procession on this day! King Ninian remains in Port Regael," Olivetan said, driving the man backward with the tip of his sword.

"No," the man replied. "Is Ninian the king over all realms, even the uncharted regions of World Over, and beyond the clouds?"

"Would you seek to steal loyalty from King Ninian, in his own country?"

"Tell me, who is King Ninian like? Is he like my king?" The man turned and raised an arm to the heavens. Lifting his voice, he spoke again to the crowd. "Does Ninian paint the sky and the hills? Does he give the sea its bounds?"

Bouts of laughter poked up here and there in the crowd. Lowering his arm, he shook a finger at Olivetan and spoke harshly. "Hear my words! For it is now that I am given words to speak. And when I am through, after I have said all the things I must say, mock on!" He dropped his arm to his side and glared up at Olivetan.

Wesley had never seen Olivetan lose his temper like he did next.

"Would you create unrest?" Olivetan shouted.

"Create it or not, it is upon us," the man said.

"Would you stir these people to rebellion? Before these young men who have sworn to lay down their lives for King Ninian, and for Nantes?"

The man said nothing else. Olivetan let down his sword, sheathed the weapon, and ordered the man's arrest. Two soldiers approached. The mountain man did not try to flee. He did not try to explain. His eyes were soft, and his rugged looks radiated a tender expression. Arms rose in willing submission, as if he were used to it.

Hundreds of eyes tensed as their leader surrendered, some sad and defeated, others sparked with defiance. One man shoved one of the soldiers and screamed, "Will you take me, as well?" Another threw a punch. Dodging the blow, the soldier landed his own fist just below the man's sternum. He was in the dust moaning before he knew what had happened.

Ignoring the growing threats, the soldiers shackled the little man by hand and foot, and they took him away to the prisoner cart. There, he would be in the austere company of the melancholy pirate troll. Over his right shoulder, Wesley lifted his chin and watched the soldier turn his key and release the latch. Pulling on the door, it fell open with a clank at the rear of the cart. Despite his chains, the man climbed inside, just as the troll had yesterday. Iron bars clamored shut behind him, rattling the entire cart.

Wesley whispered to the young men around him, "He does not look the least bit frightened."

The troll opened his narrow eyes long enough to see what was happening and then closed them again. The man settled down in the opposite corner, taking his place, seemingly without a care. He started speaking.

"Do you see that?" Wesley asked. "He's talking to the troll."

But the other boys in his cart did not respond. Wesley realized that they had their eyes fixed on the growing resistance. Murmurs in the crowd grew into shouts of opposition. "Release him!" someone yelled. The crowd taunted the king's men and demanded that their leader be set free. Some of them tore their own garments, while others picked up rocks.

Wesley shrank down in the cart for protection, leaving himself just enough room to see. His eyes looked over at his brothers, who seemed like they were doing all they could to keep themselves from starting a fight. His brothers, as well as the soldiers, knew all too well that they must wait for orders from Olivetan. That was made clear before they had left Port Regael.

Wesley caught a glimpse of someone hidden in the tall grass, his rifle poised upon a rock and aimed to fire. But before Wesley could utter a warning, the barrel exploded in a billow of smoke. One of the soldiers toppled to the ground, clutching his hip.

The sound of gunfire released a bulging fury—the crowd fell upon the royal regiment—thrusting their rocks and bloodying their fists. Fending them off with the butts of their rifles, the soldiers controlled the riot without pulling a trigger. The extent of Olivetan's retaliation was blackened eyes and bloodied noses. The soldiers defended themselves only enough for their protection. Women grabbed the children and pulled them away from the chaos. Many of the followers simply fell away from the brawl.

Wesley looked back to the prisoner cart. The ragged man had lowered his chin and covered his eyes with his hand. Was he disappointed with his followers for resorting to violence against the soldiers? Wesley thought about times when he had taken the blame for something one of his siblings had done.

"Ready!" came Olivetan's firm command.

In unison, the cavalry raised their rifles, and without firing a shot, the crowd was stilled. No one made a sound. The mountain men had not reckoned the force they were up against. This bold, yet futile uprising was over as quickly as it started.

Olivetan hollered, "You are dismissed!"

One by one, people in the crowd dispersed, dropping their rocks and their pride. The rifleman stood up from the tall grasses and, with his arms raised, slowly backed away. One arm fell back to his side, and in an instant, he drew a pistol.

Crack, crack, crack.

All three soldiers hit their target.

Wesley took a deep breath, thankful that the confrontation was over. But he would never unsee that.

9

As several men tended to the wounded soldier, Wesley and some of the other boys ran for the edge of the cliff. They picked up their own rocks and tried to hit the water in the bay. None of them came close.

"Why is it called Beggar's Bay?" one boy asked as he launched a rock.

"Because if the trolls can get into the *bay* unnoticed, you'll be *begging* for mercy," Aarn said as he and Philor strode up, just within earshot of the others. The boys all had a laugh.

Wesley spoke up, "They say that when the wall was first being built along the southern coast of the bay, forty bears came into the camp looking for food…" He grunted, heaving a rock over the cliff.

"Wesley, you dolt!" Philor jeered. "You always tell this story as if the bears were innocent."

"They took bread, game, anything they could get their paws on," Aarn added.

"They were hungry," Wesley said. "When the men returned, they began to slay the bears one by one."

"I would have done the same thing," Aarn said.

"Wesley, you are sworn to protect Nantes," Philor said, slinging his own rock. "We'd all be dead if it were up to you to order an attack on any bears that threaten us."

"I wouldn't even wait for an order," Aarn laughed.

"The bears were not a threat," Wesley said, knowing he ought not to pick a fight with his brothers.

"You were not there," Philor said.

"But there's more to the story!"

"Go on, then," one of the boys called.

"Men who confronted the bears said that the bears did not threaten or fight back. Instead, they seemed to be begging for mercy—Beggar's Bay."

"The *bears* were the beggars?" one of the boys asked.

"That's right," Wesley responded, satisfied to have shared the whole story.

"Wesley, eleven men died that day, and scores of others were injured from bear attacks," Philor said.

The eyes of the three younger boys grew wide.

"I was getting to that. The bears were only defending themselves."

"Shut your mouth!" Aarn said.

Philor added, "If we see a bear, I say we kill it before it kills us. Or, will you wait to see if it begs for mercy?" The twins laughed then took turns asking, "Teacher, how about some deadly scientific facts?"

"Oh, yes…Do go on, won't you?" Aarn pleaded, thick with sarcasm.

"Of course," Wesley said and played along. "The Agaesian brown bear is the largest known bear in the charted regions. They weigh three times one of our horses, and when standing, they're over three rods tall. They're named after the Agaes Mountains, which is where the bears are most often found."

"Why yes, you have firsthand experience," Aarn teased.

"No, but Father has friends who trap them along the Naab River, all the way to Brazenose. You've heard the stories. Remember when we found bear tracks near our home in Navarre? We weren't allowed in the woods for weeks."

"Are you even hearing yourself? Father's friends trap and *kill* them. Wesley, are you still so dull?" Philor laughed at him.

"We all saw the huge bearskins for sale back in the square at Port Regael," Wesley said. Thinking about the polished teeth in the open-mounted jaw gave him the chills. "The bears basically keep to themselves. Though I admit, I am glad for protection from the soldiers."

"*Now* he tells us how he really feels," Aarn said.

"Don't distort my words! Back in Navarre, that trader we met without a nose is enough to keep me cautious. But that doesn't mean I want to go hunt them down."

"You'll change your mind when we reach the rim of the West Agaes Mountains," Philor said.

"Yeah, you'll have bears on one side and trolls on the other. With one hand, you will be repairing the breach, and with the other you'll be fending off bears!" Aarn laughed.

Wesley ignored them. He figured they had about two hours of daylight left. They would not be far from wherever Olivetan chose to spend the night. Olivetan did not like to travel once it was dark. Darkness made the caravan vulnerable to an attack.

Soon the boys were called back to the carts and were on their way. Wesley thought of Olivetan and the self-control he modeled in the chaos. His mother had often told him that when you find an admirable trait in someone, you should keep it treasured in your heart.

"Then, protect it," she would say. "You must keep your heart with diligence."

Wesley looked toward the setting sun. Swatches of red and yellow, blue and purple overlapped across the sky. The brightest stars came into view. As evening came, the light from Beacon's Bluff—an ancient lighthouse on Telos Isle—burned vibrantly, passing along the sea. Soon, they would set up camp and settle in for the night.

But as Wesley pushed himself back into the cart, the air grew uncommonly cold.

HABORM 075

The Ol' Smuggler

10

It was close to midday when Habormoss arrived back at the shop. Despite the long ride across town, his hands still trembled from the formidable encounter with Ninian's soldiers. He pulled back the brake and set down the reins. Wary of any sign of being watched or followed, he glanced down streets and across storefronts.

Mahre stepped out from the shop, unable to straighten his smile, and leaned back against the doorframe with his arms crossed. "Ah, you've made it back. I won't have to leave without you after all."

"Lower your voice, Mahre, and move swiftly." Habs slipped from the cart and wasted no time approaching Mahre. "I fear hidden eyes covet our goods."

He held the door open as Mahre carried each crate into the shop and through to a private study at the rear. As people strode by, Habs shook hands, laughed, and boasted of the festival. Talking helped to calm his nerves.

"Take your rest, Habormoss," a slender man said, extending a hand. It was Flannery, the candlemaker from the shop next door, still wearing his apron. "Enjoy the festival! The work will wait."

"Tell that to the captain in the harbor. Where are you headed, friend?"

"Telford's Folly, of course."

"I'll be along." Habs reached into his purse. "Order a round on me!"

"If you insist, Habs!" The man eagerly accepted. He grinned, coins rattling into his pocket. "Straight off to the pub, then!"

On Mahre's last run, Habs turned and followed closely behind him into the store. Hastily, he shut the door and bolted it. Extending an arm, he braced himself against a wall, weak from relief.

It took a few moments for Habs's eyesight to adjust to the dim, silent order of the shop. Several vertical wooden looms sat motionless. Then, there was the new metal loom. Habs had hoped to purchase another one like it in three months. Financially, he had done well. But with the Underground moving so soon, he knew all too well that his business would be confiscated by Ninian. *Am I ready to leave all this behind?*

The wide-planked, tight-grained hardwood floors were swept clean. Thread inventory decorated shelves in rows of colors. Stepping through the shop, his hand brushed countertops, cleared for the next day of business. The store was closed for the duration of the festival. *The store may never open again. One week from now, it's likely that I'll be far from Port Regael.* His head swam. Nothing seemed certain now. While he knew what he had to do, the business he had worked so hard to maintain and build was coming to an end.

"What of the horses?" Mahre startled him, calling from across the shop.

Dreary, as if waking from a sullen dream, Habs replied, "Gabrell will see to them."

Habs wandered into the study. To his left, a deck of cards sat facedown on a round, maple table, surrounded by four worn chairs. There were few things for which he would trade his evenings of playing cards with friends—most of them merchants, all of them with an opinion on something. But for Sophia, for the Underground, he would give up everything.

Mahre reached over and pulled the door closed behind Habs. "You'd think, being in textiles and all, you would have reupholstered these chairs. They're spent!"

"In the dim light of late-night card games, what does it matter, Mahre?"

Straight ahead, a bookshelf covered the entire wall. Books on mechanics, history, fiction, and biographies were filed vertically or stacked horizontally when there was no more space. The five crates were stacked beside Habs's favorite chair, a walnut armchair with a tall, soft back near the fireplace.

Habs lit the lantern that hung on a piece of iron above the mantel—a little feature he designed himself. Upon the giant oak mantel were oddly shaped candles and decorative beer steins with crooked lids, made by a dear friend. Habs leaned his head against the mantel and sighed. "Life's riddles mock me, Mahre."

"Habs?"

"I'm recalling late nights with Flannery," Habs said, gazing at the mantel. Many of the candles were too wide for common use and looked like they were melting. Habs gladly received the rejects. They burned the same and had special meaning.

"The candlemaker? He was trouble! You've said it yourself."

"Shut it, and leave me to my gloom! We're all a bit of trouble when we drink too much mead."

"Your maudlin moments are becoming."

Habs's eyes drifted beyond Mahre, "It seems that I keep returning further from where I've begun."

"Now *you're* not making sense."

Habs did not expect Mahre to understand.

Hanging low in a stand near the chair were several tools: a cast-iron poker, tongs, and shovel. On the opposite side of the fireplace, a hammered iron bin sat half-filled with firewood. But Habs had his eyes on the dirty bronze andiron with its molded leaf-like arches that decorated the hearth. He knelt, reached into the fireplace, grasped the center bars, and pulled straight up.

A latch released with a clank. Mahre knelt at Habs's side, and together they reached into the firebox and pushed left. Stone scraped against stone as they slid the contrivance left, revealing a hidden chamber—a descending room.

With pulleys, rope, and a counterweight, Habs's father had built the lift some thirty-five or more years ago. He had used it for transferring supplies and equipment between the main floor and the cellar. Habs had removed the only flight of steps that led to the cellar, built walls around the lift, and installed a fireplace to hide the only way in from the shop.

The lower level was now the clandestine meeting place for the Underground. To protect gathering members and not draw attention to the store, they had linked cellars. Following this labyrinth beneath a few other shops, an inn, tavern, and several homes along the road enabled the Underground's convergence beneath Habormoss Textiles.

But the interconnected cellars were just one part of the Underground's network. A secret tunnel known to only a few select members attached the cellar pathway to an extensive cave on the edge of town. Those passageways extended into the surrounding mountains, so when the time came, the Underground could leave Port Regael without being noticed.

Habs handed the crates to Mahre one by one, and Mahre proceeded to lift each into the hidden chamber onto the narrow lift.

"These three fill the coffin. Take them down," Habs said.

The space was roughly the same length as a coffin but higher and wider. Mahre slid in and squeezed alongside the front of the crates.

"Down you go, then," Habs said, and Mahre pulled the rope to lower the compartment. Once he was out of sight, Habs stood up and paced the room, counting the seconds till Mahre reached the cellar. *Faster, Mahre.* Habs checked to be sure the door to the back room was locked. The squeaking stopped. He rubbed his hands and then brushed his hips, stepping swiftly back to the fireplace.

"Hurry," Habs called down. Taking hold of the ropes, he doubled the effort in raising the coffin. It wasn't long before Habs himself was crawling in with the remaining two crates. He now wished he had gone first. It was quite difficult to slide the firebox back into place from behind, but he managed. He moved the latch into its locked position, took the ropes in hand, and lowered himself down.

Mahre already had the room illuminated with several oil lamps. Habs rolled out onto the dirt floor, collecting dust with his overcoat. Flat on his back, he paused before standing, anticipating aches in his legs and back. He twisted sideways and pushed off the floor, incorporating his regular groans. Dusting off his coat, he was pained to know that he could likely count on one hand how many more times he would be using the coffin. He laughed aloud, realizing that he would no longer be able to boast about the thrill of being consciously lowered in a coffin.

The cellar walls were various shades of deep reddish-brown brick. Arched doorways led to multiple rooms, including a meeting room for the Underground. Hard-packed dirt floors, in several areas, were covered with wooden planks and, in a few places, stone. On the opposite side of the room was a long, wooden table covered with parchments and maps. Habs hastily gathered and set them aside, anxious to open the crates.

"With these finally in our possession, the Underground can now fly east," Mahre said as he placed what Habs had collected into a trunk beneath the table.

"And we must somehow convince the Delaine children that Sophia's collection of writings, parchments, and maps belongs to the Underground."

"We'll need William to—"

Habs raised a hand and with his eyes begged Mahre to remain on task.

"What of the message from Bela this morning?" Mahre asked, stacking the last couple crates.

Habs reached for a hammer and pry, then handed them to Mahre. He admitted, "It has burdened me all morning."

Mahre accepted the tools and positioned them to crack open the first crate. "Will you share this burden?"

Habs looked away from Mahre as his throat tightened. Mahre began hammering, while Habs's eyes brimmed with tears. He wiped his eyes, leaned forward against the table, and cleared his throat. "Do you remember when we discovered these parchments?"

"Of course, I never will forget that day. You smuggled the

informant back out of Regael in a package going to Lothian." Mahre grinned and continued prying against the nails in the crate.

Habs snorted. *That* would *be the first thing Mahre remembers.* "These pieces were moved constantly to stay one step ahead of Ninian," he said and felt the hairs of his neck prickle under his collar.

"And everything was lost for three months."

"It was a constant battle. Ninian was always right behind us. I almost gave up, you know." Recalling his frustration, Habs grabbed Mahre's shoulders and shook him. "I was afraid he was going to find us. I had the Underground gathered to move—"

"And your patience paid off. The parchments were found amidst dried spices and salt, stowed away in a smuggler's sloop." Mahre hung the tools on the wall, and with both hands, he pulled away the top of the crate. He snatched his hand back and readily pulled a sliver from his finger. Grimacing, Mahre continued, "And even better, King Ninian had no idea it was found!"

"Till someone talked," Habs added. "Ninian has eyes and ears everywhere."

"That was when Sophia allowed herself to be captured, to distract Ninian from the parchments. That was three years ago, and it still saddens me…" Mahre paused. "Do you believe there is any chance…Do you believe Sophia is still alive?"

"Indeed," Habs said. It was Mahre's love for Bela that had Habs worried. Could Mahre entrust Bela to undertake the rescue? "Blessed Sophia. She is alive and in Port Regael."

It took Mahre a moment before he blurted out, "The message from Bela?"

"Unquestionably."

Mahre's mouth fell open, but nothing came out.

"Save your words, Mahre. I have no other answers for you. She must escape Port Regael with the Underground, though I am not sure how just yet. We will make plans with Jansen." And with apprehension unavoidable, Habs said, "We need to get word to Bela."

"I'd rather not think about that right now."

"Very well." Habs reached inside the crate, removed a folded piece of fabric, and held it up. He spread it open as wide as the span of his arms. Mahre took the other end, and together they laid it over the table. Mahre remained speechless, which was good. Soon enough, they would have to plan the details of Sophia's escape.

With the corner of the fabric in one hand and a pair of scissors in the other, Habs began to cut about one half-nik from the edge on the shorter end. He continued to cut the width and then slid his hand between two pieces of fabric to the corner nearest him. He proceeded to cut down the long edge. When half the length was cut, he looked up.

"This is it," Habs said wearily, his trembling hand setting the scissors aside. He folded the top layer back, and in the dim light of the dusty cellar, Habs revealed the parchments. "These are original, penned by the hand of Gaspard. They have even been authenticated." Habs lifted a parchment and pointed to the corner. Three overlapping almonds, like flower petals—Sophia's stamp.

Mahre responded with a large grin. "Once a smuggler, always a smuggler."

The Priest

The Priest

11

Medici waited in his quarters aboard *Calbha's Curse*, docked in Regael Cave. He loathed waiting and would not be made to wait again. He was not Ninian's pawn. He could barely stomach playing the servant to that insolent king. Such nonsense. Yet, to entertain propriety, he had put up with the king's requests. Besides, he needed the king's men to do the tedious work of searching for King Gaspard's treasure. Unknowingly, Ninian was *his* pawn.

Weighty burgundy curtains were pulled to both sides of three tall, narrow windows beside him. Black mirror-like panes reflected flickering light from around the room. Several glass lanterns with burning candles hung from chains, suspending dust particles like mist in the dismal light. Across the room and above the doors hung a pair of swords. The blades held a flat luster.

He exhaled a frustrated sigh. Candle flames quivered from two brass candelabra on the desk in front of him. With long, crooked fingers, he turned the page of his book and continued to read. He held a thick, hand-bound volume entitled, *The Unknown Realms*—a philosophical and scientific work from centuries ago. It was a coveted masterpiece, stolen from the old order of priests.

The book posed the existence of worlds beyond his own—not worlds across seas, but rather worlds across time, space between spaces, new and boundless worlds. Gaspard wrote of such lands, each one more magnificent than the one before. In some of his writings, Gaspard seemed to connect these other realms to the treasure he had found. Above all else, Medici sought access to these worlds.

The current chapter, "The Birthplace of Magic," was one Medici had read too many times to count. Again and again, he searched for any clue, any intimation of how one might use magic to pass from his own world into other realms. Medici believed that Gaspard's treasure was his last chance to save himself—and his mother.

Years ago, as his mother lay on her deathbed, in a desperate attempt to save her life, he had transformed her into a malevolent spirit. Her spirit took to the vast, cold, and dark places she called "the spectral." She became powerful in many ways, most of all known for deceiving people into panic, fear, and doubt. She led entire cities astray, helping her son collect clues regarding Gaspard's treasure. Yet now, time was short. He was growing old and refused to leave his mother in the painfully empty, lonely places of the spectral. Moreover, how would he avoid a similar fate? He would find Gaspard's treasure, and Ninian would lead him there.

When Medici heard voices outside his quarters, he quickly closed the book and stored it away in a bottom drawer. Two heavy knocks thumped on the door.

"Yes, come in," Medici called, and two men entered with dark cloaks, hoods drawn. "From whom do you hide your faces in dark holes beneath the earth?" Medici asked, setting his arms on the rests of his chair.

"Even walking through the caves, should I entrust my safety to your hands?" King Ninian replied with a laugh. "It seems you keep your pirates on a very long leash."

"Have I not done what you asked?"

"I did not ask for them to ravage freely about Nantes," Ninian said impatiently while lowering his hood.

"What of your military might? Did you not request an assault?" Medici leaned forward, placed an elbow on his desk, twisted his wrist, and stretched his fingers upward. He lifted his eyebrows and said, "I think your words were, as I recall, 'Create a threat in Nantes'?"

Ninian shook his head as he slid a chair in front of Medici's desk. "Very well, but you must do something to disrupt their progress, something to slow them down," Ninian said. He loosened his cloak and sat.

"I will find a way," Medici laughed superciliously as he finished, "so you can catch up. It seems that your role as a king is faring no better than your role as a father."

"Is my package safe?" Ninian asked. His voice was even, his eyes full of rage.

Medici savored the anguish he inflicted, smiled, and nodded. "And mine?"

King Ninian looked to his companion. Jansen opened his robe and removed a small burlap sack from his belt. He tossed it forward, and a bundle of loose coins thumped heavily on the desk.

With an open palm, Medici welcomed Jansen to sit.

"We must see her," Jansen demanded, dropped to the edge of chair, and crossed his arms.

Medici untied the sack and spilled the golden coins before him.

One by one, he counted as he returned them to the sack. "Indeed. She is below."

"With a crew of pirates, no doubt." Ninian's words came off as an order.

"Yes," Medici lied. There was only one pirate guarding Sophia. Ninian would not approve. *Sophia is slippery*, Medici could hear him saying. *Her evasion methods are cunning and shrewd.* But Medici had sent the other pirates out through caves and west toward Farne. He had his own mission in Nantes. He needed to find Ipabog, a man who had been assigned to a certain task years ago, whose life depended on his progress.

"Shall I have her brought before you?"

"I should say so," Jansen quickly answered.

But at the same time, Ninian confidently said, "That will not be necessary."

Medici searched Jansen's countenance. He seemed desperate and fearful, caught between the extremes of running scared and lashing out. He appeared untrustworthy, unreliable. As a matter of fact, it seemed as if he...Medici lifted his chin and sniffed in Jansen's direction.

"Leave him be, Medici. Jansen is no rat. In fact, he knows without a doubt that Habormoss has smuggled certain writings of Gaspard's into Port Regael."

"Really? And what have you done to gather them?" Medici inquired of Jansen.

"The right time will present itself," Jansen said, noticeably uncomfortable.

"Do pray it does," Medici snarled. He turned his attention back toward Ninian. "And what of Sophia?"

Ninian stood and pulled a cork from a jug of honey wine on the shelf beside him. He poured himself a tankard. "Jansen?"

"No, thank you," Jansen muttered, staring at Medici.

"We dare not leave her behind on the ship. I fear she will find some way to escape," Ninian said.

Medici raised his voice, "Your fears are unsound—"

"I want you to bring her into the city when you come. Since Habormoss has what we have been searching for, we no longer need her. So, kill her. But kill her slowly. In her final breaths, I want her to see what we have taken from the Underground. I want her to see that she has failed." Ninian took a deep drink and added, "Now, about your mother."

"You mean *our* mother," Medici corrected. "One is adopted by the family of Ninian, presented with royalty, and given riches. The other son is abandoned with Mother on the Island of Sardis and raised by poor priests..."

Ninian ignored his comments. "I would like to request her presence in Nantes."

Medici lifted his chin. "You want Nantes thrown into a panic?"

"Yes...but only temporarily. I want Mother to play along. Make it look like my soldiers have run her out of town. Then, my citizens will see that only *I* can lead them to peace."

Medici craned his neck and laughed loudly.

Ninian stepped away from the desk. "We need Aphrosyna to influence their thoughts, create doubt in ever finding an heir for Gaspard's throne," Ninian said, his voice growing louder as he spoke. He turned quickly back toward Medici. "I need the city's full confidence in me!"

"*My* mother does not waste time with greedy kings."

Jansen slammed his hands upon Medici's desk while his rage threw him to his feet. Leaning over the desk toward Medici, his jaw tightened, and his face waxed dark red.

A deep snicker rose from within Medici. "Take this child home." He sat back, looked at Ninian, and gestured toward the door.

Ninian chuckled, unfazed. Nonchalantly, he placed his empty tankard on a shelf to his right. "I will triple your wages."

"Some things cannot be bought..." Medici said and paused. "But of course, what you have requested is not one of those things."

Besides, Mother has already arrived in Port Regael...

ith the gold paid by Ninian, Medici could have sailed away to an island and lived quite comfortably for the rest of his days. But that was not his concern. Despite the bitterness he harbored toward his brother, Medici still needed him. When the time came to go into the city, he followed Ninian's orders.

Medici strode through the dark caverns and climbed the subterranean tower that connected Regael Cave with the dungeons. Then, after making his way through the dimly lit chambers of the hidden corridor into the castle, he proceeded to the northernmost tower. His footsteps scarcely made a sound, as if he were drifting along like a ghost. The torn, ragged edges of his magical black cloak twisted and stretched, lifted and turned, diffusing a dark vapor which vanished into the air.

He stopped to peer around a corner. The cloak grew more animated as it anticipated its master's evil task. Eerie red eyes reflected in a lantern's glass, glowing from beneath his hood. As quickly as he stopped, he moved on again, leaving a cloud of black fog dissipating in his stead.

Medici's raspy breath grew heavier, for in his arms Sophia slept under a spell. She was barefoot, clothed in white linen, her hands and feet bound together. His menacing coat caught her long, braided hair as it slid from her form and then laid the braid over her body.

Across the hall from the base of the tower steps, he briefly paused, looking to the left and to the right. Down the long, cold hallways he searched for assurance that he would not be seen. Oil lamps flickered in the empty passages. Satisfied, he adjusted the burden in his arms. His cloak now helped to bear the weight, so he hurried to ascend the spiraling staircase.

The tower door flew open, nearly coming off its hinges. A blast of wind blew Medici's hood back as he carried his prisoner over the threshold. Strands of white hair lifted and danced across his eyes as he placed Sophia at his feet. With bony fingers, he pulled his hair away from his scabrous face. Atop the northernmost tower, he grimaced in the daylight then stood tall, overlooking the city.

Sophia's eyes opened to a haze. A praesidio spell... She had felt this before. It pressed hard against the inside of her skull. Bound in a dreary trance, she blinked until she gained a bit of focus. Her arms and legs would not move. She could not feel her fingers. Where was she? She did not know, but the rancid smell and tentacle-like robe gave away her captor's identity.

Few were strong enough to resist this type of spell. Most said it was better to sleep in death than to suffer its arduous load. But to her, it was worth the fight. More than one time in the past, she had escaped from under the sway of malicious magic. It was always worth the fight.

The curse pulled at her body. Her breaths were tight and heavy, as though an anchor weighed her down, as if the pull of gravity grew tenfold. The strain clenched her body and mind. She ached. Her concentration clouded. *Focus!* She could not dare to make a sound, yet she sighed. Panic ripped through her. Her arm twitched, and her fingers came together in a fist. *Move! Run!* She dared not look up, but it was too late. Her eyes locked with his, and her soul emptied...

"Em sthi!" Medici called, and with a deft curse like a tidal wave of poison, he crushed Sophia back into unconsciousness. From his pocket, he grasped a handful of glasslike beads and scattered them about while summoning a dormire spell to guard the tower.

Medici raised his hands to the sky. Calling upon the elements, he thrust forth his arms and spoke, *"Unsrhi em sool,"* casting a diabolical curse along the coastline.

The Frore Edge
of Time

13

esley sensed something odd. In an instant, a heavy dampness settled in. It was not merely the evening's cool breeze. Something had shifted in the air.

The caravan stopped. Searching through the hay, he found his woolen blanket and shook it once. Then, wrapping his head and torso in warmth, he sunk into the hay. The other boys did the same. Soldiers were buttoning their coats and slipping on gloves. Some pulled long, heavy capes out from their leather packs to cover themselves.

Wesley thought of the two prisoners. *Am I permitted to help them?* Comfortable as he was, he threw off his blanket and ran to find Olivetan. He could hear his father reminding him of his responsibility to help people in need—even prisoners. Something his father used to say came to him as easily as a song. "With a soft tongue, you'll break bones!" At first, Wesley had not understood what it meant. And when he would ask about it, his father never gave him a straight answer. Having thought about it since at least the age of seven, he had concluded that it meant something like, "A humble request can accomplish difficult tasks."

Out of breath, Wesley asked, "May I bring blankets to the prisoners?"

Olivetan paused for only a moment. Extending the keys, he lowered his brow. "Do it quickly…"

Wesley did not hesitate. He grabbed the ring of keys and bolted for the supply cart. Olivetan, still mid-sentence, called after him, "We will not be stopped for long!"

Wesley hurried ahead and passed several other carts filled with young volunteers. He hopped up on the back of the supply cart, removed the lock, and climbed inside. The cart held everything from bandages to bayonets. He grabbed two thick blankets and locked the door behind him. Off he sprinted, all the way back and several carts beyond his own, to make the delivery.

Approaching the prisoners, he heard them talking. Though he did not understand what they were saying, it confirmed what he had seen earlier—the mountain man spoke with the troll. He pushed the wad of coverings through the iron bars.

"This is the best I could bring you, sire," he said as he jumped up, clinging to the bars. The wagon creaked as it dipped to the side.

"Thank you, son," the mountain man said. "Thank you for thinking of us."

"Even enemies need care."

"And what of punishment?"

"Your punishment is imminent. King Ninian will see to that. But I'm breaking metaphorical bones." *Does that work with what Father said?* "Besides, I would certainly not release you." He sounded bolder than he was. It was a bit of a thrill to be so close to someone who opposed the king. As for the troll, it was like approaching a wild animal in a cage, only niks from danger. Clinging to the bars outside of the cage was a space that held a fierce safety.

"Yes, I suppose you would not."

"I will say this, you were wise to surrender to Olivetan. By doing so, you likely saved the lives of all those people."

The mountain man sat upright and leaned closer to the bars, spooking Wesley, to the point that his left hand slipped from the bar, and he swayed backwards, still clinging with the opposite hand. Discerning that the mountain man intended no harm, Wesley swung forward, resolved to hang onto the cart.

"So, you expect that they will disband without me?"

"It matters little. You are their leader, and you surrendered. They too will reckon the might of King Ninian and see that any resistance is useless." Wesley then remembered what the king had said during his speech and continued, "Those who dare to oppose us will contend with an invincible foe. Those who are not with us will be made to bow before us!"

The mountain man seemed undaunted. "Hmm…" was all he said.

At first, Wesley expected a duel of words, but then he immediately regretted what he said. It was easy for him to flaunt authority from this side of the bars. *Everlasting peace*, his mother had spoken of. How might he change the tenor of the conversation? How might an enemy help to achieve peace? *Wait!*

"Where did you learn the language of the trolls?" Wesley asked.

"It is my mother tongue," the man explained and tossed one of the blankets toward the troll. The troll grunted, and Wesley's heart was in his throat. The frightful beast merely stuffed the blanket behind his head to use as a pillow.

With his eyes locked on the troll, Wesley asked the mountain man, "Are you part troll, sire?"

The man chuckled. "Let's just say that they are part me." He tapped his fingers on his chest.

On rare occasions, selling produce in Port Regael, people spoke Calbharian—the language that the trolls use. As heir to the throne, if he knew the language, perhaps he could arrange a truce and avert the seemingly inevitable violence. *The Fullness of Time? A peaceful way to save the kingdom?* "Could you teach me Calbharian?"

"Well, there is much to learn, and I don't believe your ranks would permit it."

Wesley slipped off the rail and quickly bounced back up, grabbing the bars. "But if they *did* allow it?"

"Then, of course. I'll do what I can with the time we have."

"Thank you, sire. I'm—"

"Move on up to your cart, boy," a passing soldier ordered.

Wesley nodded, and the soldier walked ahead.

"Before you go," the mountain man inquired, "why do you call me sire? I am no king myself, nor am I fit to fetch my king's sandals. Look at me. I'm a ragamuffin, lad."

"What does it matter how you look? You do speak *for* a king. Does that not mean something to you? My mother told me that as citizens of Nantes, we represent our king. She said we represent our land as the king himself does."

The mountain man shot Wesley a quizzical look. "Well, young man, I would suppose so."

Wesley continued, "Does it not concern you, then, how you represent your king?"

"Certainly." The man shook open his blanket and laid it over his lap. Seeming to give Wesley his full attention, he asked, "Tell me, since you have seen me, can you describe *my* king?"

"Yes, sire. Your king is gentle and fearless, but he does not know his boundaries!" Wesley jumped down to go. But before he left, Wesley said, "This is King Ninian's country. Who is the king *you* speak of? And what would ever compel you to announce the coming of another king, into King Ninian's boundaries?"

Another soldier approached on horseback.

The mountain man waved Wesley on, urging, "Yes, yes. We shall talk more, but I will tell you one thing. The king about whom I speak, *he* established the boundaries."

Wesley wrinkled his eyebrows. This, he had to think about. And with that, he hurried back to his cart and jumped up just as they began to move forward.

14

As evening approached, the temperature continued to plummet. Wesley imagined winds racing from the tops of mountains, resolving to reach a finish line. He was merely a crude obstacle in the way. Like frozen ghosts, the winds entered one side of his body and exited the other.

Large snowflakes appeared, but they did not fall from the sky—they simply swirled into existence. Larger and larger they grew, spiraling and spinning, until they could no longer resist gravity and fell to the ground. Puddles gathered on the trail. The earth sopped up the moisture and slushed under the feet of the marching soldiers. Horses slipped, and soon wagon wheels crunched thin layers of ice over shallow puddles. It wasn't long before the ground was a patchwork of earth and snow. This continued for about a quarter hour or more, and then new spectacles brought the caravan to a halt.

Everything went completely still, as if the last blast of wind froze the moment. If time could stand still, this is exactly how Wesley would imagine it. It was as if they rode on the frore edge of time. They glided through a surreal world. No one spoke.

All at once, ice crystals appeared everywhere, wrapping the tree branches and leaves with silver rime. Icy glitter draped the equipment, the wagons, and the weapons. Frost rolled out over the grass like large, white blankets. Men brushed at their crystalized beards, but to no avail, as only moments later it grew back, doubling in size.

"What strange wonder is this?" Wesley found himself speaking his thoughts aloud. It was an instantaneous winter frost, thicker and whiter than any he had ever seen.

"Let's jump in the snow," Philor called out and leapt from the wagon. "Come with me!" He made a snowball and hurled it back at the cart.

Ready to play, Wesley and the other boys stood and dropped their blankets.

"Stay put, all of you!" one soldier ordered.

A chorus of groans protested. Philor was slow to return to the cart, testing the soldier's authority. Wesley fell back in frustrated compliance.

The wind did not blow. The sun shone brilliantly, and everything glimmered in silver diamonds. The placid sea floated golden beams from the lighthouse on Telos Isle. Like the superior mountains—superior winter! Wesley could not wait to run and play in the glacial garden. His mind raced ahead, warming himself by a fire in the camp, sipping a tin of hot tea. Wesley wondered, amazed. Could *this* be the magic their mother had spoken of?

Then, it struck him—he was the only one at ease. From atop the hill, Wesley's eyes followed the wall as it curved around Beggar's Bay. Far in the distance, on the south side of the bay, a portion of the wall lay in ruins. Beyond the wreckage, anchored in the bay, were two pirate ships. His stomach filled with dread and sank.

And where were King Ninian's ships? Olivetan had to be wondering as well. Three of King Ninian's ships were promised upon their arrival. *Where were the additional forces? Had something stalled their headway? Were Ninian's ships frozen by the magic?*

Several carts ahead, a soldier had wandered off the path and reached for large icicles, hanging like stalactites from a branch.

"Don't touch it!" a cohort shouted. Running up from behind, he knocked the soldier's arm away just before he clenched it.

Quite alarmed, the soldier planted his fist in his cohort's face, knocking him flat to the ground.

The man flopped about. "It's the dark magic. We'll all turn to ice!" Attempting to get up, he slipped and tripped, screaming, "It's all over me!"

His fellow soldier laughed.

Olivetan rode up, his horse spinning and snorting. "Enough of your foolishness. Back to your mounts, we are pushing ahead."

"But sir!" the man pleaded, holding his bleeding nose.

"Enough! Get yourself together! Your fears are nonsensical."

Wesley scoffed at the idea of the snow and frost being contagious. He had often overheard people sharing their fears of contagious dark magic on trips to market, but this was one thing he did not worry about. His father had told him it was a rare but growing phobia that stretched to Nantes from Calbha Mor.

Sailors had dubbed what was formerly known as Calbha Islay (the enlightened lands) Calbha Mor (the darkened lands). Legend said that the priests of Sargus once grafted a young sorcerer into the long bloodline of priests. Because of his prowess and elegance, they had allowed him to dabble in forbidden magic, and in doing so, he fooled them all. Many inhabitants fled Calbha Mor, but the lowest caste pleaded for relief outside the temple gates. The sorcerer answered their cries with malice and afflicted them with spells.

Those who lived through the agony of the aberrations were born a new race—trolls, who now sailed the seas as pirates.

Olivetan broke through the worry and gloom. "Gather your wits, men! Make haste! We've yet to secure camp this evening! No more delays…"

An explosion of light, followed by a reverberation of deafening thunder, cracked around them. Wesley spun around, staring over the heads of all the others who were fixated north. Black clouds instantly filled the horizon and promptly advanced, rushing toward the cavalcade.

The wind hurled its icy blast. Before he knew what had happened, Wesley was tumbling over the rocky ground, shielding his head with his arms. Rolling, he coughed and puffed as the earth jabbed and beat at his body. Screams from other boys called out around him, but everything in his sight was a whirling blur.

Jolting to a stop, he shrieked as pain shot from his ankle to his thigh. His foot was wedged between protruding tree roots. Straining to twist free only increased the pain. The wind lifted Wesley and slammed him to the ground, pushing his face against the half-frozen mud. Panting, he smeared away the muck as the wind lifted him again. As quickly as he could take a breath, the earth forced it out of him.

He crossed his arms to cover his ribs, yet his neck jerked with each thrashing. The wind whipped him again, straightening his ankle, but now his back bounced off of the ground again and again. Finally, he threw out his arms, took hold of tree roots, and forced himself against the ground.

Snow mixed with rain and washed dirty slush into his nose and mouth. Clenching his eyes, he spit out bitter grit and muck. His burning hands clasped the tree roots. Frozen raindrops felt like beestings on his exposed flesh. A loud wail came from his left, then another. He threw his head and saw men blown about by the wind, slamming against the iron barrel of a nearby cannon.

Through sheets of rain and thickening snow, a dark object spiraled and lifted through the sky. A cloak? A blanket? Wesley could not be sure. When it became tangled in tree branches, he realized it was one of the other boys. Only a moment later, the trunk snapped, and the screaming boy fell with the tree over the ridge.

Wesley began to sob. He wanted to be home!

Lightning struck horizontally. Trees exploded. Splinters flew like arrows, as if archers were attacking. Several grazed Wesley's chest. Panicked, he shrieked as a soldier collapsed to his right, filled like a pin poppet.

"Olivetan! Olivetan!" Wesley wailed.

Loud twisting and cracking sounds made him strain to lift his head and look back down the path. Frantically howling over cracks of thunder, the troll shook at the iron bars that imprisoned him. In a rush of debris, the iron cage flipped to its side and slammed to the ground. *The mountain man must be dead! Where is Olivetan? Where are my brothers?*

Angry clouds continued to grow, erupting throughout the sky. Soon the darkest clouds loomed overhead, and the day became as night. The earth began to shake as if stones were falling from the sky. Rumbling over him, pea-sized hail pelted Wesley's body and stung his face. He threw his head left and right. Risking another whipping from the wind, he let go with one arm to free a long shield that had been driven horizontally into the mud next to him. With short, persistent tugs, he freed the shield at last and covered himself just in time to fend off the bombardment of growing hail.

Hail the size of Wesley's fist assaulted him and hammered the ground all around him. Overwhelmed, breathless, and weak, Wesley surrendered to his plight. The crackling and bursting and increasing weight of the shield stole away any hope of survival. Sobbing, his body tensed with each successive blow. *I am going to die, buried in the ice! Father will die of sorrow—losing his wife and then three of his sons.*

Packed in ice, his arms were now numb, and he could not move his legs. Losing consciousness, he prayed for his father, his brothers, for the prisoners, and for Olivetan.

15

The storm had Olivetan trapped. He had taken cover under an overturned wagon. Two more soldiers worked with him to free a third, whose leg was pinned down by the wagon. Drenched from the rain, his body shivered in the wind. His clenched hands were red with cold and spattered with dirt. Pressing them to his lips, he warmed them with his breath.

He longed to act—the screams around him made his stomach turn. His throat tightened, and he could not swallow. With so many boys in the caravan, what would he find later? The responsibility for the cavalcade was his. Who was more foolish—Ninian, for sending young boys into a territory overrun with trolls, or himself for following orders?

Hail rumbled louder. Large rocks of ice shattered all around. The wagon above them held its own. Yet, his mind raced ahead, looking for the next shelter.

A loud *thwack* ignited his nerves. He knew that sound and what would follow. Timber snapped, then began a crescendo of tears like giant, ripping ligaments. He quickly flipped to his side, covered his head, and peered out from below the wagon. An enormous tree fell toward them.

"Go!" Olivetan shouted.

Into the hailstorm they leapt. Olivetan reached back and under the shoulders of the man who was stuck. Wrenching him backwards was no use. Olivetan rolled away, the tree pulverizing the wagon.

"This will be our frozen tomb!" one of the soldiers cried.

He ran in circles. His crazed eyes rolled right and left. Spouting gibberish, he took a blow to the head from a chunk of hail. Olivetan motioned for help from the remaining soldier, and the two hoisted the unconscious man. Stumbling ahead, they fell into cover and pushed their way into the branches of the fallen tree.

In one last bitter breath of ice, the sky seemed to fall upon them, and all went still. Looking up through thick foliage, Olivetan witnessed their black, icy grave fade to a lighter grey. He removed his wet, heavy cloak, pushed upward, and climbed straight up to peer from the branches. The wind lifted, and the hail passed, pounding its way down the coast.

A quick scan of the area revealed no sign of movement. The assault left but a slew of damaged wagons and scattered gear. Despite Olivetan's yearning to begin a search, something told him to stay put. The moment seemed to hold its breath, taut, as if nature itself were fighting against another force—but could not hold its own.

Lashing out again, the wind threw Olivetan back. He flung his arms forward and locked them around a thick limb. *This is enough to drive anyone mad!*

At least forty rods wide, the sea formed a path, a raging torrent of ice surging toward him from the north, thrusting and thrashing its way along the coast. The convulsing tide rushed in along Beggar's

Bay, moving with the clouds, faster than any ship he had ever seen. The pirate ships in the bay were consumed in an icy glaze and imploded from the compression.

He knew then that there was sorcery in Nantes. It had only been a matter of time before its foray came to these shores. Not only did he have to contend with pirate trolls, but Medici had also played a role in Ninian's madness. Deep inside, Olivetan had known this all along.

Dammit! he cursed to himself. He should have moved the Underground weeks ago, but Habormoss had pleaded for them to wait for the shipment. If Medici was in Port Regael, then his mother, Aphrosyna, was not far behind. The Underground could be kept safe if they could make it out of Port Regael and into the caves. Olivetan prayed that Habormoss had wits enough to move them.

The icy trail blazed on with the wind and the clouds, and soon the storm passed. The thunder hollered its evil malady back at the caravan. "And stay down!" it seemed to call.

As best he could, Olivetan looked about to assess the damage. While several wagons were destroyed, it looked like most of the caravan had found shelter among the trees. He climbed from the branches and met with other men who began to gather amidst the ice and rubble. Gear and weapons lay strewn all around. Many men emerged from the forest. Those who were able began to salvage all that they could.

Olivetan found two of his lieutenants and gave orders. "Set up camp. Look for survivors and tend to the wounded. It'll be dark soon."

A soldier called in the distance, "Here, there are voices, come help!" He had discovered the troll and the mountain man still alive.

In less than an hour, several fires were burning, and the camp fell into order. A perimeter was set, and guards were posted.

"As much as I don't like it, we are here for the night," Olivetan confided in his second-in-command. Rubbing his cold hands over the fire disguised his trembling, yet his voice betrayed his worry. "I had hoped to arrive at the breach to set up camp on higher ground. We'd at least have an advantage over our enemies. We're a few hours out from there. Let's pray that the pirate trolls are far off."

It was now dark. Soldiers worked nearby, preparing torches and awaiting orders. About a dozen boys and several men were unaccounted for, including Wesley and his brothers. This troubled Olivetan. His orders were to lead the men to repair the breach. Yet, his *true* objective was to keep Wesley and his brothers safe and somehow convince them that, when the time came, they must abandon their duties and return with him to Navarre.

Olivetan gave the order to search the trail again. "There are three boys—Wesley, Philor, and Aarn. Call for them!"

"The men have walked the trail twice, sir," one soldier argued, dragging his voice with exhaustion. "The paths are slippery, and the men haven't eaten—"

"Is that what you would have me tell the families of those who are lost? Take torches and walk it again!" Olivetan did not have to say another word. The one who questioned him made no more excuses. Olivetan began to aid in the search.

It seemed that an hour had passed before a hopeful soldier called, "Over here, sir! There's someone here!"

Olivetan ran toward a group who had cleared away shards of ice from a long shield. Three fingers clasped around the top edge. He yanked the shield up and away.

"Wesley!" Olivetan smiled and eased the boy up from the ground. He longed to throw his arms around him, but this was not the time nor place. Instead, he fought to keep the tears away. "Come along, son. You'll be all right," Olivetan said and lifted Wesley to his feet. "You're going to be all right." He looked to those around him and said, "Continue to search for others!"

Olivetan guided Wesley to the nearest fire and called for hot tea. Then he dared to ask, "Do you know if your brothers were near you when the storm hit?"

Wesley shook his head and reached his hands close to the fire. It was obvious that Wesley's mind was muddled. His floating eyes seemed to stare at nothing.

Kneeling beside him, Olivetan flattened his hand on Wesley's back, took a breath, and said, "Shared sorrow is half sorrow." No response. "Looks like we've found a place to stay for the night. You rest, and I'll check back soon." Olivetan had begun to stand when Wesley finally spoke.

"Did you see how it all began?" Wesley asked. "I thought I was finally seeing the true magic." His eyes grew large with anxiety, and his body shuddered. With his left hand, he coddled the slash across his cheek.

"True magic?" Olivetan questioned. *What does he know of true magic? How much has Sophia told him? How much can I safely share?*

"My mother..." Wesley began, then he looked away from Olivetan. His voice sounded disheartened, but he continued, "Mother said that I would recognize true magic when I saw it. I feel like I have failed her somehow. I wish I could speak with her now."

"It *was* magic. It was sorcery, however, dark magic that began in Calbha Mor." Olivetan stood and warmed his own hands over the fire. "You haven't failed her. In fact, she'd be proud of you."

"No, no, I've done nothing to gain approval. I went to the fortune-teller! She must have cursed me somehow. I heard mother's voice. I...I...I wish I understood more," Wesley sniveled.

One of the soldiers brought blankets. "Here you are, sir."

"Thank you, that will be all. Continue to help the others look for survivors."

When they again were alone, Olivetan continued, "Perhaps your mother taught you what you needed to know for the time." Olivetan longed to tell him more. He longed to tell him how close he had been with his parents, how Sophia and William had found and adopted Avlae, and more...but it had to wait. The time would come.

"My brothers..."

"We are still searching for others. Stay here and keep warm. I need to assist the men," Olivetan said.

Wesley wiped his eyes with the back of his hand and nodded. Olivetan turned to leave.

"Wait," Wesley said. From inside his overcoat, he retrieved the ring of keys, which seemed to bring him closure. With them, he offered a contented smile.

Innocent Exile

16

ipe smoke, mixed with lingering smells from the evening meal, thickened the air. Riant laughter burst above the constant chatter. The spacious room below Habormoss Textiles was filled with more than one hundred members of the Underground. Children giggled, chasing each other through the dense crowd.

Three clay oil lamps lit an alcove adjacent to the gathering. Removed from the ruckus, Habs and Mahre met privately, tracing their route one last time. Habs doubted himself, but now wasn't the time to shrink away. He worried, though. He had not heard from Bela. The afternoon's sudden winter storm changed his timeline for leaving Port Regael. With the onslaught of ice and snow, the Eve of Enrichment came to an abrupt end. While the city recovered, the Underground needed to move. Habs feared a tangle with Ninian and could risk no more delays.

Mahre's voice was somber, "It will be two, maybe three days to Merchant's Pass with the children."

"To save us time, we'll leave most of the group at Caracas, in the caves. From there, I'll send messengers to gather the others, who will lead them ahead to Coligny. No need for all of us to go north.

You and I will take a small group to the Pass to meet Olivetan," Habs replied.

"The messengers must be swift, and we'll have to pray Olivetan is on time. Once we move ahead, it will be another four or five days to Dochart's Glen…"

Habs had been looking over Mahre's shoulder through the archway and listening in on the clamor in the next room.

"Habs?"

His eyes connected with Mahre's. "Yes, yes. Or perhaps not even that long. That will certainly be a curious part of the journey."

"Indeed," Mahre replied.

Mahre continued to speak, but Habs did not catch the details. His eyes wandered away again. He tried to hide his fear, but Mahre certainly recognized his misgivings. There is a comfort with close friends that disarms one's guard.

"Who am *I* to lead them, Mahre? How many will perish on the journey? Only a fool allows women and children to travel such a perilous and uncertain path."

"I don't need to tell you that everyone knows the danger. They have always known," Mahre said and lifted a hand. "They trust you, Habs. They know of Ninian's evil intentions. If it comes to it, each of them will surrender their life for you, for the Underground."

Habs's eyes again looked beyond Mahre. A twinge of unease twisted his insides. With trolls about, how many would not make it to Dochart's Glen? Any loss would be his to bear. Yet, there was no other way. Despite his uncertainty, Habs knew that Mahre was right, and he relaxed a bit. He shuddered to think of moving the Underground without Mahre at his side.

Habs methodically rolled the map on the table in front of him.

A copper medallion, stamped numerically, dangled from a leather cord that Mahre used to bind the scroll. Habs kept all they had collected in order, and Mahre immediately left to file the map away in the trunk with other parchments.

Pausing briefly, Habs closed his eyes and inwardly bowed to the Great King. He considered the cost of the journey, as he had done so many times. It grew quiet, and he opened his eyes to see the people staring at him with hope on their faces. It was not hope like a wish, like when he hoped it would rain, but rather a hope they anticipated—a confident hope that would carry them, no matter what happened along the way.

Gabrell stepped into Habs's view and informed him, "Jansen has arrived."

"Thank you," Habs said. "Please, see to the lamps."

"Yes, sir."

Habs found his way to the head table, where he had finished his meal not long before. Habs listened and watched. The room was hot and rank. Never had the entire Underground been gathered in one place. Some cried tears of uncertainty, while others let out tears of joy. A child protested against his mother's attempts to wipe his face. Pounding the table, one man released his anger toward King Ninian. A group of young women, concerned about the trek, shared their worries. Many laughed, and most seemed eager to get started.

Fears attempted to crowd his mind, but Habs shoved them away. Calling for the group's attention, he shouted, "If your heart is cold…"

With voices as one, the group finished Habs's sentence. "There is no hope!" And they hollered and hooted.

Habs again began to speak, "Friends, today, we press on, looking for a city that is not our own. The texts we have gathered lead us to Dochart's Glen. As we depart from this place and the things we leave behind, remember, these were never ours to keep. Yet, as we look ahead, we are a step closer to peace and justice, and that, my friends, we can never lose."

Habs did not know where his words came from. He became a spectator like the rest.

"The treasure in the field holds the promise of hope—binding, like a contract. But this is not just any contract. It is the person behind the contract. I knew many men who abandoned contracts. I've dealt with plenty who have failed to keep their promises. I, myself, am prone to this and have broken promises, too. And yet, it is the Great King who stands behind *this* promise. That makes all the difference!"

"Aye!" one man cried from the back of the room. Pounding tankards against tables, the group began chanting, "Aye! Aye! Aye!"

"King Ninian is too close!" Habs shouted above the rumble. His words drew them in, and he repeated, "King Ninian is too close..." The group became somber. "Those dogs on the hill have caught our scent. The black ship has arrived. Blown in by the winds of hate, it rests, docked in Regael Cave. All of Nantes will soon sense the ire of Ninian." Habs waited as faces scowled and heads shook in disappointment. Fevered tension rose, so Habs rallied them onward. "Yet, we do not grow weary!"

"No!" a woman's voice snapped.

"We will not grow faint!"

"No!" This time it caught on with many others.

"We will not be shaken!" Habs raised his pint. "To the Great King!"

"To the Great King!" the crowd echoed.

Habs swallowed the last of his ale, then he traded his pint for a satchel. He caught Jansen's eye and raised a hand, acknowledging that they were ready to go. He carefully shouldered his way to Jansen while the others began securing what few items they could carry.

"Is everything all right, Jansen?" Habs said. "You look a bit rattled."

Jansen adjusted the slim, golden band on his head—which designated his status as King Ninian's envoy—and clasped his hands. He hesitated, avoiding Habs's eyes, and said, "Of course, of course! It's not every day you get to smuggle a hundred people out of the city. Are you not nervous? The way is clear."

"Very good," Habs replied. He paused and looked into Jansen's twitching eyes, not quite convinced that everything was okay. Jansen was not his usual self—he stammered his words and fidgeted. Still, Habs let it go and said, "It's good to see you!"

Then he reached to embrace his friend, who stood stiff as wood. Jansen was slow to return the gesture, but Habs chuckled a bit to himself, wondering why, even when crawling through the cellars of Port Regael, Jansen wore his finest.

Thin as a beanpole and several niks taller than Habs, Jansen wore a pomegranate-colored cape clipped around his neck, held in place by a gold insignia of the co-regency in Nantes. Jansen's long-sleeved white satin shirt shimmered when it caught light from the lantern. Straight, brown hair hung just past his shoulders, as smooth as his shirt. A well-trimmed goatee fashioned his narrow jaw. As a well-respected member of the king's court, Jansen held great influence over many high-ranking officials. He spoke no fewer than seven languages from across World Over.

Jansen had always impressed Habs with his professional flair for public relations. But what was missing on this night was his business-minded tact and his decisive, confident character. Then again, perhaps Jansen had noticed that Habs seemed a bit off as well.

A dark oak trunk rested at Habs's feet. He lifted the rounded cover and inspected the contents one last time. Five decorative iron brackets aligned as he closed the top. The center bracket held a key, which he attempted to turn, yet it took the strength of both hands. A metallic rasp and click secured the trunk. He removed the key and attached it to a metal ring on his belt.

"Anything to report from the hill?" Habs asked.

"Bela sends her greetings," Jansen said.

"What, no poetry?" Habs smiled. Bela had always sent poetry.

Jansen delayed and answered, "She asked to meet with me in person and said to assure you that all is in order."

That was not like Bela, but Habs continued, "What of Ninian?"

"Bela has been following him closely. There is talk of searching your shop, but with news of the breach, and the wonderful weather, the search has been delayed. And unless the king has kept it completely to himself, he knows nothing of our movement tonight."

"Thank you, Jansen. Good work. You know, I really love that girl." Habs grinned and turned to Mahre, knowing he was listening at an arm's length away.

"Yes, Bela, she is quite lovely," Jansen jumped in and played along. "But she's always going on about Mahre. 'How is Mahre? Does he ask about me?' If I could only convince her that she's in love with the wrong man..." Jansen and Habs laughed heartily together.

"That's right, go on," Mahre said, ruffled, then knelt to tie his pack.

"Did anyone warn him about the danger of playing with love spells?" Jansen asked, inflating Mahre's chagrin.

"I'm afraid he is smitten," Habs said with a sigh, then changed the tone of the conversation. "I do worry for her safety. She'll be the last to get out of Regael. And if the king discovers her..."

"She is the one for the task," Mahre leapt to his feet and spoke up. "She is doing her job. We need to do ours." He glared at Jansen, seemingly daring him to say another word about Bela.

Habs nodded in affirmation, "You are right, Mahre." Habs knew Bela very well. She was a resilient young woman. Her family had a history of serving at Regael Castle that dated back to Ninian I. Having grown up in the castle, she knew its passages better than the king himself. "She will get it done."

Habs reached down to the trunk—filled with all the parchments and maps they had collected, invaluable to the Underground and highly coveted by Ninian. The lot of them would be executed if they were exposed. He slipped his hand behind the leather handle and took a firm hold. Mahre did the same on the opposite end.

"You don't let go now," Habs ordered.

"They'd have to pry it from my dead, rigid fingers," Mahre said.

Habs turned and looked over the room. He saw mostly silhouettes now in the darkened space, but he knew the group could see him from the light of Jansen's lamp. He stood tall, for he knew that he must. Any hint of fear, an inkling of despair, and they would see it in his eyes. And they would feel it with him. He took a long look over the room, searching the faces of all those who gathered. There was nowhere else he would rather be at that moment. With new resolve, he pushed away his doubt.

"We're right behind you, Jansen," Habs said. And they began.

Jansen lifted his lantern, and in the flickering glow of dusty yellow light, they passed through a hole in the wall. Jansen showed the way. Close behind followed Habs, the trunk, and then Mahre. The rest walked behind them, one by one, stepping through openings from room to room, ambling over dirt, brick, or wooden floors. Only five or six lanterns were lit among them.

Ducking under staircases and crawling through cracks, they

moved in a long, twisting line. At times, they climbed the cellar walls to reach crawl spaces beneath some buildings. They passed their bags and their youngest children. The children did better than Habs expected. Only whispers were heard among them. The burden was carrying the ones who were sleeping. For nearly two hours they had been afoot. Twice, they stopped for water and to rest, and Habs helped entertain the restless young ones who found their path quite adventurous.

He focused his thoughts. *One goal at a time. We just need to get clear of the city.*

Years ago, shortly after Jansen had arrived in Port Regael, he had helped the Underground dig a tunnel from the last cellar of the city, under the wall that surrounded Port Regael to the nearest cave outside these city walls. The wall around the city was built like the wall that surrounded Nantes—a double wall with loose rock filling the space between, which Habs used to the Underground's advantage.

Habormoss wanted no one to be able to follow them through the tunnel. So, when the tunnel was finished, they dug straight up below the center of the wall, cleared a large area, and planted gunpowder charges. After passing that area on this journey, Habs would ignite the charges, and the loose rock would fill the tunnel with debris. If anyone were to discover the path which the Underground followed, they would be busy for quite some time clearing debris before they could pass. This would give the Underground plenty of time to disappear into the caves.

Approaching this spot, Jansen reached back and gave a hand signal for them to stop. He turned and whispered, "Did you hear that, Habs?"

Habs shook his head. He did not hear anything but a couple of children behind him asking why they had stopped.

"Wait here," Jansen said and moved ahead.

"Wait! Jansen!" Habs called in a loud whisper. But Jansen was already around the next bend. Habs heard nothing. He waited. No light shone from up ahead. He and Mahre placed the trunk on the ground and sat on top of it.

"Something's not right…" Mahre spoke quietly.

"Just give him some time."

"We are so close. We need to keep moving."

"What do you propose?" Habs asked, eyes closed, fearful for Jansen.

"Send two more to check on him."

"We will wait a bit longer," Habs said, fighting his own impatience. Deep inside, he shared Mahre's distress and agitation.

Habs stared in silence and leaned forward, drawn into a black abyss. He yearned to see the least bit of light from Jansen's lantern, hoping his very thoughts might conjure it up. Then, at last, the faintest light scattered a bit of darkness, followed by Jansen's voice.

"Habormoss!" he called out. "Move on ahead."

Habs breathed deeply and pulled a cloth from his pocket to wipe the sweat forming on his forehead. He stood, pushing back on the trunk. Mahre sat so close to the edge that he fell to the ground.

"Time to get up, Mahre. All is well."

"All right, but if anything like this happens again," Mahre pushed off the ground with one hand and shook his finger at Habs with the other, "we must send two from the start to check it out."

"I concur."

With the tension resolved, they once again secured the trunk between them and anxiously walked forward. The group followed.

As they rounded the corner, a blaze of light filled the tunnel. Habs turned his head and lifted an arm to shield his eyes. The enormous ball of light came from rows of lanterns. It seemed that many hands held lamps high. Habs traced those hands to arms, to indistinguishable bodies. Long, thin metal barrels extended beyond the lamps, reflecting the light.

With a clammy hand, Habs gripped the handle of the trunk even tighter. He could feel the blood drain from his face. An odd paralysis covered him like a cloak from head to toe. There stood a wall of men, flames dancing in their eyes. Their garments were enough to give them away—a contingent of King Ninian's soldiers.

His eyes came to rest upon Jansen, who looked at Habs with a contemptuous smile. Habs felt his mind swell, unable to piece everything together. After all they had done, all they had gathered... This could not be happening.

Disappointment droned in each of his words. "Jansen, what have you done?"

Calm as could be, Jansen said, "Sorry, it has to end like this. That trunk has more value to me in Ninian's hands. He will be most pleased, and I most wealthy."

"But...friend..." Habs begged, as if somehow Jansen might reconsider his actions this far into his scheme. *All we have worked for, dear friend. Why?* Habs's face began to burn, fueled by rage and unforgiveness.

Jansen stared coldly at Habs and ordered the soldiers, "Fire!"

Rescued

17

"Oh, Sophia, we must flee!"

Between her nerves, the cold, and the dark magic pushing in on her from all around, Bela found it nearly impossible to focus. Producing a two-fold rawhide pocketbook from her brown leather vest, she unwrapped the twine cord that bound it and laid it open before her.

With shaking fingers, she fumbled for her lockpicks, then she went to work freeing Sophia from the chains that held her.

Besides the grey in her hair, Sophia had not aged. She was old enough to be Bela's mother yet looked young enough to be her sister. Indeed, she was like a sister to Bela. She had met Sophia at the age of fifteen. Bela had had her suspicions concerning King Ninian and after confiding in Habormoss, he introduced her to Sophia. Twelve years had passed since then.

Locks were not all that kept Sophia bound, for Medici held her by a curse as well. Bela recognized the praesidio spell from Sophia's listless body and bouts of consciousness, which for Sophia came with a keen awareness of what was happening. It was a grueling curse for sure, but not impossible to come out of.

Bela knew that an evil spell was like an illness. It would attack the mind and body. In time, however, even under the influence of cruel magic, one would get better. But Bela did not have time. She knew that those with a strong mind and body could fight it off and overcome its effects quicker.

This was not the first time Medici had captured Sophia. She had escaped from his evil magic countless times before—the Rivermoore Raids, the Siege of Dalarone, even the dungeon of Ninian's castle near Cape Bede. Spell, recovery; spell, recovery. Bela wondered how Sophia did not wear out.

Medici knew Sophia's strength. And like no one else, Medici could keep multiple spells in place at once. He had cursed Sophia with a praesidio spell and simultaneously cast a dormire spell to guard the tower, intending to keep Sophia in and others out. In the cold temperatures, Sophia's body had fought to stay warm, and therefore the effects of the spells lasted longer. The intention, it seemed, was to drag out her painful death.

Sophia's mouth opened just enough to let out her voice, "Who-who's there?"

"It's Bela," she answered and kept working.

Sophia mumbled some other words and fell silent.

Bela swallowed hard, fighting to stifle her anger. Tense hands made it nearly impossible to work, but deep breaths steadied her. She owed this to Sophia. Bela, herself, would die to save her friend. The tales said that Sophia had escaped from Medici ten times. If Sophia faced Medici ten times, then Bela would face Medici ten *times* ten to rescue Sophia.

Knowing that Sophia did not have the strength to hold tight for the climb, Bela kept her hands bound. She maneuvered Sophia into a seated position and turned away, pulling Sophia's arms around her like a satchel, over her head and right arm. With sturdy legs, Bela stood, slightly bent, balancing Sophia on her back. She secured a rope around them both and eased her way to the edge of the tower. Placing one hand on the parapet for balance, Bela turned and stepped backward through the embrasure. Finally, she began her descent.

With each step down the side of the tower, Bela's neck fought the pull and pinch of Sophia's chains. Bela clenched her teeth to fight the pain. Sweat beaded across her forehead. Yet, climbing out of the dormire spell, the fog in her head slowly cleared. She gained clarity and strength and became more conscious of her surroundings. The paths in the garden far below were empty. The air was still.

Finally, they reached an open stone archway in the tower. Firmly placing her feet against the tower, Bela shrugged to adjust Sophia on her back. Though they were about the same size, Sophia was all deadweight. Bela reached high and coiled the rope around her left arm, then let go with her right. The rope twisted and pulled against her skin. Quickly, she slid her right arm down between them and lifted Sophia's legs. Pushing back off the tower, Bela adjusted her hold of Sophia and swung forward. Letting go of the rope, they collapsed through the archway to the stone floor inside the tower. Bela cradled Sophia, her rope-burned arm stinging against the cold floor. Her body and mind, which were overwrought by the spell, now lolled and cooled, the effects of the dormire spell were waning.

"Bela…" Sophia tried to speak again.

Bela lifted Sophia's shoulders and dragged her from the arched window, propping her up in the corner, where the circular tower met the castle walls. Immediately, Bela went to work separating the remaining chains, her hands quivering with urgency. Time was short. Thoughts of being detected by Ninian's soldiers tormented her. And the Underground! They, too, were moving—they must flee the city unseen.

She had only a few hours and prayed that the effects of the spell would lessen, that Sophia might walk on her own. After removing the chains, Bela massaged Sophia's bruised wrists. Then she took out a wide, thick woolen blanket from a canvas pack she had stowed away days ago and used it to cover Sophia.

"That will help to take away the chill," Bela whispered.

She reached into the side pocket of her pack and pulled out a clean cotton cloth, tied at the top like a sack. With one hand, she held the bottom, and with the other she loosened the string. Bits of dry biscuit fell about.

Bela continued to speak to Sophia, not certain if she would hear her. "Well, you can see that my mother didn't bake these," Bela said with nervous humor.

Certainly, she must remember Mother's baking. Bela's mother, Esvara, had often sent baked goods with Sophia on her missions. If Bela could get Sophia to eat and drink something, it could help to diminish the spell. But Sophia just stared at the biscuits.

Bela decided to start with water. From her pack, she took a leather pouch and removed the wooden stopper. She lifted it to Sophia's cracked lips and tipped it just enough to wet them. After a couple of tries, Sophia began to sip. Bela took biscuit pieces and pushed them into Sophia's mouth. At first, it was like feeding a corpse. But soon, Sophia began to chew and take more until she ate the entire biscuit.

"We have a few hours for rest. Then, we must get to the courier's post. Sleep if you can. It will be necessary for you to regain some strength." Bela slid herself up against the stone wall beside Sophia, covered herself with some of the blanket, and closed her eyes.

What if Sophia doesn't regain her strength? The post is too far to carry her. But if necessary, I must. I cannot fail her. I will not fail her. O' sleep, do not take me. O' sleep, do not...

Bela awoke and sat upright, trying to catch her breath. Her heart pounded in her head. *I slept too long!*

She shot forward and placed her hands on the cold, stone sill. Lifting her eyes, she searched through the archway for the moon. Her fears were allayed. There it hung, though farther above the mountains—only a couple of hours had passed.

With the moon as her only light, Bela's eyes adjusted as she gathered the cloth and leather sack. She reached to touch Sophia's cheek and was overjoyed to find that it was warm. Even in the faint light, Bela could see that her color had improved.

Without opening her eyes, Sophia spoke, "What are—you—do-doing here, Bela?" Each word pushed through the lingering spell, heavy and dry, like pushing a boulder through the desert sand. "Don't be—foolish. L-leave now and—flee—the—ci-city."

"Habs said you would be stubborn about this."

"Stubborn?" Sophia cleared her throat. *"Stubborn?"* Speaking as if through gravel, she made it to the next sentence. Opening her eyes, Sophia said, "How about sensible? Habs risks too much..." Sophia coughed and swallowed. "His masquerade in service of the king will not..." Sophia placed her hand on her chest and slowed her breathing.

"He also said I should consider myself fortunate that you'd be weak from the spell and unable to put up much of a fight." From her satchel, Bela traded the woolen blanket for a heavy black cloak.

"Thank you for what you have done, Bela, but you must..." Again, Sophia stopped.

"Sophia, please, the Underground has moved. Habormoss is leading them. He instructed me to get you out of the city." Bela folded the blanket and tucked it into the pack. Pulling Sophia forward, she wrapped the cloak around her shoulders and began, "There was a phrase he used..."

"The Fullness of Time," Sophia said as clearly as if the spell had left her.

"Yes, that was it."

Bela pulled several knives from her pack. The handles were the width of her hand. Deadly blades glinted in the moonlight as she sheathed them in leather pockets. She then proceeded to strap them around her ankles and waist.

"What of my family?" Sophia asked. She then reached into a ragged pocket and removed a necklace, from which a silver, almond-shaped pendant hung. "Take this."

"That's beautiful," Bela said. She smiled to herself—Sophia spoke as if she had had too much wine. "Your family is well. Habormoss intends to gather them on his way east."

From her pack, Bela handed Sophia a beveled triangular knife, sharp and shiny, easily hidden in the palm of a hand. She slid the handle over into Sophia's hand and demonstrated how, with a flick of the wrist, the blade would swivel outward parallel to the fingers and lock into place for quick defense. At that, Bela pulled on her pack.

She grasped Sophia's hands and pulled her to her feet, urging, "We must hurry before someone discovers you are missing."

18

y legs…I won't make it…" Sophia said as she threw an arm around Bela.

"You must." Bela pulled her close. The two made their way down the spiral staircase. She kept Sophia to her right, where the steps were wider. Even so, Sophia's feet slid along the stone. Bela carried most of the weight, stopping briefly from time to time and leaning against the wall for support. When Sophia did manage to plant a foot, she groaned and tightened her arm around Bela.

"You will get stronger," Bela said and moved ahead. If they waited too long in one place, they would be discovered for sure.

Bela had been planning her timing, tracking the guards' positions and movements to take the most favorable path from the castle to the courier's post. That was the easy part. She had grown up here. Her mother baked for the royal family. Bela still worked as a servant in the castle—a handmaiden for King Ninian, using her post as a spy for the Underground.

Reaching the bottom of the steps, Sophia looked as if she would faint from being so weak.

"I can carry you," Bela said. Panting between words, she continued, "But we…must keep…going."

"Don't carry me…just keep me close." Sophia held tight.

Bela moved forward through an unlit corridor. For a short time, they could move without the possibility of being seen. Keeping a quick pace was what mattered now. Once they reached the gardens, though, they would need stealth as well.

Exiting the corridor, they arrived at the south portico overlooking the castle gardens—a grid of pebble pathways bordering wildflowers and well-trimmed shrubs. Stone columns held heavy wooden beams and spanned the entire south side of the castle.

"Do you have a spell to conceal us—absconditus, perhaps?" Bela asked.

"Draw forth…a charm? I've barely str-strength…to…"

Bela's face distorted to a frown, giving away her jest. "The post is on the west side of the garden. We'll rest at the pool along the way."

From column to column they moved, stopping only in the shadows. At the middle column, Bela backed up against the pillar nearest the garden entrance. Supporting Sophia with both arms, Bela pursed her lips to stifle her panting. *Quiet. Remain calm.*

Stones crunched behind them.

Bela's arms tensed around Sophia. *Not now, not now!* She knew her timing was dead on—someone was not where they were supposed to be. On the opposite side of the column, someone stepped away from the garden path. The hedges to her right blocked her way into the gardens. She shrank in place, holding her breath.

The footsteps trailed off west along the portico—the opposite direction of the women. Bela exhaled and counted the steps to measure distance. Then, circling close to the column, she pushed off onto the trail and into the garden. Thick green hedges on both sides kept them hidden for a time. The first left led them along the outer circle that encompassed the pool. Any right turn would lead them to the center. They were exposed now, and her legs seemed to melt beneath her.

I just need to reach the pool! Focus!

Rectangular oil lamps billowed slightly in the breeze, illuminating the path. For now, at least, the moon was shrouded by clouds. They passed ancient statues of robed women, men of war, and even children. Ever since she was a child, the statues of the children holding hands in the garden had intrigued Bela the most. Some led dragons, some had wings, and others carried large water vessels—ancient symbols of the peace that was to come.

Bela's eyes were ever watchful. Far off, she could see the storehouse and silhouettes of soldiers carrying rifles. *These men will not think twice about killing us.* A vine-covered trellis near the pool offered cover.

Sophia's feet were dragging. Her head sagged against her chest. "I've no strength…" Sophia exhaled her words.

"Twenty paces more." Bela strained to walk as Sophia's feet slid heavily across the stones, her body slipping from Bela's hold. Nearly tripping, the two fell forward onto the granite edge of a kidney-shaped pool. Bela held tight to keep her friend from falling in.

Sophia slid her arms down through the water lilies. With cupped hands, she gently flushed her face. She repeated this several times till her hands fell to the rim. Bela bore the weight to keep Sophia upright.

"I have you," Bela assured her. Sophia's arms trembled, but Bela kept her steady. "We haven't much time—I need to say this now." Bela paused. "I'm so sorry that I failed you."

"What do you mean?" Sophia asked, sounding exasperated and confused.

"When Ninian captured you, it was my fault. I should have stayed back…"

"Say no more," Sophia said. She managed to turn her head and look Bela in the eyes. "It was Aphrosyna. I was keeping her from the city when Medici ordered his spell upon me."

"But I led him to you," Bela admitted.

"This you do not know for certain. You came to help me."

"Yes, but…"

"Aphrosyna is deceptive. Ninian will have her summoned when he finds out the Underground has made their move. It is likely that she will come to Port Regael."

"Ninian would do that?" Bela's voice was surprised, but her soul was not.

She knew Sophia was right, though she did not want to believe it. Aphrosyna—the evil spirit of Medici's mother, known for deceiving entire cities—could be summoned to Port Regael. The strength that had been leading Bela drained. Sophia would be needed right here in Port Regael to contend with her. Did Habormoss not realize this?

"Then, you must stay in the city," Bela reasoned.

"No, Bela. Continue with the plan. Habormoss will be expecting me. One step at a time."

Bela closed her eyes and thought for a moment. She nodded with new determination. "You're right. We must leave, now!"

Bela knelt beside Sophia, putting an arm around her upper back and under the opposite shoulder to guide her fragile body away from the edge of the pool. From there, a single curved path would lead them from the garden. They sidled through a narrow arbor that ran the length of the path. At the main entrance, Bela paused and leaned against a brick column, adjusting her hold on Sophia.

"We're nearly there," Bela said as she peered around the column through an iron gate.

Directly across from them was the courier's post. All shipments coming and going from the castle were sorted there. The two-story building was constructed of heavy oak beams and plaster. Its many windows were dark.

Farther down the road, the castle patrol was walking away from them. Bela reached for the latch and opened the heavy gate. Gradually, she pushed against the creaking iron, giving just enough room for the two of them to squeeze through.

"Keep going," Bela whispered.

"I'm beginning to feel my legs again," Sophia said, her face determined.

Through the gate and across the dirt road, Bela guided more than carried now. Every so often, one of Sophia's knees gave out, but Bela kept her upright. Bela prayed, *We just need to enter the post. We'll be safe in the post.*

Arriving at the entrance, Sophia let go and pulled away from Bela. She reached to the doorframe for balance. Iron braces adorned the wide oak door. Bela lifted a key from her pocket. She inserted it into the lock, twisted, and then leaned into the thick door. She gently thrust with her shoulder, nudging it open.

"Here we go," Bela said.

She took Sophia inside and lowered her to the wooden floor. Bela sloughed her pack, then immediately closed and locked the door behind them. Before she could turn back to Sophia, a light washed around her. She lowered her arms to her sides and did not move.

Behind Bela, reflected in the windowpanes of the door, were two of Ninian's soldiers looking down at her. One had his rifle aimed at her back. He chuckled and said, "A bit early for mailing packages."

"You *are* up early this morning, Miss Col," the other quipped. He lifted the oil lamp to reveal his wide smile of large, crooked teeth. His greasy fingers smoothed his beard. "Jansen said I might find you here."

Jansen? If he betrayed me, then what will happen to Habs?

Bela twisted and spun in a single motion, releasing the blade strapped to her waist. Across the room, it accurately lodged into the throat of the gunman. The soldier dropped his weapon and clasped his neck. He sputtered and spat, bouncing off the fixed wooden bench behind him, then falling hard to the floor. As quickly as he fell, the one with the lantern raised his pistol and cocked the hammer.

"You foolish girl. Now, you lift those arms high. The king ordered us to do all we could to bring you in alive, but I'd rather do things my way. Please, give me a good reason to kill you." He placed his lantern on a nearby table and clasped his pistol with both hands.

The sentry was too close. His hateful eyes told her that he would not hesitate to pull the trigger. Her only movement was her breath. Yet, her mind scrambled for anything to get out of this. She looked past him to Sophia. Had she passed out?

"Turn around!" ordered the sentry.

Bela swiveled toward the door, her head pounding with alarm. All of Mahre's fears and warnings she realized at once.

Staring at the door, she felt the barrel of the gun press hard between her shoulder blades. She prayed no one on the outside saw light coming from the post. Two soldiers were enough to deal with. Next to the door hung an iron crowbar, used to open the crates.

"Now, open the door."

His hefty hand shoved her forward, and her head bounced off the doorframe. Pain shot through her skull and neck. Yet, Bela heard the soldier screaming over her own moans. Through blurry eyes, she looked back. Sophia had jabbed her blade into his back.

The soldier lashed back, striking Sophia across the face with the butt of his pistol, and the blow knocked her flat. Before he could turn back on Bela, she reached for the crowbar and with all her strength bashed him over the head. The henchman thumped in a heap, the bar clanking to the floor beside him.

Bela took the lantern, lowered it, and dimmed the light so as not to draw attention to the post. She stepped over the body and knelt to see Sophia's right temple swelling around a sliver of her right eye. Elbows slid back as Sophia attempted to get up off the floor.

"Wait, wait." Bela took a cloth napkin from her sack and gently dabbed at the cut above Sophia's brow.

"We haven't much time. Come, Bela, get me up. We must hurry."

Bela lifted her, and the two scampered to the next room. After closing the door, Bela held the lantern up. There were no windows in the back room. She searched and found the outgoing crates from Habormoss. Finding the one marked *Coligny*, she knelt beside it and went to work picking the locks. The crate was made of thicker planks than most. It was meant for shipping artillery and cannon balls.

Once it was opened, Bela removed several layers of cerulean silks. She reached inside and twisted interlocking handles. Finally, pulling upward, she removed a wooden divider.

"Only Habormoss," Sophia said, shaking her head. "How many times has he pulled this off?"

"The Underground is moving. They will find you near Merchant's Pass and take you to Dochart's Glen, where you will be safe."

"And what of Jansen?"

"He left only hours ago. He is with Habs and the rest of the Underground. As far as he knows, these soldiers arrested us. I say we move ahead with the plan to get you out of the city. You will be long gone by the time that bastard hears of what happened."

"The Underground is in danger," Sophia worried. "There is no telling what Jansen has planned for them."

"I fear the same." Bela lifted Sophia and placed her in the crate on a bed of straw. Sophia curled up tight. Bela took a crowbar from the counter, placed it in Sophia's hands, and said, "We'll pray and trust that Habs finds you tomorrow night, but take this. If Habs is delayed, or if, Great King forbid, he does not arrive, you can pry your way out."

"From one prison to the next," Sophia said and managed a smile.

"There's enough of a gap in the slats for you to breathe, but not so much that you will be seen. Here is some water and the rest of the bread. It will help you regain some strength. And look, I've brought you this as well." Bela placed a shallow pan in the crate.

"A bedpan? You *have* thought of everything."

"I knew you'd like it."

Sophia took Bela by the hand, asking, "And what of the dead soldiers?"

"I'll find a place to ship them as well." Bela grinned. "Now, let's get you settled."

"May the Great King go with you, Bela."

"And you."

With that, Bela covered Sophia with the wooden divider and turned the handles in place. She carefully returned the fabric, then covered and locked the crate.

HABORMOSS
© 20

The Triumph of Magic

19

lames ignited one by one. Each rifle threw vivid starbursts, flaring as flints struck steel, dotting Habs's vision. He dropped his end of the crate and stumbled backward, tripping over his own legs. Slumped on the ground, one of his legs was bent at the knee in front of him, while the other hung up over the crate. After a minimal delay, each flare overlapped with a sizzle, a crackle, and a rumbling whoosh of sound.

Jansen had given the order to fire.

There was no time to run.

Yet…Habs had not been shot?

Mesmerized by his own confusion, Habs watched. Successive explosions tarried on at a deafening intensity—then dragon fire, spewing one barrel after another, burning like the sun—a sound so piercing, Habs clasped his ears and looked over at Mahre, who was bent over shielding his own ears.

Faint screams and muffled shouts from members of the Underground tore through the residual blast. Fixated ahead, Habs pushed back and used the wall to guide him to his feet. With his right hand, he reached over and grabbed Mahre's arm. Still covering his ears, Mahre finally opened his eyes and looked at Habs. Habs motioned with his hand for Mahre to look ahead.

Amidst the blinding riot of light, billows of smoke expanded ever slowly. Lead balls pierced the smoke and were rolling toward them mid-air, creeping along at chest level. With his hands glued to his ears and mouth agape, Mahre stood rigid. Behind him, people running in the opposite direction were turned around by another flash of light and expanding concussions from rifle fire. The Underground was ambushed in both directions.

Unlike the slow-moving balls of lead, the people rushing toward Habs ran speedily and freely. The lead balls continued, laggardly stretching toward him. At this rate, the Underground could run themselves directly into the line of fire.

Habs pulled Mahre's hands from his ears and shouted, "Tell them to stay low! We have to run beyond the line of soldiers!"

Despite the irrationality of it all, Habs put it together. Time itself had warped around them. Ninian's troops had fired upon the Underground, and at the same moment, something bent. Like a blade of grass in a pool of water or like light as it passes through a prism—they had time within a moment, a longer reach in the same distance.

"Warn them, Mahre! Pull each person close! We must run ahead and stay low!"

Habs began waving his arm forward and calling back to the group, "Stay low and crawl! Go! Go!" His voice echoed, and his movements blurred.

Mahre pulled one man close. "Stay below the line of fire! Crouch down and run!" Then he motioned downward with his arms, yelling, "Stay low!"

Frantic, the first man lunged ahead and immediately ran through one of the rounds. In a spatter of blood, it burst from his back and continued its languid roll toward the Underground. Reaching arms fell limp, and the man flopped against the rocky floor. Those who remained alert pulled at the frantic ones, the disoriented ones who were seemingly deaf to Habs's warnings.

Parents gripped their kicking children, who screamed and ran toward the blast. Older children attempted to run away while parents tugged them back, fighting pleas and throes of resistance. One after the other, the group plunged ahead. Figures bleared, rushing past Habs, crawling, scrambling, throwing clouds of dust, and penetrating the line of Ninian's soldiers.

Over and over, throwing his arm forward, Habs wrawled, "Move! Move!"

After securing the crate between them, Habs led Mahre ahead, sidestepping the incoming rounds. To help guide him, Habs looked back at Mahre, just in time to see him lift his hand to touch one of the lead balls. In slow rotation, it burned across Mahre's palm—he clenched his fist and cussed. Mahre's face curled in pain.

Habs shook his head, unable to hide his amusement. "A bit hot? Are you through playing around?"

"You weren't curious?" Mahre spoke through his teeth.

Habs turned to move ahead, and his eyes locked with Jansen's. The last of the Underground passed through the line of soldiers as the resounding blasts ceased. Jansen's eyes seemed alert, and his gaze averred hate. His lips slowly moved as if spewing curses. Habs now pitied Jansen. And as he stepped by, he placed a hand on Jansen's shoulder, rigid and tense, as if to feel the resentment flowing in his friend's veins.

Habs glared at Jansen. "And so, the truth has arrived to suffocate your lies. Whatever has met us here on this night, it will surely be told for generations to come. I am sorry our friendship has come to this." Habs walked on, still carrying his end of the crate filled with the parchments and maps that Jansen intended to confiscate. Mahre followed behind.

Then Habs felt a slight tug on the crate. He turned to see that Mahre had bumped into Jansen on the way past him.

"Let him be, Mahre," Habs ordered.

"It wasn't me," Mahre explained. "It was him!"

Habs looked closer. Still bound by warped time, Jansen moved steadily. His head began to turn back. His fingers released their grip on his weapon, stretched as if shaking off a cramp. Along with the other soldiers, his form eerily twisted toward Habs.

"Let's go! It seems as though our friends are catching up to us." Habs and Mahre hurried away, just beyond the border where they had planted explosives in the ceiling. Pulling the fuse from the rocky wall, Habs said, "I'm certain this was meant for our demise. They would have killed us and buried us right here."

Lifting his lantern, Habs lit the fuse. And just as the two references of time merged together, the ceiling burst with a concussive blast, burying Jansen and his men in rubble.

What Happened at Beggar's Bay

20

hile en route to the breach, the boys who were lost in the storm were found hiking south on the trail. Wesley's brothers and all the other young men had lived! Wesley jumped from the cart and ran to embrace Philor and Aarn, but they were less than affectionate. When asked what had happened, the boys said they had found shelter not long after the storm began, though each of them told a slightly different story.

The boy who went over the cliff said, "The wind carried me. It was as if I could fly!" He exclaimed, "I could see the whole of the bay! I glided in the falling snow for what seemed like hours. I came close to the mountainside, landed in a pile of snow, and rolled and rolled. It was great fun! When I finally came to a stop, the other boys surrounded me, laughing."

Another boy chimed in, "Then, this giant bird appeared. It spread its wings and came over us."

Others said the so-called "giant bird" was "more like a giant blanket."

And another said, "The bird provided shelter large enough for the entire caravan!" On this they all agreed, nodding their heads. "We tried to find a way out to come back and lead the caravan to the shelter."

"Yes, but we couldn't find a way out," another reported.

"Weren't you afraid?" Wesley asked.

They all agreed, "Not at all!"

"We could see each other well enough…"

"But," Aarn jumped in, "we didn't see a lantern or a candle or a fire."

Philor added, "It was warm. We slept well, with warm coverings."

"We even had breakfast!" a boy who had been trying to talk snatched the opportunity.

"That's right," Aarn again butted in. "A table was set, and we ate bread with honey butter, with cups of… What did we drink?"

"I don't know, but it was hot and sweet," Philor boasted.

Then they had all left the shelter, as if an exit had always been there. And though they had looked, no one saw the giant bird again. Shortly thereafter, while walking, they had heard calls from Olivetan.

Wesley found it very difficult to believe anything they said. To him, it seemed far too preposterous—which could only mean it was his brothers' doing. He wondered how his brothers had managed to convince the other boys of their tale.

That evening, when the caravan arrived and set up camp on the hill above the breach, however, Wesley's brothers decried what the others were saying. Philor wrote it off as an illusion. Aarn linked it to the bewitching effects of the dark magic. Aarn and Philor always had to have a way to separate themselves from the rest. Wesley may never know the truth of what had happened.

In the morning, regiments began felling trees and sharpening the ends. Several abatis were placed across and down the northern ridge. More cannons were placed on high ground, and bunkers were positioned to the south and west. Soldiers were told to make the posts their homes for the next several days. Throughout the morning, Wesley and his brothers worked with the other boys at clearing away the rubble from the breach—that is, until Philor and Aarn decided to go exploring. For a time, Wesley lingered behind them and remained hidden. He did not want to leave camp, but he did not want to lose his brothers again either, even if they were jerks.

Despite the snow, Philor and Aarn found what seemed to be a trail leading up and farther into the forest. Winding through hemlock and birch trees into a slight opening, they arrived at an arched fieldstone bridge, crossing a freshwater stream that flowed from the mountains. Near the banks of the stream, the water was frozen solid. The ice thinned as it spread toward the center, though, and right in the middle, the water flowed freely.

Too thirsty to stay hidden, Wesley scrambled from his hiding place.

Philor grabbed him by his shirt collar and called to Aarn, who had crossed the bridge. "Look here, we have a stalker!"

"Let me go!" Wesley tried to push himself away, but Philor held firm and dragged him toward the creek, like he may throw him in.

"That'll be enough!" a voice called from somewhere behind.

For a moment, Philor's grip tightened, and in an instant, Wesley was pulling his face from a pile of snow.

Philor shook his hands from the contagion of coming into contact with Wesley's clothing. He called to Aarn, "Seems our stalker has stalkers."

"We've been in need of fresh water," one of the soldiers said to the other. "Damn fools are worried about the melted snow being contaminated by dark magic."

The other replied, "Looks like we've found our water boys!"

The water boys were strictly warned to only enter the forest with an escort.

But the next day, on a water run, Philor and Aarn decided they needed a break and convinced the escorts to allow them to wander beyond the bridge, up into the forest where the trees grew spaciously. While he was not always quick to agree with the twins, secretly Wesley also wanted to rest and followed along without protest.

"It's getting warmer," Aarn announced and threw off his coat.

The soggy ground around them soaked up melting ice and snow. They tromped through muddy puddles, lured ahead by a rich, earthy fragrance. Piece by piece, more layers came off, and they began hanging their clothing on branches along the path.

Philor called out, "Look up the trail, I see grass!"

Springing forward at full speed, Wesley pushed past Philor and sprinted ahead. Now stripped down to his undergarments, he rushed out into a meadow. Warmth seized the air like a summer day. His brothers came running right behind him. Their escorts finally caught up with them and seemed to enjoy the weather, as well. The soldiers pulled off their boots and reclined in the tall grass.

"The spell has lifted!" Wesley shouted as he reached out through a patch of wildflowers.

Dancing bugs, grasshoppers, and dragonflies buzzed around them. While running, Wesley swung his arm forward, throwing yellow and pink flower petals into the air. The petals opened into butterflies and fluttered away. His arms fell to his sides. Baffled, he stared into the sky.

Unbelievable! Quickly, Wesley looked to see if the others had witnessed the spectacle. "Did you see that?" Wesley asked, but no one had been watching. *That had to be the magic Mother spoke of.*

Even so, that thought was gone in a wisp of time. Perhaps he only imagined what had happened. Was he looking *too* hard to see any sign of true magic? Perhaps the petals were merely blown by the wind, fluttering in the light of the sun, but this was not the first time he had seen this.

The fall after his family had first arrived in Navarre, his eldest sister Avlae, who was only nineteen at the time, had been collecting daisies. Just outside their home, she had tripped, and when the daisy stems hit the ground the petals seemed to burst open and began to flutter around her.

"Are you seeing this?" she had asked as the butterflies led her toward the root cellar. Wesley had seen it all, but he was too stunned to speak. Avlae chased after them and called back, "Are you dense? Come along, come with me!"

She tugged open the cellar door and hurried down the steps. When Wesley had caught up to her, they both stood, dumbfounded. The butterfly wings illuminated the space, and several of the strange insects lighted upon an old trunk. And in the flittering light, the two of them opened the trunk and explored.

Clinging to a parchment, Wesley looked and asked, "Did Mother ever tell you of mountains that spoke?"

Lulled by her thoughts, Avlae seemed to search her memories. "I cannot say that I remember such a thing." Her voice had inflection just like Mother's, but other than the large braid they both wore, Avlae looked nothing like her. Avlae had a narrow chin, whereas Mother's was rounded. And her hair was a light brown, while Mother's was deep auburn.

Wesley spread the writing before Avlae, who studied closely.

"Amazing!" She smiled and lifted a brittle page—a map of Nantes. She pointed, "Here, Calbha Islay. Do you recall Mother's tales about it? This is where Aphrosyna raised her son."

"Yes, of course!" Wesley told her. "The young priest grew up to become a wicked sorcerer."

"How often Mother warned us of those two…" Avlae added. "Mother said that they seek Great-Grandfather's treasure for themselves."

"Look here," Wesley said, "directly across the river from Brazenose."

"The Province Beyond the River. Oh, that sounds alluring!" Avlae said.

She reached upward, a few butterflies gathered upon the palm of her hand, and she moved them closer to the map. Smoothing her almond-shaped wire pendant between her finger and thumb, she studied the map and then the pendant. Something was testing her nerves. Wesley followed her eyes to the parchment. In the corner, a symbol was stamped. Three almond shapes, like daisy petals overlapped at the center, formed a triangular pattern.

"Our three pendants," Avlae spoke, seemingly lost somewhere in her thoughts. Her eyes began to tear up. "Mother, Jess, and I each have a segment."

Wesley took her hand, and together they lifted the parchments— one by one, each having the same stamp in the corner.

For what seemed like half the day, the boys romped through the tall weeds, chased frogs, and played with insects. It would finally be a warm night of sleep when they arrived back at camp.

However, much to their disappointment, as they made their way back and collected their clothes from the trees, the cold crept in around them. Their damp clothing only made things worse. Evidently, when they had ventured beyond the bridge and walked deeper into the forest, they had walked beyond the edge of the spell. It looked as if only the coastline was affected by the unusual winter storm.

Trying to find the bright side, Wesley boasted that they would have a warmer road home—a road farther inland, away from the coast. But Olivetan was quick to deny that request. They would return to Port Regael the way they came. That would be the safest route. And perhaps by then, the spell *would* be lifted. Wesley was not optimistic about that.

21

It was now the third day since the caravan had arrived. Wesley stood before the gaping hole—the breach at Beggar's Bay. Just enough morning light shone to view the frozen bay and the wreckage of the pirates' ships.

An ice-glazed forecastle jutted from the frozen sea as if it had broken through from below. The main mast, with the crow's nest still intact, angled out behind it. The other two ships must have been completely swallowed by the storm—crushed and buried below the ice. Other debris lay scattered about, covered with snow.

Out farther in the bay, there was open water. Wesley hoped that at any moment, he would see one of King Ninian's ships. When he saw deep purple flags trimmed in gold speedily cresting the horizon, all his nerves cheered within him. Leaping up, he stumbled forward, barely catching himself from falling. When he looked back to the horizon, however, the flags evaded his sight. Some illusion had bewitched him. The weight of gloom immediately returned.

The storm must have overtaken them. If I could only tell Olivetan of my family... Though something pulled him to do so, Wesley fought against the yearning to tell Olivetan of his relation to Gaspard. He swore to say nothing until he returned. But what if he *never* returned?

His chin sank to his chest, and he shuddered in the cold. This wintery blast was no fleeting spell. Unrelenting cold pervaded his bones. The brutal storm that had shaken them three days ago gave no signs of releasing its icy grip.

He studied the breach, which seemed so much bigger now. The last two days had been spent clearing away the rubble, and the next three to four days would be spent making repairs. He had hoped to be on his way home by now. Yet, with so much more to be done, that day seemed to extend further and further away.

Nearly stepping over him, several soldiers tromped past and through the break in the wall, relieving the night patrol. More men arrived with axes and shovels to break through the snow and ice that covered the sandy shore. They needed sand to mix with the slaked lime to make mortar. Another crew arrived with scaffolding, tools, ropes, and pulleys and immediately began to assemble their gear for the day's work. An outer and inner wall needed to be constructed. Between the two, they would dump loose rock, sticks, broken equipment, rubble, and anything else they could find to fill the space and reinforce the wall.

Wesley studied two carts sitting near the breach. One held the bodies of four soldiers who had died in the storm, frozen as the ice that they were packed in. It could have been his body lying there, or even his brothers'.

His eyes shifted to the other cart, which held the bones of soldiers who had died in the king's service over the last thirty years. It had been that long since any work had been done on the wall. The remains of those killed in combat were to be buried between the walls. This tradition dated back to when the wall was built. Even while cleaning up the debris around the breach, Wesley had found bones that must have been buried in the wall when it was first constructed. Some bones had even been gnawed on, reminding him of how the bears had to defend themselves, too. Some of the men said, and truly believed, that the spirits of those dead men continued to guard Nantes.

Were the spirits overcome by pirate trolls as well?

Wesley turned from the breach and started the uphill walk back to camp. The caravan had settled on the flat land above the breach. To the north was a large precipice overlooking the valley road they came in on. To the south and east, the land sloped slightly down and flowed into a forest. Rising out of the forest were, of course, immense mountains. Olivetan had said that this location worked to their advantage in case of an assault by pirate trolls or bears.

The camp was waking up, and Wesley could not find his brothers. Earlier that morning, it was still dark when he had seen them leave, but he had been too tired to question them. He had thought for sure he would find them down at the breach. Though, since they were not here, he had a good idea where they might be—the forest, beyond the bridge, where it was warm.

It seemed unlikely that they would have found an escort so early. Never overly willing to get to work in the morning, they must have been up to something. But Wesley was also certain that they were not so stupid as to venture off into the forest without protection.

And since they surely already had an escort, Wesley reasoned with himself that there was no need for him to find one. Moving along the perimeter of the camp, Wesley circled his way east to the trailhead, hoping he would not be seen.

22

"orgetting something, Wesley?" a familiar voice called from up the hill.

How did he spot me? That man had eagle eyes. There was no use in trying to sneak off. Wesley marched against the wind, up the icy hill, back toward camp.

A stout man holding a long, wooden pole stood near steaming pots and kettles. Two buckets were laid in the snow on the ground near him. It was Lew, preparing morning rations. *He must need water.* Slices of thick pork sizzled over fires—it smelled so good. But Lew would not let him eat before he returned with water.

"Have you seen my brothers this morning?" Wesley asked. He cupped his hands, wrapped in fraying cloths, and exhaled slowly to warm them.

"Sent them off before dawn." Lew seemed impatient, rattling dishes and digging through utensils, his layers so thick he could barely bend his short arms. He offered Wesley half a tin of steaming coffee.

"You sent them off in the dark?" Wesley asked and raised a hand, declining the coffee.

"Suit yourself." Lew sipped and set the cup aside. "Your brothers had lanterns and an escort. The sooner I get my water, the sooner we get men to the wall and the sooner we get home, boy. Perhaps you ought to catch up with them."

He never looked Wesley in the eye. Though, with such a hairy face, one could not really see where Lew was focusing. He didn't seem to care if Wesley went off alone, as long he got his water. Lew went on to say, "And while you're fetching water, you might fetch your brothers and their water as well. They've been gone quite a while."

"Yes, sir," Wesley spoke dryly.

Far too often, he took the brunt of his older brothers' irresponsibility. He reached for the pole from Lew's hand and put it on the ground. A leather strap ran from each bucket handle to an iron ring. Wesley knelt, slid each ice-cold ring into a notch on either end of the pole, and proceeded to place the pole over his shoulder. Yesterday, one of Lew's assistants had shortened the leather straps after several soldiers were mocking him because his buckets were sliding through the snow as he walked.

With a stick over his shoulder, one empty bucket in front, and the other behind, Wesley balanced back down the hill and took to the trail. Several niks of fluffy snow covered the path. The footprints his brothers had left were already filling in. He followed their trail and had not yet reached the creek when their tracks left the path. It was just like his brothers to venture off! No doubt, he'd take the blame for them being late, too.

Wesley removed the stick from his shoulder and placed the buckets along the trail, then searched ahead into the woods. *Where did they get off to?* He waited a moment and considered whether to go after them. Even after coming up with several great excuses as to why he should not, however, he reluctantly followed the tracks into the woods.

Not long after the tracks began, he came across his brothers' supplies. The trees had grown too dense to maneuver their poles. Wesley stooped under branches and pushed through the brush. Snow fell down the neck of his coat, and he shuddered. Attempting to scoop it out made it worse, as it only fell farther down. Crawling and climbing over and under downed trees, he reached a point where the footprints stopped, as if his brothers and the soldier had vanished.

Realizing what lay before him, he stepped back and gripped a nearby branch to steady himself. Footprints three times the size of those he was following had stomped around the area and trailed off into the woods—trolls! He envisioned a pirate troll picking up his brothers and carrying them away. His stomach turned, as if he could retch.

He had to move. Slowly, Wesley made his way ahead, carefully placing each step to not make a sound, terrified of what he may see—or what may see him. He pictured his father burying three of his four sons. His entire body flinched as the shadow of a bird flashed through the corner of his eye. Something rustled in the woods beyond his sight.

A bear? A troll? Brown fur launched from the snow-covered thicket… A squirrel. It had sounded much bigger.

Coming to a clearing, the prints went down into a ravine. Not wanting to follow the tracks to where they ended, Wesley decided to climb a nearby ridge off to his right. He hoped he might gain a good view from the top, but he did not anticipate such a steep bank. Using protruding roots and branches, he pulled himself up through the deep snow. Voices came from the other side. His brothers were alive! But there was another voice he did not recognize, a deeper voice—the escort?

Upon reaching the top, he slid up behind several large rocks. His heart pounded so hard, he thought for sure it would be heard. Sweat and melted snow rolled over his cheeks as he leaned in and peered around the massive stone. Wesley felt his eyes bulge. Quickly, he pulled his head back behind the rock. Trying to find a safer view, he maneuvered ever so carefully to the snow-covered branches on the opposite side.

What have they done?

His brothers stood, arms crossed and confident, with two pirate trolls and some rough-looking nomad. The soldier—their escort— was bound and gagged behind them.

"Tell them we are the *family* of Gaspard," Philor spoke proudly.

The nomad translated for the trolls, then for Philor and Aarn.

"You say this, but you have no proof," the nomad said.

"You think we would lie and risk coming to you?" Aarn reasoned without fear, seemingly upset that they would not take him at his word.

"We need your strength to establish our reign," Philor said, waving his arms before the trolls as if they would understand him better with his hand gestures. "The throne is ours to take!"

Aarn continued, "With the treasure in our hands, we can free you from your curses. And we will give you dominion over lands throughout World Over."

Wesley could not believe what he was hearing. How did the twins ever get caught up in this?

The nomad spoke again with the trolls. He clasped a walking stick in his right hand and had a rifle slung over his left shoulder.

Long, thin hair, black and greasy, stuck to the sides of his face. A patch covered his right eye. He wore black leather boots and several layers of ragged cloaks.

The trolls were hideous—caesious skin, thick and calloused, bubbled with blebs up and down their arms and legs. Veins stretched and crawled between the lumps like giant earthworms under their skin. The creatures were huge. They had to be over four rods tall, with arms and legs like trees, except for the peg leg on one of them.

Their pale-yellow eyes sank deep below their brows. Nostrils stretched the width of their eyes and exhaled the winter air. The points of their noses loosely drooped down below their chins and curled up at the ends. Wide mouths formed natural frowns. Triangular teeth randomly protruded from their bottom lips, and pointed ears stuck out of their thin, matted hair.

One yawned. His jawbone seemed to be double-jointed. The troll could easily fit Wesley's entire head into his mouth. Their necks, if one could say they truly had necks, were as wide as their heads. Both wore thick, brown cloths around their midsection. One wore heavy, plated armor that hung from his shoulders, covering his chest and upper back. Brown wrappings began a few niks above their ankles, wound down around their heels, and covered their enormous feet. One had a rifle clutched in his massive hand. The other carried a steel-spiked club.

"Look," said Philor. "We can take you to maps, drawn by Gaspard himself."

"We'll take the treasure and fill all our pockets with plunder. We'll take what we want from whomever and wherever we want," Aarn added.

His brothers had weapons. *Where did they get guns?*

"You know, boys, if you are lying to us…these trolls will tear off your limbs and leave them as a trail to your severed heads," the nomad warned and curled his lip in scorn. Taking the staff into his left hand, he extended his right to seal the deal.

Aarn reached out a hand and shook. "We'll lead you to our home in the Navarrian Hills. I know where Father has kept the maps."

"No!" Wesley shouted, not intending to speak aloud.

Immediately, the trolls' heads spun. *Their heads* do *spin all the way around!* The one with a gun fired upon him. Stone fragments shattered over Wesley. He quickly pushed himself behind the rocks and jumped down the ridge. Thwacked by branches, he spun and bounced, landing upside-down in the snow, crunching his left shoulder into the ground.

Slipping as he stood, he reached back to balance and kept himself from falling. Without looking back up the ridge, he cradled his left arm and lurched ahead with long strides. Beneath the snow, his boot caught a branch and he stepped at a frantic pace, managing to stay upright. He had not traveled very far from camp. The shot would have been heard. He needed only to make it to the trailhead. At last, he spilled out onto the main trail, crashing headfirst into one of his buckets. Behind him, branches were snapping. Scrambling to his feet, he refused to look back.

Breathing fast and heavy, he raced on. His shoulder pain faded, and a warm trickle rolled over his chin. With the back of his hand, he wiped his lip, leaving a smear of blood over his knuckles. Another shot exploded from somewhere behind, followed by a howling pirate troll. With the end in sight, his strides grew longer, and his body stretched forward. Stumbling out of the woods, he rolled to the feet of an armed soldier. Looking up, soldiers surrounded him and raised their rifles, aiming into the forest. Olivetan pushed through between two of the men.

"Wesley," Olivetan spoke as he knelt beside him. "Speak up, son! What did you see?"

Wesley panted furiously. "My brothers," he finally managed to say. "They've gone off with the trolls!"

KING NINIAN III
© 2020

Unknown Realms

23

ing Ninian closed his tinderbox and slid it back inside his leather satchel. He waited in his meeting chambers, expecting several of his advisors, and Medici momentarily. They all would be quite pleased to hear what he had learned. He was eager to announce that after three generations, an heir to the throne of Gaspard had come forward. And he was just as eager to bury that name forever. Gaspard had betrayed Ninian's family once—but never again!

Hearthside he paced, with his arms behind his back, from the table to the window and back and forth. With his chin up, his pipe hung from his jaw, leaving a lingering path of white smoke across the room. Despite his layers, it was difficult to keep warm. It was frigid in Port Regael as of late. He reached for his heavy, purple cloak, which hung opposite the hearth. Fastening the ornate metal tags, he admired his rich brocade decorated with silver vines, highlighted by the room's crimson walls.

Several paintings ornamented the room. He looked upon a portrait of his late wife. Obsessed with her beauty, he had wooed her without really loving her. Changing her proved to be impossible, and their relationship became a mere formality. Royalty did not suit her.

She had disengaged herself from her duties as queen. Committed to her vows, she stood beside him but never truly with him. She died of dysentery while serving the poorest villages throughout Nantes. He did not miss her. Her portrait had been hung only because some would ask about her, and he would lie about his broken heart. It served to keep up appearances.

Next to it was a depiction of the Lothian Victory, which ended the Bailiwick Wars of 384. Painted in 1102—308 years before he was born—it had adorned the castle walls since King Ninian I. In this painting, seven generals stood, overlooking the parched land they had conquered. Bodies were strewn over burning fields—tokens of triumph and sacrifice. The generals had just secured their victory, conquering the one who called himself the Great King. This victory had marked the end of his wicked and oppressive rule. That weak and spineless king was finally driven out. Defeated, he had withdrawn into uncharted lands.

The painting symbolized two things. Firstly, independence from tyranny. The generals had announced themselves as kings. They had drawn their own boundaries, established their own kingdoms, and written their own laws. Secondly, vigilance. The new kings had prepared vast armies, ready to defend themselves. If this so-called Great King were to ever return from the uncharted lands, the seven kings agreed to band together and meet his threat with a heavy hand.

The victory this painting displayed was King Ninian's prize—his impetus for conquest and a symbol of his own might and achievement. And with King Ninian's family being the only remaining lineage of the seven kings, he was prepared to meet any return of this Great King with his own military might.

Finally, there was the mysterious painting. A translucent man—a spirit or ghost, perhaps —seemed to be emerging into the scene. Adorned in amethyst robes, he gestured forward, as if to offer a ready hand of deliverance. Beside him reared a valiant white horse, ears back and nostrils flaring. Its fierce silver mane blazed like fire. The lighting in the painting did not come from the sides, nor above, nor even below, but rather from the face of the man himself.

It was a rare painting to say the least and priceless, or so he was told by a local appraiser. Many, including the appraiser, suspected that the man in the painting was the *numinous wanderer* from tales of old. But the man hardly fit the description. In separate stories Ninian had heard, the *wanderer* was a crazed nomad, an ugly beggar, or a filthy glutton. Such fine clothing, which he wore in the painting, did not add up. But the appraiser had insisted that he had heard other stories. And as much as Ninian would have liked to dismiss that idea of this being the said *wanderer*, he could not. The man's eyes seemed to see into him, convicting him of his devious thoughts. And that terrified Ninian. He knew the lore.

The legends said that a year after the Bailiwick Wars had ended, the Great King sent a council of peacekeepers. The kings of the land had not even taken time to hear the council. Immediately, the kings beat the peacekeepers, breaking their arms and legs. After binding them in their broken condition, they were dragged to port, placed on a ship, and sent away.

Yet again, the Great King had tried to make peace. This time, he'd sent several ambassadors to initiate an armistice. But it was no use. The kings of the land would have nothing to do with the Great King. They had responded by cutting off the hands and feet of the ambassadors. Tied to their horses, the ambassadors were sent back the way they came.

Finally, one day this *numinous wanderer* was discovered on the outskirts of Brazenose. Up to his elbows in dirt, shovel resting over his shoulder, his face smeared with mud as if he had wiped his brow with his forearm, he was seized by a local militia and brought before the seven kings. He told the kings that he came to offer peace with all the treasure of the Great King. When questioned about where this treasure was, he told the kings that he had buried it in a field, in the Province Beyond the River. And if they would follow him, he would lead them to it.

The kings scoffed at such a thing, suspecting the wanderer had come to lure them into an ambush. How naïve did he think they were? If indeed there were a treasure, the seven kings reasoned, the dirt would be freshly dug, and the treasure easily found. Since they had refused the peacekeepers and ambassadors a hearing, how much more the poor ugly beggar?

Rumors spread quickly concerning the treasure he had buried, and as a warning to anyone who would go seeking the treasure for themselves, the seven kings had impaled the man on a post at the gates to Brazenose. The seven kings sent patrols into every corner of their territories to stand alert, in case the Great King might retaliate.

But war never came.

Months went by. Extensive exploration of the Province Beyond the River was proven futile. Each of the kings died, spending the rest of their lives scouring the Province. The treasure was never found.

Memories faded. New boundaries arose. New territories were charted.

Like his father and his father's father before him, Ninian's most desperate desire was to find the treasure in the Inner Realm, formerly the Province Beyond the River, and keep it for himself. He would do anything to secure the treasure—resorting to military might, sorcery, and deception. No one would dare to stand against him. Ninian's grandfather had said that when Gaspard found the treasure in the field, he chose to sever ties with King Ninian and partner with the Great King to steal away the coveted kingdom of Nantes.

For that, the family of Gaspard would pay.

24

ing Ninian turned to his windows and looked out over Port Regael. Snow sagged from rooftops, and ice-striped roads snaked through the city. It had been several days since the ravaging storm. There were only a few days of suspicion among his people. Rumors arose about dark magic, but that was nothing new. Most talk on the street, so Ninian was told, was that people spoke of an early winter storm and resumed their lives as usual.

There were no sailing vessels coming or going, but there had been times like this in the past when ice shut down the locks and the water froze in the bay. Seasons change. This weather was certainly early but not entirely surprising. King Ninian would not have ventured such a ploy with Medici, had this not been so.

A knock came upon the chamber door, and King Ninian cleared his throat. "Come!" he called, approaching the table.

The door pushed open, and his attendant took two steps into the room. The chamberlain bowed and said, "They are present, sire."

King Ninian simply nodded and stepped up onto the dais, taking his seat at the head of the table. Five men—the king's circle of closest associates—silently entered the room. Layered as well, they were dressed in the finest garments the kingdom provided. Silver and gold weaved through their silken robes. Thick, white cuffs and tall collars were fitting highlights. They did not sit, instead waited for the king to begin.

"Come now," King Ninian called, "we will drink to the new age!"

From the doorway, the chamberlain pushed a silver cart with goblets and several bottles of wine.

"Very good, Elwic. Now, please gentlemen, be seated and take your rest. Your eyes tell weary tales. Do be forthright." King Ninian lifted his hands as if to urge them to speak. "Where do we stand with my dear friend, Habormoss?"

None of them looked King Ninian in the eyes as they took their seats. After an uncomfortably long silence, one man spoke up. "Habormoss has escaped, sire."

Ninian waited to hear more, cursing Habormoss in his thoughts, but the men said nothing else. He suppressed his rage, and after a lumbering moment, the king continued, "Well, this was certainly not unforeseen. His antics do keep things lively." Ninian forced a smile to hide his clenched teeth. His advisors scowled.

Elwic poured wine for each of them. Taking his time and stealing glances at the king. Ninian sat back in his chair, listening to the lapping of wine and shifting of chairs. He drew his breath and released a deep sigh, fidgeting in his chair. *Oh, hurry it up.* He knew Elwic was hoping to hear some of the conversation. Nosy old fool. But no matter, Ninian would wait.

"Thank you, Elwic, that will be all," King Ninian ordered. And the door closed behind the chamberlain. Ninian lifted his glass. "Here we are, men. This will settle your anxiety and restore you to clarity."

All of them drank deeply. Yet, when the goblets were placed back on the table, the silence resumed. King Ninian could have killed them all. More and more, these men displeased him with their inaction. He needed new advisors.

But he nodded and continued, "Please, go on. I want to hear more about Habormoss and how he escaped from a regiment of my soldiers." Ninian's tone mocked their nervous silence. He waited without a word, glaring over his goblet as he drank—deep red wine, dry and woody, perfect. Warmth coated his insides, adding to the fire growing within him.

"The passage below the city, my lord, it fell in upon our men," said the timid Torres.

What kind of nonsense is this? Ninian shook his head in disbelief.

"And Jansen?" the king questioned, anticipating another tall tale.

"Jansen is dead. It was quite unusual how it came about. One moment the regiment took aim upon Habormoss…"

"We more than took aim at him. We fired upon him!" Talicue interrupted, throwing his arms up in anger and spilling his wine. He snagged a cloth napkin and clumsily began soaking up the spill, then slammed his hands upon the table. "It was as if we watched the whole of an instant stretched out like a canvas over a frame. If I had not fallen backwards, I too would have been buried in the rubble! We saw each detail of the moment, and yet, the moment was gone! There was some type of magic woven in time!"

King Ninian stood, tipped back his goblet, then placed it on the table. He stepped down from his dais and took several steps toward the hearth. *Deep breaths.*

"Forgive my protest, but what sort of tangle is this, my lord?" Torres spoke, his voice shaken with uncertainty. "What is this otherworldly realm that impedes our law? What is it that Medici wields? It's terrifying!"

"Medici?" questioned the king. He spun quickly around and stared down his advisors. "I do not contend his involvement in this matter. You are all privy to his service on our behalf."

"Sire, if you please, it is Medici whom we have come to fear..." Talicue said. With a tremble in his voice, he added, "And his sorcery."

Refilling his spilled goblet, Torres spoke again, "If we are speaking openly, it is the alliance you have made with him that defines our contention."

Ninian tapped his pipe on the stone above the fire, emptied the ashes, then looked back toward the table. *Cowards!*

"Gentlemen, we were unanimous in our decision to seek Medici's help." Ninian shrugged, raising his arms to emphasize that they had known about this all along. "Now, your unease is unarguably decided..."

"Decided?" Talicue objected. Immediately, he pushed back and stood straight up, knocking over his chair. "Indeed, I should say imposed!"

"Now, now, I want to assure you men that Medici does not lift a finger without our orders." Ninian paused and walked back to the table. Leaning forward and looking directly at his advisors, he raised his hand, pointing his index finger in scorn at each of them. "His license is at our discretion!"

But Talicue could not let it go. "Again, sire, permit me to question, but does the trouble elude you?" His small voice quavered. "How will the one you *claim* we tame interfere with this seemingly untamable realm?"

Pitiful man. How did he ever end up as an advisor?

Ninian employed his golden tongue. "Gentlemen, I know there is much mystery, but that should not deter us. Rather, it should drive us on to victory and discovery." Ninian raised his arms. "Lift your eyes, men. The laws of our world do not bind us. Old letters tell us that the unknown realms are controlled by the one who has the treasure. When *we* have the treasure, we will control all realms. We will establish the law as we see fit. Gaspard sought this for himself and in his weakness surrendered his reign to another king. Is this what you would have me do?"

Ninian would not be moved. Yet, he also did not want to lose the loyalty of his advisors. He could not let distrust from his advisors contaminate his people. He thought long about his words, puffing away on his pipe.

With a lighter tone, he continued, "Accept my word that you have nothing to fear in Medici. The Underground has nowhere to go. Though they have gotten away, that is but a small matter. We will find them. I mean, really, where will they go? Who is sovereign here? The Inner Realm will be secured, and the lost treasure of Gaspard will be ours. You must consider, now, your own allegiance."

"We are loyal to you, my lord, and all you stand for," Torres said, and he stood to honor the king.

"We are with you," another vowed and stood.

King Ninian stepped back upon his dais. "Very well, gentlemen. Then we must move forward. Who will lead the charge into the Inner Realm?" the king asked. He began to repack his pipe. For a long while, he waited. After all, he must at least give the *impression* that his advisors had some say.

"Let me speak boldly," Torres said. "It is time to claim the treasure in the field. We must move swiftly."

"I agree," a third said and joined the other two standing. "All ties to Gaspard must be severed. In the meantime, preparations should be made to sail to Orhe Mireth and onto the Inner Realm. It is time we secure the treasure."

Typically quiet but always honorable, the one whom King Ninian trusted the most, Ezra, stood from his chair—the fourth to stand.

"Bold indeed, and we shall not delay. Your words have been my thoughts of late," Ninian answered.

Talicue said, "Sire, if I may, there is more."

"Proceed," Ninian said. His fingers tightened into fists as he obliged the seated rebel.

"You would do well to think on the things we've spoken of, my lord," Talicue seemed to warn the king.

Daring fool! This man is seeking his own execution! Ninian's entire body became rigid. With his jaw so tight that he had to force out his slow, accusing words, Ninian asked, "How do you mean?"

"We do not know the bounds of other realms, nor do we know the extent of evil magic. I fear where the treasure will lead."

"I will hear no more of this!" Ninian screamed. He thrust the table toward Talicue. Goblets clanked to the floor. Talicue fell from his chair, his tunic soaked with wine. Ninian stomped off to the window, "It seems you are ready to put limitations on my reign! With Gaspard's treasure in our possession, Nantes will extend into the uncharted lands and even the unknown realms!"

Soon. Soon she will be here. Soon all of Nantes will lose hope of finding Gaspard!

Without looking back, he hollered orders. "Pull together your men. I will personally accompany you to Orhe Mireth. From there, we will set up operations to thoroughly explore the Inner Realm. And Medici has a plan in place to keep others out of there." With shaking hands, Ninian messily repacked his pipe.

"And what of the pirate trolls gathering to the east?" Talicue once again questioned the king.

King Ninian casually turned his head to see Talicue still on the floor. "Ezra!" Ninian called. "Arrest this man. He will hang for his insolence!"

Without hesitation, Ezra grabbed the scrawny Talicue by the shoulders and yanked him to his feet. The other advisors threw threatening glares, seemingly tempting the fool to say another word so that they might slay him immediately.

Without removing his pipe, King Ninian spoke, leaning ahead with his arms behind his back. "Those pirates do not concern me. They are no match for our might. Some things must first be put into place, for this is why I have called you before me today." Shifting his demeanor, Ninian removed his pipe and set aside his anger. "I nearly forgot the reason I called you together." *You idiots distract me so.* All eyes followed him as he stepped. "There is a new development that will give us critical advantage. It seems that I've found an heir to the throne, a son of Sophia."

Now, Talicue laughed aloud.

"So, you doubt what I say?" Ninian frowned at Talicue. "You will not live long enough to meet him."

Torres spoke up, "Do tell, King. Three generations have searched for the family of Gaspard, and he appears *now?* In Nantes?" His voice betrayed his disbelief.

"The heir came to me," King Ninian said as he strode, chin up, back to the table. "His name is Derian Delaine. It seems that

Sophia married some time ago without our knowing. Her husband and children are living nearby, in Navarre. Derian spoke to me of writings from the hand of Gaspard himself. I am preparing to—"

The door to the king's chambers swung open. Medici stormed into the room, emanating his vaporous stench. Often agitated by the sorcerer's lack of propriety, King Ninian was not surprised at the intrusion. The advisors seemed to hold their breath, though, as if fear were strangling them.

"She is gone!" Medici announced in a cold, loud voice.

Ninian could feel his face flushing, burning. *One day, I'll figure out how to have Medici put to death.*

Of course, he knew what Medici was talking about, but Ninian grinned and played along. "Would you care to elaborate, my friend?"

Medici was not amused. "Sophia is gone, my lord."

"Perhaps you ought to arrive on time for our gatherings, or even come before me when summoned. Then, you would be better informed."

"I do not—"

"Come, will you not join us?" Ninian welcomed Medici yet clenched his hands to hide his shaking. "Take your rest."

His advisors were quick to lift the table upright and gather chairs. Elwic stood at the door, his countenance attesting to his discomfort as a result of Medici's intrusion.

King Ninian spoke, "Sophia cannot be far, my friends. In fact, considering her options, we'll most likely find her at the Delaine home. Where will she go when we bring a full battalion to her doorstep? And if she is not at home, *someone* will be…"

The Heir of Gaspard

25

ollowing a vibrant, yet waning display, the last of the sun's gleaming rays surrendered below the horizon. Wesley's eyes finally relaxed from squinting. He sat slumped near the campfire, unable to eat, addled by his foolish brothers.

After dinner, men smoked their pipes and would tell stories until sleep pulled hard at their eyelids. Wesley sat with them, shivering, dinner plate in his lap as he played with the gristly meat, which had long gone cold.

A heavy hand came down upon his shoulder and startled him. He looked up to see Olivetan's hairy face, with a long, curved pipe hanging from his grin.

Olivetan removed the pipe and said, "I've seen bed warmers back in Port Regael, but this is a new touch."

Immediately, Wesley jumped back, while flames seared the edge of his blanket. His tin plate clanked against the edge of the fire pit, and his food spilled over the ground. He threw off his heavy linen and stomped out the fire, irritated by the men cackling all around him.

"The boy has nothing on his bones to keep heat in," gibed one of the men. The others laughed along.

Agitated and embarrassed, Wesley draped his still-smoldering blanket over his shoulders and pulled tight. He had had enough of their banter for the evening. Yet, he was not ready to leave the warmth of the fire for his frozen bed.

How could Philor and Aarn betray our family—even Nantes and King Ninian? What about Avlae and Jess? Who would protect them from the pirate trolls? What about Father?

Wesley's chest tightened. His face flushed, and his breaths were short. If he could only speak with Olivetan, he would pour out his heart. His brothers had broken their promise. Did that make it right for him to break his? Perhaps *this* was the Fullness of Time? He had always pictured it as a momentous ceremony, a celebration very much like the Eve of Enrichment, not a scramble in the shadow of fear. He trembled for his family. How could he get home? Again, he remembered words from his mother. *"You need to learn the sound of your own heart, so that you may follow what it says."*

His heart became clear. He must get home before his brothers.

"What is the best protection from pirate trolls?" Wesley asked.

Several men chuckled.

Olivetan lifted his eyebrows and looked very serious. He bent over close to Wesley and answered, "The best armor is to stay out of range."

Wesley didn't laugh. Instead, he merely blurted out, "My brothers are fools!"

"I am afraid for them," Olivetan's voice became stern, "and their treason is the least of my fears. Pirate trolls move with more strength than the bears, and without their armor, they could easily outrun them. That is why I've taken so many precautions. Without proper defense, those trolls would roll over us like a rockslide."

Why did their heritage have to be a secret? *Forget the promise!*

Wesley reasoned with himself. He could no longer remain quiet with his family in danger. It was the only chance to save them.

"Sir…" Wesley said.

"Yes, son," Olivetan answered.

Wesley waited. His heart jumped and skipped as he began to sweat. "There is something I need to tell you."

Olivetan said nothing, as if he had not heard him.

"I…I…" A pang shot through Wesley's gut. He had never spoken a word of this to anyone outside his family.

"You're tired, Wesley. We'll talk another time, perhaps after you get some sleep. Things always seem ten times worse when it's late and our bodies are not fully rested." Olivetan moved toward him and offered a hand. "Come, I'll walk you to your tent."

What is wrong with Olivetan?

"No, you need to hear this now," Wesley demanded.

"Let him talk," one of the men suggested, sliding closer, as if not wanting to miss what Wesley had to say.

"Yes, go on, lad. It'll help just to get it off your mind," another said. Leaning in, he rested his forearms on his thighs.

The men's prattle gave way to sympathy. Or perhaps they were mocking him. It didn't matter to Wesley now. Olivetan sat again, seemingly put off, as if Wesley were wasting his time. This seemed out of character for him. *Once I speak, he'll certainly understand.*

Wesley took a deep breath, then began, "I've longed to tell you…I mean, what I need to say is…"

"Oh, my." One of the men shook his head. "Out with it already!"

Olivetan stared at the ground, picked up a stick, and poked at the fire. The others sat wide-eyed, leaning in so far that Wesley thought they may fall over.

"I..." Wesley lowered his head. "I just want to get home."

Wesley looked around. Their eyes said it all. Most straightened their posture and moaned. Others fell backwards in hysterics—this was surely not the climax they had anticipated.

One man constrained his laughter and said, "Olivetan, would you please hitch up the horses and take this lad home?" This set off the lot of them in riotous laughter.

"Come with me, Wes. We need to talk." Olivetan stood, put a hand on Wesley's shoulder, and led him away.

"Wait, where are we going?" Wesley asked. Quickly, he twisted and pulled his shoulder away from Olivetan.

"Keep moving," Olivetan ordered.

Wesley did not like this. He held back, a few steps behind Olivetan. "Why are we leaving?" Wesley worried. "Where are you taking me?"

"There are things you need to know, things that will be troublesome to hear." Olivetan was short with Wesley. His pace quickened, tromping through the snow until they were quite a distance from the fire. Clusters of stars lit the sky, and with the moon nearly full, one could see clearly down the hillside and into the valley.

Without breaking his stride, Olivetan said, "I am trusting that the time is right for you to hear some truths." Olivetan waited for Wesley to catch up and looked him in the eye. "Wesley, you need to know..."

Bright lights flashed out of the northeast. Before Olivetan could finish his sentence, their heads turned in unison. The next ten seconds seemed like an eternity to Wesley.

A triplet of resounding blasts followed the lights. In an instant, Olivetan knocked Wesley to the ground, falling on top of him.

Wesley lost his breath and gasped for air. A whoosh of cannonballs tore through the trees around them. Branches burst, and Wesley threw his head to the side. Squeezing his eyes closed, Wesley's face was spattered with shards of wood.

Three times, the insides of his eyelids flashed red, and the deafening sounds ripped through him again. Chaos echoed from the hill—the camp had been hit. In a blur on the hill above, silhouetted horses were tromping and whinnying alongside men rushing to arms.

When Wesley came back to real time, Olivetan was dragging him by his shirt through tall grasses and down into a damp gully. With both hands, Wesley grasped at his collar to pull it from his neck. He twisted his body and kicked his floundering legs, trying to break Olivetan's hold. Dropping to the slushy ground, his body reeled. Now flat on his back, sucking in air, he huffed and panted.

Up and behind, at the camp, Olivetan's men returned fire upon the trolls. Scores of flaming arrows lit the sky, and it seemed they would fall upon him. There were too many arrows. Wesley covered his face with his hands.

"Stay down!" a voice called, a voice Wesley did not recognize.

Through his fingers, Wesley saw three soldiers appear out of the darkness, raising heavy wooden shields. Sheltered beneath the protection, he listened as successive thuds thumped into the thick wood. As fast as they had arrived, away the soldiers flew, rising above the grasses, unhindered by the trees, absorbed by the night sky.

Wesley gasped, and he finally called, "Olivetan! Olivetan! Did you see—"

"On your feet!" Olivetan ordered as he jerked Wesley off the ground. Stumbling and tripping, Wesley could barely keep up, his wrist twisted in Olivetan's grip.

Mortars raged from the hill. Olivetan's forces unloaded their massive guns. Wails carried across the cold nighttime air—the pirate trolls were too close. Several units of soldiers rushed upon the furrow below the cannons and fired their rifles as fast as they could reload them. More arrows and flares were launched overhead.

I have to see this.

Wesley spun around as the flares exposed a field of pirate trolls. With blazing shots, the hill erupted in artillery fire. Several pirates appeared over the abatis. A burst of rounds assaulted them, followed by more mortar fire.

"Incredible," Wesley said, gaping at the trolls.

Seizing Wesley from behind, Olivetan pulled and rushed him into the camp.

Out in the field, far off behind him, the trolls returned fire. One of the caissons had caught fire, burning not far to Wesley's right and then abruptly exploding. The concussion kicked him to the ground. Flames licked his back, whisked around him and upward into oblivion. Shattered planks hurled past, while hot coals and ash scattered around him. With mortars ringing in his ears, he crawled, dragging himself from the debris.

His vision teetered, and all went black.

26

chill awakened Wesley. He lay on his back, covered with a heavy blanket. His eyelids strained to open. Through bleary eyelashes, his surroundings were fuzzy shadows. His dull mind stretched to remember anything. Was he home? It certainly did not smell like home. It smelled like unwashed clothes and ashes. Both his head and neck ached. Breathing sounds crept around him, a loud snort and cough. Lantern light flickered in a low, vertical slit on the wall. A doorway?

Flaming arrows.

Pirate trolls.

The explosion that had knocked him to the ground.

Finally, his mind caught up. The camp was attacked. He had been laid among the wounded.

Wesley pulled his arm back to push himself up but was stopped short. He tugged against an iron clasp around his wrist. Chains clanked against the side of the bed. Moments later, lantern light leapt across the room.

"Can I help you, boy?" a gravelly voice asked.

"Why am I chained to the bed?"

"Those were my orders, lad. Do you need water?"

"No, I..."

"Another trip to the latrine?"

Another trip? "No. I need you to..."

"You get some rest, then. It's nearly dawn. They'll come for you soon enough." The soldier pulled away the lamp and flapped the canvas closed.

Who would come for him? What had he done? They must have feared he would try to get home. *Oh, what a dumb thing I said. But this matters not. I will find my way home. My family needs to know what happened. I'll leave while it's dark and sleep during the day, as we did years ago, finding our way from Brazenose. Magic will protect me. Or maybe...*

Clasping the iron band with one hand, he pulled with the other. His skin folded and tore as he twisted his wrist back and forth. Having a small frame had its advantages. His hand jerked free, albeit cut and bleeding. Gently, he placed the iron clasp upon his bed, tore a strip of linen from his sheet, wrapped his hand, then silently slid to the floor.

Crawling on his belly from bed to bed, he made his way beneath the sleeping wounded. At the end of the room, he crawled under the canvas. Staying low, he ran bent over from tent to tent until he reached his own. Grabbing his pack and two heavy blankets, he hurried to find bread among Lew's provisions. Two loaves—no, three—would get him home if he rationed his portions.

By now, the faintest light of day was creeping into camp. He fled from the cookery and down the hill, toward the trail that led to the stream. He ran along the south end of the hill to keep out of sight. Scampering across the main trail that led back to camp, he then entered a small section of trees just north of the prisoner's cart.

Safely hidden in the trees, he stepped cautiously, coming up behind the two captives. Ever slowly, and without a sound, he crept close to the cart.

"Sire," Wesley breathed a whisper. "Sire. Sire."

The man stirred and lifted his head while the weak pirate troll tossed about, then returned to his slumber.

"Come now, you've awoken me. What is it you want?"

Perhaps I've acted too rashly? Wesley did not say a word. He was about to conspire with the leader of the Underground. *How can I trust him? Do I really have a choice?*

"What is it you are after? I know who you are."

Wesley held his breath.

The mountain man chuckled and said, "Who else calls me 'sire'?"

Finally, Wesley pushed himself from the snow-covered shrubs, stood, and stepped up to the bars.

"Well," the man said. "It's the young boy who brought us blankets."

"Yes, sire. Now, I need *your* help," Wesley said. "I am leaving."

"And where do you intend to go?" The mountain man sat up, crossed his arms, and rubbed his shoulders.

"I must return to Navarre. My family needs me."

"It's a dangerous road back to Navarre." Rubbing his eyes with his thumbs, the man yawned. "You intend to travel alone?"

"Yes, sire. Or perhaps...perhaps you would be my guide?"

Seeming to consider Wesley's words, the mountain man stared off in another direction for a time. He then cleared his throat and looked back at Wesley.

Wesley added, "Before you answer, know this. I can set you free. I can promise you a pardon from the king!" Wesley could not believe what he was saying. Judging from the mountain man's expression, *he* could not believe it either.

"So, you want to help the Underground?"

"No, I want to help *you*."

"You are close to King Ninian, are you?"

"No, not at all," Wesley admitted. The man frowned, and Wesley explained, "What I mean is…I am close to the throne."

Now the man seemed confused.

Wesley leaned in, his lips nearly touching the bars. The mountain man met his gaze. Clinging to the bars of the prisoner cart, Wesley's knuckles ached. His jaw began to quiver. Then, under his breath, Wesley said, "My brothers and I, we are heirs of Gaspard. That is what my brothers told the pirate trolls, that is why…"

The mountain man reclined, his disbelief evident. "Oh, really?"

"It is true." Wesley begged, "You must believe me."

"So, if I help you…" He eyed the sky and dropped his gaze back to Wesley. His large eye seemed to open even larger. "You," he pointed at Wesley, then back to himself, "will pardon me?" Laughter began to shake him. "All these years the kingdom has searched, and the heir of Gaspard comes to *me?*"

"Well…I am not first in line for the throne. But Derian, my eldest brother, seeing that you have brought me home safely, he will pardon you."

"Ah, yes. This will bode well. A leader in the Underground helps an heir to the throne commit treason!" He choked back his amusement.

"Please, sire."

Finally, the mountain man seemed to consider his options. Certainly, he could not pass up such an offer. The man's face became grim, and he said, "So, you are an heir of Gaspard." Wesley nodded, and the man crossed his arms. "You seem to speak of this rather carelessly."

Wesley burst, "What do you mean? Do you know how hard it was for me to tell you? My brothers and I made a pact. I was sworn to secrecy!"

"Well, so much for your oath!"

"No, no, it's not like that." Wesley ran his fingers through his hair and kicked at the wheel of the cart. "Look, are you going to help me or not?" *Slow down. Try another approach.* "You speak the language of the trolls," Wesley said. "You could keep me safe!"

"Yes, yes, you're very observant, lad. However, I'm far too old to make the trek." The mountain man lay back as if he were going to try and get back to sleep. Yet, as soon as his head hit the wooden planks, his eyes popped open. The man sat straight up and said, "You have given me an idea. This troll, *he* could guide you. He's not much for strength, but he is a friendly one."

Wesley considered the mountain man's offer and quickly agreed. "Then, I need you to teach me some words right now. If I can communicate even the smallest bit and perhaps even make it look like I've befriended a troll, I believe I'd have a chance."

"You mean to learn Calbharian this morning?" the man chaffed.

"Only a few words, like, uh…'friend' and…'peace' and maybe a sentence or two…Like, 'Don't eat me!'"

With that, the man laughed aloud, and the troll opened his eyes. "Do you want to go free?" Wesley pressed.

"With my record, it really makes no difference. Besides, who is ever *truly* free?" The mountain man examined Wesley. With narrow eyes, his face tightened, and his voice became strict. "If you are indeed an heir of Gaspard," the man poked his index finger at Wesley, "you'd do well to keep your mouth shut. There are men here who would kill you if they knew that."

"Are you mad? If they knew, they would honor me. They'd bow before me!"

"You are quite ignorant and arrogant."

Wesley shook his head and shrugged.

"Tell you what…if you keep your mouth shut about this heritage of yours, I will help you."

Wesley reached up and again grabbed the bars of the cage. "I will not tell anyone else. I swear!"

"I feel so much better." The mountain man rolled his eyes. "Okay, let's not rush, though. The camp will be awake soon, and you won't be able to leave without being seen. Allow a couple days to learn."

Wesley blurted out, "But I need to leave this morning. My family is in danger!"

"Let's do this right. I will teach you and even speak to this young troll about guiding you, but you must wait for the opportune time."

"I don't have time!" Wesley argued.

The mountain man's face softened like Wesley had never seen it before. "If you want to help your family, you must be sure not to get caught leaving this place. You could be arrested for treason, you know." The man seemed thoughtfully concerned for him.

Wesley ignored the implications. "But, what of my brothers? I need to get home before them, and they are already a day ahead. To wait is too much to ask."

"Too much to save your life? Too much to spare your family from having to collect your pieces from the trail?" The mountain man smiled and nodded his head. "Give me the day. Leave on the morrow before dawn…"

"But…"

The man raised a hand, signaling to wait. "I know a path to Navarre that is rarely traveled. Provided you are not caught, you'll arrive home before your brothers."

Seeing that his arguing was not getting him anywhere, Wesley decided to trust the mountain man. "Very well. We'll leave at the third watch."

"Very good. Where do we start?"

"How do you say, 'friend'?"

The man stood and stepped over toward the troll, pointing. "*Aderlos*—friend."

"*Aderlos*," Wesley repeated.

The troll questioned him, grumbling, "*Aderlos?*"

Though Wesley didn't have the accent, he was confident this was going to work.

27

Tall, sparse grasses poked through the snow against Wesley's face. Though chilled, he lay out of sight, wrapped in a blanket below the prisoner cart. He had just shared a meal with the mountain man, and his eyelids were sagging. Worry had worn him thin. He only needed to close his eyes for a bit. The cart creaked above him, and his body jolted, then tensed, opposing all drowsiness. Turning his head, he shifted his eyes toward the rear of the cart, where he saw dark blue pants covering black boots—someone resting on the edge of the cart.

"Have they been feeding you well, old friend?"

Friend? Wesley knew that voice. It was Olivetan!

"A smiling face is half the meal!" the mountain man quipped. And he repeated what he had said in Calbharian, translating for the troll. The cart shook from the troll's laughter.

"And what does this one have to say, Quesnel?"

The mountain man's name is Quesnel. Wesley became rigid. *Did Quesnel point me out?*

"He is very fearful for a troll and unsure of their numbers, but it seems that he's telling the truth."

Wesley breathed again, but suspicion had all his nerves dancing beneath his skin. *Olivetan has known Quesnel all along?*

"He says more trolls are en route. Though, it is uncertain when they will arrive." Quesnel's plate clanked above. "There is more you must know, which is what brought me to you."

The cart sunk lower in the corner as Olivetan leaned back. "Yes, I do suppose you deserve the credit for your own arrest. If there is one thing you know all too well after these many years, it's how to avoid Ninian's soldiers."

What is Olivetan saying?

"The black ship is docked in Regael Cave," Quesnel warned.

"I figured we had Medici to thank for the exquisite weather we've been having," Olivetan said with a laugh. Adjusting his position against the cart, he continued, "Is Habs aware of this?"

Habs? From the market?

"Bela sent him word. The Underground is to be moving soon," Quesnel answered. "Upon our return to Port Regael, we must break off from the group, make our way to Merchant's Pass."

"And pray we stay clear of trolls," Olivetan added.

Olivetan? A spy for the Underground! No! No! Keep still. Sweat dripped from his nose. *I trusted Olivetan. I nearly told him who I was.*

"Yet, I've another problem," Olivetan said. "Have you seen a young boy wandering about?"

Wesley locked his arms at his side. His heart throbbed in his ears. *I should have hidden in the forest.* His eyes squeezed closed. *Keep still. Keep still.*

"His name is Wesley, and it seems he has gone missing."

"Yes, yes, the boy who brought blankets. I've spoken with him three times today. He arrives shortly after the food," Quesnel chuckled. "I'm quite hungry, but I've kept him here all day."

Quesnel's been deceiving me!

"Well done."

"He says he is an heir of Gaspard."

"He told you this?" Olivetan sounded unnerved, but he quickly let it go. "It's true, he's Sophia's youngest boy."

What? Olivetan knows? How? Wesley had to get home, had to get to King Ninian. Clearly, he could not trust anyone in this regiment. *Ninian needs to know about Olivetan!* Suddenly, his thoughts seemed loud enough to be heard. Olivetan and Quesnel were no longer talking. *Don't look back. Remain still! I will run for the forest. Just... remain...still.*

Something clutched his ankle. Dragged backward, his blanket rolled away, and he had no time to grasp anything. Jerking him to his feet, Olivetan leaned into Wesley with one arm while nursing his own ribs with the other.

"What's the matter, old man?" Quesnel quipped.

"I broke some ribs last night and..."

"How do you know who I am?" Wesley broke in. He shoved at Olivetan, but Olivetan was quick to seize him.

"Wesley, I have no time to talk right now..."

Attempts to spin, kick—nothing worked for him. Wesley shouted, "You're with the Underground! Let me go, you traitor!"

One of the guards heard the yelling and came running.

"He's a traitor!" Wesley exclaimed. "He speaks against King Ninian!"

"Now take it easy, son," Olivetan spoke in his typical, calm demeanor.

"Don't call me son!" Wesley would have no part of it. He fought against Olivetan's grip. "I'm no son of yours. Gaspard would have you removed from Nantes!" Wesley freed an arm. Reaching it back and then flinging it forward, he clipped Olivetan across the jaw.

"Solider, arrest this boy," Olivetan ordered.

In one swift move, Wesley's arms were up behind his back, and his face was pressed into the metal bars.

"Let me go! No! Olivetan is working against King Ninian! He would betray the king!" Wesley was no match for the viselike hold of the soldier, who wasted no time securing Wesley with Quesnel and the troll in the prisoner cart. The iron bars closed with a clanging latch.

Grasping the bars, Wesley cried, "Olivetan is a spy for the Underground!"

Olivetan stepped up close and whispered, "You will be safer locked up here." Olivetan then raised his voice. "And King Ninian will have *three* to hang for treason!"

"King Ninian will find out the truth about you!" Between the bars, Wesley swung his arm as far as his reach allowed.

Olivetan turned his back to him and walked away, ordering the soldier, "I want eyes constantly on this cart."

Wesley glared at the mountain man. "And you've betrayed me, too!"

At the command tent, Olivetan's thoughts whirled over what had just happened. How painful it had been to treat Wesley that way. If he had gained any trust with the boy, it was surely lost. For now, at least he knew Wesley was safe.

A sentinel came running up the hill, calling toward Olivetan. "Pirate ships in the bay! There are pirates in the bay!" Bent over and panting, the soldier repeated himself, over and over.

Olivetan sprinted, ignoring the stabbing pain in his ribs and scrambling down toward the breach. A stark group of soldiers stood at the base of the scaffolding.

"Stand alert, men!" Olivetan ordered, climbed up behind two others, and stood atop the scaffold. Taking up his spyglass, he searched across the ice-covered bay. Scores of pirate trolls had disembarked, unloading cannons and artillery. Some were already advancing across the ice towards the wall. Mere minutes separated them from an attack.

Olivetan swallowed hard and brooded over the moment. He had only one option. "Looks like plans are changing again." Back he scurried, skipping bars as he flung himself down from the scaffolding. Before his feet hit the ground, he was shouting orders. "I want this hill behind me lined with mortars! Men, to your posts. The rest of you, pull together the others, ready the horses and wagons. We make for Fehrael!"

Rushing to his bunk, he heard mortars exploding from far out on the ice. Skimming his supplies, he gathered an extra cloak and rounds for his rifle. He cinched the pack and slung a rifle over his shoulder. Ignoring the pain from his broken ribs, he hurried to speak with his commanders.

"When the pirates are in range, unload all the firepower we have, and then move out as fast as you can!" Cannon fire shook them again from the northwest. Pirate trolls had them on two fronts. "Load only the weapons you can carry. Get the young boys out first. Our route is all downhill. The last of the troops will be at the wall. When the trolls are in range, rain as much firepower as you can upon them! Then fly out of here!"

Olivetan dashed to the prisoner cart. He ordered the guard to open the cage and free only the boy and Quesnel. He grabbed Wesley by the arm and escorted him to the edge of the forest.

"Wesley, I do not have time for talk. You need to trust me!"

"How could you betray us all?" Wesley shouted, attempting to twist free from Olivetan's hold.

"Shall we execute them now, sir?" the soldier asked all too willingly.

"You must stand down, soldier," Olivetan ordered. "There is no time for explanations. You must run to Fehrael with the others. Now, hurry!"

"I'm not sure I understand, sir."

"I am taking charge of these two prisoners," Olivetan said.

"What? Are you abandoning your troops?" the soldier asked, his eyes beginning to blaze. "You are going to run like a coward?" He lifted his rifle, this time with Olivetan in his sights.

"Leave us, soldier. That is an order!"

"Oh, I have orders for what to do with your likes." The soldier smirked. "Seems the boy is right."

Olivetan stared down the barrel of the soldier's rifle.

"Alive or dead, the three of you will pay some high bounty when we return to Port Regael," the soldier said, pulling back the hammer on his rifle.

"This is your last chance to flee." Olivetan demanded, "You must move out while you have time. You'll find safety and more soldiers in Fehrael. I say this for your own protection."

"Back to the cart!" the soldier said and tossed his head.

Olivetan looked straight ahead into the forest. With the sun nearly set, all he could see was shadows.

"*A kosd an et seun,*" Quesnel inflected his voice into the forest.

A monstrous brown bear stepped out from the tree line, jaw hanging wide. Releasing a howl, the bear lunged toward the soldier. Its giant claw knocked him over, the rifle exploding toward the sky. Clinging to his weapon, the soldier stared up from the ground with the snout of the growling bear drooling only niks from his face. The soldier lumbered backward, fumbled to his feet, and ran toward camp.

Olivetan looked over at Quesnel, who had already mounted another bear, and he smiled, "Thank you for calling the bears, friend."

"One must always be prepared," Quesnel replied.

Olivetan looked down and saw that Wesley had fainted. He threw the boy upon the bear like a sack. Grabbing handfuls of fur, he then pulled himself up behind.

Into the forest they fled.

The Crooked Garden

28

According to their plan, Habs would be the first to climb out of the cave and hoped to establish a pattern for the rest. He tied the rope around his waist, gained some leverage, and pulled himself upwards. He had made this climb before, though it was daylight then. It was steep, but the layout of rocks and roots worked in his favor and made for a confident climb.

It was not long before Habs had climbed the eighteen to twenty rods and lifted himself out of the hole, into the cool air of a garden, beside a gentle stream. Huffing foggy breaths, Habs walked ahead in the dark and searched for a place to tie off the rope.

This garden was one of pine trees with an unusual growth pattern. The trunks of these trees somehow grew with a natural curve, creating an eerie surrounding as clouds hid the moon. Habs chose one particular tree trunk, which came straight out of the ground but then immediately curved north, parallel to the ground, then curved and bent back, shooting toward the sky. All the trees in this garden followed the same pattern—some larger and some smaller, but the basic shape was the same. Though Mahre thought the place to be rather frightful, last time they were here, Habs had

had no problem napping on the natural bench created by a tree trunk. Habs had dubbed it "the crooked garden."

Thick clouds cloaked the moon. Habs had been relying so much on the moonlight that he didn't think to light a lantern. All the better, for the less likely he would be seen by pirate trolls or anyone else that may be about—like spies for Ninian. They could be anywhere.

A speck of rain dotted his forehead, then another. He tied the rope around the base of one of the largest trees and, allowing the rope to glide along his hand, followed it back to the hole.

Peering over the edge into the abyss, Habs called, "All secure, Mahre!"

He found firm footing and grasped the rope, pulling one hand after the other. Mahre was to climb up beneath the trunk, following it as Habs pulled, lifting it over rocks and guiding it around roots and branches to keep it from getting snagged.

Raindrops swelled and slapped at the ground as if Habs were surrounded by applause. With every second or third pull, the rope slipped in his hands, but other than that, he heaved the trunk with relative ease—easier than when he and Mahre had practiced, anyway.

Letting go with one hand, Habs drew his forearm across his face, wiping the rain that blurred his vision. His other arm continued in its pulling motion until the trunk jerked to a stop. Immediately, he strengthened his grasp and tugged again to overcome whatever held it up. Attempting once more to break it free, he yanked hard and lost his footing. Habs fell back, and his leg slid out in front of him. Slopping down into the mud, the rope whizzing out of control, he landed on his bottom.

"Mahre!" Habs called.

Before Habs heard an answer, the rope went taut.

With his voice faintly ringing out above the deluge, Mahre called from below, "The knot king reigns!"

Habs pushed his hands into the muck on either side of him, twisted to his knees, and stood with a stumble.

"Are you going to help me?" Habs drew deep breaths.

"Says the one who cannot hang on from above. The trunk is below me."

"Pull with me, and when the trunk reaches you, be sure it doesn't get hung up on anything!"

"What happened?" Mahre called.

"Just try to hang on!" Habs would say no more. Anything he said now would be an open invitation for Mahre to keep jabbering. Now was not the time to talk—they had to keep moving.

The rain shower ended as quickly as it had started, and moonlight edged the breaking clouds. Habs bent over and lifted the rope, which was dripping with muck. He found his stance and pulled again. On his third pull, the trunk seemed weightless.

Immediately, Habs was jerked backward and sloshed once again into the mud, his hands stinging. Flat on his back and staring up at the sky, Habs watched as the trunk flew out from the hole and over him. Somewhere behind him, it came down with a thud and— *thump, thump, thump*—rolled to a stop.

Lying still, he soaked up the muck. Strewn throughout his bleary thoughts, Habs could hear Mahre calling, shouting. Rattled, he could not make sense of what had happened. Rolling out of the puddle, Habs again lifted himself from the ground and took steps toward the trunk. Something in the shadows captured his eye. He could not quite make it out.

"Habs!" came Mahre's call again.

Habs knelt beside the trunk and examined it. There seemed to be no damage, only pieces of grass and mud from when it had rolled along the ground.

His breath became raspy. Was he wheezing? He wasn't struggling to breathe. He tried several times to clear his throat, until he realized that it was not *his* breath he was hearing. Suddenly, a monstrous face lunged out from the shadow, the muscular features highlighted in moonlight. His double-jointed jaw opened wide. The troll roared in disdain.

Surely, this would be Habs's demise. At least he had gotten the letters and maps out of Port Regael. Mahre would have to take charge of the Underground. This was the end of his journey.

Protect the writings! Habs threw himself down and clung to the trunk.

Mahre had made it to the top of the hole. His voice was not far behind. "Habs!"

But Habs did not utter a word. He just lay upon the trunk, clutching it, protecting it with his life. Nothing happened. Reluctantly, he lifted his head and found himself nose to nose with the pirate troll. After hollering something in his own language, the troll ran from him. Or at least, he was *trying* to run. He had an awful limp. What was wrong? Then, Habs spotted it. As the troll shot out of the moonlight, he saw that the rope was tied to his leg.

"Oh, damn! I tied the rope to a troll," Habs uttered to himself. "Mahre!"

"Habs!" Mahre was close.

The troll was running for the river. Habs tried to undo the knot, but his hands were cold, and they stung with rope burn. There wasn't enough time. He fell back upon the trunk and held on tight. Launching forward, the pull strained ligaments and tendons in his arms. Bouncing off the ground, he spat and coughed. Rolling and tumbling with the trunk, rocks bruised him, while broken branches scratched and punctured his exposed skin. The troll fought, yanking the trunk in stronger bursts. Yet, Habs was resolute—he would not let all he had collected be given over to trolls. He would die first.

Rebounding off the earth, he bounced high, sailing forward and splashing mid-river. Down he went and just as quickly found himself bobbing on the surface. Panting, he rolled sideways as the troll pulled him. Side by side with the trunk, he skipped along the surface. With river water spraying his eyes and filling his mouth, he gagged until he collided with the shoreline. Head over heels, he flopped forward and landed face-first with a thud in the sand. He had lost his grip on the trunk. He could not even lift his head.

The trunk was gone—the writings were lost.

Unable to breathe, he managed to lift his chin against the ache in his neck. Pressure pushed at the back of his eyes, like they were bulging. His sinuses stung, filled with river water. Gritty with sand, his tongue tasted like dirt. He lay with his eyes shut only for a moment. Then, he heard the troll bellowing somewhere in front of him.

"Habs!" Mahre called from the other side of the river.

Habormoss pushed with his left arm to roll onto his back. There was Mahre, along with three others, all trying hard to conceal their laughter.

"The trunk is behind you!" Mahre shouted and laughed all the louder.

Habs slowly turned to look. In relief, he rolled to his other side. He buried his head back in the sand, then looked up, spitting sand with each breath. On his belly, Habs pushed and pulled his way to the trunk. The troll grumbled louder, moaning from somewhere out of sight. Habs worked quickly to untie the knot, ignoring the pain in his bleeding hands. Mahre and several other men splashed their way across the river.

One man pulled a knife from his belt.

"Allow me," the man said.

Mahre picked up the other end of the rope. "Look at this. It must have frayed."

"Very good," Habs said and collapsed again to the ground.

"Shall I go and kill it, sir?" the man with the knife asked.

"No, let him be," Habs spoke between breaths. "I think…he's wounded…must have been…left behind."

"Yes, but with the ruckus he's making, we'll have some of his healthy friends here soon," another man said.

"Mahre?" Habs asked. "How is your Calbharian?"

"You want me to *speak* to it? I think you swallowed too much river water!"

Habs turned, succeeding in rolling onto his side. "If we can somehow offer him help, it would be quite advantageous to have a troll on our side."

"And you want me to befriend him?" Mahre questioned. "I knew Quesnel should have come with us. Don't you think that the people are distressed enough, after what we went through with Jansen? Now you want to welcome a pirate troll among us?"

"Well…you may have a point." But Habs had his mind made up. "I'll send the group ahead to the caves at Caracas. They'll be safe, and we'll take a small cohort to gather Sophia. No one will know about the troll, at least for now."

"You have no idea—"

"You know what we can offer him."

Mahre paused, shook his head, and crossed his arms. Like a child, he stomped around before he finally said, "All right then, I will say my farewells to you now. Just don't bury me in your crooked garden. I would like a dignified funeral. Yes, in the Glen. That would be appropriate. You must carry my body to the Glen and have the priests bury me properly."

The troll continued to bawl.

"You're stalling. We really need him quiet," Habs said.

"Yes, yes…" With his pack and a lantern, Mahre left to confront the troll.

All But His Braies

29

esley awoke in a swelter, his eyes compelled to squint. Wrapped tightly in covers, his body had been thawed by the direct sunlight. He had forgotten what it was like to awake and not be frozen. With the corner of his blanket, he wiped the sweat from his face. Loosening his covers, he welcomed a comforting breeze.

For a time, he did not know what day it was. It did not matter at that moment. It seemed he was somewhere beyond the spell! The sun was well above the mountains. It must have been near midday. The scent of pinesap on his blanket, mixed with lavender on the breeze, was soothing.

He breathed deeply and realized that he could not remember the last time he had slept this late into the morning. Attempting to recall any trace of where he might be, he jumped as if spooked by a shadow. He had been clinging for his life, racing through the forest while slumped over a bear!

To his terror, there it was again, stretching out its legs and yawning. The bear turned toward him. Wesley's body stiffened, his breaths shallow and shaky. The bear's hefty head plopped down in the dust directly in front of him. Its cool, moist nose met with

Wesley's. The beast's warm breath was like a blend of compost and rotting rabbit. Wesley swallowed against the rising content of his stomach and braced his sweaty hands against the ground to keep himself steady. Straining against his petrified state, he finally broke free and flung himself backward out of his covers, falling upon what felt like a tree limb.

"Careful, boy!" Quesnel scolded, pulling his arm away. Turning over, he settled down again. At his feet slept another bear.

Wesley twisted left. Spinning his head, he tried to piece together his surroundings. He was atop a small plateau, far above a valley of giant trees. Something slid across the loose stones behind and to his right—he jerked around. It was Olivetan, rolling up his blanket.

"Sleep is the poor man's treasure," Olivetan offered with a smile. He brushed pine needles and broken leaves from his blanket and secured it to his pack with twine.

Wesley wanted nothing to do with Olivetan. He imagined fleeing. *The right time will come.* "Where are you taking me?" he demanded.

"We are on our way to your home in Navarre, just as you requested."

"You are deserting your troops? Running from Ninian? You found an heir of Gaspard, and you're afraid. Do you think you can use me for leverage? Do you plan to hold me for ransom? When King Ninian finds out who I am, he will protect me." Wesley threw out his arm and grasped a stone the size of his palm. He flew to his feet and craned his arm back in defense.

"Cork up, boy!" Quesnel grumbled and pulled his blanket over his head.

Olivetan sat down upon his pack, and his arms fell into his lap.

"I would say that you are free to go your way, but we are sworn to protect you and your brothers *from* Ninian—and any other threat."

"Sworn before who, the Underground? You're the threat!" Shifting his feet, Wesley secured his stance, turning the stone in his hand till his grip was just right.

"I swore an oath on my life to keep you safe, before the Great King…" Olivetan paused and studied the ground. Twice, he opened his mouth to speak, until finally, looking directly at Wesley, he shrugged and said plainly, "And before your mother."

Wesley dropped his arm to his side, and the stone fell from his fingers. "My mother?"

"Yes, I know her well."

"You mean, you *knew* her well. My mother is dead."

"That's what we feared, as well, but—"

"That's absurd!" Wesley began to sob. For three years, he had believed his mother was dead. The memory of losing her wrenched him. *What is Olivetan playing at? How does he know anything about my mother? Does he really think I'll fall for such nonsense?* Immediately, his sadness flipped to anger.

"How do you know this? Why not come and find my family? There are nights that my sisters still weep, and my father has long been numb. Why should I believe you?" Wesley heaved, out of breath.

The care in Olivetan's eyes was unmistakable. "I have protected you thus far."

Wesley was quiet, for he could not argue that. But he still could not bring himself to trust Olivetan.

"The news of your mother has only recently reached me. Anyway, the Underground had already planned to move, and I would have been in Navarre to gather your family in a week's time, had Nantes not been attacked by pirate trolls."

"Are you saying that my mother stood with the Underground?" That thought was like a thornbush inside his mind.

"Wesley…" Olivetan seemed to wait. "I have many things to tell you, things that will not be easy for you to hear."

"Do you think I'm a child? Tell me the truth!"

"Your mother *created* the Underground."

Wesley's face flushed with heat. His heart could have burst. *The Underground is against all that Mother stood for!* He tromped past Olivetan and climbed a narrow trail leading away from the plateau.

"Suit yourself!" Olivetan called from behind.

Olivetan's words are a snare, but he won't trap me. I will convince Father that we must go to King Ninian. This trail will have to cross a road at some point. From there, I will travel northwest and find my way back.

The path crested, then twisted down away from the mountainside. Only minutes into his hike, Wesley came upon a shady area and realized he had walked off without a pack—no water or food, no blanket or cloak. Below the low-sprawling branches of a stout tree, he found a place to sit. While uprooting the weeds around him, he cursed Olivetan. He missed his mother so much. Could she really be alive? And how would this traitor know anyway? He knew his family kept secrets, but *dark* secrets? *No way! I will get home. Father will set things right.*

No more than a quarter hour had passed when a canvas pack bounced off his shoulder. Olivetan approached. Anger and confusion were so loud inside of Wesley that he had not heard.

"I thought you might get hungry."

"What do you care? It didn't seem to bother you that I left." Wesley looked up and lashed out, "Where are we? I need to get home."

"Let us take you, Wesley, and when we arrive, you can confer with your father about all I have told you."

Why would Mother not tell me these things? Why did Father keep so much from us? Why the hell would my brothers betray the crown? Wesley wanted answers—now!

"I would rather be dead than believe..." Wesley stopped speaking, as if fingers gently pressed his lips. What had come over him? Mother had taught him better.

Wesley closed his eyes, inhaled slowly, and sighed. It was as if his mother had breathed into his ear, "What is most important for this moment?" *Traveling home with Olivetan and the mountain man would be safer than traveling alone.*

"How do I know I can trust you to take me home?"

Olivetan seemed to ponder Wesley's words. Then he asked, "What do you know of the Fullness of Time?"

Olivetan's words gave Wesley gooseflesh. Many times, his family had debated the *Fullness of Time*. After Mother died, those conversations had become contentious. His guard dropped a bit at the thought of discussing it with Olivetan.

Curious but cautious, Wesley said, "My oldest brother, Derian, said that the Fullness of Time will begin with the restoration of the co-regency."

Olivetan removed his scabbard and reclined in the tall grasses across the trail from Wesley. "And your father?"

How much more do I tell him? What does he know of the prophecy? What does he want from me? If he wants to use me to bargain with Ninian, he'll need me alive. Considering this boosted his confidence.

Wesley continued, "My father refused to discuss it. After the death of my mother, he was forced into a dark place." It felt good to talk about this. "To help my father and to bring rest to our home, Derian reasoned that when all the brothers were of age for the crown, that would fulfill the prophecy, and together we would go before King Ninian."

"And you are soon to be fifteen."

"Yes, and I have a responsibility to act on what I know to be true." Wesley's tone grew stern.

"That I do not argue," Olivetan said. "Tell me, where does the prophecy have its origin?"

"With Gaspard," Wesley answered too quickly. That answer was only the surface of something he did not quite understand. Even King Gaspard yielded to the authority of the Great King. But Wesley had no clear answers.

"King Gaspard, your great-grandfather. Tell me, what do you know about King Gaspard?"

Wesley did not speak a word. This conversation was over, for Olivetan had asked too many questions. Several silent minutes passed.

"Look," Olivetan finally said, "perhaps a clue to my truthfulness is that your mother had you keep your royal bloodline secret. Isn't that correct?"

Wesley conceded that point. But still, it was not enough. He shot back at Olivetan, "Or perhaps she wanted us to wait until we were all of age to take on such a responsibility!"

Olivetan sat up, resting his elbows on his knees. He spoke with his hands, "I need to tell you, the dark magic from Calbha Mor has arrived on the shores of Nantes. Ninian is—"

Wesley cut him off, "I am loyal to King Ninian. Nantes is my home."

"Your honor for your country is to be admired. Your father has brought you along well."

"Repair the breach and steal me away to collect the parchments for yourself? You're as bad as my brothers." Wesley's heated tone returned, and he refused to look at Olivetan. "Was this your plan all along?"

"There is certainly a plan, though I'm discovering it as I go." Frustration began to edge his words as Olivetan added, "Please listen. It's because of Ninian's obsession with the treasure that the wall has been breached."

"What?"

"Yes! This attack is a distraction as he seeks the treasure. He never trusted Gaspard. Furthermore, if Ninian knew that you are the great-grandson of Gaspard, you'd already be in a cell below Regael Castle."

Wesley's jaw tightened. "The line of King Ninian has always searched to find an heir!"

"I'm sorry to tell you that those closest to the king have orders to—"

"That's nonsense!" Wesley shot back. "The people seek an heir to restore the co-regency."

"True enough, but you need to know that the king will do whatever he can to keep that from happening."

This was too much to process. Two days ago, he would have trusted Olivetan with his life. Now, who could he trust? What could he believe? Wesley wished he were home. He wanted to forget about the breach and get back to his life in Navarre. There was no fixing this. He lacked sleep, and his stomach moaned of hunger.

"I thought you were courageous, but you deserted your men and ran from pirate trolls!"

"May I explain?" asked Olivetan.

Wesley did not answer. Instead, he lifted the sack Olivetan had thrown at him, dropped it in his lap, and loosened the tie. Tucked in below a blanket, he discovered a chunk of stale bread. He broke a portion to eat and stuffed away the other half.

"Your great-grandfather's journey began as a survey of the island. No one knew why Gaspard ventured into the Inner Realm. Perhaps he sought to acquire more land. We don't know for sure. Gaspard sent word back to Ninian, crossed the Diachrieno River, and entered the Province Beyond the River —or as it came to be called, the Inner Realm."

Wesley nodded with a mouthful of stale bread. He had heard of that province.

"Gaspard's trip, which was meant to take only a few months, lasted two years. No one knew what happened to him. At first, King Ninian I was concerned for his safety, but his concern soon turned to distrust. In his absence, Ninian grew suspicious and feared that Gaspard had found the Great King's treasure and set out to build a kingdom against him."

Wesley uncorked a skin of water and washed down his bread, eyes focused on Olivetan.

"Gaspard knew nothing of Ninian's growing rage. He wanted to share the treasure he found with the Kingdom of Nantes. When he sent word home, this time Gaspard asked Ninian to leave Port Regael and join him. Gaspard wrote that he was going to sell all that he had, find the owner of the field, and purchase the field from him."

Here was a chance to test what Olivetan knew. Wesley leaned forward and asked, "He sold *all* that he had?"

"Old parchments say he sold 'all but his braies.'"

That's what Mother would say. Wesley kept a straight face.

"Ninian was outraged! Gaspard's wealth would have been supreme. Ninian feared he would lose his reign. He feared that Gaspard would grow mightier. He decided that he would forcefully take the Inner Realm—the Province Beyond the River—while he had the chance, and all the land surrounding the field would be his. But though Ninian never found the treasure in the field, it hasn't stopped three generations of searching."

Wesley now realized he had been twirling small sticks in his fingers and stopped. "And what of my great-grandfather?"

Olivetan stood and said, "The stories conflict. Some say he was assassinated by King Ninian I. Others say he was driven out of the Inner Realm, found passage aboard a merchant ship, and sailed to the uncharted lands. I believe it was there that he secretly dispersed writings and maps concerning the treasure."

Wesley argued with himself. *Could Olivetan have made all this up so quickly? Lies can come easily when someone is in a difficult situation...*

"Look," Olivetan said. "There is more I could say, but we must make our way to Navarre. We are racing your brothers, along with pirate trolls. Ninian will soon hear of who you are and of my desertion. When he finds out that the family of Gaspard has been living so close all these years, you can be sure that he will be on his way to your home as well. We must move quickly to collect the writings before the others arrive."

"All too easy for you and the Underground."

"I will get you home, and you decide what to do with the parchments."

Wesley reached for a limb, pulled himself to his feet, and slung the pack over his shoulder. "I will go with you to Navarre. From Navarre, I will make my way home on my own. You will not include me in your treason."

"Very good," Olivetan agreed.

Suddenly, a loud snap sent birds scattering from a cluster of trees. Olivetan hunched and put a finger to his lips. He had Wesley crouch low as he searched out across an open area beyond the wide tree. A large doe gently stepped into view, putting her head down to drink from a stream.

Relieved, Wesley and Olivetan exchanged a smile.

In a streak of grey, two trolls rushed in, the doe bleating its last breath. Effortlessly, the trolls tore off her legs and gnawed them like Wesley would a chicken leg. Wesley dropped his head, for the sight was unbearable. Knowing the trolls could sense the slightest movement or sound, Wesley waited with Olivetan. After what seemed like an hour, Olivetan tapped his back then stepped over to gather his belt and scabbard. Without a word, Wesley stepped backward toward the trail. As he turned, he choked back his screams and leapt behind Olivetan. When he looked up, Olivetan had his sword drawn but started laughing as he sheathed the weapon.

Quesnel had arrived, sitting upon one bear while he escorted the other.

"Thought you may be in danger," said Quesnel. "Our friends here noticed the peculiar smell of fresh troll scat."

Olivetan smiled and mounted one of the bears. He offered a

hand to Wesley, who hesitated but finally accepted. Then, Olivetan instructed, "Grab the fur and pull yourself up."

With one hand in Olivetan's and the other clenching fur, Wesley climbed up behind him. The bear trudged forward, and as Wesley slid back, he flung his arms around Olivetan. He never thought he would be so happy to see a bear, let alone ride on one. Tilting side to side with each step, he thought that at least fur made for a comfortable seat. Though wary of Olivetan, Wesley would accept his escort to Navarre. They were a long way from the Navarrian Hills, and it seemed as if trolls roamed everywhere.

Unlikely Friendships

30

ahre lifted his lantern, throwing light upon the frantic pirate troll. Hanging upside down between the trees against a narrow, rocky ridge, the troll flung his right arm about, unable to free himself. His other arm was caught behind his back. After several failed attempts, the troll ceased his struggle. The soggy beast panted, staring directly at Mahre, his floppy nose dangling between his eyes.

It had been so long since Mahre spoke Calbharian. He struggled to come up with the words. *Brother...what is the Calbharian word for brother or friend? Ah, yes...*

"*Aderlos toomaian.*" He spoke again, but slower. "*Aderlos toomaian.*" He hoped he was telling the troll, "Be still, friend."

As he spoke, Mahre motioned downward, hoping to calm the befuddled troll. A wide gash bled above the troll's right knee, and again the creature began to bellow.

Quiet! Be glad you didn't hang yourself.

"*Terraiven due ginbanaien. Aderlos toomaian,*" Mahre said. "*Aderlos, aderlos!*"

Again, the troll continued to twist and struggle, throwing threatening shadows, making the beast seem four times larger than he already was.

Mahre hung the lantern from a branch and with the tips of his fingers tapped his chest, saying, "Friend, I am your friend. I want to help you."

This is getting nowhere...Wait!

Mahre removed a bottle of whiskey from his satchel and held it up.

"*Aderlos*," Mahre said.

The troll became still and stopped his wailing. Eyes darting between Mahre and the bottle, he finally asked, "*Aderlos?*"

Mahre smiled. "Now we're speaking a common language." He balanced the bottle on a pile of rocks, then walked toward the troll. Keeping his distance, Mahre climbed the ridge until he was slightly higher than the troll's feet and the rope was within his reach.

"So, this is how I'm going to die. I free the troll; he kills me and steals my whiskey."

Mahre pulled a knife from his belt and put it to the rope. One cut at a time, Mahre pulled the knife toward him. The rope frayed and turned, then finally snapped. Headfirst, the troll slid down the rock and landed in a heap on the ground. He immediately jumped from the loosened ropes, and using his arms and legs, he backed away, keeping his eyes on Mahre.

For a moment, neither of them moved. Cautiously, Mahre returned the knife to his belt. The troll dropped into a seated position, spooking Mahre. Mahre grappled for a hold and nearly fell from the ridge. Bracing himself, all he could do now was wait to die. He was just hoping it would be quick, leaving his arms and legs intact.

The troll looked up. "*Aderlos?*" he said.

"Yes, yes, right." Mahre quickly maneuvered back down the ridge.

"*Doami ech estaiven*," the troll spoke, holding out his hands.

Mahre thought hard to translate, for the troll spoke so quickly. Repeatedly, he worked over the troll's words in his head. When he figured it out, he said, "Of course, a drink!" Mahre reached for the bottle and pulled the cork with his teeth. He offered it to the troll, who only pushed it back.

It only took a moment and Mahre understood. "Oh...*Estainan!*" *At least I've befriended a cordial troll...* Mahre thought and lifted the bottle in gaiety. "Bottoms up!"

He swallowed a mouthful, and his face rushed with heat. Liquid fire spread through his insides. Coughs burst uncontrollably. Mahre preferred his ales—whiskey was for wounds. He once again offered the bottle to his genial new *aderlos.* The troll finished half the bottle before taking a breath. Reaching down, he dumped the rest over the gouge in his leg. Whiskey lapped loose-hanging skin, and Mahre cringed merely thinking about the sting.

"*Aderlos, due weri ithroainan loi ahech,*" Mahre pleaded for the troll to come with him. He warned that they must leave immediately and get to a safe place. "*Due eigeraien sai semaien?*" Mahre wanted him to get up. Unmotivated, the troll sat in a slump. Then Mahre remembered what Habormoss said to offer. He tried, "*Helephimai due nent kartathezaien.*"

"*Elephaios?*" the troll asked.

"*Aderlos, elephaios.*" Mahre assured the creature of freedom from the curse that bound him as a pirate troll.

P hilor and Aarn sat before a pile of carcasses. Half-eaten deer legs, some gnawed to the bone, buzzed with circling flies. Broken ribs had been licked clean, and the tails of small forest creatures had all been tossed aside after the pirate trolls had their fill.

"I'm so hungry," Philor finally confessed to Aarn.

For the last two days, they had only eaten berries and water. Soon the sun would set, and he would lie awake with stomach pangs, praying for sleep. Aarn lay in the damp forest grass beside him, moaning. He had eaten a slice of raw deer liver an hour ago and was not well.

"Are we not kings, Aarn?"

Just then, Aarn rolled to his side and vomited his dinner. He threw his arm back for his canteen, so Philor pushed it within reach. With shaky hands, Aarn removed the cork and attempted to drink, lying on his side. Some of the water made it into his mouth, but most washed over his sweat-pearled face. The canteen fell from his hand and glugged upon the ground.

"We are kings and should be served as kings," Philor demanded. "I'm starting a fire and *cooking* my dinner."

Black knee-high leather boots draped by a tatty overcoat stepped into Philor's view. The filthy mountain man with long greasy hair, Ipabog, stood in front of him.

"You'll do no such thing," Ipabog scolded. "I will not have you risk giving away our position."

"We're through with your cowardice. No one will ever find us this far out!" Philor yelled.

"You know little of Ninian, boy. He has spies high and low. Even creatures of the forest," Ipabog warned.

Philor's eyes drifted back to the heap of animal parts.

"We can never be too certain," Ipabog said. "You claim to be a king of Nantes, yet you are oblivious to many things."

"It is *you* who lacks understanding!" Philor leapt to his feet—raging ahead and shoving Ipabog to the ground. "I am king, and it's time you bow before me!" Drawing his leg back, Philor aimed to kick Ipabog below the rib cage, but his leg got caught up. "What?"

Philor spun his head and was met by a snarling troll. Yanked backward, Philor dropped, his head thudding against the ground. With his tongue, he collected blood from the sudden gap in his teeth. Through a blurry stupor, he watched as Ipabog knelt beside him and leaned forward.

"Remember this, *king*—I found you. You will heed me, or you'll find yourself in pieces with the rest of the animals. You have our protection...for now. You will have our allegiance when you prove Gaspard's writings do indeed exist." Ipabog stood and left him.

By then, Aarn had sat up and was patting Philor on the back. "You should have eaten dinner."

"You idiot!" Philor shouted. He pushed off the ground, spun, and found a backrest against a tree.

"You look terrible. You ought to go over to the river and get yourself cleaned up," Aarn replied.

"And what of you? Dried blood on your face and chin." Philor scoffed and said, "You've really taken to troll etiquette."

"Ipabog is right, you know."

"A king does not have to earn his place. They came to us!" Philor argued.

"They would have killed us had we not told them of Gaspard!"

"Shut up, Aarn. You long for the throne as well. We need them only to secure our birthright, and that is all." Then, Philor lowered his voice. "I will not forget Ipabog's imprudent ways. When I sit on the throne, he will pay. Along with any pirate troll who opposes me."

"It's time you wise up, brother. These trolls will be our army, Ipabog our commander. With the trolls on our side, we'll be unstoppable." Aarn jumped up and pulled a blade from his belt. He stepped over to the raw leftovers and cut off a chunk of meat. "We have a new life, Philor. Get used to it." Aarn sank his teeth into the bloody flesh and turned his head, tearing it in two. He offered half to Philor. "Share this with me, and may it be a pact between us—the new co-regents!"

Philor slapped away Aarn's hand. "I would not be so stupid as to bring such shame on the name of Gaspard." He let his head fall back against the tree and squeezed his eyes closed. For the first time since he had run away, Philor began to doubt what he had done.

Lost

32

illiam Delaine cradled his head in his hands and covered his eyes. There was nothing to see anyway, as darkness always settled quickly in the mountains. The days never measured up, especially in autumn. His knees pushed up tight, niks away from this chest. He joggled and bumped along with a wagon full of men returning home from the mines.

As a child, William had lived on the coast, and he could count on one hand the number of nights he missed the sunset. Now, he did not care if he ever saw the sun set over the sea again. He had never imagined that he would be hiding with his children in the Navarian Hills. Sunsets had lost their beauty. There was no pleasure in even dreaming about them.

When Sophia was alive, they had traveled as a family east of Coragaes Pass. There, they picnicked overlooking the River Naab until the sun went down between the mountains. Days like that would never come again—never. There was no comfort in those memories with his wife and their family. Leisure time strangled his mind with what was and what would never be. Every day, he fought to see beyond the grief of the past but brutally lost.

Mining was his only reprieve. The darkness of the caves soothed him, and the constant hammering filled the hollow inside of him that otherwise echoed with worry and fear. It was less confining in the mines, so he had signed on for more work.

The children were getting too old, too curious. He should have fled Nantes after Sophia died. But where would he have gone? How would he explain to the children that they must leave their home? And what of the Fullness of Time? His sons kept asking, but he had nothing to tell them. He had no idea what it meant, or if it meant anything at all. He feared what it might mean… A confrontation with Ninian? A public shaming and punishment? Banishment to the uncharted lands? The day would come when the children would need to know why they must run from Ninian. How would he ever explain that they must hide for the rest of their lives?

Each day, he thought of Philor, Aarn, and Wesley. William wished now that he had traveled with the children to Port Regael on the Eve of Enrichment. And now, with the news of the storm that tore along the coast, he feared that he may never see them again.

To restrain his spiraling thoughts, William trained his ears on the rasping and grating of the wheels. The clomping of horses provided a mechanical rhythm—however, it was not to last. The cool cadence collapsed and quickly fell out of tempo. The horses stirred. Something had spooked them. The men began to mumble amongst themselves. William lifted his head.

"Giddy 'p!" the driver called.

Pulling against each other, the horses grunted and groaned.

Gunfire cracked, and William's whole body jerked as the horses lurched forward. With arms clasping the edge of the wagon, he spun his head to see the driver slumped in his seat. Screams yanked his attention to the rear of the cart. Two men had rolled out and now fell farther behind the quickening cart. The others were linking arms and clenching whatever they could to hold on. He had to get control of the cart.

William stood, teetering side to side. One step, regain balance, then another. The wagon bounced, throwing him forward. With one arm, he grasped the back of the slatted seat. Taking hold with the other arm, he pulled himself up, climbed over, and dropped down beside the lifeless driver.

Below, the flapping reins were just out of reach. Pressing one arm against the driver, he reached down with the other. The reins danced across the tips of his fingers, the ground whizzing by underneath. The shaft buckled, flipping him back and upward. The driver tilted sideways and flopped off the seat. Clasping the arm rest, William whirled his head around. The rear left wheel had broken free—behind them, scores of pirate trolls were in pursuit.

Flaming arrows arched overhead. William leaned forward, covering his head with his arms. Blazing shafts peppered the ground all around him.

Thwump! Just barely missing his leg, an arrow pierced the buckboard seat. Angry flames leapt up and bit at him. He threw off his canvas cloak and beat wildly. After smothering the fire, flames from behind snarled and sparred. The wagon had caught fire! Fanned by the wind, it blazed and swelled. Soon, the whole cart was engulfed. Panicked men rolled back and forth to extinguish the fire, while others leapt from the wagon. If the fall did not kill them, the trolls certainly would.

The wagon zigzagged, bouncing down the path. Finally, the other wheel flew from its hub. The rear of the cart slammed to the ground in a burst of sparkling cinders. The recoil put the reins into William's hands. *Won't do much good now.* He found himself balancing on the edge of a flaming chariot. The horses raced, as if they could outrun the fire.

Not far ahead was a bridge. If he could just hold on, he could jump and let the river waters carry him away. *It's too late! I'll never make it!* Again, he was showered with flaming arrows. Yet, none struck him.

Nearing the bridge, he prepared to jump. With extra propulsion from the wheels hitting the ramp, he leapt, sailing upward with his arms extended to the sky. In that moment, searing pain split between his shoulder blades. His entire body flashed with heat. Twisting in the air, he brought one hand to his chest as an arrow shot through him, still throwing flames.

When he hit the water, the cold suffocated him and pulled him under. Fighting for the surface, he broke through and stole a breath before the current seized him, dragging him under again. Caught in the torrent, he hacked and hemmed, swallowing mouthfuls of water while trying to get another breath. The river turned, throwing him toward the shore. Caught between rocks, fighting for every breath, the current pounded him. But the water soothed the burning.

Pirate trolls ranted somewhere behind him. Clinging to a rock, he tried not to move. He hoped they would think him dead. He wondered if maybe he *was* dead. Feeling his chest for a wound, he found nothing. Not even a tear in his shirt—still breathing, still conscious.

He waited and waited, hoping the pirates had moved on.

Replaying the whole episode, he thought about the arrow. Had it missed him completely? No, it had passed right through him. He had felt it—*seen* it—leave his body. But it did not harm him. Was he a ghost? Perhaps he had died before the arrow hit…

Just then, he was lifted from the waters, placed on his feet, and ushered beyond the river's edge into the dense trees.

"Move ahead quickly and do not look back," a woman said from behind—steady, calm, direct, and urgent.

"Am I dead?" William asked his abductor.

There was no answer at first, only what he thought to be a bit of snicker.

"I am breathing, and I can see my breath…" William stepped fast, water sloshing in his boots.

"Do you have a pulse?" the voice asked.

William placed two fingers on the side of his neck just to be sure. "Okay, I'm alive, but that arrow…I saw and…*felt* it go through me! Yet, I have no wound. Who are you? Where are you taking me? Will I live to tell the tale?" Silhouettes of claw-like branches lifted and drooped all around him. Chilled by the breeze, he clenched his own shoulders.

How did I slip away from the pirates? How did they not see me—us? He did not bother to ask his silent captor.

And the night tarried on.

Finally, after what had seemed like hours of bustling about the woods, the woman behind him spoke. "Listen well. I will speak, and I will be gone. Do not return to your home."

"What are you saying? You're mad! What about the children?" Infuriated, William lurched at shadows, spinning in circles and attempting to seize his abductor.

"They will be cared for. They will be safe." The woman's presence warmed him like a fire, and she continued. "Trust me, William."

"And you know my name…"

Leaving the children alone was not an option. Panicked, and

with no sense of direction, he ran. Tripping forward, he fell. His head thumped off the ground and split with pain.

Yet again came the voice of his captor. This time, her voice surrounded him…or was it within him?

"Make for Merchant's Pass. Stay in the wood. Do not take the road." Each word was like a salve for his pain. Yet, with each word, he also fought for consciousness. He longed for the woman to keep speaking to ease his agony, but he also feared he would fall asleep. "A trail will be marked for only you to see, until you come upon a friend. Be moved by nothing—keep to the path."

The pain in his head was gone. He breathed easily again—it felt as if he were floating above the ground. Was he under a spell? Poisoned?

"Show yourself!" William called out. "Don't leave me here! How will I find my way?"

William could not lift his head. His resistance against sleep was futile.

A Language from the Mountains

33

It was now the eleventh hour. Face scorched and arms dangling, Wesley leaned into Olivetan, mounted on the back of a bear. Quesnel was close behind, not much for words these last few hours. The trio had been riding since morning. Olivetan had said that bears were the quickest way back to Navarre, exceling over rocky terrain better than any horse could. Another night and most of tomorrow would be spent riding. With few stops, they would arrive in Navarre in approximately one day.

The plan was to get home before the twins, but Wesley secretly hoped to see them, talk to them, plead with them to honor Gaspard. If only he could convince them to go to King Ninian, that would solve everything—clear up all misunderstandings. *King Ninian will certainly honor my family.*

Nearing the edge of the Timaru Desert, soon they would stop for water and, with any luck, some sleep. After the temperature dropped, they would move northwest, staying along the mountain range that spanned the desert.

"Did you ever meet my great-grandfather?" Wesley asked with his cheek pressed against Olivetan's back.

"Our paths crossed decades ago," Olivetan said.

"I wish I could have met him. But with all the stories Mother told, I feel as though I have. How did you meet?"

"I was only a boy, younger than you. He didn't see me at first, but I knew it was him. Our meeting was short. I was in the Reynes Islands with my father as he led a regiment of soldiers."

"But I thought your father worked the lighthouse on Beacon's Bluff?" Wesley asked.

"That he did, but only after he'd fulfilled his time with Ninian II. As a young man, my father sailed with the king's fleet. He was highly trained in covert missions and was one of the king's best assets. In fact, Quesnel here was my father's bagman for some time."

Wesley was rising, twisting, and leaning with each step of the bear. Looking back, he questioned Quesnel with his eyes.

"I bribed the authorities, boy, to allow Gaspard passage. And I did my job very well."

"Yes, until Ninian discovered what he was doing. Many times, Quesnel used the king's own treasury to lead his abductors farther away from your great-grandfather," Olivetan said and laughed. "Quesnel spent months locked away in Regael Castle."

"But if I didn't escape, Ninian released me," Quesnel stated proudly. "And then I was snared again. Those actions repeated for the next twenty years."

"At least he was consistent," Olivetan laughed.

"Why would King Ninian let you go?" Wesley asked.

"After he released me, Ninian secretly had me followed, hoping I would lead him to Gaspard. He never knew I was onto his schemes." Quesnel hacked and spat.

Olivetan continued, "It's true. In any case, my encounter with

Gaspard was brief. After hearing all the stories from your mother, I am certain your knowledge of Gaspard is far richer than mine."

Beneath a grove of wattle trees, Wesley slid from the bear and followed Quesnel to get some water. Quesnel plunged his worn leather costrel with one hand and cupped water to rinse his face with the other. He took a long drink before unfolding his blanket. With a groan, he stretched out to sleep.

"Quesnel?" Wesley asked. There was no answer. "Quesnel?"

Through a yawn, Quesnel replied, "Get some rest."

"Did you know my *grandfather*?"

Keeping his eyes closed, Quesnel answered, "For many years, I worked to keep your grandfather's family hidden. Eventually, it was best I didn't know where they were. And now..." Quesnel rolled with his back toward Wesley, wrapping himself in his blanket. "Here you are."

"There is so much I long to know. I have only the piece of a memory, of meeting him." Olivetan opened a sack and broke some bread. He offered a piece to Wesley, who immediately devoured it and then spoke through a mouthful, "What of the Great King?"

Olivetan reclined against a rock. "How do you mean?"

"Certainly, Ninian honors the Great King. I've heard him say so."

"I will answer your questions, Wesley, but you will not like my answers."

"I presume nothing," Wesley stated.

It was time to allow Olivetan some chance at explanation. Besides, anything Olivetan said could be compared later with what his father might say.

Olivetan reached over and scratched one of the bears behind its ears. The bear gave a yawn and a yawp, not wanting to be bothered. "You know of the Bailiwick wars?" Olivetan asked.

"Of course! It's the earliest story Mother shared and quite often repeated."

"Then you know that after the Great King had been driven out, memories of him faded, new boundaries arose, and new territories were charted. The Great King seemed to have been forgotten."

"Yes, but King Ninian has not kept this hidden," Wesley said with a defensive flare on his tongue. Olivetan would not sway him to side with the Underground. "King Ninian often testifies to the influence of the Great King."

"That is true. I will only say that Ninian likes to keep up appearances. He fears the Great King's return. He fears the old myths."

"I don't understand..."

"Ninian speaks of restoring the co-regency, but like his grandfather, Jurias Ninian I, he is jealous of Gaspard. He fears he'll lose the kingdom. He'd rather the tales be forgotten."

Wesley argued, "Yet, they're not forgotten. We are speaking of them now."

"Indeed, as Gaspard wrote, they *cannot* be forgotten."

"Now you lost me," Wesley said.

As if on cue, Quesnel drew a long, deep, chiding snore.

Olivetan rolled his eyes. "Gaspard wrote that if ever there came a time when the old myths went untold, the mountains would cry out."

Wesley had no idea what Olivetan meant by that. "You spoke to the bears. Do you also speak to rocks?" Wesley's thoughts were becoming muddled.

Olivetan laughed and went on, "Listen carefully, Wesley. Your great-grandfather wrote down what happened, just as the Great King said it would."

Despite his burning eyes begging for rest, Wesley needed to know and would hold Olivetan to everything he said. "What happened?"

"The mountains trembled and shook, as if a voice from deep within the earth broke through the stone."

Avlae and I talked about the mountains that spoke.

"The words were heard by the wind as it raced around the peaks and above the valleys. The wind carried the words to the birds of the air. The birds shared the message with the smaller creatures in treetops, who then whispered to the beasts of the field. With the treasure—all the wealth of the Great King that your great-grandfather found—he learned the language and spoke with the animals. He then shared the message with King Ninian, who was very much offended."

"But why? Why be offended?"

"Ninian and Gaspard had built the greatest empire that World Over had ever seen, and the thought of giving it up repulsed him. He longed for the old myths to be put away. He looked to his own rule."

Olivetan's words trounced all Wesley knew. Had he believed some illusion? He asked cautiously, "My father knows all of this?"

"Indeed. Ninian continues to hollow out the mountains and build his empire. He mines deeper and deeper to silence the stone. If he could kill Gaspard and gut the mountains, he believed that the reign of his household would then last forever. He would become the *new* Great King. What he doesn't realize, though, is that in their pain, the mountains cry louder and wail all the more."

Words eluded Wesley. He held his costrel against his chest and lay back as if on a bed of nails. Except, Olivetan's words stabbed at him from the inside. He shut his eyes, thinking he may never sleep that night. The world pressed in around him, spinning him, throwing him.

Father will prove that Olivetan doesn't have his story right. Somehow, all of this is a misunderstanding, and soon life will go on as it always did. One day soon, King Ninian will celebrate with the heirs of Gaspard, and Nantes will be at peace.

Found (Part One)

34

K eeping off the main roads, Habs, Mahre, two trail scouts, and their new friend the troll hiked along the trail of an overgrown cart path. Habs chose the longer route, as it offered the most cover. As for the rest of the Underground, Habs had sent them to the cave near Coragaes Pass, where he planned to meet them later at the Caves of Caracas for some rest.

Well, we've found camaraderie with a pirate troll. Did you consider what it would take to feed him?" Mahre asked, glancing back toward Habormoss across the waist-high grass that separated them. Mahre's facial features were lit by the glow of the deep blue night.

"Have you considered *what* he eats?" Habormoss said with a smile in his voice. "So far, I've counted four bats, a fox, two raccoons, and ten squirrels. And there was no preparation or cleanup. He ate them whole!"

"Good point, we're not likely to run out of squirrels. It's his uncanny manners that don't suit me, I suppose. Makes me a bit queasy," Mahre said. Several steps ahead of the group, Mahre seemed to keep his distance from the pirate troll.

"Don't fuss. If you're so put out, give him your tea towel next time he eats."

"Of course, where are my manners?"

"Anyway, be glad he offered to carry the trunk," Habs said. He wished that Mahre would show more empathy, knowing what it was like to be under the curse of being a troll.

"How much farther?" Mahre asked.

"We're close."

Habs's boots were no longer sloshing, though his wet undergarments still stuck to his skin and chilled him. No doubt, the others suffered the same. But his body ached, as well-worn as an old garment with its threads pulling apart. Rest will come.

Thankfully, the moon was a ready guide. Habs knew exactly where he was. Thick trees on either side hid them well. They had a day's lead on the king's men. And with a pirate troll among them, he hoped to keep the group safe, should any of the same kind cross their path.

Coming around a bend, the main road came into view. Habs's eyes strained, searching shadows to make out any sign of a package alongside the road. *No, no...* His thoughts surged, and his heart added beats between beats. This was too much to risk. One unmindful delivery driver, and Sophia could be halfway to Brazenose by now. Looking back to where he had started, he spotted the package, right where it was supposed to be delivered.

Habs assessed the road for any sign of trouble, then he stepped fast toward the package.

Habs tapped—two quick knocks, pause, one knock, pause, two quick knocks. He waited. No response. Mahre was about to speak, but Habs raised a hand to keep him silent. Finally, the reply came—knock, pause, knock, pause, two quick knocks. Sophia was safe. He mentally checked off the second leg of their journey.

"We'll have you out soon, Sophia." Habs looked to Mahre. "We'll take the maps and writings from here. Have our new friend carry Sophia." With the trunk again between him and Mahre, Habs led the way into the forest. He continued, "We'll move toward the caves. Thanks to Jansen, Ninian's men are too close. No doubt they will make their way to Merchant's Pass."

"I suppose it's too late to send a message to Olivetan?" Mahre asked.

"Yes," said Habs. "We'll be cautious."

Soon they found themselves wading across a wide, shallow river. Once across, the pirate troll placed the fragile parcel on the sandy shore.

"Os-ostit...titaian due," Habormoss thanked the pirate in broken—yet his best—Calbharian.

Taking the key that was strung around his neck, Habs unclasped the lock and pulled up on the latch. He handed the key to Mahre and opened the crate.

"*Ses ibdromet?*"

"What is he saying?" Habs asked.

"He wants to know what you have."

Habs emptied the textiles and removed the divider.

"Sophia." Habs reached in and placed his hands behind her shoulders. Their eyes connected, and she beamed, more intense than the moon that night.

"It's been too long, cousin," Sophia whispered and extended her arms from the crate.

"Indeed."

Habs lifted her from her folded position, and she immediately threw her arms around his neck. He stepped ahead and carefully placed her in the sand along the banks of the river. Sophia straightened her legs and eased herself back with thin, shaky arms.

Mahre brought her water and a wetted towel.

"Thank you, Mahre." Sophia placed her hand on the side of his face. She drank deeply and handed the leather pouch back to him. "I've been gone too long," Sophia said and proceeded to wipe her neck and face.

"Your return has us reeling. There have been a few changes as of late…" Habs began.

"So, I see," Sophia jumped in. She paused at the sight of the pirate troll but did not look surprised in the least. Softly, she said, "Help me to my feet."

Mahre and Habs each took a hand and eased her up. On either side, they guided her. Stepping and pausing on unsteady legs, she moved toward the troll. Without a word, she smiled and touched his arm.

"Did you tell him that we will help?" Sophia asked.

"Yes, we did," Mahre answered.

Sophia's expression warmed, and her eyes did not waver. Looking directly at the troll, she spoke, *"Ses ou ton suphon dwe?"*

Habs looked at Mahre, who whispered, "She asked its name."

"Callas," the troll answered.

"Elephaios, aderlos," Sophia said and looked back at Mahre. "For that is why *he* came, correct?"

"Yes, my lady," Mahre answered.

"I promise. *Ouschenomon,*" she said and slid her hand from the pirate's forearm. She looked to Mahre. "Bela sends her love."

"I worry about her," Mahre admitted.

"She is a sensible young woman. She will make her way."

"That is my prayer."

"It is so warm here. Snow arrived early on the coast," Sophia commented. "If I were to venture as to why, I would say Medici had something to do with it."

"Indeed. And other strange activity…There is much to share," Habs said but hurried as he spoke. "We must keep moving to stay ahead of Ninian's soldiers."

Habs briefly spoke with his guides and promised sleep when they reached Caracas. On the way to the caves, Habs told Sophia of their journey. They grieved over Jansen, wondered about the magic that had come to their rescue below Port Regael, and celebrated the narrow escape.

The Navarrian Hills

35

Dense foliage in the deep wood kept the three of them in a daylong twilight. Wesley swayed as he rode upon his own bear now. Up ahead, a circle of light suggested their path was finally ending.

The musty smell of the valley reminded him of the fruit cellar back home. He pondered how certain scents had a way of sparking his memory, and his mind was quickly down another path. The earthy aroma of hay—where he had slept while he rode in the back of the cart—had him recalling working the mow back home. And after drinking sweet tea, provided by the chef at the camp back near Beggar's Bay, he had so much appreciation for how Avlae made tea. His mind continued to make connections. Before he knew it, he was on his way out of the woods and into an open meadow…a very familiar meadow.

With both hands, Wesley clenched fur on the nape of the bear's neck. Leaning forward, he slid his legs together and dropped off the side. Slightly annoyed at the sudden tug and pull, the beast twisted its giant head back and growled. Wesley thought nothing of the bear's grunts and grumbles, for they had become all too common while riding. Besides, he was home.

"The Navarrian Hills!" Wesley shouted.

He tore ahead through the prairie grasses, squinting in the late afternoon sun. Bugs and insects fluttered and jumped from the golden fields around him. These were the hills he loved. The mountains farther south had seemed to close in around him, like he was trapped. Here, he was free.

"Get back here, foolish—" Quesnel spouted in a low voice, unable to finish his sentence.

Wesley immediately swung about and hurried back as Olivetan and Quesnel dismounted.

"My home is not far," Wesley answered with considerably less volume. "Not far at all. Beyond the creek is the road my father takes to the mines."

"Keep quiet, keep still!" Quesnel spat as he spoke. "We are not far from Port Regael. Ninian's soldiers guard these roads."

"Certainly, you know an off-road route?" Olivetan asked.

"Yes, but we will have to cross this road just the same. My home is that way." Wesley pointed northeast. Then in a loud whisper, he added, "And there is a place I would like to stop that's not far out of the way, if it's all the same to you."

Olivetan paused. "It's urgent that we collect the writings and maps, but tell me, where is it you want to go?"

Quesnel shook his head. "There'll be no time for frolicking about the—"

Olivetan raised a hand to cut off Quesnel and urged, "Go on, Wesley."

"There is a cairn I placed in my mother's memory. I would like to see it again."

"Very well, but we mustn't tarry in the meadow. Quesnel's right."

"It is not out of our way. Up ahead, on a hill, in the wooded area north of the meadow, there is a small cemetery."

"Lead the way," Olivetan answered, and then he spoke to the bears. "*A limt sdu. Ses lo ek tnikloj.*"

Wesley had caught onto some of the language from the mountains. He understood that Olivetan had said *quiet* and something about a *dumb animal*. Olivetan, it seemed, had made a joke, and if the bear could laugh, it certainly seemed like it did. He was not sure what Olivetan was planning, but as Wesley found out later, the bears could easily cross the road openly because, well, they were bears. Most men avoided them or were fixated upon them— from a distance, of course.

Stumbling ahead, Wesley snatched a handful of wildflowers and led the way.

Far off, hanging thick above the western shoreline, thunder rolled through dark clouds. And if Olivetan was correct, it was a relentless reminder of the chthonic spell that loomed along the coast of Nantes. To the right, while still some distance away, the road came into view. Thankfully, it was unoccupied.

With his bear beside him, Wesley strode through the meadow. He glanced back and forth between the road and their goal. For some time, it seemed as if they were not getting any closer. Growing deep inside was an ever-increasing awareness of how vulnerable they were. Spooked by Olivetan's words, Wesley thought that the meadow seemed longer and wider than it ever had before. A bird, a deer, any movement out of the corner of his eye, and his stomach leapt. His ears caught every sound, every step—branches lifting, leaves fluttering. The rushing river, like a continual roll on a snare drum, enthralled him. Splashing waters stole his focus like some kind of charm.

But ever so slightly, the rhythm changed, bringing in an offbeat blend of rattling and creaks. He was hearing two sounds. Soon, one cluster of sound broke away from the other, and by instinct Wesley fell to the ground. With his face only niks from the dirt, dry grass poked at his nose and eyes.

"Olivetan!" Wesley spoke.

"Quiet," Quesnel snipped.

"Don't move!" Olivetan warned.

Wesley, Olivetan, and Quesnel lay low in the tall grasses of the meadow. The bears held still. On the road, wagon wheels rolled to a stop.

Heartbeats pounded in Wesley's ears, and grasses tickled his nose. Attempting to shake off a sneeze and realizing it was not going to work, he reached over and snagged the back of the bear's leg. The bear immediately looked down and recognized what was happening. It lifted its head and released a growl. Wesley stifled a laugh as he sneezed into the bear's paw.

Gunfire cracked. The jolt seemed to bounce Wesley off the ground.

"Off with you!" a soldier shouted.

Stepping slowly forward, the bear again moved across the meadow. Feeling a tug on his pant leg, Wesley craned his head back and saw that Olivetan was urging him ahead. On his belly, Wesley crawled, keeping pace with the bear beside him until he was out of the meadow and well into the woods.

Once he was certain that he would not be seen from the road, Wesley stood and searched his location. Twenty or so paces away was a trail of carefully placed flat stones that led up between two stout oak trees. Their thick branches formed a door-like entry.

From stone to stone, Wesley jumped until he stood, arms stretched between the trees, and leaned through. Golden leaves domed a small parcel of thin grass around the cemetery.

Like so many times before, Wesley stepped past five other grave markings and knelt before the cairn he had placed. He removed several leaves and sticks, revealing the center stone he had had etched in Port Regael. He had saved his money for several months, working at the market.

The stone simply read, "Sophia, beloved wife and mother 1577–1621 A. Kom."

Wesley paused only a moment. Would he really get to see his mother again? This thought filled his daydreams. He prayed he would.

Something tiny seemed to jump from the stone as Wesley stood to leave. Curious, he knelt back down and looked closer. It could have only been a bug. Yet, he was compelled to search.

A small burst of light, about the size of a pinhead, jumped from the dirt to the edge of the stone, where it shook and shimmered. Another appeared then, rolling steadily in the dirt around the stone. Suddenly the dot burst, exploding into brilliant specks. Sparks fell to the ground and surrounded the stone. Light cast a glow over the stone and radiated warmth in the cool air of the early evening. The glow warmed him—not merely on his skin, but on the inside as well.

Light blazed across the etched stone. It filled in the numbers and stopped. In the glow, he saw his mother's face. He lifted a hand to reach for her cheek, and immediately from behind came a cold blast of wind which drew away his breath. Like candles, the warm glow was blown out. Wesley became paralyzed. Only his eyes moved, darting back and forth in a frenzy. Fighting hard against whatever held him in place, his body went rigid.

White frost appeared on the ground around him, just as it had on the trail several days ago. It grew closer and closer as if to consume him. This time it was more jagged, like broken glass. As it lurched, it changed color from white to grey to black.

The black frost attached itself to Wesley's knees, then crept up his legs to his torso and his arms. He tensed and pulled, fighting against paralysis. He yanked and tugged and finally wrested away from whatever held him. He threw his arms forward to shake off the frost, and as it fell from him, it became like chains—thick chains latching into the ground in front of him. Shackles twisted around his wrists. With both hands, he seized one of the chains and jerked it. The extreme cold was like needles to his palms and fingers, yet he heaved it back to tear it from the ground. He stood and regripped. Again and again, he tugged with burning hands, but to no avail.

Sinister visions filled his sight, but he could not turn away. He closed his eyes, yet the malevolence remained. He saw burning parchments and caves, breaking ice and floodwaters. The water seemed alive—it reached out and snagged his feet, dragging him into the current.

He heard his name, "Wesley!" as if someone called to him from spans away.

"Wesley!" He heard the voice again, closer than before.

"Wesley!" This time it shook him and broke the trance.

He opened his eyes.

"You fell hard, son. Are you alright?" Olivetan asked, kneeling beside him.

The back of Wesley's head throbbed, his ears rang, and his eyes saw double. "Did you see the burst of light?" Wesley asked.

Olivetan shook his head.

"What about the frost, the chains, the…"

"It must have been meant for you alone. We watched you fall back and hit your head. You've been unconscious for at least ten minutes."

"It began so magically. I saw my mother and felt her warmth. I could even smell her hair. Then it grew dark. I saw things I've never seen, places I've never been. Could this be the magic my mother spoke of?"

"Your mother knew it well, Wesley," Olivetan said.

"It seemed like she was right here with me."

"I believe that time will come."

"But it wasn't *all* so warm. I was trapped and couldn't move. I think I felt what it is like to die."

"You know nothing of death, boy," Quesnel said and turned back to leave.

Still trembling, Wesley asked, "Will you accompany me to the farm?"

Olivetan offered a hand and pulled Wesley to his feet. "Of course, we will."

36

oving farther north and staying west of the creek, Wesley's eyes searched the surroundings. He led Olivetan and Quesnel to where the creek had higher banks with overhanging brush and fallen trees. Here, they could get closer to the road and still stay hidden. The problem was that although they were hidden, the thick brush kept them from getting a good view of the road as well.

The river rushed alongside them. It was too fast and too wide to wade across. But Wesley knew of a footbridge, and it did not take long for him to find it.

He looked back at Olivetan and Quesnel. "We can cross the river here, then the road."

"Stay as low as you can on the bridge," Olivetan said. "I'll cross first." He moved beyond Wesley, crawling on his belly. "I will signal if it is safe."

Rattling along, another cart approached. The three sank low and watched it pass. Olivetan sprang over the bridge and across the road as the cart came to a stop not far from them. Olivetan motioned for the other two to cross. Wesley shook his head. No way was he moving with the cart so close. Olivetan motioned again.

"He's quite out of his mind," Quesnel muttered.

Olivetan tilted his head as if Wesley should look again. Wesley crawled upon the footbridge, stretched forward, and peered around the corner post. There, beyond the cart in the middle of the road, were the bears—five of them now, holding the attention of the soldiers. Wesley looked at Quesnel, smiled, and gestured for them to go. The two of them crossed the road with ease. Wesley found the trail, and they were off. The bears soon joined them.

Growing anxious at the thought of seeing his father again, Wesley wondered how he would ever explain the bears, Olivetan, and Quesnel. Would his father be angry? He had so much to say. Where would he start? What would Father think of him bringing members of the Underground to the doorstep of their quiet home?

Wesley began to hope his father would not be home. But at the same time, he needed confirmation. He could wait. Or could he? What if his father was *not* home? Not seeing him would make his heart ache. King Ninian had regiments all about, and they could come across pirate trolls at any moment, but what worried him most was the thought of seeing or not seeing his father.

Wesley began to regret learning about the Underground. *Why couldn't I just remain ignorant of the Underground, and life could go on as usual?* He then remembered something Mother had often said. *"Only one sort of worry is permissible—to worry because one worries."* But with the king's men so close, he and his father together could hand over Olivetan and Quesnel. King Ninian would reward them, and they would celebrate the return of Gaspard's family, the Fullness of Time!

Cresting the hill, the path narrowed, and trees grew thick, yet the decline was gradual. Wesley waved his hand to Olivetan and Quesnel, who were single file behind him.

"Come look," Wesley said. "*E seiv*," he whispered in the mountain language, a message that meant "to slow" or "be calm," depending on the context.

"*Osvris fy eledl*," the bear said, seemingly annoyed.

Unable to position itself to lie down, it awkwardly trod, lifting its legs like a march before settling on the ground. Wesley slid off, took several crouching steps, dropped to a crawl, and crept to an opening. Without saying a word, Wesley looked on with his companions over the apple orchard to his home. The fieldstone house, the barn, the garden, the orchard—all was still. Smoke lifted from the chimney, hanging in the still air. His sisters must be baking.

"We can approach the barn through the orchard," Wesley said.

"Agreed," Olivetan answered. "And where will we locate what we have come for, provided your brothers haven't made it here first?"

He had not made any promises to Olivetan. But to keep the parchments out of the hands of pirate trolls, he would trust Olivetan to help. "As long as Father hasn't moved them to another place, the crate will be in the left stall at the back of the barn. Feel for the loose floorboards. Beneath, we'll find the crate."

"As we make our way, stay with your bear. If there is any sign of Ninian's troops or your brothers and their troll friends, you must be ready to flee and meet where we have planned," Olivetan said. "Understood?"

Wesley's stomach clenched, and his shoulders tensed. If he saw King Ninian's troops, he may just run to them for protection from pirate trolls *and* the Underground. He nodded, then continued his crawl. Besides the soft sound of their cautious movements, only an occasional bird chirped above. They made their way to the edge of the orchard in single file.

With a sudden crack, swoosh, and crunch Wesley dropped to the ground. It sounded as if a branch had fallen behind him. After what seemed like minutes, Wesley looked back at Olivetan and Quesnel. Olivetan shrugged, and they did not see or hear anything more. The three sat still for another ten minutes of silence before Olivetan signaled to move ahead.

Again, a *thwack* and *thud* came from behind, closer than the first time.

"Can you see anything?" Wesley quietly asked Olivetan.

"We need to keep moving to the orchard. We are vulnerable in this brush," Olivetan answered. "Keep moving."

Within minutes, they had reached the edge of the apple orchard. Wesley started breathing again. Olivetan seemed to be constantly planning a route for escape. He put his hand on Wesley's shoulder, comforting him. They both looked back to Quesnel.

He was gone.

Found (Part Two)

37

illiam awoke curled up against a mossy log under autumn leaves. All around him, the woodlands seemed to glow yellow and orange. It had to be late in the afternoon. Warm and comfortable, he had slept so deeply. As William drew a breath, the cool autumn air forced a cough. He tried to recall what had happened, and the trickle of a memory turned into a flood of remembrance.

"Oh, no…" he said aloud.

The children.

Pirate trolls were so close. He then remembered what he was told. *"Do not return home."* But everything in him wanted to go home. Who would possibly lead him to safety but then keep him from returning to his children?

He sprang from his floral coverings and searched for footing, wobbling on numb legs. Two side steps, then dropping to sit, he nearly rolled backward off a log. Remembering the arrow, he grabbed at his chest. There was no tear in his tunic. Quickly, he unbuttoned his shirt—no bruises, no scars. Had he dreamed it? Had some strange charm tended to him?

No matter, he would find his way home. Steadily rebuttoning, he stood, searching all directions for anything familiar. The woman who guided him had said something about a path being marked. But how? And if he did find it, where would it lead him? Yet, he would do anything now to get to the children. This path might at least lead him to a place he recognized, and from there he would find his way home.

In his muddle, he noticed something that had changed in the wood ahead of him, but then it was gone. A brighter color? A clearer view? William stood, leaned forward, and then stepped. He leaned slightly left. There it was! And then it was gone—not an extraordinary change, but just enough to notice, as if somehow his vision was corrected when he saw it.

He leaned right and slightly back again. This time, he was able to stop and focus. A path came into view. He took one step and then another. He took several more and then lost it. He adjusted his position, and there it was again. William walked on, and after some practice, whenever the path would once again fall out of focus, he would find it.

It was not a worn path along the ground, nor was it markings in the trees. It was not something dropped, like popcorn or breadcrumbs in the fairy tales he had read to his children. It was nothing like that. The direction he followed was slightly brighter than any other way. And because it was narrow, it required his full attention.

Though the sun shone in his eyes, the path he followed was brighter still. It was as if light shone from behind him, reflecting off leaves and branches and stones, illuminating the way. Every so often, he would turn around—not intentionally, but instinctively— to look for a light coming from behind. But there was nothing.

He went on for quite some time, all the while hopeful to find a landmark he knew, forget about this *friend* he was promised. He needed to get home. Besides, any true friend would have shown him the way home, not left him to play stupid games.

Then, he stopped. A monstrous brown bear blocked the path.

He tried to make the trail move with his mind to go around the bear. Yet, the way was so clear now, so visible that he could not lose it, and it led straight to the bear. William remembered the woman's words from the night before. "Be moved by nothing—keep to the path."

This is madness.

He left the trail and hoped to pick it up again once he made his way beyond the bear—counting his steps so that he might find his way back. Each move crunched the leaves no matter how slowly he lowered his feet. After fifty torturous paces, he turned, hopefully parallel to his path, and moved on hurriedly through the trees. Ducking under low branches, tripping on snags and fallen limbs, he dashed ahead. Breathless, he bent forward and rested his hands above his knees, the leaves below him catching drops of sweat. He lifted his tunic to wipe his face and decided to count his steps back to where he hoped to find the path.

Trudging ahead, a slight breeze rustled leaves and soothed him. Fifty paces back, and he began to search for the trail.

Nothing.

Waiting.

Leaning.

Stepping.

Focusing.

Squinting.

Had he gone too far? Not far enough? Maybe there never was a trail. Maybe it was just a play of light from the sun. How would he know where to start looking again? Pacing in circles, he clenched his arms, cursing himself. Where was he going? He never should have left the path. When he came across the bear, he should have simply waited for it to move on. *What was I thinking? Dammit. What am I doing here?*

Branches lifted, and he staggered backward, the wind nearly sweeping him over. The sound of marching echoed from the treetops as the bear came lunging toward him. Bounding along, its burly legs carried it faster than William thought possible. Before he could react, he was pummeled to the ground, pinned on his back.

He was merely a one-hundred-and-eighty-pound raw piece of meat. Unable to even tremble, he waited to be devoured.

A hand appeared around the shoulder of the salivating beast. Then, a face—a familiar face with a smile that sent William back twenty years.

"Hello, friend. Decided to leave the protection of the spell, did we?"

In a strained breath, William spoke, "Quesnel?"

Bickering Brothers

38

From where the forest met the orchard, it was slightly downhill through rows of apple trees. Wesley rushed toward the barn, darting from tree to tree. At each break, he looked over his shoulder to be sure Olivetan was close behind. They had already lost Quesnel, and it was getting dark. A couple of days ago, he would have been glad to lose Olivetan, but not now. Not this close.

Sprint—stop—look—safe—go—sprint—stop—look—safe—go...all the way through the orchard to the fence line. Dreading how he would explain being home to his father, he waited. A trace of light stretched from a crack between the barn doors. Was his father inside? Down the cart path in the opposite direction was his home, windows glowing yellow.

Go!

He planted his hands on the top rail and threw his feet over. Landing with his feet crossed, he tripped head over heels onto his back. He was sure that he heard Olivetan laughing. Lifting his head, he peered over his knees toward the house. Two figures had emerged from the falling darkness and were walking toward him.

With a thump, Wesley let his head fall to the dirt path. Staring into the sky, Wesley's head throbbed, and his stomach whirled. He had arrived too late. The twins were coming for the parchments. No doubt, pirate trolls were close. He had no chance of securing the writings by his great-grandfather.

Aarn stepped up beside him and reached down. Wesley lifted a limp hand, and Aarn yanked him to his feet. The three brothers stood silently. Wesley searched his brothers' eyes, desperate for any sign of comfort or care, but he found neither.

"Wh-what have you—" Wesley began to ask.

"How did you get here?" Philor broke in.

"Never mind that! I know what he's up to," Aarn said. "He thinks he will keep us from what we've come for."

"You are fools!" Wesley shot back.

"It is *you* who lacks understanding," Aarn said.

"Soon you will honor us as kings," Philor added. "With Great-Grandfather's treasure, the kingdom will raise us to our rightful thrones."

"Indeed, you are standing before the new co-regents of Nantes," Aarn said, hands on his hips.

Jaw tight and fists clenched, Wesley argued, "The throne is already yours! There is no need—"

"*Humph*…We will no longer wait in line behind Derian," Aarn said. His grin always made him look like he was up to something devious.

"Derian is unreasonable, and Father is too cowardly to act on what is ours. It's time we do something," Philor said. "And you would do well to join us, Wesley."

"Yes, we will need advisors," Aarn continued. His words were hollow, "Besides, you're family."

"It seems you have adopted a new family," Wesley shot back.

Just then, light washed over them as the barn door swung open. In the doorway, light traced Derian's silhouette.

"Who's there?" Derian called and stepped out from the barn. With widening eyes and a growing grin, he welcomed them. "Brothers!" Throwing out his arms, he hurried toward them. "Welcome home! I have much to share. There is good news to tell."

Wesley rejected all the enthusiasm that Derian afforded. He longed to land a fist across Aarn's jaw, then tackle Philor to the ground.

"Well, you all look a little worse for wear. But hey, you're home!" Derian attempted to gather them in his arms, but they all pushed back. "What is wrong?" Derian asked, still smiling. His eyebrows raised in concern. "And how did you get home? I expected to meet you in Port Regael."

"Go ahead. Tell him, brothers. Tell him how you've abandoned King Ninian." Wesley stood with crossed arms.

"The truth is, Ninian abandoned us long ago," Philor argued.

"I watched as you swore allegiance to the pirates!"

"And what are *you* doing here?" Aarn countered and shoved Wesley's shoulder. "How is it that you have arrived in Navarre so soon?"

"Whoa, slow down...You mean you've all walked off the mission?" Derian asked. "This will not sit well with King Ninian, nor with your new king."

Wesley and the twins stopped their bickering and stared blankly at Derian.

"New king?" Wesley asked.

"That's what I'm longing to tell you," Derian explained. "My coronation is in three days!"

Aarn reached out and clutched Derian by his tunic. Pulling him close, Aarn spit his words into Derian's face, "You've gone too far, brother!"

Derian shoved him away. Stumbling backward on his lanky legs, Aarn barely kept himself from falling. Derian may have been shorter, but Aarn was no match in physical strength.

"*I've* gone too far? I work to restore what is rightfully ours, and what have you done? What is it called? *Treason?* This will not bode well in the public eye, especially as heirs to the throne yourselves."

"What do—" Wesley tried to speak.

"The public knows nothing of what is true," Philor said and laughed.

"On this day, you have made us enemies," Derian said. He shook a condemning finger at his brothers. "You three have betrayed the trust of your kings." Derian paused and sighed deeply. "If, indeed, you have made allegiance with pirates, as your brother and king, I tell you to withdraw from this foolish pledge, and I will advocate for your exoneration."

Wesley tried again, "Wait—"

"Listen to this aristocrat, Philor." Aarn was barely able to speak amidst his laughter. "Not yet a king, and yet our brother extends us pardon. Ha!"

"I am King. All that remains is the ceremony," Derian said.

"Well, *King*, you should pray that you might receive such mercy when *we* sit upon the thrones of Nantes!" Aarn threatened.

Finally, Wesley shouted, "You? King? How?"

"I sent word to King Ninian about our heritage. I told him of the letters, the maps, the writings," Derian said and straightened his tunic.

"But we made a pact!" Wesley protested.

"And which of us has kept that pact?" Derian asked emphatically. "What about you, Wesley? Are you not guilty as well?"

"No…well, yes…but let me—"

"Then, we have all failed each other. None of us could have known what was about to happen. Unable to communicate with you, I needed to decide. Mother said that we would know when it was time to go forward. With the attack of the trolls, I felt this decision was perfect to lift spirits in Nantes. The Fullness of Time has come, and King Ninian agrees with me. It is time to restore the co-regency in Nantes."

"To be sure, the Fullness of Time *is* upon us," Aarn said. "That is why we have returned. Philor and I are seizing the crown."

"For three generations, Ninian has held the throne. Nantes needs new blood," Philor added.

Derian's eyes stared beyond Wesley and the twins. "It seems you've already considered the cost—new blood for *spilled* blood."

Wesley spun his head around. Several pirate trolls had emerged from the growing darkness and were walking the cart path toward them.

"So, it is true. You've gone off with the pirates," Derian said, and his stance shifted. He lifted his chin, straightened his posture, and glared at the twins. "And somehow you think you have a chance of usurping the throne?"

"Yes, just step aside. We will spare your life and take what is ours," Philor said.

"And we'll be on our way," Aarn added.

With both hands, Derian clutched Aarn by his tunic and pulled him close. "Brothers or not, traitors will not sit upon the throne. You leave quietly and quickly. I will give you this one opportunity to flee. Leave these shores. As your king, pray I do not find you before then." Derian shoved his brother. Aarn stumbled backward and fell.

Philor rushed upon Derian, only to be met with a hard left across the jaw. Immediately, Philor flopped to the dirt beside his twin.

"No!" Wesley cried.

"And why are *you* here, Wesley? Have you found your own band of pirates? Are you here for Great-Grandfather's letters as well?" Derian asked.

"You do not understand—"

"Don't be stupid," Derian snapped.

Wesley looked back. Steadily, the pirates continued their approach.

"Derian, please trust me. I need time to explain. We need to talk with Father. We must protect the writings!"

"And how do *you* plan to stop us?" Philor chuckled from the ground, wiping his bloodied lip.

Derian began to plead with his brothers, "Listen, it seems we are all here for the same reason. We all seek answers. Stand with me, and the writings are already yours. You have a choice to make. I am not against you."

The threat of trolls loomed. He longed for Derian to understand. He begged, "You mustn't do this, Derian. You need to speak with—"

"You have all brought shame to the name of Gaspard," Derian scolded.

"Listen, please!" Wesley cried. *Where is Olivetan? Did he leave me? Did he trick me?*

Derian took several steps to his left and reached into the horse cart. He drew out a rifle, lifted the barrel, and took aim at his brothers.

"In the name of King Ninian, you are all under arrest for treason."

Wesley put his hands on his head in surrender. "This is a mistake!"

"Last chance," Aarn threatened.

Wesley looked at Derian and threw his head around toward the trolls, then back to his eldest brother. Several scraggy men now accompanied a growing number of trolls. In less than a minute, the monsters would be upon them. It was time to surrender to the mercy of Philor and Aarn.

"Will you allow me to stay here at the farm with our sisters?" Wesley pleaded. He could sort things out later. Father would help them understand.

"Of course," Aarn replied. "We only want the writings, and we'll be on our way."

"Lay the rifle down!" Wesley cried. "Save your life, for the sake of your family!"

"Wise words, Wesley," Philor said. "You will make a fine advisor."

"I will not cower to these foolish devils. They know nothing of mercy." Derian drew back the hammer on his rifle.

One after the other, like giant fireflies, small flashes of light burst across the blackness of the forest beyond the barn. Yet, each was followed by a savage boom. The blazing blasts sent Wesley whirling. In an instant, he dropped to the ground, shielding his head with his arms. The pirate trolls raged aloud. He pictured Avlae cradling Jess, covering her ears, and doing all she could to comfort her, like Mother used to do with him on stormy nights.

What of Olivetan? Had trolls captured Quesnel? Was Father running to them from the house?

Spattered by bits of earth, Wesley squeezed his eyes tightly and covered his face with his hands. His body jumped with each successive blast. Rolling onto his side, he peered through spread fingers to see two fallen trolls and pieces of at least one of the mangy men. In more flashes of light, he watched as others groped over the ground, moving toward the orchard, attempting to flee from the heavy, unyielding bombardment. More mortars erupted, blurring his sight.

A growing and rolling tremor shook the ground beneath him, like boulders toppling forward to crush him. Turning his head, he stretched his chin. Hesitant, he finally looked to see what he thought was certain to kill him. It was King Ninian's regiments, rushing from the black smoke. Horses charged upon the trolls. Like bursts of lightning, rifles ignited. One man bellowed, confidently ordering through the chaos, "Kill the trolls! Spare the men!"

Rifle fire split Wesley's ear, and he spun his head to see that Derian had fired his weapon.

"Run while you can, brothers. You've chosen your position!" Derian ordered. "From now on, you'll be hunted as wild game!"

"You ready yourself, *King*, for we will soon return!" Aarn gave the final word. He and Philor ran from the attack. Battered trolls and men followed, all absorbed by the darkness.

Rifle flares ceased, and the rumble halted. With his elbows digging into the dirt, Wesley pushed himself up to see. Smoke dissipated, and the enormity of King Ninian's military might advanced before him. Soldiers leapt from steeds and beat down a few resistors with the butts of their rifles. Wounded men wailed as heavy boots pushed into their backs and chains bruised their wrists and arms. Far off, Wesley heard cries from his sisters, weeping and calling to Derian.

Derian's voice brought him back to the moment. "Now, you must act, Wesley. Come with me, and I will say nothing of your treason. We can tell King Ninian you were a captive of the pirates."

"Are you asking me to lie?"

"No, I am telling you to. I do not want to arrest you."

Where was Olivetan? Where was Father? He longed to console his sisters.

"Wesley! We haven't much time. Are you listening to me?"

What had just happened? Why would Derian arrest him? His ears were ringing, his thoughts strewn about. Wesley shook his head. No time to reason. Instead, he chose to test his brother. "Would it not be suspicious if an heir of Gaspard was taken away in chains?"

"I must act according to my role as king. Again, I do not want to arrest you!"

"Arrest me, then. Take me with you, but I'm not going to lie!"

"You are a stubborn fool!" Derian said in a loud whisper as several soldiers approached.

"What of this boy, sire?" one of the soldiers asked as two others yanked Wesley to his feet.

"Bind him!" Derian ordered.

"Where is Father?"

"He did not return home last night."

"Did he know of your plan?"

Derian did not answer.

"Did he know?" Wesley again implored.

"Step away," Derian commanded the soldiers. After the soldiers had walked out of earshot, he spoke, "He would never have permitted me to reveal our heritage. You know that."

"Did you have him arrested as well?"

"Of course not! I don't know where he is," Derian argued. "I've heard rumors today that a group of miners was attacked by trolls while returning last night. What would you have had me do? Jess screams in her sleep each night. She has nightmares of trolls carrying her away! I need to protect our family."

"I'm coming with you, even if you take me away in chains. I need to speak with you. There are things I have heard as well," Wesley pleaded. "Can you at least stay this night and hear me?"

"For all I know, Father has been killed. We must get to safety in Port Regael."

"But, Derian—"

"You listen to me. I am the heir, and only in my place will you reign. I will hear you when we reach Port Regael. I'll do what I can for you." Derian shouted over Wesley's shoulder, "Guards!" He moved quickly back into the barn, and in a moment, he appeared with a leather-strapped crate—Great-Grandfather's writings. "Take him away."

Wesley was led away from the barn. Soldiers lined the cart path securing the property. Lanterns lit up the farm like a festival—a festival of sorrow, if there was such a thing. Men hurried to attach cannons to carts, and others reloaded their rifles. Farther out, King Ninian's purple flags were lifted high, held in place by keepers to mark the king's present victory.

What was now to become of him? How would things have turned out if Father had been home? *I have failed. Derian will never listen. As the youngest heir, will anyone listen to me?* He looked toward the house. *Avlae!* He had to find her.

Wesley was quickly pulled aside. Guardians marched in step, their rapiers drawn. Tall, tasseled hats rested on their brows, and their eyes were trained forward. On the opposite side of the path, between the swinging arms and stolid faces, he saw Derian carrying away the writings.

Wesley searched for his sisters. He needed to speak to Avlae before he was taken away. Up ahead, a line of prisoners waited with iron rings around their necks and chains down their backs, fastened to their wrists. Each prisoner was chained to the next.

Just then there was a tug, a pull, and a clamoring about his leg. He nearly fell over.

"Wesley! Wesley!" A young voice cried out. "How did you get here?" His youngest sister, Jess, had clenched her arms around his leg. Right behind her was Avlae, who also threw her arms around him. She let him go and put her hands on his shoulders.

"Are you not going to hug me back?" Avlae asked. But then she looked down. "Why are you bound? What is going on?"

"I don't have time to explain," Wesley said. "You must find me when we reach the castle. I have much to tell."

Avlae searched the area. "Where is Derian? You must be freed at once!"

"Avlae, please listen."

"Release him!" She shouted to a passing soldier.

Reaching a hand to her shoulder, the man spoke, "My lady, what you ask, I am unable to do. You must seek out King Derian."

Avlae threw his arm aside. "I certainly will." She was about to leave that instant, but Wesley stepped into her path.

"May I speak with my sisters?"

"Very well," the soldier obliged, yet held him tightly.

"Don't fight this now, sister. The time will come."

"King Ninian himself has come to escort the writings back to

Port Regael. Whatever this misunderstanding might be, the king will rejoice to know you are safe and have returned from your mission."

Wesley looked deep into Avlae's eyes.

"That is why you are back, isn't it?" Worry framed her eyes. "The breach has been repaired, right?"

Wesley looked directly to Avlae. He whispered, "Promise me that you will come to me in secret once we reach the castle."

"He has chained you like you are some kind of threat…"

"Avlae," Wesley said. "Please, promise me."

"Yes, I promise."

"Sisters, we must leave, now!" Far ahead on the path, Derian waved, motioning them toward him.

"Good-bye, brother. I will find you." Avlae scooped Jess into her arms. Jess began to cry, her little hands wiping away tears.

A tug on Wesley's arm pulled him back, and he was led away with the other prisoners.

Olivetan must have deserted me. And to think, I almost believed him! At least Great-Grandfather's writings are on the way to the castle. Now, if Derian will only hear me!

Lifting Shadows

39

In the early morning hours, while it was still dark, the Underground reached the Caves of Caracas. Too tired to argue, Habs agreed to keep the pirate troll out of sight of the others…for now. He had Mahre explain to Callas that he must remain hidden and that they would come for him. *Poor Callas.*

After finding a quiet corner within one of the caves, Habs took his rest, doing his best to ignore the rocky, uneven floor beneath him. Amidst his earnest thoughts of putting on dry clothing, sleep overtook him.

Later, Habs awoke to the sound of people grumbling about not having enough to eat. Others protested about having to live in darkness for several days, not being allowed out during daylight hours. Despite the complaints, the caves were the safest place until they could reach Dochart's Glen. Somewhere southwest of Farne? Northeast of Coligny?

Scouts had been commissioned to secure the surrounding trails. Throughout the day, there were many times when Ninian's soldiers came uncomfortably close. Habs positioned others to survey paths that led to Merchant's Pass with hopes of finding Olivetan.

Merchant's Pass was part of the old trade route, only accessible by foot. Surrounded in all directions by mountains far above the valley, they would have an advantage should Ninian's soldiers come looking for them. The escape routes were many and well hidden. Habs knew Olivetan would be cautious. Yet, it is what Olivetan did not know about Jansen's betrayal that made Habs wary.

When scouts returned the next evening, Habs listened to discern the best route to the Pass. After issuing strict orders that no one leave the caves, soon after dark, Habs, Sophia, and Mahre introduced Callas to a dozen others who would transport supplies. Quick and to the point, Habs issued a terse explanation for the presence of the pirate troll and answered no questions—they made for the pass.

Following three dark hours of tense but fortunately uneventful trailblazing, they approached a unique, arched bridge that stretched up and over a flume. Illuminated by the aurorean light, the bridge seemed to float above the valley. There were no less than ten different tales that described such a scene, but Habs was not inclined to tell any of them in the moment. Twisted tree roots had gathered and coiled, stretching out and up from both sides of the ravine, creating a wide span—a natural bridge. Habs directed the others to cross one at a time. Once across, the path zigzagged, sloping upward until they overlooked the valley from precipitously high above.

Behind them, a deep cove in the side of the mountain formed a natural shelter. Mahre immediately set to kindling a fire. Sophia collected sticks and joined him. Habs ordered Callas and several others to take shifts scoping the area and watching the valley, while the remaining few settled in, preparing a meal. When things were in order, he returned to speak with Sophia and Mahre, who were warming themselves near the fire.

"It has been three years…Jess has doubled in age," Sophia said, tightening her cloak.

Sparks scattered as Habs stacked a couple logs on the fire. "I have often purchased produce from your children at the market."

"How difficult it will be for the children and William to see me again…" Sophia shook her head and tucked her hands into large pockets. "There is no easing into this. They've thought me dead all this time."

"Your children have done well. It is they who have taken care of William. He has brought much pain upon himself," Habs said and poked at the fire with a long, crooked stick. "We advised him to speak openly with the children and flee from here after you were captured. He'd often remind me that he must wait until the Fullness of Time. I think he chose to stay and sulk in his pain…" Habs threw his stick to the ground and looked away. He had never understood William's mental state. His voice became more earnest, "I pleaded with him, for the sake of the children, but he would not hear me."

"You mustn't blame him. His days will get brighter. I believe it. He may have worn thin, but he will hold together. He will see that mercy can be severe. Do not doubt, cousin. You could find yourself in his place."

Sympathy was far off when Habs thought of William. The one time he had held his tongue was when Sophia married the milksop. That was when he should have said something! Habs could not hide his feelings. No doubt Sophia could read him.

"Habs, you are very quiet."

She knew him all too well.

"Of course, I know," Habs replied, and he reached for another stick to stir the fire, avoiding eye contact with Sophia.

Sophia stood to stretch and took several steps away. "Tell me about Callas, Mahre. He says you saved his life."

"Well, to be honest, Habs put me up to it," Mahre confessed.

Habs went on to explain how he had tied a rope around Callas's leg, thinking it was a tree, and the adventure that followed.

Sophia laughed aloud and said, "You have not changed at all!" Her voice then became grim. "Pirate trolls in Nantes…"

"Word arrived during the day of the celebration that the wall had been breached. We were attacked. Ninian sent men to expand the kingdom as planned. Others, including Philor, Aarn, and Wesley, were sent with the group led by Olivetan to repair the breach. His plan—"

Sophia broke in, "The breach was not unexpected, was it?"

"Not at all. Only wish the timing could have been different." Habs continued, "Olivetan planned to break off from the group with your boys and bring them here."

"I can tell you that they will not be so easily persuaded." Sophia strolled toward the edge of the cliff and stood with her back toward Habs, the moonlight outlining her silhouette.

"Aye, that was his fear as well."

Sophia's voice was shaky with regret as she said, "My intentions of keeping the children safe from the exploits of Ninian—"

This time, Habs stopped her. "Do not pick up that burden."

Her voice cracked in amusement. "Can you travel the recondite paths of a mother's heart?"

"Well, no, but…"

With a careful lift of her arm, Sophia steadily waved her hand, calling Habormoss to come to her side. Habs stood and stepped promptly toward Sophia. Resting a hand on her shoulder, he leaned forward to see what she saw. In the glow of the midnight moon, two figures were crossing the root bridge.

Swiftly, Habs was up and moved to a hidden path. Mahre, Sophia, and Callas followed closely behind. Between trees that lined the path, Habs climbed a narrow, rocky lane. Moonbeams invaded the path through holes of missing foliage—a testimony to the coming winter. Habs looked at the autumn leaves, hanging like men, clinging for life, high above their doom with no option but to let go at any moment. On his worst days, that was how he had envisioned the Underground.

The trail grew steep, and every third or fourth step, his boot slid, sending stones rolling behind him. If Habs timed it right, they would curve around and come right up behind their two mysterious guests.

At the highest point, Habs leaned into a tree, stopping to catch his breath. Catching it just as the others reached him, he bounded off again. He knew they did not have time to stop if they wanted to keep up. Yet they were younger, and for Callas it didn't matter much. One step for him was three for the others.

Trees provided the needed leverage as Habs bounced and slid toe to heel down the slope. Arms out, his hands caught tree trunks to break his descent. Slowing his pace as the path leveled, he approached the main trail. He stopped short, bent one knee, then the next, and lay flat on the ground. He panted heavily with exhaustion, watching each warm breath rise and dissipate into the night. In shadows behind him, he heard the others find their positions.

They listened.

And they waited.

Things fell into place just as he had planned. The two came and went. Between their voices, the shuffling leaves, and the kicking of stones, Habs knew they were not particularly concerned about stealth. In fact, the two were laughing rather loudly and taking their time, chatting like schoolboys. Anticipating his move, Habs waited, thankful to have a troll on his side.

Counting off a minute in his head, he jumped up and called back in a loud whisper, "Callas…Callas!" Habs's heart stopped, realizing the pirate stood only several paces away. Hardly able to speak, Habs managed, "Now…go!"

Callas fled out onto the main trail, and Habs followed. After three long steps, Callas leapt, landing right behind the men. The thump from his monstrous hands would have knocked the two over if he had not grabbed their garments. Tripping over the foliage along the trail, Habs stumbled while trying to catch up. Callas lifted the men off the ground and growled, as Habs had ordered, to add to the fear. The men kicked and threw their arms a bit, but they did not seem frightened—merely annoyed.

"Put us down, you bulging ruffian!" one man yelled.

"So, this is where you have brought us to die, friend?" the other asked with blithe.

The first spoke again, directly to Callas in Calbharian. The troll seemed stunned and stuttered a bit as if he did not know what to say. Then, a conversation ensued between the two. Habs understood the word *aderlos*. And it was not long until Callas started laughing right along with his catch.

What is this all about? Habs had instructed Callas to knock them together so he could tie them up and question them later. But instead, the men stopped kicking and just hung there as if it was a relief to get off their feet for a while. Habs walked closer. Callas turned around with the two men dangling from his grip. Habs's jaw went slack.

"Aderlos!" Habs bellowed and threw his arms in the air.

Callas repeated, *"Aderlos!"* and threw his arms higher than they already were. Flopping like marionettes, the two laughed all the more.

Sophia and Mahre rounded the corner and immediately ceased their pursuit. Sophia just stared ahead. The silence that followed drowned out all sounds of the night.

"Sophia!" one of the men wailed. The man's reaction nearly sent him falling to the ground. In the air, his legs were already running. In the tone of that one word, *Sophia*, Habs had heard the joy of a thousand shadows lifting at once.

Callas regained his grip and gradually set the man back on his feet. Still, the man nearly fell forward in his haste. He ran toward Sophia and embraced her back from the dead. Locked in each other's arms, they wept and laughed and lived again.

"Oh, William!" Sophia cried.

"My one desire was to see you alive again." He held the sides of her face. "It was another spell, was it not?" William kissed her forehead and pulled her close again.

"Yes, a spell. And thanks to Bela, I am here with you now."

William turned to Habs and asked, "So, you've known she was alive all along?"

"Well, we *hoped*..."

"No need to explain, friend. I understand. And where is Bela? Is she with you?" asked William.

Sophia looked to Habs.

"No, but she'll be along," Habs answered. With his arms outstretched, he then walked up to Callas and had his own reunion. "I've missed you, Quesnel," he said.

"*Due Phithien*," Quesnel spoke quite casually to the troll, and Callas put him back on the ground.

With both hands, Habs grabbed Quesnel just below the shoulders and looked him in the eyes. "What are you doing in Navarre? I didn't expect to see you until we reached Brazenose."

"Navarre? Is that where I am? It's so easy to get turned around in these bloody mountains."

Habs bolstered a laugh and put out his hand, offering the way back to camp. Side by side, they walked together. Habs threw his arm over the shoulder of his friend.

"It is good to see you without your iron jewelry," Habs said.

"Yes, yes. I suppose so, though I do feel a bit naked without it."

"Mahre!" Habs hollered back. "Do you not have some menial tasks to attend to?"

"Right! Off we go then, Callas. Good to see you, William." Mahre slapped him on the back and nodded at Sophia. "Ma'am."

Habs knew that Sophia and William needed some time alone together. He left them behind and, with the other three, made his way back to the camp.

When the others saw Quesnel, they pushed in around him. Someone brought him a coat and a cup of hot tea. When the tears were wiped away and greetings were complete, Habs sat down near the fire next to Quesnel.

"I'll tell you, I didn't think I'd see William alive again," Habs said.

"The wind will blow, my friend. You'll indeed hear it, but you won't know where it is coming from or where it is going," Quesnel responded, then sipped his tea.

"And have you happened to find yourself this way by the wind?" Habs asked.

"It was most sublime. I was with Olivetan—"

"Olivetan?" Habs interrupted and jumped, just about knocking the cup from Quesnel's hands.

"Yes, Olivetan. And the Delaine boy, oh…what is his name… Westcott?"

"Wesley."

"Yes, Wesley. We were near his homestead, not far from the apple orchard."

"Are they far behind? Were you separated somehow?"

"Yes, you could say we were separated, as I was carried away."

"Carried away?"

"Well, I was with Olivetan, but then all at once I was on the western edge of the Sea of Trees—carried away. I'm not sure how else to say it. I was in one place, then another. I found myself far away from where I was just a moment before."

"Why the Sea of Trees? What good is the Sea of Trees?" Mahre said, removing a mandora from its case.

"Quite odd, don't you think? I think perhaps it was in a dream or vision. It's all a bit muddled now. Somehow, I knew that I needed to find someone."

"You *are* like the wind!" Habs paused. "You know…it has begun."

Quesnel raised a single eyebrow and smiled. "Yes, I know."

"Are there not some who await your arrival in Brazenose?" Habs asked.

"I've sent them a letter." Quesnel shuddered in the cold night and closed his eyes as he swallowed. Finally, he said, "I told them I would be delayed. Ninian's couriers are very reliable. Olivetan made sure it was on the cart."

"One could not plan *your* travels."

Habs chuckled and was glad to hear Mahre beginning to sing. Mahre plucked notes on his mandora and transitioned into a strumming melody as another joined him on the dulcian. It was a well-worn and sturdy song. There was not one person among them who didn't know the words, nor anyone who grew tired of singing them.

Mahre led them, and they sang.

On the road to the ol' field mine eyes ever onward
Whence the night comes the light, stays my heart to the dawn
And we'll drink to the beauty and warmth of the morning
When at last the golden lands welcome me home

On the road to the ol' field mine hands they're ne'er idle
My gains are but loss and my loss only gain
Though the weight of the harvest bears down on my shoulders
We'll tread paths of hope with steps lighter than today

On the road to the ol' field mine heart prone to wander
For despair would have me succumb to the throes
But from anguish of night comes the warmth of the morning
And at last the golden lands will welcome me home

40

The tinnient sound of music fell like mist from above. Sophia and William had made their way to the center of the root bridge in a glowing gamut of blue shadows. William caressed Sophia's hands in his own and peered into her round, hazel eyes. Her fair complexion and youthful appearance had not changed since the day they met. Just to have her close was remedial, and her touch, salutary.

"Despair has been my torment for far too long, my days bleak and weary. Doubts have left no trace of joy. And peace…peace I have not known in years." William ached. His chin fell to his chest. "Forgive me, Sophia."

Sophia reached out and lifted his chin. "Can one forgive malaise? How do you forgive one for being ill?" She hugged him and added, "You will heal, William."

"But *three years*. For so long have I wallowed in the blood of my own misery, that I'd forgotten the pain of others—even their happiness." Willian threw his arms out and stepped away. "Yet, two nights ago, I was purged of this wretched self-pity. Returning from the mines, pirates ensnared our cart. Flaming arrows showered upon me, and when I leapt to save my life, one pierced me." Telling the tale was like reliving the event. He began to sweat and shake. "My insides burned, for it felt as though my blood boiled and my organs had melted away. But the arrow did not tear my skin."

With a gentle touch on his shoulder, Sophia spoke tenderly, "It has begun—the Fullness of Time."

Willian pulled away from her touch and wrung his hands. "Then, why the agony? Why do we flee? Why the mystery?" Recognizing his rashness, William slowed his breaths. In a thready voice, he said, "My hope is small."

Sophia raised her finger to her lips to quiet and calm him. "But you have acknowledged a turning around. Doubt is not weakness." Again, they embraced and kissed. With yearning in her voice, Sophia said, "Tell me of the children."

"I have not stopped thinking about them since yesterday. Oh, I have watched how they've longed for a father. When I was attacked, I could think of no one else. The pirates were so close, but I could not get home. My only desire was their safety."

"This trial has led you—"

"But I felt so helpless. I could not get to the children, Sophia, for I was led away from the wreckage by a stranger in the night. I never saw her face. She promised that the children would be safe. I could have killed this wretched woman for leading me away." Again, his arms whipped in furor. William thought again, poised himself, and grabbed Sophia's hands. "Yet, I've been led to you… You need to see Avlae, for she has your spirit…What is it?" Sophia had let go of his hands and turned away. "What's wrong?"

"I…I…What you said, just now, I dreamed it."

"You what?"

"I dreamed it. I directed you through the forest, told you to not return home…" Sophia shook her head. "When I awoke, I was so angry at myself for what I had said to you. I knew the danger that the children were in, yet I told you they would be safe! I was furious—"

"But it was a dream. We can go to them and bring them here!"

"Let's leave now."

"I'll find Mahre," said William. "We could use his help."

"No, no," Sophia said and pulled him back. "We'll leave a note and meet up with the rest on the way to Dochart's Glen. This journey must be ours. After all we've been through, Habs would not agree to this."

"And neither would I," spoke a confident voice behind them.

William caught Sophia as she jumped backward into his arms. Mounted upon a bear, Olivetan appeared from the shadows. Several other bears stalked behind him.

"Our boys? Are they far behind?" Sophia asked, stealing glances beyond Olivetan.

"I have much to tell. Please, come." Olivetan increased his pace.

"But the children?"

"You will not find them at home," Olivetan said and moved on.

Instinctively, Sophia reached as high as she could on the neck of a passing bear, grabbed tightly, and threw her leg over, like she had done many times so long ago.

William watched proudly. While he had no trust for the creatures, he knew this situation was unavoidable. And before he thought twice, he found himself with a mouthful of fur, dangling from the side of a bear. William was not as graceful as Sophia, but he managed to pull himself up.

The bears did not have time for the trail that diagonally crossed the side of the mountain. Instead, they went straight up and over the rocks, between the trees and through the brush. Those in the camp must have heard the ruckus, for they waited at the edge of the wood, gaping as the giant paws tromped and the bears appeared before them.

Olivetan slid off and walked directly to Quesnel. "So, this is where you've gotten off to."

"Something tells me we are not leaving for Coligny in the morning," Quesnel said. With a stick, he pushed himself up to greet Olivetan.

"Good to see you alive!" Olivetan wrapped his arms around his friend and said, "You can tell me later how you arrived at Merchant's Pass. I'm certain it's a wonderful story."

Quesnel only laughed. He and Olivetan shared a deep friendship. When they communicated, it was so much more than just words. There was a tone, a look, a random reference that only the two of them knew. William used to accuse them of conspiring, not in spoken language, but merely because they were in sight of each other.

"Great needs grow from great possessions," Olivetan began. He lifted off his satchel and placed it on a boulder, which substituted for a table. He opened it and began to lay out the contents. Others crowded in close with lanterns, eager to see.

"These are my personal writings from Gaspard," Sophia said. She stepped back and placed her fingers to her lips. "Tell us of the children. How did you come to possess these?"

"This will be difficult for you to hear." Olivetan wasted no words. "Philor and Aarn have betrayed the crown and seek to force a new co-regency."

Olivetan then spoke of all that had befallen them. Sophia sank in William's arms.

"I knew I should have accompanied them to Port Regael," William bemoaned.

"And what would that have achieved, William?" Habs accused. "You should have fled with them years ago!"

William's face flushed with heat. He stood rigid and let go of Sophia.

"Stand down…" Olivetan warned Habs.

But Habs would have none of that. "All this time, you have cowered in Navarre—"

"Habs!" Olivetan blared.

"You hid away, unwilling to protect your children! Frail and weak, you—"

"Habs! No more!" Olivetan ordered.

Silence twisted the moment. William seethed but managed to keep his mouth shut.

"Tell us more," Sophia pleaded.

"Derian had sent word to Ninian about being heir to the throne, but Aarn and Philor were determined to get what they came for. They brought a few troll friends. Poor Wesley, no one was going to listen to what he had to say. After all, by now, each had broken the oath they made to each other."

"And you didn't intervene?" Sophia asked.

"But I did. How do you think I came about with the writings? While the boys fought over them, I slipped into the barn and took the writings myself. About that time, Ninian's men attacked and drove off the trolls—along with Philor and Aarn. I fled from the barn and watched from the woods. Ninian had come to escort the writings back to Port Regael. The girls were quite shaken by all of it, and it looked as if Wesley had a moment to talk with them before…" Olivetan seemed to suddenly realize the shock of what he was about to say.

"Before what?" Sophia demanded.

"Before he was taken prisoner. Wesley would have no part in what Derian was doing. Avlae and Jess took their seats with Derian in Ninian's carriage. They are all on their way back to Port Regael."

"Derian is only acting on what he knows. He'll see that no harm will come to Wesley," Sophia said.

"Yet, we cannot leave for Dochart's Glen without the children," William demanded.

"Indeed, some of us will have to return to Port Regael. Yet, we must also keep the parchments and maps moving toward the Glen," Olivetan agreed, but then his chin sank, and he gritted his teeth. "There is one more thing we all know but have left unspoken."

"We're listening," Habs said.

Olivetan seemed to consider his words carefully. "We must take into account the exigent circumstances that often accompany Medici's presence."

Sophia looked up at William, took his hand, and said, "Aphrosyna."

The Advent of Kings

ing Ninian's entourage crested a hill on the main road overlooking the city of Port Regal. To the east, sunrays pierced clouds, lifting the haze. Eager to arrive, Derian's stomach twinged with elation as they neared Port Regael. It would not be long before they entered the city.

The weather did surprise him. Although he had heard stories from those who passed through Navarre of the long-lasting winter freeze along the coast, he really did not believe it until now. He had never seen this much snow and ice.

Derian was accustomed to this route. Soon, the scene came into view. When taking produce into Port Regael, it was in this very place that he and his brothers and sisters would stop to rest. Stretching out in the grasses, he would marvel at the entire city in all its grandeur. But he would not be sprawled out in the sloping meadow today.

Glistening snow doused fiery autumn trees. The three rivers that twined through the city were icy paths. Rows of shops and homes peaked like whitecaps, rolling up to Regael Castle—brave and bold upon the hill. Derian dreamed of royalty, and how appropriate it seemed for the snow to have arrived, a symbol of purity and truth. Even nature honored the restoration of the co-regents.

Rising above and beyond the castle was the statue that guarded the harbor. Throughout all these years of coming to Port Regael, he could only look upon the back of the statue. Now that he was king, he imagined sailing out beyond the harbor and for the first time looking his great-grandfather in the eyes.

Guilt wrenched his gut. *First, Wesley will be pardoned, and he will join me.*

The streets of Port Regael were already overflowing with what looked like more people than the crowds of the Eve of Enrichment. King Ninian told Derian that before he left the city, he had made a public announcement and sent riders to tell the news. The heir of Gaspard had been found, and King Ninian was accompanying him back to the capital city! Derian sat tall and lifted his chin. *All this for me!* A king must look dignified. There never had been, nor would there ever again be, an event like today. He imagined the applause and the accolades—the honor, glory, and privilege. He was king.

"It is beautiful, Derian," Avlae startled him.

He had not seen her wake. She was gazing out the quarter light of the carriage, running her fingers through her sister's auburn hair. Jess was sleeping soundly with her head in Avlae's lap, both of them wrapped in heavy wool blankets. The girls sat to the right of King Ninian, who was directly across from Derian. King Ninian had slept for most of the ride from Navarre. Overwhelmed and restless, Derian could not sleep.

Avlae whispered sternly and nodded her head sideways at the sleeping king. "You must speak with him about Wesley. You are king, too!"

Derian raised his hands to quiet her. "At the right time, sister," he whispered back.

He already felt the embarrassment of having a traitor in the family of Gaspard. Even *three* traitors! King Ninian had not spoken a word, but his eyes…his eyes said it all. Derian made up his mind not to even mention Wesley's name publicly until he could sort things out. Keeping Avlae quiet would prove to be impossible. He needed a plan. He would secretly order that Avlae and Jess be kept in closed quarters for a time.

Dipping to the right, the carriage jarred and rocked back in place. King Ninian awoke. His face was lit with a smile, and he stretched his arms as far as he could in the little space they had.

"I see we are close to the city!" His gruff voice awakened Jess. "Countless people await your arrival!"

"I'm hungry," Jess said, rubbing her eyes.

"Yes, yes! You all must be very hungry. A wondrous feast is prepared for you."

"We should like that very much, sire, but tell me, will Wesley be joining us?" Avlae asked.

"Wesley will be treated with special care, young one. Your brother, Derian, and I have much to talk about. It's important that we discuss the details of last evening. I do need to know why your youngest brother was in Navarre and if anyone else knows of his relation to your great-grandfather. I want only to protect him, Lady Avlae. We need to protect the good name of Gaspard. We wouldn't want any gossip portraying Wesley as a traitor."

"Wesley is not a traitor," Avlae said sharply.

"Of course not," the king agreed. "Of course not, but it is a delicate matter. It deserves our careful attention. Your family deserves special attention. We must craft our public responses carefully."

With a nod of agreement, Derian lifted his chin and asked, "How do you mean, sire?"

King Ninian leaned forward as if he were about to tell an age-old secret. "Well, to begin, you must learn to temper the truth by manipulating the facts." His brows fell just over his narrowing eyes. "Even trivialize and leave out certain aspects that would only confuse people."

"That just sounds wrong," Avlae snapped.

King Ninian gave her a forbearing smile. "Of course, there are lines we don't cross, dear." He reached an arm around Avlae.

Her eyes filled with resistance. Derian warned her with his own eyes to keep still.

"But as royalty, we have influence. We draw the lines!" With a laugh, King Ninian drew his arm back, pulled down his sleeves, and continued, "You will learn about having authority."

"I'm afraid I've much to learn, sire," Derian admitted.

"All in time. Answers will come, young ones, but now is a time for rejoicing! This day has been declared the *Advent of Kings*. Nantes has searched for three generations to share the crown again with Gaspard. Let us bask in the glory!"

Ninian straightened his collar. He then reached to pull a cord that rang a bell, alerting the coachman to stop.

"Come now with me, Derian," King Ninian announced. He opened the door and stepped out of the carriage. Looking back inside, he said, "You and I will arrive in Nantes in the open carriage. Young ladies, please remain here. For it is only proper, and tradition has it that a princess—or in our case *princesses*—should arrive in the closed carriage. High propriety and all, ladies."

"Yes, sire," Avlae answered. Jess sat upright in her seat. Ninian chuckled and stepped forward.

42

everal paces behind King Ninian, Derian followed. Large, spoked wheels carried the dark maroon open carriage. Gold elegantly trimmed the edges, and the symbol of the co-regency emblazoned the door. King Ninian turned and faced Derian.

"All will set their eyes on the heir of Gaspard. There is much to be done, and there are many celebrations to plan. We'll certainly need you to make appearances in cities throughout Nantes. But, one day at a time. I want you all to enjoy this extraordinary season."

Behind the king, a man approached with a garment folded neatly over his arms. The wind lashed out and lifted it away. Ninian snatched it back from the gust and shook out the fold. Stretching his arms around Derian, King Ninian placed it over his shoulders, latching it around his neck.

"Here you are, Derian. The amaranthine robe, symbolizing the everlasting reign of the co-regency. This robe was once worn by your great-grandfather, and on the day of your coronation, you will receive his crown."

Derian bowed. "Thank you, sire."

King Ninian chuckled. "You are welcome, of course, but arise, son. We are equals!"

Reaching back, King Ninian pulled open the door. Stepping aside, he gestured for Derian to enter first. King Ninian climbed in beside him on the rear seat facing the coachman. Tipping his head to the driver, Ninian ordered them forward.

First lesson as king learned. Derian mentally made note of King Ninian's response to his sister's question. A king must manipulate his words to his own advantage.

"Tell me," Derian asked. "How do I learn to craft my words for the public?"

King Ninian seemed to ponder the question and said, "Well, ambiguity is one of the best tools. It is really just a game of words."

"Good, ambiguity..." Derian responded. He had an idea about what it meant but would seek to understand it better.

Derian repeated the king's words to himself. *"Enjoy this season!"* Any reservation and tension he had about hiding Wesley no longer concerned him. Wesley was safe, and that was enough for now. Soon all would be resolved. Besides, he had immediate concerns. Derian knew nothing of governing a country. He needed his own advisors, and he would appoint Father as one of them. His first decree would be to send for him. Father was wise, and appointing him as advisor would get him out of the mines and heal his gloom.

Drawing near to the gates of Port Regael, the jubilation swelled toward them. Entranced, Derian became inert. Ahead, Port Regael's iron gates opened wide. This was it—life how it was meant to be years ago. Why had he waited so long to speak with King Ninian? Had he really waited for the Fullness of Time, or had the Fullness of Time waited for him? For the last three years, he had been of age for the throne. What foolishness had he bought into? Why had he waited so long? Never mind, he knew better now, and now he was king.

As they passed through the gate, the crowd erupted in acclamation. Streamers flew, flags were raised, and chants proclaimed a new age. The carriage rolled ahead, parting the mobbing crowds. Derian sat with his arms at his side and shoulders up to his ears, stunned. Many hands reached to embrace him.

"Go on, son," Ninian said with a large smile as he waved to the crowd. "Greet your kingdom! You've nothing to fear. This is all for you!"

Derian shook off his dreamy spell. Raising his arm, he greeted his people in wide, dramatic waves.

"Welcome home!" the crowd shouted.

"Thank you! Thank you all!" Derian's voice was drowned out by the roar.

A chant arose among the people, "Hail to Gaspard! Long live the king! Hail to Gaspard! Long live the king!" Little children called from the shoulders of adults. Young maidens leaned from windows and waved kerchiefs up high above the streets. Bells continually rang in the harbor.

Entering the narrow passage that led to the castle, they passed below stone arches. This was the same path Derian had walked with his siblings in the rain on the Eve of Enrichment. The carriage stopped at the steps before the main entrance to the castle. Immovable soldiers stood at attention along both sides of the stairway. Ninian's advisors were present to greet them. Before Derian could reach for the door handle, an attendant appeared. After bowing, he opened the door and offered a hand. Derian readily accepted and stepped down from his royal ride.

Ninian escorted him before his advisors. Derian stopped in front of each of the five men and shook their hands. Several wore black, wide-brimmed hats with a narrow stack. Most had long hair that bushed out from under their hats. Others just had bushy hair without the hat. White flaps that rested below their chins were held up by the long collars of their moss-green overcoats. Derian laughed on the inside—they looked so much alike.

A tall man stepped before Derian and led them up the wide, deep steps. Soldiers stared straight ahead with rifles tucked tightly at their sides. Derian preened several steps ahead of King Ninian, processioning up to the castle. *Once again, two shall rule as one!*

Through giant oak doors, the marble foyer expanded. Derian seemed to float over the threshold. Mirrored staircases curved to the next level of balconies, doorways, and halls. Up a short flight of shining marble steps and through another doorway, they entered a narrow corridor. On Derian's right, light flooded through tall, arched windows. To his left, elegantly carved statues of serpents, women in long robes, and hooded men lined the passage. Leafy plants sat on short granite columns and hung from the ceiling.

Sounds of a garrulous crowd came from the other side of another set of doors. Two doormen nodded and opened the way. The throng applauded and praised their arrival. Lively music played in celebration of his presence, and the smells tortured him, for he was famished. Derian's throat tightened, and his glands salivated at the spread of food—roasted duck, seasoned potatoes, and hearty rolls of bread. Then, there were the sweets—cinnamon cakes, fruit tarts with cream, sliced peaches in wine, and custard pies.

The accolades were incessant as Derian reached the head table. Beyond the gathering, windows overlooked the eastern highlands.

The sun just began to show itself between two mountains and blinded him.

King Ninian leaned in and said, "We are seated here, intentionally facing the sunrise." Derian must have looked confused, because King Ninian then explained, "We are illuminated before the people."

Derian nodded and confided, "Small price to pay as king!"

King Ninian chortled and threw an arm over Derian's shoulder. "Indeed! Royalty suits you well!"

Derian sat with King Ninian to his right and his sisters to his left. King Ninian remained standing and lifted his arms to silence the guests. It took several tries before they finally sat still.

In a loud, bold voice, Ninian spoke, "Today, we continue what we have long held as the guiding principle of our land. The two will rule as one!" The crowd rose to their feet and clamored. They eventually quieted but did not sit. "This celebration will be like no other. Today we honor and welcome home..." Derian felt a hand tug on his shirt, and he stood. "...King Derian Delaine Gaspard!"

With that, the guests could not be quieted. Derian's face flushed, and he wiped his sweaty hands on his pants. Nodding, he waved and lifted his hands to quiet the ovation. He began to sit, but someone lifted him from behind.

"Remain standing!" ordered a voice.

Derian did not look back. He reached his hands forward to balance against the table and smiled while studying hundreds of eyes. When things finally calmed, Ninian spoke one last time.

"Derian, you have given Port Regael—even all of Nantes—a renewed sense of joy and prospect that will reach throughout World Over." King Ninian put his arm around Derian's shoulders. "The breach will be repaired, the wall will expand, and the country will grow. As it was intended from the beginning, the co-regency will reign!"

The entire room shook. Some started singing. Others were in tears. Derian was seated, and he ate like never before. Pastries, duck, potatoes, eggs, bread—it all kept coming.

Between courses, Derian leaned back in his chair. Immense wooden chandeliers hung high above them. Music pleasantly rained down from the minstrel's gallery that wrapped around the upper portion of the hearth. A large fire roared, drying the cool dampness of the morning. He lolled in the moment—the lively crowd, the jubilee, the feast—until a sharp kick under the table disrupted his pleasure. He looked over at Avlae.

"What?" he snapped in an exaggerated whisper. Immediately, he was sorry for how he had responded.

"When will you speak to the king about Wesley?" Avlae said, seemingly disgusted with Derian's lack of concern for their brother.

"I am king—"

"Do you know where they've taken him?"

"Will you keep your voice down?" Derian looked around to see if anyone was watching.

"He must be with us this evening, or Jess and I will not attend dinner. We will be off looking for Wesley." Avlae warned him through her polite smile and kicked him again under the table.

Following the feast, Derian greeted guests alongside King Ninian as they filed out of the banquet hall. Some recognized him from the market, but there was no time for explaining the details of his lineage. Ninian told his guests this would come at the coronation speech and kept the line moving. When they had finished with the pleasantries, Avlae and Jess were escorted to their room, and the king led Derian to the library.

Derian fell into a chair—exhausted, amazed, and full. Finally, alone. How would he ask the king to keep his sisters away from the public for a time? *Wait. Why should I need to seek Ninian's permission? I am king.* Ninian certainly understood the need to know if Wesley was indeed a traitor. Avlae no longer concerned him. She may be his older sister, but he was king. He gave the order to a nearby soldier that for the time being, his sisters were to be confined to their room—for their safety, of course. He was beginning to understand how to manipulate others with his influence.

King Ninian walked from window to window, tying open the thick red curtains and immediately filling the room with sunlight. Derian slouched in his chair and pushed away his concerns. No more secrets. He would take his seat on the throne with everything now in the open. His eyelids fell, and his thoughts blurred.

"Gaspard!"

Derian jerked upright in his chair. King Ninian stood across the table from him, examining parchments. With both hands, Derian delicately lifted a thick page. He recognized the handwriting of his great-grandfather. He set it down and took another. It seemed that Ninian had his own assortment of Gaspard's writings.

"I've been collecting them for years," Ninian said. "I've taken missions across World Over and even into the uncharted lands. And yet all this time, the route to the treasure in the field has been right here in Nantes…"

"I've been feeling foolish for not coming forward sooner," Derian admitted. "I am very eager to share my great-grandfather's writings. When will we open the crate?"

Just then, an armed guard entered the library, leading the five counselors, followed by two men carrying the crate and another soldier at the end of their party. The king gathered his letters and moved them to an adjacent table. The men placed the crate on the table before Derian and formed a semicircle barricade. The guards waited, and the council members looked on.

"Here we are. The honor is yours, Derian." The king held out his hand.

Derian stood from his chair, reaching for the brown leather strap securing the crate. Pulling up against the iron buckle with one hand, he slid the prong from the notch with the other. Glancing up, he noticed that every soldier and council member seemed to scowl at him.

As he lifted away the cover, pieces of straw floated down to the table and floor. Derian had fulfilled the Fullness of Time, and now he would lead his subjects to the lost treasure of Gaspard. Taking his time, he carefully began to remove the straw and place it aside. Not a breath was heard in the room. Everyone towered higher above him and moved in closer. Soon he was halfway into the crate—but no parchments. He did not look up but worked a bit faster. He pushed his hands through the remaining straw, reaching for something…anything!

"This is not right!" Derian said. He grabbed the cover and had to restrain himself from throwing it. Calmly, he set it back on the table. He looked up at the king, who remained silent. Turning the crate over, he dumped the rest of the stubble out. The crate was empty! Derian threw it to the floor. "Wesley did this!"

"How can that be, King Derian?" Ninian asked. "Wesley has been in our custody since we left the farm."

"He must know something!"

The Meeting at
Merchant's Pass

43

aces glimmered yellow and orange as the fire popped and crackled, lobbing single sparks which floated aimlessly upward. Silence seemed to flaunt its grip on their voices, but Olivetan would have no more of that.

"The day I left Regael, Bela sent word that we must meet. She insisted that we meet in person, so I—"

"Oh, out with it, Olivetan! We all know Sophia must go back into the city," Quesnel spat.

Reluctantly, Olivetan's eyes shifted from Quesnel to Sophia. Reticent tension contorted the mood. Olivetan knew that Sophia would waste no time going back for her children. Painful looks from the others avoided eye contact with Olivetan.

William placed a hand on Sophia's shoulder. She reached across her chest and laid a hand on top of his. Sitting tall and lifting her chin, she locked eyes with Olivetan. "We'll go together."

"I will not leave her side," William asserted.

Olivetan did not want to send her back. After all she had endured—three years in Medici's vile hands, the strain of being under numerous spells, a day locked in a crate. To return to the city would mean an encounter with Aphrosyna. And that was exactly how the Underground had lost her three years ago.

But with Sophia, Olivetan knew those were just small afflictions compared to what really pained her. It was not for herself that she worried. Her intentions were pure, and her acts were selfless. She feared for her children, for William, for the Underground. She would risk facing Aphrosyna seventy times over to protect what Gaspard had discovered and those she loved. Sophia understood the prospect of what was happening. If, indeed, Aphrosyna presented herself in Port Regael, Sophia would act. Olivetan and Sophia had spoken of it many times.

William may have been moved by his experience in the woods, but Olivetan could not risk sending him back to Port Regael with Sophia. His instability would impede the mission. He may have new determination, but not for this. On her own, Sophia would be swift and focused. With William along, Olivetan feared she would be spread too thin. Of course, William's reaction was the same as that of any husband whose wife came back from the dead, only for him to send her back into the cords of death. He wanted to protect her—they all did. But this encounter demanded Sophia's full engagement.

In the search for Gaspard's writings, Ninian would send Medici to subdue anyone or anyplace that was thought to have information about Gaspard. And when the spells were not enough, Medici would call upon his mother, Aphrosyna. Her spirit could sway the minds of the populace, weaken them, deceive them, and rip them apart with fear. Though, at first, it was never obvious.

Aphrosyna worked in very subtle ways. Ever so slowly did she lead people on, and by the time they knew any different, it was far too late. Her ways were so appealing, for her effect always looked, smelled, and tasted so good. When her influence left and the spell wore off, those she had enticed found themselves bewildered, wondering how they had ever given in or strayed so far. Many gave away what mattered most for a moment of desire, an hour of fame, or a day of power and were left empty. In guilt and shame, they sputtered, and they wept, utterly forsaken by Aphrosyna.

Sophia had saved many who were lured in and tempted—from individuals to entire cities. Before Sophia had met William, she had traveled closely behind Medici. Even then, she was part of a rising rebellion initiated by her father, Bishop Gaspard. Across the seas and over the lands, they fought against Medici on the frontlines of his invisible assaults. So often did she confront his sorcery that she grew immune to some spells and was able to work herself out of others. People began to come to her for protection. She had a way of counteracting and reversing the effects of spells for others as well.

Olivetan remembered when she had saved him. Sophia's voice severed an evil enticement. It was the last time they were both in Brazenose, only months after the birth of Jess. William had gone to Emden on assignment with the mining company. Sophia and the children were being kept in a safehouse. Olivetan had been sent by the Underground to smuggle Sophia and the children out of Brazenose and travel west to South Fehrael. There, they would start again.

It was then that Ninian had received word from an informant about the possibility of an heir to Gaspard in Brazenose. Ninian never took chances with information like this. He ordered Medici to summon Aphrosyna, who through the citizens of Brazenose spread rumors about a ruler that would rise up against Ninian and seek to oppress Nantes. Soon gossip had spread across the city, and many were fooled, seeking out this ruler to bring him before Ninian. Neighbors grew suspicious of each other. Olivetan, himself, had to fight against Aphrosyna's sway.

It had become more and more difficult for him to keep Sophia and her family hidden. He soon began to think twice about what he was doing. Why take the risk anymore? All he had to do was turn Sophia in to the authorities.

Late one night, he entered the safehouse. Sophia had been up feeding the baby. He grabbed her, bound her hands, and told her he was taking her to Ninian. Those she was staying with awoke when they heard the clamor. They restrained him, keeping him away from Sophia. She recognized Olivetan's severe state. At first, he resisted her salve, but then it soothed him, removing his confusion and lifting his fears. With a clear mind and new discernment, he was able to move Sophia and the children to safety, keeping their identities hidden.

"Our children will need us in Port Regael," Sophia finally spoke, nabbing Olivetan from his thoughts. "It's nearly morning. We will take our rest, and in the afternoon, we can make our way back to Port Regael under the cover of night, far from the main path. I'll begin at the east gate of the city. Aphrosyna will find me."

"And I will—" William began, but Olivetan did not let him finish.

"Please, hear me." Olivetan said. "You know Sophia will need all her wits about her."

William opened his mouth yet remained silent as Sophia clasped his hands.

"And now we'll hear from the benevolent dictator," Quesnel mumbled about Olivetan.

"You will protect her best by allowing her to return to the city while you lead the Underground and the parchments east, toward Coligny."

"That is what you call 'protecting' her?" William raged and pulled away from Sophia's tender hold. He protested, "I will do no such thing."

William, you selfish idiot. Have you so quickly abandoned the Underground's intent? Olivetan fought the urge to put William in his place. Not that long ago, he would have lost that fight. But he reminded himself that William spoke out of fear, out of his depression. William was healing. How might Olivetan help that healing?

"We've all sacrificed, and we've all suffered loss. We have families with us who have left everything behind. Some of us are going back to the city; there are always setbacks. But we need to keep the group moving east, protecting the parchments and leading the Underground closer to Dochart's Glen." Olivetan preserved his disposition.

William's face was tight, as if his words were being tied in knots behind his teeth.

Olivetan continued, "We'll need to get a message to Bela. Have her gather the children. Send Jansen to fetch her." Olivetan paused. "Where is Jansen? Did he not flee the city with you, Habs?"

"Well, our journey started out that way," Habs replied. "And the tunnel is no longer passable."

"How do you mean?" Quesnel asked through his teeth, not removing the pipe from his mouth.

"It was all quite peculiar," Mahre offered.

Habs went on to explain Jansen's betrayal and death, as well as their most curious escape. "You know, it has begun," he finally said.

Olivetan agreed, "The Fullness of Time is upon us."

"Yes," Sophia said. "William has quite a story to share as well."

"You can be sure that Jansen has kept Ninian informed, which means that the king knows much more than we thought." Olivetan stressed his concern.

"And Bela is not safe," Sophia added.

"It also explains our interrogation at the docks the other day," Habs said. "Jansen knew about the shipment and stalled, knowing he could catch the Underground fleeing."

"And the king was waiting all along to take it from us," Olivetan answered.

Quesnel spoke, "The king is sure to find us here before too long. Really, I am surprised he hasn't found us already."

"I think we have Derian to thank for that," Olivetan said. "Gaspard's writings rank a bit higher than finding us, but Ninian will soon discover an empty crate."

"How much does Ninian know?" William asked.

Olivetan stole a quick glance at Habs, who raised his hand and nodded, letting Olivetan know he would answer. "Well, Jansen knew we'd be traveling toward Farne…" He began to gather his items as well.

With all diffidence aside, William said, "When you leave for Port Regael, Habs and I will gather the Underground and make our way east, taking the north side of the Timaru to avoid being seen from the main road."

Olivetan was taken aback but did not show it. His decision to not fight with William had paid off.

William continued, "I know the area well and will be able to make changes at a moment's notice. We will meet on Arbor Hill, just outside the city of Coligny, in three days' time. From there, we'll make our way to the Glen."

"Very well," Olivetan agreed, and he quickly continued, for he did not need anyone questioning William about his sudden change of mind. "Sophia, we have trackers and trailsmen among us. Seek out whomever you need."

"If he has summoned Aphrosyna, Ninian knows that I will respond—not only for the sake of the city, but also for my children."

Mahre stood and approached the group. "I do not doubt your abilities, Sophia, but after all we did to get you out, how will you ever flee the city? If Ninian knows you are coming, he'll have scouts everywhere."

"This is where *our* mission begins, Mahre." Olivetan grinned. He looked around, and everyone had stopped what they were doing, waiting for him to explain. "You do speak very fluently with our troll friend. What is his name?"

"His name is Callas, and we have promised him freedom from his curse."

"Freedom will come, but not just yet. We need him for our part of the journey. You'll have time to explain all of this to him on our way westward."

"That would be the wrong direction, friend," Quesnel added while stroking his beard.

"We'll scale the wall near the Silesian Foothills, just south of Port Regael." Olivetan untied a blanket from his pack.

"And how do you plan on crossing the frozen coastline?" Habs asked. "You know you'll be walking targets out on the ice!"

"The children will never make it back across the ice," Sophia argued.

"Quesnel," Olivetan continued. "Do you remember the stories I told you about my younger days, living on Telos Isle?"

"Yes, yes, we've all heard the sappy stories about your boyhood," Quesnel bemoaned.

"Remember what we ate throughout the winter months?"

Quesnel thought for a moment, his pipe still clenched in his teeth and pinched between his finger and thumb. He took the pipe out of his mouth, and his lips unwrinkled and stretched upward.

"What did you eat?" Mahre asked.

"Mussels," Sophia said.

"So what?" Mahre shrugged in frustration.

"Where do you find mussels?" Quesnel enquired of Mahre.

"On the sea floor. I'd really like to know what you..." He paused. "We're going *under* the ice?"

The Petulant King

44

"I don't understand," Derian said to himself under his breath. His aspirations fell from soaring heights and shattered into thousands of pieces. His insides shrank around his turning stomach. Stares from Ninian's advisors fired alliterative backlash—*inept, insufficient, incompetent, inadequate*. He poured anger into the hollow feeling within him. He was certain that Wesley had something to do with this.

"Now, Derian..." King Ninian glared down at him. The king's tone demanded that someone be held accountable. "You assured me of the contents within this crate."

"Yes, sire. I opened it yesterday morning and all was in order, just like I've left it so many times." Derian cowered. *What if the king thinks I made this whole thing up? He will never trust me again. But I am king! I have equal authority to Ninian. But without evidence, he'll send me away, and I'll end up in the mines!*

Ninian strutted away, and with his back toward Derian, he asked, "Tell me, King Derian, what direction do we go?"

He's asking for my counsel? Derian's confidence surged, and he kicked at the crate, knocking his chair over behind him. He blurted the first thing that came to mind. "I must speak to my sisters and then to Wesley." Time would help him think this through. And right now, he could not think in the presence of the king.

Without wasting a moment, Ninian turned and called out, "Guards!" And he looked back at Derian. "These men are at your service. Ask of them what you wish."

"Take me to my sisters," Derian ordered.

The guards nodded and filed out.

"I will settle this!" Derian announced and stormed out of the library.

Why did Wesley do such a thing?

At the end of the hall, they came to an open space that overlooked the entry where they had arrived that morning. Derian stopped walking, recognizing a young man coming up the main staircase to his level. He had seen him before, but where? The young man stepped past Derian and the sentries without saying a word, then continued in the opposite direction down the hall. Then, Derian remembered. This was the young man whom he had seen with Avlae from time to time at the market.

"Who was that?" Derian asked.

"His name is Torres, and he is an advisor to King Ninian," one of the sentries answered.

And therefore, an advisor to me. This may play well for me to keep Avlae out of my business.

Around the corner, they ascended another flight of steps. Each step echoed down the wide hallway. The shining floor reflected his image as if he were walking on a mirror. The ceiling was high with elegant moldings.

His thoughts jumped back to Wesley. *How did he get to the*

writings? He better have some answers! Wesley had made him look careless and irresponsible before King Ninian. *I should have known that the life of a king would not be so easy.* The guards came to a stop before a door. Derian proceeded to knock, and Avlae answered.

"Hello, brother," she said dryly and immediately walked away. Derian followed her, closing the door behind him.

"Look at this place!" he exclaimed. A huge window flooded the room with sunlight. "Ornate carvings, decorated dressers, elegant bed stands, and look at this drapery!"

"Oh, shut it!" Avlae exclaimed, busying herself by placing clothes in a dresser drawer.

Jess poked her head out from under the covers, jumped off the bed, and ran toward Derian, beaming with delight. "Can you believe that this used to be the queen's chambers?"

"Well, how fitting, Jess!" Derian said, hugging her.

"Our maid said," Jess giggled and mocked a royal tone, "'Would you like me to draw you a hot bath, dear?'"

"Your highness!" Derian exclaimed haughtily and bowed, placing an arm over his abdomen.

"And look…" Jess snatched his hand and ran toward a wardrobe. "New clothing!"

"What of Wesley?" Avlae asked. Her arms were now crossed, and her lips pursed. Her expression reflected one who had swallowed a mouthful of vinegar.

"That bugger made me out to be a fool," Derian blurted out, pulling away from Jess's hand.

"What are you saying?" Avlae rolled her eyes and proceeded to straighten the covers on the bed.

"The crate was empty—none of Great-Grandfather's writings, no maps."

"But I saw them as you closed the crate."

"Yes, I put them in order yesterday morning. Was Jess playing in the barn at all during the day?" Derian was reaching for anything, but he already knew the answer to his question. It had to be Wesley.

"Jess was with me all day. Do not blame her! We were packing for this foolish trip."

"Yes, but—"

"And Father must be worried sick, as if he hasn't enough to weigh him down," Avlae lashed back. "Now his children have gone off and left him behind…"

"But you left him a note and—" Derian began, but Avlae did not pause to let him speak.

"This whole idea of yours is proving to be quite preposterous. I must talk to Wesley. You need to find him!" Avlae pointed sharply, her finger shaking. "I am very concerned for him. I have asked to see him and was told, 'We are here to honor you. You must remain in your quarters, *m'lady.*' What foolishness! Such ostentatious flattery. In fact, we were told that we must not leave this room. For our protection? Drivel and drool! Something is not right, Derian. You *will* find out what is going on!"

"When I leave here, I am going to see Wesley."

"So, you know where he is?" Avlae said, her voice softening. Clasping her hands, she stepped closer to Derian.

"No, but he can't be far," Derian spoke confidently. He had to try and make it seem as if he had things in order.

Then, she let him have it again. "After you find him, perhaps you can return and have us released from our opulent prison.

There is far too much secrecy around here." Avlae waited with hands on her hips.

"They are taking me to him now," Derian said. Hoping that he might leave with some leverage, he added, "I understand Torres is an advisor to King Ninian."

Avlae was speechless.

"What, nothing to say?"

"Don't you dare use him against me!"

"You allow me to rule as I see fit, and I will consider not having him locked away!"

Derian left without another word and followed his silent servants down the hall. *Avlae does not understand what it means to be king. No matter. I am king, and I will set all this right.* Derian walked, now arguing with Wesley in his head. *You better tell me where you put the writings. I am king now. I'll have you locked up until you talk. Oh yes, I would even do that to my own brother. What would Father have you do? You insolent fool!*

Derian had not been thinking about where he was walking. Finally, he asked the sentry, "Where are we going? I thought you were taking me to Wesley." They were descending, and the air had become dank, stale, and still.

"We are, King Derian," one guard responded.

King Derian. He liked the sound of that. Derian walked a bit taller for a while. He nodded quite assuredly at those who passed by. He was in control. No one was going to question him. He was going to see his brother and get some answers. Wesley would not dare to question him. *He* gave the orders now.

But soon, they entered darker tunnels. After unlocking an iron door, the sentry dragged it open. Derian's eyebrows loosened.

His proud demeanor vanished, and he felt as if there were a tail between his legs. He found himself in a bleak and gloomy passageway—alone.

The sentry remained behind, and Derian was ashamed of all he had been thinking.

Instructions echoed from behind, "Fifth cell on the left!"

45

esley is in a cell? If Avlae could do it, she'd have me sent to the dungeon for this.

Figuring that Wesley would at least be placed in a palace room like his sisters, Derian had not feared for his brother. He had never imagined the dungeon.

With fragile steps, Derian moved ahead on the wet, uneven stone floor. The dim flicker from dying torches lit his path. There was a stench in the air, like rotting compost mixed with the bog back home. Dying moans ached deep within the first cell. It was too dark to see even a figure. Torchlight outlined the cell but barely entered it. Although, it went farther in than *he* would have chosen to go.

His ears stayed with the moans, so much so that his whole body turned as he passed the cell, and he found himself walking backward. One long, passing groan was exhaled. Derian paused. He strained to hear anything—even his own breath became a distraction.

Enough! He had to get to Wesley.

Spinning around, he found himself face-to-face with a yellow-toothed beggar behind the next set of bars. With a half step back, his other foot slipped out from under him. His hands slapped against the floor, stinging and slipping through the grit and grime. Leaning back on his elbows, he found himself looking up at the deplorable creature. Soiled black, greasy fingers clung to the bars, while torn and filthy rags hung from his body. His eyes were desperate. Was he trying to speak? Dry caws came from his empty mouth—he had no tongue! Derian could not bear to look. He moved himself back along the floor and crawled away.

Decrepit singing languished from dying vocal cords in the next cell. He stood and moved onward, willing himself not to look. Ahead, some off-tempo clanging tripped over and over, seeming to fight for a rhythm. Approaching those bars, he saw an old woman walking back and forth, dragging her tin cup against the black iron. She did not look up, and Derian was not going to wait around to see if she would notice him.

If he had counted right, Wesley would be next. He ran and grabbed the bars, forgetting all about the missing parchments.

"Wesley," Derian said in his loudest whisper. "Wesley, it's me. It's Derian!"

"Derian?" a voice rasped within the cell.

"Yes, it's me." Derian reached for a torch, took it from the wall, and stretched his arm through the bars. Curled up in the back corner, Wesley sat on the floor with his arms on his knees.

"Derian!" Wesley shouted, jumped to his feet, and charged the iron gate. He threw his arms between the bars and attempted to pull his brother close.

Derian slid away, avoiding Wesley's stench and filth but still feeling remorse. "Who did this to you?"

"The guards told me that *you* sent me here," Wesley said and quickly added, "but don't worry. I don't believe them. Even if you did, I forgive you. You needed to sort things out, I get it! I've been praying you would come and see me, come and take me to King Ninian to explain!"

"I…" Derian began, but he thought twice. Perhaps it was best for now that Wesley believed Derian had him placed in the dungeon. *Yes. "A good leader must be ambiguous," King Ninian would say.* "I need to know how you arrived home. Why did you abandon the mission?"

Wesley drew his arms back and leaned closer to the bars that separated them. His eyes shifted to the floor, as if he were ashamed. "Members of the Underground led me home."

"So you—"

"No, no, listen." Wesley pleaded. "We fled an attack from Pirate Trolls. I had no other way to get back. I only went with them for safety. I planned to go right to King Ninian and turn them in!"

"You led the Underground to the parchments! Mother would—"

"I know, I know…but believe me, I had no choice. They deceived me. Please, bring me to King Ninian! He will understand."

"You *are* a traitor!" That was enough to end the pity Derian had begun to feel. Again, he lashed out, "Wesley, you did this to yourself. You abandoned your mission. Now, tell me what you did with the parchments!"

"What are you talking about? I was with you. The trolls were going to kill us!"

"You're hardly in a position to put on an act." Derian decided that his loyalty to the crown trumped any feelings of sympathy for his brother. "First you abandon the mission, and then you steal Great-Grandfather's writings. You are making it extremely difficult for me to help you."

Wesley sighed. "It is true that I came for the writings. But I also came for you and Father, Avlae and Jess. There is much I need to tell you, if you will just hear me."

Derian felt like he could vomit. Between his anger and the stench in the tunnel, he was ready to turn and storm out. Yet, he would oblige Wesley and then give him a final warning. "I'm listening."

"I'm telling the truth. I want to set things right! Maybe... maybe..."

"What?"

"It could be that the Underground took the parchments while we—"

"So you told them where to find the writings?"

"I did, yes, but—"

"Did you want to be the hero? You want my place on the throne, don't you? Well, you're not going to get it!"

"I never meant...You must believe me! You need to get me out of here. Bring me to King Ninian!"

"You've sided with the wrong people. The Underground would only divide Nantes. They're just some crazy sect from the mountains, and one of my first acts as king will be to hunt them down!"

"Derian, wait...listen! I want nothing to do with the Underground! Listen to me!"

"Now *you* listen, Wesley. I am going to King Ninian. If the Underground knows about the writings, then it is likely that they have stolen what belongs to me. If you know anything about where they might be, you will lead us to them!"

46

Bela slid closely along the polished stone wall, listening outside of the library as Ninian spoke with an advisor.

"The boy is of no use to us, sire. But now we have announced that an heir has been found, and the coronation day is—"

"Do not be hasty, Ezra. Derian is innocent. His intentions are pure. Don't read too much into this. We need to let him sweat this out a bit. He may be able to get information from his siblings that *we* would not so easily retrieve."

"And when he finds his brother behind bars?"

"Wesley needs to be held for questioning. Derian knows this. This is normal procedure for anyone who is guilty of desertion."

"Something is not right. How did the younger brother get back here on his own?"

"You still think he did it on his own?" Ninian snickered. "You know the Underground has their own among our ranks. It's likely that he was led back by one of them. In any case, we have him now."

"But it's what he may know that I fear!" Ezra raised his voice to Ninian. "Suppose the Underground has convinced him of their rebellion?"

"These young minds are very pliable. Given time, he will believe anything we tell him. We must simply help him through this… misunderstanding."

"Please pardon me, King, but I am finding your frivolous nature quite upsetting."

The silence repressed her. Bela tensed, ready to run at the sound of footsteps, should they come toward the doorway.

But Ninian proceeded, "If you are to serve beside me, you'd be wise to be thinking a bit *frivolously* yourself. Right now, we need answers that won't come with threats. We remain firm but understanding. We give the new royal family some space in the castle. We show them about the town and have the people fall in love with them and have them fall in love with the spotlight."

"That's too long. Torture them all till we have the writings!"

"We must wait. When we have what we need, we'll send the heirs of Gaspard out to sea for, say, a tour of Telos Isle. And the country will again mourn when they hear of the accident at sea, where every one of them will be lost!"

"Yes, I see, my king." Ezra sounded all too eager for Gaspard's demise. "You will gain the sympathy of your citizens. There will be no more talk of finding Gaspard's family, and we'll take what is ours within the Inner Realm!"

With the wall as her guide, Bela stepped back gently, her eyes fixed upon the library doorway. She would send word to Olivetan and get Avlae and Jess out of Port Regael. Wesley and Derian would be much more difficult to get out, however. She would focus on the girls. Olivetan would have to come up with a plan for the other two.

The tips of her fingers reached the corner of the corridor behind her. Spinning around, she collided with Derian, who immediately grabbed her wrists.

"You're spying on the king!" Derian raged.

"I..." Bela started to speak. She pulled back hard against his grasp. "I was merely leaving the room..." *That was a dumb answer.* She could easily handle this situation, but she did not want to hurt Derian.

"It seems that we haven't been formally introduced." Derian tightened his grasp and shook her arms.

"Well, I know who you are, Derian Delaine—or should I say, young heir of Gaspard." Bela stated plainly. Kicking off her shoes, she used her bare feet to gain a bit of leverage on the glassy floor. "Your mother has told me quite a bit about you."

Derian let go with one hand and attempted to get an arm around her. When that failed, he again grabbed her wrist. "What do you know of my mother? She died three years ago."

"I know that she would want you to listen to Wesley." Bela gave in just enough for Derian to think he had her handled.

"My mother would be ashamed of what you are doing. You are one of them, one of the Underground. And what do you know of Wesley?"

"I know he has his mother's eyes. You should have paid attention to where they took him. You could have kept him from the dungeon. You should be ashamed!" Bela had to stall him a bit longer. "You would be wise to release me." Bela took control and began pulling Derian out onto the upper tier, overlooking the castle entrance.

Derian's voice grew louder, "You're another traitor. You sound just like my imprudent brothers!"

"*You* sound like a spoiled child!" Bela scolded.

Bela was way ahead, already planning her escape. But the louder Derian shouted, the less time she knew she would have to make her move. Surely, Ninian would hear the commotion. She checked her surroundings. No one had yet come out of the library down the hall. All was clear in the next corridor. She was not concerned about finding a hiding place, only the time needed to get there.

"Where will you run, traitor? You have nowhere to go," Derian warned.

It was time for her to make her move. Bela stiffened her fingers and spun her wrists, pulling at the weak points of Derian's hold. She lifted away from his grasp and sent him spinning. Bela slid in the opposite direction, but she had spun too quickly. Derian stepped fast, trying to regain his balance. He hit the banister, arms whirling, and flipped backward over the railing. Reaching out, he caught himself with one hand.

Bela sprang forward to help. Derian's body writhed as he tried to grab hold with his other arm. But his fingers were losing grip. Out of the corner of her eye, Bela saw something move in the hall. A quick glance confirmed that Ninian and Ezra were running toward her. She looked back to Derian. Between the railings, she connected with helpless eyes. If she stayed to help him, she would be arrested. If she fled, Derian would fall to his death.

Dammit! She threw an arm forward to pull him in—but just as their fingers touched, he slipped away. His shriek echoed throughout the entryway as his body collided with the marble floor below.

With Ninian closing in, Bela pushed herself away from the banister and fled.

Trolls and Tiaras

47

For days, the pirate trolls had been adding to their numbers. *When will it stop?* The gathering made Philor sick to his stomach—he barely ate. The smallest noises made his stomach lurch. He could not remember the last time he had slept through the night.

On the fringes of the coastal spell, the group had converged in a thick tangle of trees not far from Port Regael. Most of the trolls wallowed beneath the moss-covered soil, an earthy vault filled with grubs and worms and burrowing varmints—plenty to eat. Yesterday, as Philor had made his way through the forest, he stepped on the head of a pirate and nearly had his leg bitten off. He refused to meet with Aarn that deep in the vale again.

"Lack of communication," the one-eyed man had tried to reason with him. Philor had strictly warned Ipabog to make it clear who was king, but Ipabog laughed him off. Philor wanted to kill him. Ipabog had the allegiance of the pirates, and this meant Philor was constantly watching over his shoulder.

Encountering King Ninian's soldiers back at his home had scared the hell out of him. He did not want to fight against the king, and he certainly did not want to be known as someone who opposed the king. If he were in charge—and he should have been in charge—he would have taken the maps and went directly to the Inner Realm. Consuming his thoughts was the glory of returning to Port Regael and sharing Gaspard's treasure. It had never occurred to him to consider what would happen if they did not gather the maps and writings.

How would he ever rule over the pirate trolls? Once they secured the treasure, it seemed that nothing would stop them from putting Aarn and him in the dungeon—or worse, they could have them hung! All that Nantes had become would fall into disarray.

Philor put his face in his hands. Aarn was ready to storm Port Regael with the pirates, but he was not. No more playing games. The glory he had been seeking was not true glory at all. It was time to begin plotting his escape. It was the only rational thing to do. He must flee to Port Regael and surrender himself to King Ninian. Port Regael would be saved, and perhaps his honesty would lessen the punishment for his wrongdoing.

Late that evening, on the northern rim, away from the trolls and high above the royal forest, Philor waited.

Soon Aarn approached from behind and said, "You've asked to speak with me. What's on your mind, brother?" Aarn sat down next to Philor and tossed his legs over the edge.

The moon's glow highlighted the tops of pine trees below them. It took several minutes before Philor found the courage to speak.

"I cannot continue with this madness."

"Look, if it makes you nervous to stand watch, leave it to the trolls."

"It's not that…It's this whole quest."

"What…What do you mean?" Aarn straightened his posture.

"I mean that what we are doing is going too far," Philor explained.

Aarn raised a fist. "We've sworn allegiance to the pirates. There is no backing out! If you sever this pact, they will kill you."

"The pirates owe us *their* allegiance!" Philor argued through his clenched teeth. "Besides, it's better to die a traitor at the hands of trolls than hang for treason before all of Regael."

"You are such a fool! I cannot believe I am hearing this from you."

"Keep your voice down. We need to flee while we can." Philor took hold of Aarn's arm. "We need to get out of here and make our way into the city to warn them. Surrender…seek pardon…save the name of Gaspard."

Aarn pushed away Philor's touch. "And leave all this behind? In one swift battering, Port Regael will surrender, and I will sit on the throne that is rightfully mine."

"*You* will sit on the throne? Don't you mean *we* will sit on the thrones?"

"You are obviously not ready. Listen to your spineless talk. It is mine, and I will take it."

"What are you saying?"

"You want to run? You'll never get away from here alive." Aarn's face twisted. He meant every word.

Have I been this blind all along? Philor wondered. He grabbed Aarn by the collar of his jacket and leaned in close. "Your words betray you! You leave me no choice…" At that, Philor pushed away, launching himself off the edge of the cliff and hurling himself into the darkness.

"Philor!" He heard his brother scream from behind. "You spineless ass!"

In less than the span of a breath, Philor found himself breaking branches of tall fir trees. Flopping about, his body bounced off limbs until he managed to grab hold. Hanging far above the forest floor, his feet kicked around.

"Philor!" His brother's voice echoed through the black void above.

Philor hustled downward, limb by limb, ignoring his brother's calls. He knew that the words Aarn had spoken were no idle threat. If the pirates caught up to him, he was as good as dead. But even that was better than betraying the king. At least he would die knowing that he was doing the right thing.

He swung from the lowest limb to the ground and ran hard. Though the moon was bright, the forest was thick, and Aarn would never see him from above. At first, the darkness forced a slower pace. He felt like he always needed to duck. He ran with his chin down and raised his arms to protect his head, unsure of what he might run into.

It was not long before a loud blare from a horn sounded from high above and behind. Its bellow cursed the midnight air. It was the call to rally the trolls. In his mind, he pictured them easily jumping from the cliff and falling upon him in minutes. With quick, shallow breaths, he pressed on—temples throbbing and palms sweating. His fast and steady pace only fell off tempo when he slowed to sidestep rocks and fallen limbs.

Cold nipped at him as he neared the edge of the spell. Fog had gathered in the valley. Out of the woods and into a marsh, he tumbled face-first into freezing water. He jumped to his feet and splashed through the fog.

Soon, thin ice slowed him, catching each step before breaking through into the water. Moving along, he found that the ice merely cracked and sunk a bit. Thirty more paces from there, and the ice was solid. Several times he slipped, bruising his knees and hips, elbows and ribs. Eventually, there was enough snow to give him some traction. The fog was behind him now, and the ice sparkled and glowed in the light of the moon. He trudged through deepening snow until he made it out of the marsh and into another group of trees.

Which way?

He looked up to the splatter of stars across the sky, hoped he was going northwest, and rushed ahead. Running at full speed, he was yanked aside as a hand slapped over his mouth. Stinging pain shot along the sides of his head. He could taste blood when he swallowed. Whoever it was, they had caught him with one hand and kept him from falling with the other.

Being dragged away, Philor flung his arms and twisted his body, hoping to break free. But the grip was like steel, and he could not get his feet below him. He flopped and pulled and kicked. Nothing worked.

His captor took long, fast strides. After stopping, Philor was pulled around and held up, the hand remained in place over his mouth. One of his abductor's fingers pushed up below his left eye, giving him double vision.

Someone lifted a lantern, and in the same moment a face appeared. The hand over Philor's mouth muffled his shriek. With each breath, he exhaled a successive scream. He could not run, nor could he move. When he finally wore himself out, his body went limp in his captor's arms. Fear fell to despondence, his eyes filled with tears, and everything was blurry. Had he seen a ghost? He began to sob.

It was his mother.

Sophia reached out and pushed her fingers through his frozen hair. She smiled at him and lifted a finger to her lips to quiet him. When he calmed down, the hand that held his head slowly let go. He fell forward, embracing his mother.

"All is well, Philor," she assured him. "All is well."

Her voice only made him weep more. Memories of another time doused his thoughts. Her chin rested upon the top of his head, and she held him close. She stroked the back of his head, calming him. Philor lifted his head and simply looked his mother in the eyes. He had so many things to say and ask, yet he knew where he must start.

"Mother, all is not well. You don't know what I've done."

"I know enough," she said.

"The pirate trolls?"

"Yes. You must put this behind you," Sophia encouraged.

"But how? How do you know? What are you doing here? Why are you—"

Sophia put two fingers to his lips and whispered, "I will be brief, and we will talk soon. We heard the horns. The trolls will not be far behind you. These men will take you to your father."

"But I—" Philor tried to speak, but she quieted him again.

"I have a mission in Port Regael. I will meet up with you in three days. I will be safe. My friends will protect you with their lives. I know this is difficult, but when I see you again, we will find rest. Now you must go. Do not be afraid."

48

I f Derian is king, does that mean you are queen?" Jess asked Avlae with inquisitive eyes.

Avlae smiled, though her thoughts were tangled like Jess's hair in the morning, and she knelt down beside Jess. "No. When Derian marries, his wife will be queen."

"That is not fair!" Jess protested and stomped.

I'd like to stomp out of here and demand that King Ninian take me to Wesley. Let me tell you what is not fair!

"Your temper does not befit your nobility, young princess." *Nor would mine if I had Derian alone.*

"I am a *princess*?"

"Indeed, you are. And I am a princess, too." Avlae poked Jess on the nose and stood again.

That suited Jess well. "We will need tiaras," Jess continued. She leapt up on the bed and rolled over the blankets.

"Yes, we will. Do you suppose there are dried vines in the courtyard?" Avlae plopped down beside Jess.

"Yes, and flowers from the breakfast table!" Jess giggled.

Flowers…Torres always brings me flowers when we are in Port Regael. He must know I am here in the castle. Why has he not come to see me? Or at least sent me a note? He would never give in to Derian's threats. I'm sure of it.

"We shall make tiaras ourselves, just like we do at home."

"Right now?"

Avlae did not know how to tell Jess that they were not allowed to leave the room. Luckily, she did not have to. The door to their room opened, and in slid a young woman, out of breath, who quickly closed the door behind her. Avlae leaned back, guarding Jess. The young woman held out her hand and fell to her knees before them.

"Please hear me, daughters of Gaspard," the woman spoke breathlessly. "The castle guards, even Ninian, will be here in less than a minute."

"What—" Avlae tried to get a word in.

"Allow me to hide, and I will explain. I know your mother, Sophia, and your father, William. I know that even now the king holds your brother, Wesley, in a cell below the castle."

"Who are you? We need to—"

"Please, trust me!"

Avlae did need answers, but she saw urgency in the young woman's eyes.

"Very well. Where will you hide?"

Bela quickly climbed up the bedpost and hid within the custom frame on top of the canopy. Avlae grabbed Jess and tucked her in beneath the blankets.

"You pretend to be sleeping," Avlae ordered Jess just as a heavy hand thumped the door.

Terrified, she took several slow, deep breaths and smiled at Jess. "Not a word about the young woman and no snoring," she softly warned.

Repeatedly telling herself to stay calm, Avlae approached the door. She breathed deeply, inhaled through her nose, pursed her lips, and blew out through her mouth. As she turned the handle, another heavy knock thudded.

"Quiet!" Avlae spoke in a forced whisper. When she opened the door, there stood King Ninian with several guards. *I pray my eyes do not give me away.* "Oh, sire! I am sorry. Jess has just fallen asleep. Forgive my impatience. Please, come in."

She stepped back from the door and allowed the king and his men to enter. Many eyes surveyed the surroundings.

The king spoke gently, "Young Avlae, I do not mean to frighten you, but it seems we have a fugitive running about in the castle." Avlae put on her best look of concern, and Ninian continued, "Have you heard anything unusual, or has anyone come to your door?"

"No, sire," she said without a pause.

The sentries slowly walked about the room with rifles held up in their arms. Despite her answer, they looked under the bed and searched the armoire.

"Are we safe here?" Avlae asked.

"Well, this person is extremely dangerous and cannot be trusted. She may try to manipulate you. You'll be safe, but please do something for me."

"Yes, sire. Anything." Avlae clasped her hands.

"You will do well to report anything you hear or see," King Ninian warned.

"You are frightening me, sire. It is enough that we are in a new place."

"I assure you that I will not be far, and I will leave a guard outside your door." He looked deep into her eyes. "Remain here, and you will be safe."

The men left, followed by the king. Avlae fell back against the door. With her heart pounding and throat tight, she walked back across the room and sat on the bed.

"May I sit up?" a small voice asked from the pillow.

"Yes, come over here," Avlae answered, and Jess crawled up onto her lap.

Two bare feet dangled above them. With hardly a sound, the young woman leapt to the floor. She wore a dark green linen kirtle. Her eyes matched the color of her clothes, and her dark brown hair bounced off her shoulders. She adjusted her hood and looked at Jess.

"I don't believe we've met, young miss. My name is Bela. Your sister would call me Aunt Bela when she was your age." Bela smiled and took Jess by the hand.

"Is this part of your manipulation?" Avlae asked. "What you say, I do not remember."

"Right, then. Let me start with this." Bela took a deep breath. "Your mother is alive."

"I'm not sure if that information is any easier to receive…" Avlae hesitated, caution guarding her demeanor. "And we should just believe you? What do you know of Mother?"

"I know that I rescued her from the north tower of this very castle four days ago. She was on her way to you." Then Bela added, "And I know you are adopted."

Avlae frowned, speechless.

Bela reached behind her head and under her hair. She parted a chain, pulled it off her neck, and took Avlae by the hand. She placed the necklace in her palm, folded her fingers over, and let go. Avlae pulled back her arm, opened her hand, and looked down. There, she saw an almond-shaped pendant, a match for hers and the one Jess wore. All her doubts vanished.

"What must we do?"

"We need to leave Port Regael. I will take you to your mother."

Jess began to cry, and Avlae reassured her, "We'll be all right. Bela will protect us."

"But Mother's dead," Jess cried. She would not be consoled.

"Oh, my dear…" Avlae pulled her sister close and rocked her back and forth.

"Take nothing with you," Bela said.

"The halls…Soldiers will be everywhere," Avlae said, and her eyes stayed on the door.

"We will flee through a back passage."

"And what of Wesley and Derian?"

"I must get you two to safety. I have close friends who can help them."

Avlae took Jess's hands in hers. "I need you to be strong, Jess. Can you do that for me?"

Jess nodded and sniffled.

At that, Avlae spun Jess around and tied up her hair.

"Will we still wear tiaras?" Jess rubbed her moist nose with the back of her hand.

"Are you a child of the king?"

Again, Jess nodded.

"Then, tiaras it will be." Bela now knelt to speak with Jess. "And nothing can change that."

Avlae stood and moved toward the door. She looked back at Bela, who simply nodded. After a slow turn of the knob, she drew back the door just enough to peer into the hall.

Pushing in upon her, the blow from the door knocked her off balance. Avlae threw out her arms, leaned forward, and shoved, shrieking as she slammed someone's forearm in the doorframe. Even with her firm stance, she was no match for the might from the other side. Her feet slipped, shambling backward with each successive thrust from the other side. While dodging an arm that groped about, trying to grab her, she kicked at a foot planted firmly in the doorway.

Bela sprang across the room and wrenched the arm upward. The door swung in, thwacking Avlae's head and flinging her to the floor. Bela gripped the man by his collar. Lifting her leg and pulling him down, she bounced his head off her knee. Avlae rolled aside as the man collapsed forward, his pistol sliding across the floor. Regaining her wits, she scrambled for the weapon.

"Toss it here!" Bela ordered. She clasped the gun and lunged through the doorway.

Avlae snatched Jess's hand and followed Bela into the hall. Bela already had the pistol raised and fired a killing shot at the soldier near the end of the short corridor.

Jess howled—aghast, weeping, screaming, wailing in a panic.

"Look at me." Avlae recomposed herself, cradled Jess's cheeks, hugged her, and whispered, "Stay with me, and keep your eyes closed."

Bela flung the gun aside and ran. Jumping over the downed body, she was quick to grab the dead soldier's rifle and level herself against the wall.

Partially carrying and dragging the livid child, Avlae struggled to move ahead with Jess. Stepping past the grisly scene, Avlae hid Jess's eyes, then fell against the wall beside Bela.

"Stay close. Don't look back!" Bela ordered.

Under the Ice

49

ahre loosened the upper strings of his black, bulky cloak, and warm westerly winds blew his hood off his head. It was a welcome salve against his numb face. Clumps of heavy snow fell from high branches, sloshing to the ground or even on him. The bear he rode slogged through deep but melting snow in the valley of a thawing riverbed. His clothing absorbed moisture from the bear's wet fur. With no change of clothes, and an hour from sunset, it was sure to be a cold night.

Farther ahead and out of sight, Olivetan pushed on. Keeping up with him was a burden.

Callas was around somewhere. Every now and then, he bolted from the right or left across the path. This unnerved Mahre every time. Yet Callas was the lookout, and despite Mahre's leaps of anxiety, he was glad for the protection. Mahre did not know a pirate troll could be so sprightly. He bounced and rolled, bounding and swooping about. Mahre could not figure him out. When he had been under a spell, his mind was plagued by such darkness.

In those dismal days—the days when Mahre languished as a pirate troll—he was never content. Why him? Why did he have to live with such a burden? Back then, his thoughts stayed only on returning to what he was before. Though he begged for sympathy, no one cared for him. He separated himself from others who suffered the same fate and faced each day alone. Callas showed no signs of suffering, if he suffered at all.

Why is he not stricken with misery? Does the spell not torture him? For Mahre, each day under the spell he had awakened with a raw, deepening mental wound. *What heals Callas's mind? Has he found a charm to soothe his logy life?*

Coming around a curve in the riverbed forty to fifty rods ahead, Olivetan had dismounted his bear and was now peering over the shallow trench. As Mahre approached, Olivetan was right on task.

"This is where we enter," Olivetan called back.

Mahre slid off his bear, sloshed into a snow and mud mixture, and traipsed up beside him. Across the ice and snow-matted weeds of the bog, Mahre surveyed a guard tower in the stone wall. Soggy, wilted vines masked the entrance and climbed the tower. One sentry kept watch along the rampart.

"So, you think that if I walk over and knock on the door, they'll just let me in?" Mahre asked. Suddenly, black clouds released a downpour of sleet, blurring his sight.

"That's what I'm counting on," Olivetan said, wiping his eyes with his forearm.

"You know, it's quite unlikely that the door will even open."

"You just get one of them to unlock the door, and Callas will take care of the rest. Now, we are a bit pressed for time, so off with you. The tide won't wait for us."

Mahre crawled from the riverbed, stood up, and took large steps. He sank with each stride, and murky water pooled around his boots.

Raising his arms at his sides, he tilted to find his balance until he treaded on solid ground.

Grasping and tugging at clusters of vines, Mahre cleared the foliage from the iron door. He wiped his hands on his outer garment and shot a glance back at Olivetan. From his pocket, he pulled out a stone slightly bigger than his palm and pounded it against the door. After striking the door three times, he waited.

Nothing.

Two more times, and midway through the third slam, a voice came from above. "Who's down there?"

Mahre looked up and saw the sentinel leaning over the top of the wall. "Uh…uh…" Mahre had not thought about what he would say. "Help me?" It was not supposed to be a question.

"Walk east and you'll go beyond the edge of the storm!" came the reply.

"I…I've no strength! If you would, please, allow me to rest for the night, and I will leave. Perhaps in…in the morning? Yes, at first light, I will be gone."

"Walk east! Warmer winds are blowing, and the cold is lifting," the man called back again.

"I am not asking for food, only a place to lay my head." *I'm getting good at this.*

"I have my orders. We are not a refuge for lost men!"

Mahre stared up and had to shield his eyes from the blinding sleet. He waited. The sentinel stepped away. *This plan never had a chance.* Mahre looked back to Olivetan, offering his empty palms. Callas, now at Olivetan's side, shrugged his bulging shoulders.

Olivetan thrust his fist like he was pounding the door.

Annoyed, Mahre continued, and ten more minutes of pounding

seemed like an hour. Just as he cranked his arm back once more, an aching creak and deep clank reverberated from the door. Then, the door pushed out ever so slightly.

"Thank you, sir! Thank you!" Mahre called out.

"For a man with no strength, you are persistent," the man behind the door said. With each shove, the door slid only niks.

Mahre reached out his arm and motioned for Callas to come over. The door opened enough for Mahre to get his arm inside to pull while the sentry pushed from the inside—yet, now it did not budge. Callas landed behind Mahre and stuck his huge fingers between the door and the frame. Mahre jumped to the side as Callas flung the door open with ease, nearly taking it off its hinges.

Motionless and gaping, the sentinel was incapacitated. With his immense hands, Callas reached in, grabbed the man by the collar of his coat, and lifted him off the ground. Without the slightest opposition, the man passed out and hung in the troll's grip.

"I think you've killed him!"

"*Witotien, witoten,*" Callas cried.

"*Ovbrituin hels,*" Mahre said, telling Callas that the man had only fainted, hoping to resolve any fear that Callas had caused any serious injury to the man. After spending several days with the pirate, Mahre had learned he had a soft heart.

Reaching up, he guided Callas to gently lay the man down. Mahre stepped through the door, hoisted the man from under the shoulders, and walked backward, dragging him to the corner of the small room.

In moments, Olivetan joined Mahre in the narrow tower.

"We've got one of them," Mahre said. He slid the downed man's gun from his shoulder.

"Very good. I knew these fellows could be quite hospitable."

Olivetan accepted the weapon from Mahre and led the way up circling steps to the lookout.

"Callas! *Espos lataian?*" Mahre asked, and the pirate squeezed himself inside. "If we could avoid any gunfire, I'd find that most agreeable." Mahre leaned back against the wall and waited to see what Olivetan would do.

"Have Callas tie that man up and wait while we search the tower!" At the top of the steps, Olivetan pushed against a wooden door in the floor above him and scrambled up through the opening. "*Enichrian to're sai thoai!*" Mahre shouted and leapt up to follow Olivetan, skipping two or three steps at a time.

Boosting himself through the doorway in the floor, his achy arms strained. He lifted himself into the living quarters, and with a proud lunge, he stood by Olivetan's side, examining the dim stone-walled room. A small fire heated stew. From chains hung a thick wooden plank, covered with animal furs. Then he noticed an ale barrel, tapped and ready to drink.

"You know, I think I could…"

From the next room, someone called, "Have our guest remain below the…" And in walked a sentinel, staring straight into the barrel of Olivetan's rifle.

"Tie him up, Mahre," Olivetan ordered.

Mahre pulled a rope from his satchel and began to tie the man's wrists behind his back. Out of the corner of his eye, he saw something moving in the doorway.

"There are three of them!" Mahre shouted.

A third guard appeared, reaching for his pistol. With one quick stroke, Olivetan lifted his arms and crushed the man's nose with the butt of his rifle. This distracted Mahre long enough for the man he was binding to pull away. With his arms tied behind his back, he jumped down through the open door in the floor.

Mahre kicked the door shut, looked up, and smiled at Olivetan. He laughed, "And there are three of us."

After a bit of a fracas below, the tower was theirs.

"This should do it, then," Olivetan said as he dragged the third unconscious foe to the door. He and Mahre handed the body down to Callas. "Bind them well!" Olivetan ordered. "No need for them to be wandering off before we return. I'll meet you on the ice."

"But I was hoping to stay for a pint or two," Mahre protested.

Olivetan shot a smirk at Mahre and left the quarters, walking out onto the rampart.

Hurriedly, Mahre clanked a mug below the tapper. With a long drink, his insides warmed. Looking through the opening, he watched as Callas finished tying up the three men. Callas then stepped out of Mahre's line of sight.

"Let's go, then!" Mahre called out in his own language, not really thinking about who he was talking to. In a moment, Callas reappeared with an axe in his hands.

"Yes, very good. *Ithroaian, ithroaian.*"

The axe blade broke through the floorboards, splinters flying. Floundering backward, Mahre dropped his mug through the hole in the floor. In his twisted position, he looked straight ahead through his gnarled knees. Callas reached up through the floor, breaking away several boards and making a troll-sized hole. Straggly, wet hairs atop the troll's head appeared through the opening. Then, Mahre saw a rumpled forehead above narrow, yellow eyes. Finally, there came a troll-sized smile.

Mahre laughed and laughed.

50

Atop the wall, Mahre raced to catch up with Olivetan. Leaning through the embrasure, he took hold of the rope, climbed through the crenel, and spun. He pushed off the wall, sprang down, and dropped with each leap. Above him, Callas jumped, sailing over the edge and swooping past him. In a final thrust, Mahre released the rope and launched himself backwards.

Throwing his arms out for balance, he landed, crunching through broken ice and snow. One leg buckled, while the other slipped straight out to his side. He then toddled down over a jagged slope beyond the shoreline. Directly below him, under thick ice, the tide had gone out, and the large slab of ice had sunk, buckling and converging upon itself. Not far out, with Olivetan guiding, Callas had already begun breaking through, creating an entrance to the frozen, narrow tunnels beneath.

A shadow from the wall loomed overhead, as if it were threatening their fateful scheme. Yet, in contrast, the brightest stars began to make themselves known across the darkening skies. Mahre breathed the salty air blowing against his face. Far in the distance, uneven ice met the emerald sea.

In his mind, Mahre was drawn to Bela's green eyes looking up at him from her small frame. How he wished to be with her now. Was she hiding? Had Ninian captured her? Would he torture her—kill her? She had rescued Sophia, and now Sophia was on her back way to rescue her. How much longer till he would know something? He longed to protect her. He pictured them together at Dochart's Glen, lying beside a stream or warming themselves by a fire in the great room of the castle. He had no idea if that's what the Glen would be like, or if they would find it at all, or if it even existed, but that is how the legends explained it, and that was enough for now.

The sudden silence pulled him from his musing. Callas had completed his task. Olivetan had tied an extension of rope and released it through the opening.

"*Ses pereth?*" Callas asked.

Mahre translated for Olivetan, "He wants to know how far to Regael Cave."

"Not far, shouldn't be much over an hour's walk." Mahre asked if Callas understood, "*Insoduenan?*"

Callas nodded.

Olivetan added, "The journey back will likely be faster."

Mahre's expression was enough to tell Olivetan that he needed to explain.

"We'll be running! We've only several hours till the tide comes in and fills the tight corridors below," Olivetan said. Carefully finding leverage, he stepped downward through the hole and under the ice. "Keep moving! Follow me!"

When Olivetan had spoken about how to find an opening—a weak spot that formed when the ice buckled as the water receded—Mahre shrank at the through of it. He had dwelled for too long, analyzing Olivetan's obviously misguided and ludicrous plan, and eventually his apprehension had become sheer panic.

Now, he latched onto the rope, and even his *thoughts* buckled as he found himself climbing through the crevice. Wresting hysterical voices within, he was certain that Olivetan would hear the calamity of his inner resistance. Around him, the shimmering slab of ice became a drab green, filtering what remained of the daylight as he descended. Warmer air pushed up and around him as his passage narrowed. Unsure of his footing, he braced his back against the seemingly shifting block of ice behind him and dipped himself into erratic subterranean corridors.

With his leg now taut and cramped, he groped with the tip of his boot until he found a secure hold. With both feet hopefully uncompromised, Mahre crouched and maneuvered himself around what seemed like a giant icicle. He then slid into the eerie, pulsating glow of Olivetan's lantern.

Within the small circle of dim light, the icy ceiling glowed. Water slurped out somewhere beyond his limited vision. A strange hush pressed his ears in the small triangular chamber, which only exacerbated the weight above that sought to crush them. Slightly hunched, he took steady strides upon slick, kelp-covered rocks, one hand reaching up against the sloped ceiling to give him balance.

A sudden *crack* and *pop* came from overhead, and Mahre threw out his other arm to hold himself firm.

"The tide is still on the way out is all," Olivetan explained. He lit a candle from his lantern and placed it among rocks. "The ice is settling."

"Well," Mahre said, "you've eliminated all my fears."

Crunch. Mahre gulped as light from their slippery entrance was cut off. He squeezed his eyes closed and waited to be flattened by the massive slab of ice over his head.

Whoosh and then…laughter. Troll laughter. Callas slid through the opening and joined them, squeezing into the frozen crypt.

That troll finds too much pleasure in this.

"Ah ha, Callas!" Olivetan said, and he handed his lantern to the troll. "You'll be leading the way, and I'll place candles to light our way back."

Mahre translated.

"*Sai*, Mahre?" Callas asked.

"He wants to know what I'll be doing."

"Oh, I understood." Olivetan winked at Callas. "We'll give Mahre time to sort out his uneasiness."

"He's only smiling because you are. I'm not going to translate that." Mahre said. He turned to Callas and nodded ahead. "*Eistisa.*"

Olivetan followed Callas and Mahre along the periphery of the faint light. In places where the frozen walls expanded, the icy ceiling drooped, almost reaching the seafloor, and the three were forced to crawl through scummy seaweed and puddles. In other areas, the ceiling rose, and they had to sidestep, pinched as if by a glacial crevice.

Mahre found himself least anxious when daylight shined through thinner ice, illuminating cracks with a cloudy green glow. He supposed it was the feeling of being closer to the outside that helped. The sun, however, had set, and those areas were darkening. What then would soothe his misery?

Soon, they came to a long stretch, wide enough for them to walk side by side.

"Did it smell this bad when you walked below the ice with your father?" Mahre asked.

"Yes," Olivetan said, wandering aside to place another candle. "The sulfuric smell comes from the seaweed."

"How old were you when your father first led you to this haunting place?"

"I was eight, and I fought my father the whole way!" Olivetan laughed. "He cut a hole in the ice and lowered me down despite my protesting. But he jumped in right behind me and began placing candles on the seabed. He lit the candles, then handed me my first mussel pan and chisel. Father said to watch, and he went right to work, gathering strands of mussels."

"And you *ate* them," Mahre stated and lifted his upper lip and splayed his tongue.

"All the time. Can you believe that in Port Regael, for many years, people *refused* to eat them?"

"I can believe that," Mahre said, taking a long step over a puddle in the sand. A twinge of jealousy pinched him. Mahre had spent most of his childhood as a pirate troll. Kidnapped by slave traders, he had been taken to Calbha Mor at the age of seven. Escaping at the age of nineteen, he suffered the spell for another five years before Habormoss rescued him.

"Only in the last six or seven years have mussels been considered a delicacy," Olivetan said.

Mahre's stomach turned at the thought. He shuddered. "Slimy shellfish."

"You mean *succulent* shellfish. Cook them right, and you get a taste of sweet with the salty. If we had an extra hour, I'd fill a bucket with the beautiful bivalves!"

"If we get back early, you can do just that."

"Just thinking about it makes my mouth water. Father had one rule." Olivetan held out his arm, clenched his fist, and raised his thumb in the light of his lantern. "He'd squat down in front of me and say, 'Tanny, take only the mussels the size of my thumb or larger. Leave the smaller ones to grow.'"

Olivetan stopped, knelt by a small pool of water, and waved the other two over. He had Callas lower the lantern to show tiny shrimps swimming about. Callas pointed to something in the water.

"Yes, I see," Mahre said. He'd had enough of the troll's optimism.

Callas continued to point in anticipation.

"What is it?" Mahre huffed and finally crouched.

With his nose almost in the water, he searched but saw nothing more than the shrimps. Swiftly, Callas brought the palm of his hand down into the water, soaking Mahre's head. Olivetan spit out the water he had been swallowing and nearly fell over from laughing so hard.

"*Aderlos!*" Callas bellowed.

Mahre knew better than to retaliate. He just accepted the troll's prank and said, "I guess that means we've bonded."

Moving on, they reached an uncomfortably tight space, from which it seemed they could go no farther.

"We've arrived," Olivetan said. Reaching ahead, he braced himself to rest against the ledge of a seemingly dead end. The natural rock formation of a sea cave stopped their progress.

"How do you mean? There is nowhere to go from here."

"Look here—we follow this ridgeline," Olivetan explained. Though the ice leaned in from behind them, there was a cavity one could barely squeeze through, however harrowing and grim.

"You want to go out toward the sea? Toward the tide?"

"We need to go out and around. It's the only way into Regael

Cave, my reckless friend." Olivetan stifled his laughter and continued quite optimistically, "It's narrow, but Callas will be able to squeeze through. We'll be a couple rods off the seafloor, above the incoming tide."

Callas quickly clambered to the ledge, then extended an arm and pulled Olivetan up. Mahre hesitated, watching them maneuver along the uneven footpath until they were absorbed in the blackness of the unwelcome rift.

Mahre noticed a strong, familiar taste in his mouth. He had thought he tasted it the moment he joined Olivetan in that dreadful chamber for this ludicrous rescue, but now there was no mistaking it.

"Olivetan, Olivetan!"

"Come along," a voice called back toward Mahre, barely escaping the dismal vault that Olivetan had slithered into.

"Do you taste iron?" No answer. "Olivetan! Do you—"

"Do you think?" Olivetan sounded bemused, but Mahre had no time for his sarcasm.

"No doubt, it's a dormire spell," Mahre stressed his pessimism.

"I have been feeling sluggish…"

"But why here?"

"It is a sign we are in the right place." Now Olivetan sounded as if he were farther away. "Medici has been near here. Regael Cave must be on the other side of this wall."

"But who could he possibly want to curse out here below the ice?"

"I can't explain it, but you'll need to warn Callas. He may have to carry us part of the way."

"If you are feeling the effects already, it'll only get worse. And we still have to come *back* this way!"

"We have no other options."

Damn. Soaking wet and sweating, Mahre began to pace. Of course, the spell would affect Callas the least, if at all, but Mahre had extremely keen senses, both as a troll and as a human. Thinking about the feeling of the dormire pressing against his skull, he imagined something like being crushed by a giant slab of ice over the course of hours and hours. Mahre gasped to get a breath, as if a massive stone hung from his neck, as if a mooring line were wrapped tightly around his chest, as if...

"Come along!" Olivetan called back through the gap. "You need to see this!"

Mahre threw himself down and doused his head in a puddle of sea water. Panting, he pulled his hands across his face.

"Mahre!"

Push past, push past it. Mahre scurried up, squeezed his eyes closed, and sidestepped the ridge, sliding through the crevice. It was not long until the ice no longer pressed against his back. Mahre opened his eyes to a wide space.

"What the..."

Callas, a stone's throw ahead on the ridge, had lifted a lantern, illuminating an icy ceiling. Mahre lowered himself from the ridge and joined in Olivetan's befuddlement.

"Now, how do you suppose that happened?" Olivetan asked. With his hands on his hips and lantern light sparkling in his eyes, Mahre could tell Olivetan already knew the answer to what he had asked.

At least thirty rods above them, a ceiling of ice seemingly hung upon nothing, leaving a wide-open space in the absence of the tide.

"This section did not sink with the tide. You think Medici did this?" Mahre tried but could not hide his amusement.

"What else could it be?"

"But why?"

"I'm sure we'll find something to Medici's scheme." Olivetan shrugged and moved on, tracing his hand along the ledge. "At least we've much more room to walk."

"*Loi ahech, ithroaien,*" Mahre said, stepping up to walk beside Olivetan. Callas fell in step behind them and hoisted the lantern high, throwing light ahead. Though the popping and cracking from the ice had ceased, outside the throes of their light, the silence had teamed up with the darkness to taunt them.

Another several minutes and the rocky wall curved north; then it curved again, back in the direction from which they came. Although the trek became less difficult—they were treading upon more sand now than rocks—Mahre was feeling winded, and his body was spent within the proximity of the dormire spell. Olivetan plodded along without complaint, and Mahre alerted Callas to the possibility of him having to carry them somewhere beyond the spell. But because Mahre did not know *where* that somewhere was, he had a difficult time translating.

The three continued along the ocean floor into what they hoped to be Regael Cave. Some thirty rods above them, the ceiling of ice hovered like a massive granite slab of what was sure to be their tomb. Then, not far ahead of them, a large object seemed to be hanging from above, frozen in place.

With his arms and shoulders aching, Mahre pushed back against the weight of the spell. His curiosity about the object ahead was enough to keep him on two feet. Looking upward, even his eye sockets strained against the spell, and unless he was seeing some type of mirage, it seemed as if he could make out the hull of a ship.

Olivetan was the first to speak. "I do believe we are in the right place."

"It's the hull…" Mahre found himself needing to take a breath. "…of Calbha's Curse."

"So…this is what Medici…has devised…" Easily within his reach, Olivetan rapped his knuckles against the thick wood and continued to walk below the ship, noticeably struggling with each step. "Held…in place…with the dormire spell."

"What do you…think…he is hiding?"

"Well…for one thing, he…he is hiding…himself." Olivetan tripped forward and quickly stepped, saving himself from a fall. "But also…to st…stave off any damage to the…the ship."

Not wanting to stroll below the hull, Mahre joined Callas, who was exploring the outer edge and otherwise would have had to crouch to fit underneath. Between deep breaths, he explained more to Callas about the spell and the ship.

Beyond the stern, Olivetan pointed up. "Right here…This is the bed of the underground river…that flows to the tower, which stretches…up to the dungeons…in the…the mammoth cave beneath Regael Castle." Olivetan stood at the bottom of a drop-off, bent over with his hands on his thighs. "It will be a steep climb… but manageable. Our hidden route to…to…retrieve Wesley."

"I need to…to…get away from this spell." Mahre glowered.

"Of course…We've no time to sulk. Up we go, then."

Mahre began a sluggish climb after Olivetan, but Callas pulled him back.

"*Thoaien!*" Callas shouted and placed his lantern on the seafloor.

"*Due…Terriaet inso…insoduenen?*" Mahre asked.

"What is it?" Olivetan called down.

"*Ech leptierai*," Callas said and held out his axe.

Mahre shook his head. "It seems…that Callas has…contrived…a plan of his own."

On the side of the hull, near the stern, Callas began hacking away.

"He'll bring that ship down…on top of us! Wait, Callas! Stop! You'll—" Mahre's inner urgency did not match his spoken words. Panic lit his nerves, but he could not move fast enough.

Olivetan slid back down toward Mahre. "It will take much… *much* more than that to…break the curse." Olivetan limped away from the slope but kept enough distance from Callas to avoid the scattering wood chips. "That will slow…our enemy a bit. And… come to think of it, it may…it may…be worth…" Olivetan lifted a finger to demand patience. "May be worth a quick search…of the cargo area…"

"Wait, you just said…we have no time!" Mahre pleaded, pressure growing on the outside of his head. "Suppose…there is someone… onboard?"

Olivetan looked as if he may faint in exasperation. "Sometimes… necessary risks pre…present…themselves."

It was no use arguing with Olivetan, so Mahre retrieved the lantern and wobbled toward Callas to give him a bit more light. In no time, the troll had gouged a hole wide enough to climb through into the hull, which had to be over a half-rod thick. Just then, Callas broke through the bilge, lowered the axe, and stepped aside, panting. Against the weight of the spell, Mahre lifted himself to his toes and leaned to peer inside.

"There's a…a flicker of light," Mahre observed and looked back at Olivetan for direction.

Olivetan met Mahre's eyes, then peered around him. "What… what was that? Something is there…"

"What is it?"

"Here, take this." Olivetan slid the rifle from his shoulder and handed it to Mahre.

"You have…no strength…you don't…know what you'll…."

"Better…to find out now than later."

"Fool…"

"We don't…don't need anyone privy to our arrival. C…Cover me." Olivetan pointed to himself, then to the hole in the ship. Callas figured out what he meant and hoisted him through.

"Wait, wait, wait!" Olivetan shouted, and he began coughing faster than he could take in breaths. Troll arms latched hold of his shoulders—from inside the ship!

"*Haisren, Callas!*" Mahre called.

Callas pulled back once, then released, but it was too late. Olivetan was yanked into the hull.

"What…are you doing?" Mahre shrieked. But then he realized it was a wise move on behalf of Callas not to play tug-of-war with another troll using Olivetan's body.

Callas barreled through the hole in the hull. Mahre slung the rifle forward and teetered, trying to take aim in case their enemy tried to escape.

"Olive…Olivetan!" Mahre called.

No answer. Mahre only saw the light casting shadowy throws of the brawling beasts. From the clamor, he worried that this just might bring the whole ship crashing down upon him. Working to keep his rifle raised, he stepped away from the ship. Suddenly, his heel struck a rock, and with the spell having slowed his reactions, Mahre fell flat onto his back. He fumbled for the rifle, but it bounced straight off the sand, and when he finally caught it, he accidentally squeezed the trigger. Mahre pinched his eyes closed, anticipating the immediate flash and *crack!* Around him, the blast echoed, and he lay still.

Olivetan's voice called listlessly yet loudly above him, "Mahre! What…are you…"

"Well, I—"

"Never mind, you need…to see what's…in here!" Olivetan smiled. A bottle shattered behind him, and he shielded his eyes from shards of glass. "Callas has this…almost wrapped up."

Despite his many aches, Mahre managed to stand on his feet and got a whiff of what was in the bottle. "Breaking that out…a little…a little early?" When he lifted his head back to the hole, Mahre saw that Callas was staring at him with an arm stretched out to help him. He reluctantly accepted, and Callas pulled him aboard.

Olivetan was busy examining the contents of a barrel.

"Don't you think…think we ought to leave…before more… of the green hospitality crew…arrives?" He wrested a breath, as if Callas had sat on his chest. "And didn't you say…some…something about the tide…not waiting for us?"

Olivetan was slouched against one of the barrels. "Do you know what…is in here?" he asked.

"Whiskey?" Mahre guessed.

"No, the whiskey is there…" Olivetan pointed across the room. "In the crates. In these barrels…is gunpowder. And…and look here." He clung to a long, iron cylinder.

"Hand cannons," Mahre said. "You want to lug…those around?"

"No, no...But remember, if we break what the curse binds... then we will break the curse."

"And?"

"And? And? We must rest...Have Callas get half of these off... these barrels off...the ship," Olivetan said, more so mumbling than ordering. "I have a plan...a plan...to help our escape!"

KING NINIAN III
© 2020

The Rise of Ninian

51

erian's murder was just what Ninian needed to expunge any skepticism. When the city would discover that Bela and the Underground were responsible for the death of the long-awaited heir, the people of Nantes would worship Ninian as a god for her capture. With overwhelming support, he would sever the co-regency forever.

My reign will only grow from here.

"Your kingdom awaits you, sire," Ninian's attendant informed him.

My kingdom, indeed.

Ninian cleared his throat, took a deep breath, and put on his best look of concern. He nodded, and the attendant pulled aside the tall, golden drapery. Ninian took several steps forward onto the balcony, overlooking throngs of applause which filled his courtyards. Even beyond the courtyard, the streets of Nantes were filled with people waiting to meet the heir. Many messengers would carry his words to those far off.

Ninian remained sullen.

The crowd would not be quieted. A chant arose, "Gaspard! Gaspard! Gaspard!"

After a minute or so, he raised his arms to silence them, but his attempt was useless. Howls and bellows, cries and croons—the people were restless for the coronation. Ninian leaned forward on the railing in front of him, raising a hand of greetings to his loyal following. "People of Nantes! Hear me now! Hear what I have to say!"

After minutes of intractable acclamation, the crowd calmed.

"It seems there are those among us who continue to threaten Nantes and all she stands for—those who seek to sever the co-regency. Derian Delaine, the great-grandson of Francis Gaspard, our long-awaited king, the one who would restore the co-regency to our good kingdom...was murdered within these castle walls at the hands of the Underground!"

Shouts of disdain for the Underground arose from below.

"We are tracking the murderer as we speak. We will find her, and she will hang!" Ninian added to the unrest, "And it seems Derian's brothers, all three of them, his own flesh and blood, have defected to the pirate trolls!"

The crowd moaned in disbelief.

"Hear me well, for there are members of the Underground among us—even standing beside you on this day!" The crowd became silent and seemingly suspicious. Ninian could not have better planned such a moment. "There are those who oppose Nantes, oppose Gaspard, oppose the co-regency, and even oppose the Great King himself."

"Burn the Underground!" someone called out.

"To hell with their anarchy!" another shouted. The crowd wailed and hissed.

"The Delaine sisters, Avlae and Jess, have asked for time to mourn their brother. They send blessings and greetings to you all." Ninian feared his subjects would find him completely incompetent should he also tell them about the missing girls. "I will grant their request that Derian be buried in the Reynes Isles, alongside the memorial of their great-grandfather. I will personally escort them to the isles."

"Hail! Queens of Nantes!" someone yelled. And a chant began, "Hail! Hail! Hail!"

"The weather warms, and the ice begins to thaw. It will only be days before we shall set sail for Reynes. When we return in the months ahead, our queens will greet you! They will meet with counsel and help to lead us against the Underground, against the pirate trolls, and out of these dark days!" Ninian surprised even himself with those last words. The crowd needed something to hope for. He was free now to do away with the name of Gaspard. And how easy it would be to conjure up a tale of an accident at sea that takes the lives of remaining heirs. "I bid you farewell."

At that, Ninian stepped away from the crowds, through the curtains, and made his way down a corridor. Two men joined his side.

"All is in order now," Ninian gloated.

"But the Delaine girls," Ezra buzzed. "We've no idea—"

"I bought you time to find them. So go! Find them!"

"Sire." Ezra nodded to accept the mission and walked ahead.

"And you!" Ninian stopped and turned to Medici. "Can you not render the spell complete?"

"I *have* ended the spell. The waters will soon be passable, as you have requested."

"How much longer must I wait?"

"Can you enlarge the sun to increase its heat, oh great king?" Medici mocked him.

Ignoring the sorcerer's pittances, Ninian continued, "In three days, I *will* sail to Orhe Mireth. I hear that pirates have gathered east of the city?"

Medici nodded.

"Now is the time. The people of Port Regael are vulnerable, so we must use this to our advantage. What of Mother?"

"She is here, in Nantes."

"Very good." Ninian wrung his hands. "Sophia will not be far behind."

SOPHIA
© 2020

Gifts at the Gate

52

ight from snow-covered lamps at the city gate silhouetted several men who stood watch. Sophia peered from the shadows of dense foliage thirty paces away.

She turned toward her guides and whispered, "Thank you all. This is where we part."

"But we have yet to make contact with the messengers," a troubled companion said.

"Trust, they will find me. I bid you farewell. May the Great King go with you."

Lifted by the wind, a flurry of snow swirled before her. She gathered her cloak, pulled cover over her head, and stepped onto the path. With a charm, she guided the spindrift to hide her approach. When she stood before the gates, she dismissed her guise. The sight of her dark form left the men scrambling for weapons. Two of the soldiers had her in their sights, their jittering thumbs locking the hammers. The others fumbled about, eyes betraying their terror.

"Hold it! What's your business here?"

Sophia did not answer. She merely looked down and waited below her hood. Lifting only her forearms with her palms toward the men, she paused as if to surrender.

"Identify yourself!"

In silence, she delayed—needing the full attention of each of them, she wanted the moment to reach a certain level of tension. Well, at least it was a balance between that and the possibility of trembling fingers accidentally pulling a trigger. The thought made her smile to herself.

Before anyone uttered another word, she lifted her chin and pulled back her hood. Their eyes widened, and their backs straightened. Falling naturally at ease, they lowered their guns. Her face grew warm and bright. Yet, her light was soft—the men did not squint. She held them in the light of her incandescent beauty. One by one, she searched their eyes.

And one of them finally spoke, "Sophia?"

"You know this woman?" another said, the first to take his eyes off her.

"Well, yes, I know her. I thought she—you—were dead."

"It is a ghost then. Do not let her speak!" the angry one sizzled.

Sophia did not grant him attention. She turned to the one she knew. "Hello, Ezra. I am no ghost." Sophia spoke confidently, hiding her uneasiness. Uncertain of Ezra's allegiance, she waited to see his next move. Certainly, among the king's inner men, there was a competition for her bounty. Would he arrest her?

"I watched your coffin arrive in Brazennose three years ago. I was among the mourners that..." Ezra spoke, bewildered.

"My coffin, perhaps, but not me. Now please, I have brought gifts, and I need passage through the city." Sophia reached into her satchel and withdrew a laurel wreath, its dark green leaves glossy in her light. If it were possible, the men's eyes might have widened even more. She stepped toward them with ease and placed a wreath on the head of the angry man who had first spoken. Then, returning to her satchel, she placed one on each of them.

Ezra's jaw hung open till he finally spoke, "You have been to the Province Beyond the—"

"Dead or alive, no one is allowed into Regael without a letter from the king." The angry one could not be swayed. He threw the wreath from his head. "Now," he looked right at her, "do you have your papers?"

In silence, Sophia waited to answer. Her aura of warmth encircled them. One by one, the wreaths began to melt. Fragrant oil fell over the faces of the men, bringing gladness to their gloom. These were costly gifts—she knew that each of them would be aware of this. Smiles displaced scowls…on all but one, anyway. The men rubbed the oil over their faces and around their necks. Their skin shined. Weariness was put at ease. It was not a spell. It was not a trick. She did not seek to woo them, only to give them rest and protection.

"It was a sorrowful day in the city, the day we laid you to rest. Yet, seeing you alive…While I don't know how, perhaps this could be why you are here now, arriving on yet another day of mourning." The others waited for Ezra to explain. "Friends, this is Sophia Gaspard."

One took a knee. "Forgive us, my lady."

"Our queen," another knelt to give homage.

One fell to his face and reached to cup her hand into his.

"*You?*" The rude one's eyebrows lifted with a curl of disbelief as he let out a laugh. "Queen of Nantes? I will give you passage, escorted in chains."

Ezra placed a hand on Sophia's shoulder. "It's Derian, is it not, Sophia? That is why you have come to the city. Did he know that you are alive?"

She began, "Well, I do need to speak with my son—"

"*Speak* with him?" asked Ezra. "Then, word has not reached you."

"Well, yes. He is to reign as king…"

All were silent.

Reluctantly, Ezra went on, "Your arrival has me perplexed. I do not know where you have been, my lady, nor how you have arrived alone at the gates of Port Regael. Please pardon me, but my first thought was that you have come because of Derian's death."

Her look must have spoken for her.

"Derian was murdered in the castle—"

"She is fooling you, Ezra. How much time will you give her to draw you in? If she is indeed who she says she is, then we'll let King Ninian decide."

"Enough, Maltoun. I know this woman. My eyes do not deceive me," Ezra said.

In a hushed voice, she said, "Even *I* was thought to be dead, yet here I stand before you. Could it be that there is more we do not know?"

Maltoun complained, "That, gentlemen, is enough to connect *her* to the Underground. Have you come to play us with your reproach of the king? What is this poison that runs down their heads?" He reached down and pushed his fingers through the oil on the ground where he had thrown his wreath. Examining the substance, he slid his thumb over his oily fingers. "To speak against the king is to speak for the Underground. This sedition is reason for arrest." He reached to take her but was met with resistance from the other men.

Calmly, Ezra said, "Let her speak."

Maltoun threw his arms away from their grasp. "I will not be had by this sorcery. You will all answer to King Ninian." Taking his keys, he let himself through the gate, leaving a clamor of steel behind. "You will all soon find yourselves begging for forgiveness."

Ezra glanced at one of his men. He turned his head, motioning for him to follow Maltoun.

"Ezra, I look to you for help. Long ago, we spoke of a day that would come. Please hear me based on what you know. The king himself pronounced me dead. Yet, I stand before you. I speak only what is true."

"I know a safe place."

That was the phrase she had waited for. Ezra was the messenger. Sophia told him, "I must go to the children and find Bela."

One of the other men broke in, "When the people see you, they will lay down their cloaks to make you a path to the castle."

Her eyes searched Ezra's as she spoke. "I fear that Aphrosyna is here, in Port Regael. It is now that we must look to the Great King. Our enemies will seek to close in around us, for there is more I know—"

Ezra broke in and ordered his companions, "Watch the gate!" Reaching for keys from his belt, he paused. His eyes locked back with Sophia's. "Can you feel that?"

The feeling was all too familiar—it rumbled within her chest, starting as a deep, vacillating throb, accompanied by a low, muffled bellow. Working its way up to her head, her eyes blurred, and she nearly lost her balance. Three times it came and went.

"Did you bring friends?" Ezra asked with a smile.

"Well, I was just getting to the part about the pirates."

"Let's go!"

Trembling, it took him several attempts to get his key into the lock. Sophia and Ezra sprang through the iron gates. The other men followed and raced to sound the alarms.

Closely behind Ezra, Sophia followed down dimly lit, slippery streets. Leaping forward through the snow and ice, she landed each step with care, anticipating a fall.

The peal of bells signaled the city of the looming threat of pirates. Lights began to flicker in windows above. Distracted and tumbling forward, she cried out. Ezra pulled her to her feet and escorted her quickly into a doorway. He held her tightly, then looked back the way they came and ahead to where they were going.

"Ezra, what—"

"I know why you are here, Sophia."

"You are hurting my arms!" Should she have trusted Ezra? Was he going to betray her to the king? Ezra forced her back and once again searched his surroundings.

Sophia blurted out, "Please, just tell me the children are safe."

"There is more I need to share now that we are alone. I was assigned to gather the children, to protect them from Ninian. Hear me well, for Derian is indeed dead. I am so sorry, Sophia." Ezra moved his hands to her shoulders.

Stifling her urge to weep, she raised her shaking hands and put them on the sides of Ezra's face. "I began to think that you betrayed me."

"Never."

"Go on then, Ezra. We will mourn Derian in time."

"Avlae and Jess are safe. I've had them sent to the northern slopes. It was too risky to take them to Olivetan."

"What of Bela?"

"She is with them. Now, you are aware that the king knows you are coming, and you were right to think that he has invited a special guest in your honor."

"Aphrosyna," Sophia answered.

"No doubt she will find you. Now, I cannot go back to the castle, for I fear Maltoun has heard too much. But, I have a commitment to my troops. We will meet soon."

"Be safe, Ezra."

"And may the Great King protect you. There will be many to save. Regael must not fall."

"Thank you, and know that the oil will protect you from Aphrosyna."

Ezra examined his surroundings one last time. "Torres will find you. Go with him."

"But I—"

"Whatever happens, go with Torres. Trust me! We've a plan to get you to the children."

He let her go and fled. Sophia leaned back into the doorway. *The girls are safe.* She massaged her frozen cheeks and pressed into her temples. *Focus.*

You've no business being here, Sophia… A voice floated around her, prickling her flesh. Pangs launched every direction in her gut. It had been three years since she had last heard that voice. It grew more intense. *Your mind is old…weak…fragile! I will gather your children, and they will watch you die!*

Sophia flicked away the threats as if they were bugs crawling on her skin, one at a time until she silenced them. Then she stepped back out onto the frozen road.

As Sophia reached the town square, more bells continued to ring out. One soldier arrived, huffing and out of breath. Then another soldier, and then many were clamoring past her in a jangle of sloshing boots and clattering supplies. At first, Sophia feared that they came to capture her, but she soon realized they sprang to their posts, not even concerned about who she might be.

A leaping shadow fled in the corner of her eye. Not wanting to lose it, she spun her head, attempting to stay slightly ahead of it. It eluded her focus until all at once she could see it straight on. Sophia watched a gloom so black that it contrasted the night. It took on the appearance of a park bench, a lamppost, a bird.

Mental torment began.

Hollow.

Helpless.

Hell.

Oozing from the darkness like a rotting wound, Aphrosyna's presence spurned Sophia's soul.

KING NINIAN III
© 2020

Betrayal

53

roning bells made King Ninian pause for only a moment. On the table before him, he lifted another parchment, adjusted his glasses, and continued his review. Two servants worked nearby, packing parchments and scrolls between old linen and sawdust in wooden crates.

"King Ninian!" a frantic voice broke from the doorway. It was his new regent, Maltoun. "Trolls invade from the east!"

Ninian rolled his eyes. "So I've heard," he said in a staid voice, not even looking up. *How many times have I asked not to be disturbed in the library?* He continued to carefully trace his finger over words he had read so many times before. "Where did I read it?" he mumbled to himself.

"My king, there is something else."

Ninian released a long sigh. Pirate trolls did not unsettle him, but Maltoun certainly did. There were tasks to complete. As of late, his mind had been troubled with the capture of the Delaine children, and now his plans for them were within reach. The ice could not melt quickly enough for him to sail. Once he found them, he would snatch them out of Port Regael and take them out on the sea, where there was no chance for escape.

Yet, currently, he was burdened by something he had read—a prophecy perhaps? These words had explained that there could come a time when the co-regency may end. *Either way, it is coming to an end and soon!* But if only he had those words from Gaspard... It did not matter the context. Gaspard's words pulled the weight and gave him the platform to bolster his claim. Of course, he would have plenty of time to read once they sailed. But, oh, how his mind would be settled to have it now.

"May I speak with you?" Maltoun's irksome voice interrupted again.

"You may." Ninian pulled another parchment from under the one he had been studying and continued his search.

"Alone?"

Irritated, Ninian set aside his work, pushed up from his chair, and ordered his servants. "Just pack all of them!" He gestured to the parchments he had been examining. "But mark the crate somehow, and I will continue my reading en route to Orhe Mireth. See to it that more empty cartons are brought to this room. You two will make sure that all of these are meticulously packed and delivered to my quarters aboard the Canberra."

"Yes, my king," one of them confirmed.

King Ninian escorted Maltoun just outside the library and motioned for him to explain.

Maltoun laced his fingers. Groaning, he looked past Ninian and down the hall. "Pirates have—"

"Are you unclear of your role as regent?" Ninian huffed and crossed his arms.

"No, sire."

"Then perhaps you can give me more information than what the bells have told me to justify this dilatory visit of yours."

"Sire?"

"Trolls do not concern me. You have the entire military force of Port Regael at your disposal."

"I do not intend to lose the city. Our weapons are in place, the troops are moving into position, and your council awaits your address, sire."

"I am growing weary—then, what do you want? My ship will depart the day after tomorrow." Ninian swatted at his coat, unable to find his pipe. He had no time for this conversation.

"There was a woman at the gate, and quite frankly…" Maltoun floundered to find a place for his hands. "She seems to have cast some kind of spell on those who guard the gate."

Frustration lit a boiler in Ninian's belly. "Yes, yes, go on!"

"It was Sophia, my king." Maltoun's words trailed off. His restless arms fell to his sides. "I believe Ezra has allowed her passage through the city."

"Good, good. Then he's done what I have requested."

"But, there is more…"

Ninian resisted the compulsion to strangle his regent. "Proceed."

"It's Ezra, sire. I do not trust him. He seems very close with Sophia."

"You feel he may be a spy for the Underground?"

"You did say that they are everywhere, sire."

Maltoun clenched his teeth and added ever so carefully, "Ezra is to escort Sophia to you as well." He avoided Ninian's eyes.

"Well then…" With both hands, Ninian clasped his overcoat and pulled it forward. Securing a button, he calmly instructed, "Send men to follow Ezra. Alert the posts."

Maltoun seemed to unruffle a bit, nodded, and stood straight. "Very good. And what of the—"

Lashing out, Ninian snatched him by the collar and lifting him from the floor. Now nearly chin to chin, Ninian spat, "See to it that no harm comes to Sophia. And when you do find her, have her followed at a distance. She will lead us to the children!" Ninian thrust Maltoun away. "Do not fail in your duties."

"Ezra will pay with his life," Maltoun spoke, suddenly confident. Promptly, he straightened his shirt, bowed, and stepped away from Ninian's presence.

Ninian proceeded to the war room, where some of his advisors awaited his address. Medici reclined at the table, while Ninian's men stomped over each other's words. One by one, the expletives ceased as they noticed him.

"I will hear each of you, but know that Regael will not fall. I have complete trust in Maltoun's abilities to overcome and outwit our invaders."

A hefty man with thick eyelashes at the opposite end of the table spoke first. His facial expressions lifted his brow, turning and twisting his glasses as he spoke. "My king, if we evacuate the city through the mountains and up the—"

King Ninian did not allow the man to finish his words. "Ailmere, I do not intend to evacuate Regael."

"People are begging to flee!" shouted another.

"Care for the women and children, fit the men to fight," Ninian spoke calmly and directly.

"And you will send them off to their deaths. We are no match for trolls!" Ailmere proclaimed. He stood, making himself the unofficial spokesperson for the group.

Who chose this man to take the place of Talicue?

The king waited and, as usual, took a moment to find his pipe deep within a pocket. Smoking helped to stop him from reacting. Instead, he told his men they were trying his patience by saying, "Men, I recognize the threat—"

"We know! Is this not why Medici sits among us?"

Silence. The king took a long draw off his pipe.

"His foul magic—"

"He brought these beasts here—"

"Has he taken hold of your mind—"

"Are you mad, Ninian?"

Their clamor filled the war room.

"Enough!" Ninian raged. "Know this, each of you. If you flee, you flee on your own. Who will protect you beyond the city gates? Yes, of course, Regael and even Nantes as a whole will suffer at the hands of the trolls; there is no doubt about that. Yet, I will triumph. No more of this nonsense!" Ninian glowered at his advisors. Very soon, one by one, he would have the members of this group eliminated. *Very soon.* "Now, I believe you all have soldiers to rally against our foe."

Each of the advisors left without a word. Medici stood and walked to the windows overlooking the city. Ninian joined him.

"Mother is close. Sophia is well within our grasp!"

"That is well and good, but it's Sophia's elusive nature that concerns me. Your mother will certainly help to keep her occupied for some time, adding to the drama of my victory, for sure."

"But it is because of my mother that she now comes to us," Medici boasted. "My mother will snare her. She has no hope of fleeing again!"

Ninian threw his pipe across the room and exploded, "Mother cannot touch her!"

Medici cowered in silence.

"You know that I am right, Medici, though you would never admit it. Aphrosyna can lead men away, even delude entire cities. She can turn men into beasts, but she has no sway over Sophia. You know this well. Sophia comes to counter Aphrosyna's spell. Sophia is key to my victory, but it is her children we must dangle before her now. She'll save Port Regael, but she will not leave without her children. We need her to come to us."

"Then, what do you wait for?" Medici shouted. "Expose the children!"

Ninian laughed loudly. "Friend, you speak in haste. You are far too careless." Medici tried to speak, but Ninian raised his hand to stop him. "Hear me now, for the children have proven to be elusive as well."

"Then we have been set up. You fool of a king! Sophia may already have the children."

"No, no, no. You must wait and watch. Follow Ezra, for he will be with Sophia and will lead you to the children. If any of my men get in your way, kill them. I am growing more uncertain about which of them I can trust." Ninian chuckled to himself, wishing now that he had not thrown his pipe. "However, do not move too early. If Sophia knows you're watching, she will die before she gives up the children. Do not let that happen!"

Medici folded his hands and turned away. "Very well."

"One more thing," Ninian fussed. "Following tonight, you will end this rampage of trolls. Poison them, curse them, strike them down however you wish. They are such a nuisance."

Medici groused. That was enough for Ninian to know he understood.

"I have cared for the family of Gaspard. All have seen it and know it. The heirs have made a triumphant return and soon will meet a tragic end. Nantes will raise me up as sovereign king. The co-regency will be irremediably severed. All will look to me now. I am their savior!"

Temptation

54

ophia…

The haunting whisper of a woman's voice came from all sides and repressed her. Though a mere whisper, it bore into her ears like a scream. Sophia clasped the sides of her head and fell to her knees. With the heels of her hands, she pushed against her eyelids in an attempt to clear her mind.

Abruptly, she was struck from behind. Driven to the ground, her head slammed against the brick street. She spit blood from her lower lip and wiped the slush from her cheeks.

Clops, stomps, and snorts threatened her from above. She rolled onto her back—the evil was upon her in the shape of a horse. Suddenly, a soldier wielding a sabre stepped up.

"My lady, we're here to protect you!" he called out.

"Get away!" she tried to warn him. "You mustn't even touch—"

Another soldier attempted to grab the reigns of the wild stallion but stumbled forward and toppled to the ground. In a cloud of black haze, half of the horse's torso was whisked away.

"It's a ghost!" the one with the sabre cried out.

The soldier on the ground trembled. His eyes bulged. "Help me!" He shook and shuddered. "Fire…I'm on fire!"

Sophia recognized the spell. A blaze grows from within. Rolling and flopping over the ground, the man drenched himself in snow, seeking to soothe the burning. At first, he seemed relieved, using the snow as a salve. But Sophia knew the worst was yet to come. After a hellish scream, the man fell unconscious. Heat from his body melted the snow and ice, steam rose from the water welling around him.

Seizing Sophia's attention, the black shadow of a stallion walked forward from the haze, seemingly whole again—and yet not quite the same. The creature reared, and its hind legs shortened. Its front legs reached high and grew claws. The hair of the horse's mane spread all over the body of what was now a bear. Glazed, solid black eyes cast hate. Its head contorted and shook, snarling through dripping saliva. Rifle fire exploded, and the round pierced the bear as it would a cloud of smoke.

"Run!" Sophia cried. Bruising her elbows, she pulled herself backward on the brick street, slipping over icy patches. The one who had pulled the trigger stood dazed. His eyes shifted to his fallen friend. Sophia warned, "Run! You cannot help him now."

Another shot detonated, and the soldier before her toppled over. Sophia lifted her arms and groaned as she caught the body and thrust him aside. Someone had tried to shoot the bear from behind, but the iron ball had passed through the apparition, killing the soldier instead.

Sophia sprang to the first man who still lay suffering from the spell. Contusions had already begun. The man writhed upon the ground. She fell upon him to hold him still and quickly drew a glass flask from her satchel. Pouring oil over his head, she prayed silently that it was not too late to counter the spell. "Shhh…slow your breaths," Sophia pleaded, wiping the man's face.

Fiery snarls licked at her ears. Its shadow lifted, obscuring the nearest light. Its claw fell as if to split her in two. She stood tall and lifted her chin as the ghostly appendage passed through her. "You cannot touch me, Aphrosyna!"

Poising eloquently, Aphrosyna altered her appearance from a bear to that of a woman. Stepping forward from a shadow cloud, her pale skin glowed against her ebony gown. White patterns decorated a transparent scarf that shaped her narrow head. Thin, dark brown eyebrows peaked above her diamond eyes.

Melting snow dripped from Sophia's face. She clenched her fists. Trembling, she called, "Your spell has no sway over me!"

As delicate as lace, Aphrosyna spoke, "No, but you have come back, Sophia. That is enough for Ninian." Her crimson lips formed a saccharine smile. "He will not delay your death." She stepped nonchalantly past Sophia.

"Your words are empty," Sophia warned.

"And who will help *you*?" Aphrosyna spun around, her long, black fingernail only niks from Sophia's face. "Pirates have come to your doorstep. You have saved many for sure. Do you think you will save Port Regael? Do you think they will turn to you when trolls threaten the honor of Ninian?"

"They will defend the honor of Nantes!" Sophia cried. She understood Ninian's ploy to draw her back to the city. *Ninian will be watching. I must be cautious.*

The square began filling with people. Women and children ran in the direction of the castle. Soldiers arrived, their carts filled with guns and ammunition. They began to arm men in the streets.

Aphrosyna's shoulders were pushed forward by the curling of her back. Her face shriveled, and her clothes became rags. She stooped forward and limped hesitantly, as if she were blind. "You all must flee! How will you fend off the trolls?" she called out. Above the chaos, her voice traveled on the wind through the city streets.

"Do not fear! Defend your city!" Sophia's voice carried as well, filling the square and echoing down alleyways.

"We must leave these forsaken lands! The pirate trolls will have no mercy!" Aphrosyna pleaded. Many heard and fled for the castle. Several came running to help the old woman.

"You must come with me, for protection," a soldier instructed.

"Help me," she begged.

"Please!" Sophia interrupted. "To arms. I will care for the woman."

"She needs help now," the man said and reached for Aphrosyna. His arms went right through her, unable to take hold. Evoked by Aphrosyna's spell, others panicked and ran to the aid of the old woman.

"To the locks! The ice will thaw. Sail away. Flee while you can, or the pirates will come for you!" Aphrosyna cried in dire, wailing tones. She crept about, wobbling on her crooked stick.

"We are defeated!" one man called, and those who were swayed began to flee.

But they did not make it far. Sophia's ears ached with cries as Aphrosyna's spell took its effect. The men who had tried to help the old woman began to spin in confusion. Blue and purple patches appeared on their skin, as if they had been pummeled by rocks. It was now only a matter of minutes before Port Regael would have trolls growing inside the city walls.

"Do not submit to fear! Save your land, and I will care for the woman," Sophia pleaded with those who would hear. She countered

Aphrosyna, "Look to reason, find discernment in your heart! The locks are frozen. The king will not desert you. Stand for Regael!" Sophia found herself defending even Ninian.

Aphrosyna began to crawl on the street, reaching out her hand for aid. Men came one after another to help her up. And one by one, they stumbled away in a stupor, immediately subdued by her incantation. Scores of men began fleeing the square.

Sophia again called, "Take heart, take courage! Uphold your city!" Her voice fell from above, as though she stood on the city walls.

Sophia ran to a soldier who had fallen nearby, whose clothes began to bulge. She reached into her satchel and removed another laurel wreath, placing it on his head. His body shook. Muscles began to knot under the skin of his neck. She closed her eyes as the warmth from her face melted the wreath, and she spread oil over his face and neck. Soon he was able to stretch out from his cramped posture. She had reversed the spell.

Clasping his chest, the man seemed to wrestle himself into consciousness. "What happened?" He paused. "What have you done? You saved me!" The man lay on the ground, heaving breaths, his uniform soaked with sweat and snow.

"Hear my words and keep them in your heart. Fix your eyes ahead, honor your city, and do not flee. Protect your women and children."

With that, the soldier stood and began to rally men to himself. "To the gates!"

Despite the old women's cries, men now left her in Sophia's care.

Yet, now Aphrosyna's hair began to grow long and wavy as she walked away from Sophia. Ragged clothes fell away, her bare skin young and radiant. Whisking a silk cloak out of the air, she covered herself. As she reached a corner house, lights in the windows began to glow with warmth. Aphrosyna spun around, lifting her chin and throwing her hair back. Her arms stretched outward, pushing against the doorframe on either side. Her cloak fell to her feet, exposing her shapely body. She was no longer a mere wisp of smoke. She had taken on physical form. With the index finger on one hand, she traced an invisible line up her thigh—and with the other, she beckoned men to herself.

This time she multiplied. Women appeared throughout the square, dropping their clothes and lifting their breasts. Like sirens, they seized men as they passed, kissing and caressing them. And as Aphrosyna spoke, so did each of the women. "With silk sheets, I have opened my bed to you. I have poured out sweet spices. Come with me! We will fulfill our passions till the dawn. The city is lost. You'll not survive the night. Take me and lie with me!" Men crowded doorways, even attempted to crawl through the upper windows.

Throwing her voice in the path of the winds, Sophia called, "Hear my words—keep your honor, for it is of more worth than gold! Fly to the gates! Fortify your city!"

For many, it was too late. To embrace the women was to embrace death itself. Screams told of agony like no other. Men jumped from windows as quickly as they entered. They rolled across the ground as if on fire. Their limbs contorted and stretched. War broke out in the streets around the square. Scores of men had suffered the spell. Soldiers pulled triggers on fellow soldiers, defending themselves from pirate trolls growing before their eyes.

Sophia ached and wept. Her shoulders slumped. Helplessness set in. Alone she stood amidst the frenzy. She closed her eyes, unable to bear the misery, but suddenly cold iron stung her wrist, and her body was jerked backward.

Sophia spread her heels to catch herself, and her eyes flew open. "Torres, what are you doing?"

"You will come with me!"

With her free hand, Sophia grabbed a flask from her satchel. She pulled the cork with her teeth and poured oil over her right wrist. Then, spinning her hand and pulling hard, she wrenched it from the iron shackle with a shriek of pain. The bone in her thumb snapped, and pain rushed over her body.

Immediately, Sophia scuttered away, lifting her voice, "Defend your city!" Then louder, "Look to courage!" And like wind shaking trees, "Honor your king!"

Over the calamity, her words fell like ten thousand charms, enabling resistance to the provocative spell. Many now fled to Sophia. Instinctively, men crowded around her and cupped their hands. Endlessly, oil poured from her small flask. No fewer than one hundred men were given healing ointment. The more it was shared, the less it took to spread healing.

As a disembodied spirit, Aphrosyna leapt above the city. Like angry clouds, she threatened the masses. "Sail far from these lands! You will never last…" Fading, her words became mere rumblings of thunder growing farther and farther away.

Soldiers now surrounded Sophia, yet she called joyfully, "Folly will not lead you astray! Folly will not lead you astray!"

High above, Aphrosyna had gathered herself at the peak of the city. With a shriek of anguish, she threw herself down and disappeared, filling the streets with a choking fog. For a moment, all remained still—no movement nor breeze. Then there was pounding, clamor, and uproar. Men and horses pushed onward and rushed forward to protect the city from the invading pirate trolls.

Sophia's legs gave way to exhaustion, and she fell into the arms of Torres. Her night had just begun. Torres held her fast, binding her with chains.

I must get to the children.

Aarn's Blight

55

From the safety of the wood, Aarn reveled in the siege before him. Scores of pirate trolls scaled the wall of Port Regael with an ease reminiscent of jumping a garden fence. The assault was swift and oppressive, and he commanded it all. Without time to prepare a counterattack, battered soldiers dropped from the wall.

Regael will fall. I am taking what is rightfully mine—the throne of Nantes, the writings of Great-Grandfather, and with those writings, the treasure. My brothers have betrayed me. They will know nothing of mercy. I will trample upon them along with the rest of the city. Philor is a coward. I'll make him sorry he fled.

Cannon fire fractured the thick wall of his thoughts. Spooked by the blasts, the creature he sat upon sidestepped, nearly tripping over its six legs. Aarn tugged hard with both hands on the butt of his rifle. At the far end of its short barrel was a goad hooked into an iron ring, which was attached to the leather collar that was strapped around the neck of the bukavac. The beast jerked him forward. Pulling back against the reins, Aarn prodded the creature beneath him.

The weapon Aarn wielded served many purposes. Controlling the animal while keeping one's sights forward was all that concerned him for the moment. Some of the weapons had a hook on the end of the barrel, while others had an axe. Aarn particularly liked the crossbow combination but did not have the strength to pull the arrow into place.

The stock of the rifle was crescent-shaped with a hidden trigger, flush with the curve of the wood. The trigger became accessible when the gun was cocked. Though sized to fit the hand of a troll, with two hands, Aarn could manage.

After regaining his balance, Aarn reached forward and scratched the creature on the nape of its neck while speaking to it, "You'll get used to that. This is just the beginning." He spoke as if the beast could understand.

Though not as bulky as the bears of Nantes, the bukavac were taller and faster. It had six spindly but powerful legs. Its short, solid torso had a texture and shape not unlike that of a pig—tough grayish or tan skin with thin, wiry hairs. Its neck and head were the width of its body and level with its backbone. Narrow eyes sank beneath its thick, wrinkled brow. Razor-sharp teeth—far too many to count—lined its extended gums.

Aarn poised high upon the bukavac, nearly two rods from the ground, his rifle aimed forward between two long, gnarled horns. Another beast stepped up.

"King Gaspard, I have received word that…"

King Gaspard. His hands found a firm grip on his rifle. He was in control. The throne belonged to him, and he was ready to take command of the kingdom. Pirates were clearing him a path to the castle doors. Soon his army would lift him to the throne.

"…more pirates are arriving. They will cross the ice from the northwest and lay siege over the frozen bay into the city," Ipabog said.

In the language of the trolls, *Ipabog* meant *man of the hunt*. Ipabog had said his ancestors were from Calbha Mor. He had also boasted that he was the one responsible for the pirate attack on Nantes. Aarn was not so sure. He doubted that Ipabog was the sole architect of this coup. The pirates seemed only to tolerate him, and none were willing to allow him to lead. At times, he even seemed fearful of them. Aarn was certain there was another connection.

Twice during their short journey, Ipabog had gone missing for over half the day. Both times, Aarn began to think he had abandoned them, but just when he became overly frustrated with his inability to communicate with the trolls, Ipabog had returned. Despite Aarn's apprehension of Ipabog, he addressed Aarn as King Gaspard. Very soon, all would be calling him king.

Since Philor had run off, Aarn was the one from whom the pirates now sought information. It was him they needed now. Without him, they had nothing. He was the only heir that mattered.

Ipabog's voice became urgent, "You need to come with me, my king."

"What do you mean? The attack has begun. They will call for me at any moment!" Aarn said, making it known that he was put off.

"There is someone you must meet, sire. Please, only come back into the shadows." Ipabog pleaded with his hands.

Who would seek audience with the king at such a time?

Aarn gave a huff of contempt. "You have lost your senses. It will not be long, for I am about to take my throne."

"Please, a new matter is at hand. I would not take you away from your victory. You are king, whether you sit on a throne in Port Regael or sleep in the frozen marshlands of Navarre. Nothing will change what is true, sire. Now please, I beg you, this requires your immediate decision."

"Very well, but know that soon, I will have advisors to handle these menial tasks." Aarn turned his beast away from the onslaught and followed Ipabog into the shadows of the forest.

Searching his memory for any clues to what this might be about, Aarn's mind raced. Ahead, he could make out the shape of a man among the silhouettes of the trees. He unhooked his rifle and dismounted the *buke*, as he had gotten used to calling it.

"Lower your weapon, my king," Ipabog warned.

"I will not," Aarn answered. He stepped high through thick grasses laid flat from snow.

As they walked, Ipabog leaned in closely to Aarn, speaking in a harsh whisper, "This man is here to report to you. He is our spy."

"You have said nothing of a spy," Aarn chided. "Why have you kept this from your king?"

"Please, sire, hear your servant's report," Ipabog begged, bowing again and again.

Aarn raised his sights to the dark figure. "Let me see your hands."

The man lifted his arms away from his sides.

"You'd have done well, Ipabog, to inform your king of those in his service," Aarn said, making sure the mystery man could hear him.

"I have—" Ipabog began but was cut off.

"I am here to report, my king," the dark figure said. He dropped to a knee before Aarn and raised his hands high. His head fell forward, conceding his allegiance, and he waited in silence.

First one, then another bead of sweat trickled down Aarn's forehead. He prayed his apprehension would go unnoticed. Yet, ever so slightly, his arms began to tremble.

"Speak!" Aarn ordered. "I will not lower my weapon!"

"As you wish, sire." Keeping his arms raised, the man in black lifted his head. "You must end this attack, my king."

"You are mad," Aarn retorted. He regripped his rifle and stomped his feet, securing his stance.

Desperately, Ipabog pleaded, "King Gaspard, please hear your servant. You must understand that we had to be certain of this information. Suppose you had run off like your brother? This attack has proven your loyalty."

That was enough for Aarn to know he was respected. His anxiety left him. "Do not doubt me again," Aarn warned, glaring at Ipabog. He quickly turned back to the mystery man. "Go on then, *spy*. Do you have a name?"

"Cid Mei, sire. I've come to advise you regarding recent events."

Behind Aarn, a round of blasts and accompanying explosions lit the wood, allowing him a glimpse of Cid Mei's face. Muscles tightened throughout Aarn's body. He fought against his urge to draw back, relieved that no one could see how fearful he must have looked. The spy's face was contorted, stretched with age, and... and...*evil.*

Determined to suppress his panic, he stood tall and stepped forward, looking down on the spy. "Then, do tell me, Cid Mei. What have you to report that would convince me to retreat from my victory?"

"Please don't hear me wrong, sire. We do not flee from Ninian. Think of it more as a strategic maneuver," Cid Mei said with a snicker in his voice.

"And leave behind the writings of Gaspard? We'll not find the treasure without them!" Aarn argued. For the first time, Aarn lowered his rifle and felt as though he could bash Cid Mei over the head.

Cid Mei lowered his arms and with his palms up claimed, "That is why I come before you, sire."

"My brother, Derian, delivered Gaspard's parchments to Ninian. I will take them back! Even if I have to kill Ninian himself to do so."

"My king, I am sorry to report that Derian is already dead, and the writings were not among his belongings." A faint blue luster appeared from Cid Mei's quivering hands.

Aarn's stomach twisted. Heat flashed over his head. "That can't be. Don't take me to be a fool!"

Strands of sapphire curled from Cid Mei's begging hands. "Sire, Derian's crate was empty. I watched as it was opened. Not long afterward, Derian was thrown to his death. The—"

"Are you saying that Ninian is responsible for my brother's murder?"

"No, sire. Please hear me." Drawing back his left hand, Cid Mei coiled his fingers. "For there is more. It was the Underground. They also came for the writings. When the Underground realized Derian had nothing, they wasted no time seeing to his demise."

Cid Mei reached out with his luminous right hand, which somehow seemed to channel sympathy—Aarn's temples prickled. But like cobwebs, the sensation stretched down his neck with intensifying heat. In a flare, the ardor lit the nerves of his arms like fire!

Aarn seethed. Then, he put the pieces together. "That is why Wesley returned to Navarre. He has joined the Underground. He wants the throne for himself!"

"The Underground pursues the treasure, my lord."

"What else do you know, spy?"

"My king, I have received reports that members of the Underground have been hiding at Merchant's Pass. They may already have the writings. We are now tracking a small group of men who, earlier this evening, set off from a hiding place just outside Port Regael, not far from here. They will lead us to your great-grandfather's writings! They are quickly fleeing east."

Inside, Aarn raged, but his composure remained as stone. Derian was dead. Ninian did not have what he came for. He did not need Port Regael to establish his throne. He would hunt down the Underground.

He looked to Ipabog. "Call the pirates out of Regael. We move east!"

The Incursion
of Trolls

56

Ezra led his men down empty, dark streets, snaking their way to the front lines. The sound of mortar fire racked the air around them. Somewhere nearby, desperate soldiers heaved gruff commands. The wailing bellows from trolls sought to steal his courage. Then, explosions were followed by avalanching stone.

Ezra's troops hid themselves in the cross streets. Once in position, Ezra waited for the signal. At last, a flare launched overhead. This was their time. Ezra and his men needed to intercept the trolls before they could fall upon the soldiers who were reloading the mortars.

A scout ahead signaled that there were nine trolls. Ezra searched the faces of his men. All of them were focused, ready to move. Ezra had eight pairs of men. In each pair, one carried the fire lance mounted to a long plank, and the other held a burning wick. Five other men were ready with sabres. Ezra's heart throbbed in his ears, and his fingers tightened around the hilt of his sabre. With his other hand, he motioned for the first wave to go. Four pairs of men shifted as one, leaving the cross street onto the main road between the mortars and the approaching trolls.

"They are giants!" a soldier yelled.

"Stay focused!" Ezra answered.

It had been years since Ezra stared up at a pirate—now nine of them were running toward him and gaining speed. Each man with a plank jabbed a pointed end down into a snowbank. They clung to handles steadying the boards, which they balanced on their backs. Others waited to light the fuse.

"Fire!"

The lances exploded one after the other. The sheer intensity of the sound forced Ezra's eyes closed. When he opened them again, smoke clouded around him, then dissipated. Of the nine, not a single pirate troll was standing.

The men with lances and wicks withdrew and began to reload while the next wave entered the streets. Ezra pulled his sabre from its sheath and ran with the others among the downed trolls. Several of the pirates coiled in pain. Shards of iron had torn deep into their faces, arms, and legs. Others lay motionless. Either way, soldiers lopped off the heads and moved to the opposite side of the street. Next, they retreated again into the shadows. Ezra lit off a flare to alert others that his troops were clear. With that, the mortars resumed on the main road.

Ezra once again moved his men forward. Between flares and mortars, he repeated the same offensive strategy. Finally, it happened that fire lances were not a match for the increasing troll army. Ezra found himself in a duel.

He was fired upon by a combination musket, battle-axe. When the pirate missed his mark, Ezra charged him with his sabre. It was a foolish thing to do, but he had nowhere else to go. Full-on, Ezra ran and leapt aside, avoiding a strike from the axe. Before the troll could reposition his weapon, Ezra thrust his sword, piercing the pirate below his shoulder blade. The troll stretched tall and hollered.

Clinging to his sabre, Ezra was lifted from the ground. Hanging, Ezra twisted the blade. At last, the beast lost his strength and fell.

Hitting the ground, Ezra's knees buckled. With no time to move, the pirate troll collapsed on top of him. Smothered, Ezra strained to get air into his lungs. *What a foolish way to die!*

Though it felt like minutes, it was actually only seconds before the dead weight was rolled off. His men, once they saw he was alive, burst into laughter. Ezra sucked in a deep breath. Then, coughing and hacking, he clenched his ribs against stabbing pains. After catching his breath, Ezra sniggered with a rueful smile, partly because he was glad to see his smiling comrades. But mostly because there were so many trolls crowding them now, and death was imminent.

Respite to Revolution

57

So my father, while I was pushing against him with all the might that a seven-year-old girl could exert, carried me the entire length of the ridge."

Sophia laughed and was glad for a time of respite, however brief. She and Torres anticipated Ezra's arrival at any moment. Covered in heavy blankets, they waited in the windowless upper room of the west gatehouse. They waited even to light a candle.

"I've heard so much about your father. He endured much strife for your family's safety, and here you are," Torres said.

She knew he was referring to how she was just like her father—all she was risking by coming back to Port Regael. It was the last place she wished to be, but it was also the place she needed to be right now.

"I've seen these same qualities in Avlae," Torres said.

"You love her," Sophia answered gently.

"She has held my affection for a long time. I have loved her from a distance. We could not risk meeting together. We continue to write to each other, but I burn her letters. When I write, I encourage her to do the same. But that's not the worst of it. Even when speaking to Avlae, I have had to remain silent about the

Underground and all I know of her and her family, things she didn't know until the last few days."

"How the heart longs for truth. But now all will change."

Both remained silent for some time.

"Thank you, again, for coming to my aid, Torres. I expected to be back under some new concoction of Medici's spells by now."

"Sorry if I may have jumped in a bit too soon."

"All the more convincing for Aphrosyna to witness."

Sophia nearly dropped her sconce. The sound of an opening door came from the room below. Footsteps climbed the stairs, followed by a pattern of knocks on the door. Torres stood, turned the lock, and pulled. A light appeared, illuminating Ezra's smiling face.

"You look terrible," Sophia said, and when he was close enough, she pressed her lips against his cheek. Ezra closed the door and lit Sophia's candle with his own.

"I didn't expect you so soon," Torres said.

"The pirates are withdrawing, but not pleasantly."

"You mean *retreating*."

"I wish that were so. Having lost all my strength, I was waiting for my own death at the hand of the trolls when a call rose among them. It traveled through the troll regiments—a shout commanding to pull out of the city. We continued our bombardment, and soldiers chased them away. Celebration has already begun in the courtyard. But let's not be fooled. Something called them away. They do not run scared…" Ezra paused. "They run in pursuit."

"They must have discovered that Gaspard's writings are not here," Sophia said.

"But how?" Torres asked.

"Medici," Sophia replied. "It has to be him."

"Does he not work for the king? Whose side does he take?" Torres seemed baffled.

"His own side," Ezra answered. "If they know the writings are not here—"

"They are in pursuit of the Underground. We must get word to Olivetan." Sophia reached for her satchel. "It's time."

Ezra took Sophia by the shoulder to restrain her haste. "There is more you have to hear. Please listen."

Like a poison, worry spread through Sophia's veins. "The time is short, Ezra. We know what we must do. Olivetan will be waiting—"

Ezra interrupted, "By now, Ninian will know that I have betrayed him. I've been reckless in these final hours."

"But the children are safe, for you did what was necessary," Sophia encouraged him.

"Yes, and that is why they're after me." Ezra leaned back, his shoulders sinking.

"What do you mean?" Torres asked.

"I was followed to this tower."

Torres became livid. "And yet you've led them to us?"

Sophia broke in, "The king knows I am in the city, so it matters not. He will have people watching everywhere."

"We can be sure they will be waiting for us. But I believe we can make it to the dungeon and escape with Olivetan," Ezra said.

"Then, we must be ready," Torres stated.

"Do pray that Olivetan is ready as well," Sophia added.

"Indeed," Ezra agreed. "Now, this is what we will do…"

edici was glad to have ended the winter spell. His bones were cold, and he knew of no spell to warm them. Of course, he could conjure up a fire and stay warm aboard his ship, but now was not the time. He dared not entrust this task to another.

Sophia was close. Somehow, he sensed it. It was a dreadful feeling, like when she looked at him, unafraid. It made him feel... small. Like a speck in a pile of waste. His fingers prickled—even began to glow—as he pondered a spell of death. But he quickly hid them away so as not to give away his intentions.

Ninian is foolish to wait. "She must be kept alive," Ninian had said. *Well, no more. Sophia and the children will die. I will kill them all.*

From his hiding place, he watched the door of the west gatehouse creep open. Two hooded figures veiled in long, dark cloaks slid out from the doorway. The first took the second by the hand, and they moved through the city gate into a growing celebration.

"They're moving toward the castle," Medici said and ordered soldiers behind him. "You three, lock down the gates. Post men to stand watch. No one leaves the outer courtyard."

The three immediately went on their way.

Medici turned to five others. "Spread out and follow them. If you are noticed, hold back, yet continue to steer them to the southeast entrance. Once they are inside the lower eastern walls, do not hesitate to kill Sophia and drag Ezra to me!"

Medici and his men crept out into the street to the gate tower. One at a time, they wove themselves into the lively assembly. Tall enough to see over the crowd, Medici watched the cloaked pair meander through the gathering. It seemed they were in no hurry. Stopping for a pint of ale and then another, they leisurely drank, chatting with those around them. Even taking time to dance, they were pulled in by others and spun in circles around fires.

Medici grew aggravated. He pulled his hood tight. Ezra and Sophia were tarrying on like children. Too many people jounced about, running into him and even reaching for his hands, attempting to whirl him into the jubilee.

"Leave me be," Medici threatened and yanked his arms away. "Fools!"

Medici scorned them from below his hood. Sophia would not make a mockery of him again. The thought of her murder satisfied him. No more useless spells. Sophia would not fight her way out of death. With Sophia out of the way, his mother's work could not be resisted, and village after village would fall to Aphrosyna's sway.

It seemed that Ezra and Sophia took notice of one the soldiers who had stepped a bit too close. Indeed, Ezra even went so far as to pull his hood back a bit, seeming to offer a bit of whimsical humor. The cloaked person's profile revealed his sizable nose and a long smoking pipe. The man removed the pipe from his mouth and nodded at the soldier's recognition.

"You'll soon be mine, Ezra," Medici mumbled.

But is that Ezra? He shared the pipe with the smaller person next to him. *Sophia?* Then he turned and scanned the crowd. Looking directly at Medici, the man lowered his hood. It was indeed Ezra. Taunting Medici, he lifted his pint as if offering good cheer. Tilting back, he drank long enough to finish his ale. Then, he jerked his chin up in Medici's direction. *Does he think he can taunt me?* Sophia remained seated, puffing away on the pipe, blowing billows of smoke.

Medici did not flinch. He signaled for his men to stay put. *Enjoy your smoke and ale. All too soon you will be chained and tormented in the dungeons of Regael Castle, and Sophia will be dead.*

Ezra turned back and lifted his hood over his head. He took the pipe from Sophia and helped her up from where she sat. He placed her hand in his, and they continued toward the castle. Ezra kept checking over his shoulder, but Sophia never looked back. Medici motioned for his men to push ahead. With a quickening pace, Medici shoved aside those in his way.

Now only twenty steps behind the couple, Medici and his men had them surrounded at the east gate to the inner courtyards. Ezra stopped before the sentry to retrieve and display his papers. The sentry gave his approval and signaled for the gate to be opened.

Chains rattled, and the black iron gate lifted—one quarter of the way…half…Medici lengthened his strides. Ezra pushed Sophia through and drew a pistol from his cloak. Now a mere five paces away, Medici seized a woman in front of him to use as a shield.

Ezra pushed his gun into the sentry's chest and pulled the trigger. A rushing chaos erupted among the crowd and pushed back against Medici. Enflamed with rage, he tossed the woman aside and thrashed his way forward against flailing limbs. He lunged over the bloodied sentry and chased through the eastern gate.

Into the Reins
of Regael

59

Bearing the weight of the tree that stretched upward from his palms once again proved to be too much for Wesley. Just like last time, the giant came to his aid. Huge palms and fingers rested below Wesley's hands. The burgeoning tree grew broad and bushy. Birds arrived in brilliant harmony, hopping from limb to limb. They flew back and forth, retrieving grasses, strings, and sticks to build their nests. Buds burst into bloom—more colors than he could name. All began to grow brighter, brighter…

The echoing clank of a metal latch chased the birds away. The spectacle fractured, and he fell into consciousness like one would fall over backward in a chair.

Seated upright, Wesley's back pressed against the stone wall. He reached to rub the back of his throbbing head. Straining against the weight of his eyelids, he saw the blurry likeness of a man pulling open the iron bars to his cell. The sound of scraping metal resounded within his chamber.

Has Derian betrayed me to King Ninian? Will I be escorted to Regael Cave? Put on a ship? Sent off to a place where no one will ever find me? A place where I'll never find my way back? Will I see my sisters again? My brothers? My father?

"Take me to King Ninian. I can explain, he will understand!" Wesley's voice was hoarse, but even knowing how frail he sounded did not deter him. He shook his wrists, rattling chains to augment his muffled shouts. His chest swiftly rose and fell with heaving breaths. "I will lead him to the Underground! This is not over. I am loyal to Nantes! I am Gaspard's heir!"

For a moment, the man said nothing in return. Then, he spoke, "And what do *you* know of Gaspard, boy?"

"I know he is my—" Wesley stopped. He knew that voice.

The man spoke again, "I see the king has restored you to the throne."

He sought to respond, but his lips stuck together, obscuring his voice. "Ol–live–tan…"

Olivetan reached forward, took hold of Wesley's forearms, and lifted him to his feet. Wobbling, Wesley leaned back, his legs numb and weak.

"Tip your head back," Olivetan said. "And open up!"

Water flowed over Wesley's cracked lips, across his shriveled tongue, then seeped down his constricted throat. He coughed and spat at first, but soon he swallowed with ease.

Suddenly, his insides felt like his legs. "My great-grandfather's writings…" Wesley sputtered. "Do you have them?"

"I promise you, they are safe."

"So, you *have* stolen them. You deceived me! Derian was right. Are you going to kill me?"

"Why would I kill you? I'm rescuing you." Olivetan lifted iron chains and wrenched a key inside the rusty locks.

"What have I left? What of the hope of Gaspard, the restoration of the co-regency? Derian has condemned me. It seems King

Ninian has condemned me! All I've anticipated, all I've dreamed... Who will hear me?" Clangoring chains piled at Wesley's feet.

"Do you *want* to be rescued?"

"And so, I should just entrust myself to you?"

"Do you have an alternate plan?"

Wesley did not want to believe that Derian had abandoned him, that Ninian had given up on him. Yet, Olivetan was the only one who seemed to want to help him.

"Look, our time is short," Olivetan said. "The tide will not wait for us."

"Tide? Where are you taking me? Will we go to my mother?"

"I have much to share, but right now we must flee, unless you'd like to stay. Do you expect Ninian to come for you soon?" Olivetan turned to leave and had one foot out of the cell when Wesley lurched ahead and seized his arm.

"Wait...wait. My sisters and Derian, they are here... somewhere...in the castle. I cannot leave them."

"And I would not leave them behind. Passage has been arranged for your sisters."

Passage where? Will we be together again?

Olivetan turned and knelt down, looking eye to eye with Wesley. "We must be on our way. Trust me."

Wesley was caught between two minds, but no more. Derian had never returned. Ninian had never called on him. Olivetan came for him. No more wavering. He could be loyal to Gaspard and trust Olivetan.

Wesley limped forward, following Olivetan out of the cell. He stopped short of a downed soldier, flat out on the stone floor. A giant hand came around him from his right side and lifted him over the body. Before Wesley could recover from what he saw, all at once he was tucked up and underneath the arm of some kind of giant. This was not like the dream!

"Whoa! Olivetan!" Wesley shrieked.

Olivetan glanced back but kept moving. "Oh, I forgot to mention the pirate troll. He's with us, no need to worry!"

Wesley was not reassured. He refused to look up and see what was carrying him. Like a thick snake, the giant's arm constricted around his torso. Wesley's arms were crunched up tightly, and his shoulders were pressed into the sides of his jaw. Bouncing down a gradual descent over crags and pits, Wesley's legs flopped about. Peering out, he could only catch glimpses of what they were passing. A cell to his left, another on the right, then two more on his left…

How many are captive here? Do others suffer as I did?

"What…do you know…of other…prisoners here…at Regael?" Wesley asked in bursts of breath.

"What do you mean?"

"Do they suffer unjustly? Can we help them?"

The cave began to narrow, and they stopped before an iron door.

"Indeed, many here suffer unlawfully."

Wesley craned his neck, trying to look Olivetan in the eyes. "Then we must bring them with us!"

"You can put him down, Callas. *Witotien, witotien.*"

Deep, heavy breaths wheezed above him. Still not quite ready to see what had been carrying him, he continued to plead with Olivetan. "Will we not release the other prisoners?"

"We will not." Olivetan seemed frustrated. He searched through bars in a small opening in the upper center of the door. "Most would be too weak to make the journey. Others would not come even if we begged them. The stronger ones take care of the weaker ones, who would die if the others fled."

"They stay to bury the dead and then die themselves? If you are truthful, then why do you not free *them?*" Wesley squared his stance and became rigid. "As heir, I would order them to come with us."

Olivetan looked down at Wesley. "To command the competent ones to leave would be to steal compassion from the weak." He then put his face up to the iron bars and in a loud whisper called, "Mahre! Mahre!"

"Is that all you are going to tell me? Do you not think I have a hundred more questions for every word you say?"

Olivetan looked down and frowned. Wesley quickly realized that now was not the time.

A whispery voice dissipated like a puff of smoke above. Olivetan spun his head. From inside of the door echoed a loud rattle and clank.

"*Aderlos!*" came a loud, gruff voice from the giant. Now, Wesley *knew* he did not want to see what had carried him.

"Hello, friends!" Mahre announced, pulling open the door.

"Keep it down, both of you. Where did you get off to, Mahre?" Olivetan asked coarsely.

"Well, there's—"

"Let's go then." Olivetan pushed past Mahre and proceeded ahead on a narrow bridge that led to a tower in a large, cavernous space. Without losing stride, he began to make his way across. "Be sure to lock that door."

Mahre looked down at Wesley. "You two have met, then?"

Wesley began, "No, we—"

"Well, Olivetan can be hasty at times, leaving the formal introductions to me, of course. I have heard much about you,

Wesley. I am Mahre Laereles, and the tall green one behind you is Callas."

Wesley turned ever so slightly. His eyes caught sight of the beast's legs then continued following its form until they were looking eye to eye. If a pirate troll could indeed smile, this one certainly did. The troll reached out a hand. One of his fingers was the width of Wesley's wrist. In an awkward sort of slap, the troll swatted Wesley's hand. *A troll greeting?*

"You boys can play later. Let's be off, then."

Wesley followed Mahre, who followed Callas, who followed Olivetan.

"Where are we?" Wesley asked. He glided his hands along a railing on either side, trying to see what was ahead.

"We're leaving the lowest cells of the dungeon at Regael Castle," Mahre said and pointed. "Look there."

Wesley lifted his eyes. Across the bridge, arched doorways in the tower provided their only light in the vast expanse. At least twenty rods below was the cave floor. And stretching upward, absorbed in the vast darkness, Wesley could not see where the tower ended. But there were other bridges, one perpendicular and above them, seeming to stretch from the cave wall to the tower and out the other side to the opposite wall. And he could barely make out another bridge above that one. Caves near Navarre were barely wide enough for two side by side. This cave was mammoth!

"Someone is up ahead!" Olivetan called back.

"That's what I was starting to tell you," Mahre replied, annoyed.

Wesley pushed past Mahre and darted beneath Callas's legs. The troll's hands floundered to grab him. Twisting and pulling, Wesley slipped from the troll's clumsy attempt, and he ran to Olivetan's side. In the arched doorway, where the bridge met the stone tower, Olivetan was kneeling. Wesley leaned over his shoulder.

"Looks like you have brought quite the arsenal," Olivetan said to a man who lay bleeding.

Several rifles were leaning against the wall, and two fire lances were laid beside him. Blood soaked his right shoulder, and with his left hand, he applied pressure to a wound in his lower chest. His breaths were uneven and shaky, but he looked at Olivetan with gladdened eyes.

"Wesley," Olivetan said, "this is Ezra."

"You must hurry!" Ezra's look was now as urgent as his words. "They are not far behind. All is in place. The children and Bela have been taken to the northern slopes. Sandy and Irene have arranged passage for them." He gritted his teeth, pushing back against his distress.

"And Sophia?" asked Olivetan.

"Sophia?" Wesley broke into the conversation, pushing Olivetan off balance. "You mean my mother? Where is she?"

"Sophia was with me. She is on her way—" Ezra began.

A bright flash accompanied a jarring blast. Wesley swung his head around and looked to the bridge above them.

"Mother?" Wesley cried. Someone in a hooded cloak appeared out of a smoky haze and was running toward the tower.

"Run!" Ezra called out.

With a clap of gunfire, the one in the cloak tripped forward on the bridge. From seemingly nowhere, a second and third shot resonated throughout the cavern. The twisting body slumped forward over the railing and fell from the bridge.

"No!" Wesley called out, throwing his arms forward as if he could catch her.

The whir from the flapping cloak trailed off, and the body plummeted to the rocks. Wesley was grabbed from behind. More rounds exploded.

"You must move now! Take the rifles and wait for my mark!" Ezra ordered.

Gunmen were hidden above them. Wesley could not tell from which direction the shots were coming. Quicker than he could run, he found himself enclosed in the clammy arms of the pirate troll. With his face pressed into the troll's sweaty skin, he was unable to pull his nose from the stink. Frantic sounds became muffled. The jerking and jostling could only mean they were rushing away.

When Wesley stood again, he was tight in Callas's grasp, peering through the archway at the base of the tower. *That was fast*. His eyes scanned his limited field of vision, searching for a body. Rifle fire clapped continually somewhere above, and Callas restricted Wesley's frightful lurches.

In the space between blasts, the tower steps above him rattled with movement, till finally, steady and certain came Olivetan's voice. "No one move. Ezra will blow the tower passage above him, delaying our pursuers. We wait for the signal, then fly back the way we came."

Mahre squeezed down next to Wesley, gave him a wink, then focused on the riverbed, clenching his rifle.

"For Gaspard!" Ezra bawled. His turbulent voice was overcome by the roar of his fire lance.

Shaking and convulsing, the tower cracked. Crumbling stone fragments showered them. At once Wesley was crammed against the troll's belly, his nose again pressed into rank sweat. As the troll bounded toward the riverbed, Wesley's face slid back and forth in it.

Then, Callas stumbled. *I'll be flattened for sure!* But even as Callas tumbled, he threw his elbows out to break the fall. Wesley slid from his grasp and was launched forward, rolling across the rocky floor. Immediately, Wesley lifted his shirt and wiped slime from his eyes. It was then that he saw his chance. Quickly, he jumped to his feet and rushed toward the body that had fallen from the bridge.

"Wesley, no!" Olivetan called.

Wesley dashed for the contorted body lying upon the rocks. A blast of gunfire distorted his eardrums. He glanced up to see soldiers racing back across a bridge high above him. More gunfire showered from above, and he instinctively put his arms over his head. He fell to the rocks beside the body just as a large, concussive sound exploded above. That was the second fire lance. Ezra was out of artillery.

I just want to see her face one last time.

He reached out for her hood as Mahre snatched back his arm.

Wesley broke away. "I need to see my mother!" Grasping the hood that covered her face, he closed his eyes. Knowing Callas would be dragging him away any second, he forced himself to look. Without another thought, he opened his eyes and lifted away the hood. Wesley jumped back. "It's not her! It's…"

Olivetan had raced up behind him and knelt beside the body. He mourned, "Farewell, Torres."

"Oh, Avlae, I'm so sorry…" Wesley looked over to Olivetan. "But my mother, where is she?"

"Ezra assured me that your mother is making her way to the northern slopes, where she will reunite with your sisters. It was for her own protection."

Thank you, thank you. Avlae and Jess must be overjoyed. I wish I were with them.

"What is this?" Olivetan reached for an envelope which extended from inside the man's coat. He pulled it out and placed it within his own. "Callas!"

And the giant's arms came over Wesley, picking him up again.

"You know, this is nothing at all like the vision I have had," Wesley found himself saying out loud.

"All of you, follow the riverbed!"

Slumped over Callas's large, green shoulders, Wesley glimpsed many soldiers lining the bridge above the one they crossed. Olivetan raised his rifle, took a killing shot, and hurried away. Gunpowder from Mahre's pan exploded as Wesley was whisked past, clinging to Callas—eyes burning, ears ringing.

SOPHIA
© 2020

The Northern Slopes

60

Sophia dashed uphill beneath sparse foliage. Frosted leaves crunched under her bare feet. She had placed her ragged leather shoes, too worn for running, inside her satchel. Time would come soon enough for mending. Sparkling ice crystals dazzled tree limbs and lit her path. Moonglow made for an easy passage but also made it easier for her to be seen. She prayed that no spies watched the northern slopes on this night.

Though she was exhausted, adrenaline pushed her. The safe house was not far now. She clenched her hood, moving in long strides from shadow to shadow. Each step moved in cadence with her resolve. The last eight hours could have been days. Yet, everything had happened so quickly.

Ezra and Torres had led Medici away while she fled the tower. "Into the dungeons and out through the caves," Ezra had said. He had made it sound far too easy. If they could make it as far as the dungeon, they may have a chance. Yet as Sophia fled to the slopes, somehow she knew that their story ended another way. Only by some miracle would Ezra and Torres flee under the ice with Olivetan. She prayed for their safe passage.

As cold as the evening was, she wiped her sweaty palms on the sides of her cloak. Fingers throbbed with her pulse. It was not merely her escape that had her reeling. Avlae had been eighteen when Sophia saw her last, and Jess was only two. So much change in so little time.

Will they remember me? Will they be angry with me? How will we begin again?

Thirty paces out from the safe house, she waited as instructed. Perspiration dripped off the tip of her nose. A gust of wind sent chills from head to toe. She wiped her face with her scarf and leaned her head back against a tree.

"Sophia, my dear," lifted a low voice.

Though startled at first, she quickly fell at ease. Into the moonbeams leaned a face drooping with over one-hundred years of age, brandishing a warm, wide smile. Stepping closer, he reached out his arms and embraced her.

"Sandy," Sophia was glad to say, knowing he preferred his nickname, which was short for *Alexander*. She returned the hug. "I had heard you left Nantes."

"And where would I go?" Sandy answered. "Come, let's get out of the cold."

Sandy leaned on his walking stick and began hobbling toward the cottage. Sophia matched his slow pace and knew better than to ask if he needed help.

"The girls are asleep, and it wasn't easy getting them there. How they long to see you."

"Thank you," Sophia said. "I do hope they can understand how this all came to be."

"Oh, your girls are strong. Avlae has learned much discernment.

And Jess, she keeps asking questions about her *secret* family. They won't let you sleep a wink on your way to Farne." Sandy lifted a branch, and Sophia walked under.

"I don't think I should want to sleep." Sophia laughed. "You know, Bela has risked her life for my family over and over again."

"So I have heard. Your daughters adore her."

Sophia took two steps up onto a small porch. Taking the rail in one hand, Sandy limped up one step at a time behind her. Warm light from the windows softened the already cozy cottage.

Pulling a handkerchief from his coat, Sandy's eyes wandered down. "Sophia, you need shoes!" He shrugged, then slowly bent over and measured her foot with the span of his hand. "Irene can fit a pair of boots for your size."

"Mine only need mending," Sophia insisted. "I'm sure she will see to it at once."

Sandy covered his nose and mouth and snorted like an angry goose. Stuffing his handkerchief back into his pocket, he asked, "How's William?"

"William is recovering. His burden is lighter." Sophia paused and said with a smile, "Quesnel found him, lost in the wood."

"There must be a wonderful tale about that." Sandy chortled. Placing a bony hand on Sophia's shoulder, he continued, "He has done well raising the girls."

Aged with spots, his other hand turned the doorknob and let her inside. Stepping across the wooden floor, her feet warmed. Before her, illuminated by the hearth's flitting orange and yellow glow, her girls slept beneath brindle blankets. Bela was cuddled upon pillows beside them. Sophia's eyes began to swell, choked up by memories, and she put her fingers to her mouth, restraining her sobs. Sandy's wife, Irene, smiled from across the one-room home as she hung a teakettle over the fire.

On the left was an oak table for two. Several shelves built into the walls held sparse belongings—animal carvings made by Sandy, a few books, writing materials, blankets, and sheets. Irene's paintings decorated the walls.

"Tea, dear?" Irene asked. Without waiting for an answer, she took clay teacups from her only cupboard and placed them on the table.

Between her daughters, Sophia knelt and sat on her feet. She lifted Avlae's light brown hair, tucking it behind her ear. With the backs of her fingers, Sophia traced her daughter's cheek. The young lady stirred awake. Like frost in the moonlight, her wide eyes sparkled.

"Mother!" Avlae flew from the blankets, throwing her arms around her mother.

"Avlae, how wonderful it is to see you and hear your voice!"

Avlae sobbed, clinging to her mother.

We will take the time. We will get to know each other again. We will start anew.

"Mother?" sang a little voice. Slowly, as if stretching from a dream, Jess's face brightened. She crept from her coverings, lifted her arms, and fell forward against Avlae.

"Look at you! My little lady," Sophia said and gathered her daughters tighter. "How I've longed for this day!" She kissed them both on the tops of their heads.

Suddenly alert, Jess pulled away from their embrace and sprang to the table for her satchel. She flopped it open and reached inside. "We made tiaras!" Leaving a trail of leaves, she scurried back to her mother and placed a tiara on her head.

"Thank you, dear." Sophia removed it and looked closely. "It's lovely! You made this?"

"Avlae helped," Jess admitted. "She told me you taught her how."

"Yes, yes, that's right."

Avlae clung to Sophia as if she would never let go. Suddenly, Avlae sat upright and pulled Sophia's hands together in hers. "I knew something was wrong, Mother, the moment we left our home. King Ninian treated Wesley like a prisoner. I am so angry with Derian, and now…now he's…" Her head fell forward into Sophia's lap, and she wept.

Sophia placed a hand on the back of Avlae's head and whispered, "I am so sorry." Sophia caught Bela's eyes, took her hand, and squeezed tightly. Neither spoke a word. Bela returned a squeeze.

Sophia looked over and beamed at Jess. "It's a new day, my dears, and we soon must be on our way."

"Where will we go, Mother?" Jess whimpered. "Why must we leave so soon?"

"You let your mother rest, young miss," Irene interrupted and reached into Sophia's satchel. "There will be time for talking later. Sandy tells me I've some work to do." Irene examined Sophia's shoes. "I will get these mended."

"Come here, little dear," Sandy called Jess over to the table. He began spreading elderberry preserves over a chunk of bread and sang:

Elderberry, berry bush
Elderberry, berry
A twist, a pull, fill your mouth full
You may be dead by morning

Sandy laughed, for Jess had already pushed the bread into her mouth and chewed with a purple smile.

Irene groaned at his choice of poetry as she diligently made repairs to Sophia's footwear.

Once her sobs softened, Avlae wiped her eyes and again took her mother by the hands. "Bela helped us escape. I was so afraid but knew I must protect Jess."

"I am so thankful you are safe," Sophia said.

"Ezra helped us, too. He said he had seen you! His eyes held true. Somehow, I knew I could trust him," Avlae continued.

"Sandy tells me you have grown in wisdom." Sophia held Avlae's hands. "And I see it, too!"

"Bela has said many things about the Underground," Avlae stated sternly. "I want to help."

"Me, too!" Jess called from the table.

"Indeed, you shall, my dears." Sophia cradled Avlae's chin in her hand.

"Now, warm your bones. Drink some tea, Sophia," Irene insisted, working swiftly while sitting upon her little, cushioned chair. "You've only the span of an hour before you must leave."

"Thank you. Thank you both," Sophia said. "You know that I desire to stay and—"

"None of that now. I have bread, dried meats, and a few apples prepared for your journey. We'll share a cup of tea, and off you'll go... *Ow!*" Irene pricked her finger but kept working.

"Slow down," Sandy said. His tone proved his impatience with her. He moistened a cloth and dabbed preserves off Jess's face.

Three heavy knocks shook the door to the cottage.

Avlae's face tightened, and her eyes became fierce. In a startled whisper, her words were sharp and quick, "Mother, they've found us!"

Jess nearly screamed aloud. Sandy reached over, covered her mouth, and put a finger to his lips. He motioned for Jess to step aside, and he moved the oak table. One of the clay cups fell to the floor and shattered. With the side of his foot, he kicked a rug out of place, then lifted a trapdoor. With the other hand, he waved them over. "Let's go, let's go!"

Bela quickly climbed down. Reaching up, she took Jess in her arms and whispered something in her ear. Avlae grabbed her mother's arm and forced her to go ahead. Irene crammed Sophia's boots into the satchel and tossed it through the hole in the floor. Climbing down, Sophia saw lines of tears streaming down Jess's cheeks. Avlae landed in behind, then darkness.

The table dropped back into place above them. Leaning into one another, they held each other closely. Jess trembled in Sophia's arms.

"Mother? Mother?" Jess spoke too loudly.

"Quiet, my dear. Hold tight. We are safe."

"Is there another way out?" Bela breathed out in a whisper.

"Yes, but we must wait. Irene will signal if it is safe," Sophia answered. Deep breaths helped to keep her from shaking.

Knocks pounded louder. Above, floorboards creaked. Footsteps made their way to the door. It seemed as if every muscle in Sophia's body had constricted. She began to plan her route to the caves. An eternity had gone by. Had someone answered the door?

"Well, well. You want to wake the dead?" Irene said. "Come in, then. You scared us half to death with your battering."

Above them, the floorboards creaked as the table slid. Irene moaned as she pulled open the trapdoor, and Sophia poked her head out from the crawlspace just in time to see Sandy returning his gun to the wall mounts.

Irene looked down at the huddling women and smiled. "You called for the post?"

Sophia lifted Jess, grabbed the satchel, and followed her up. The rest climbed out behind her. A young man, merely a boy, stood at the door with a small leather bag over his shoulder.

"I am so sorry. I had completely forgotten," Sophia said, relieved. "Ezra promised to send you here. I must get a letter to William."

"Thank you, ma'am. Only, make haste. The slopes will be crawling with soldiers yet tonight, and I could not linger in the shadows any longer," he said. Sophia did not even know his name, but the patch on his cloak identified him as a letter carrier for the Underground.

"Very good, then," Irene said. She snatched the satchel out of Sophia's hands, fell back into her cushioned chair, pulled out Sophia's shoes, and carried on with her work. Focused on her task, she ordered, "You heard the young man, Sandy. Fetch paper and ink!"

Back Under the Ice

61

queezing his burning eyes shut, Wesley clung to Callas. But just as quickly, fleeing through the cloud of white smoke, a choking cough forced them open again. Watering eyes blurred his vision. Attempts to wipe his face were useless. Callas had an arm secured around him, and Wesley's arms did not budge a nik. Muffled pops of gunfire clapped his ears as they dashed into the tunnel of the riverbed.

On both sides, near the ground, a jagged, horizontal ridge of ice ran parallel to their escape. Callas trod upon shards of ice.

Olivetan must have broken through on his way in.

Wesley remembered puddles frozen over with thin layers of ice. On early spring mornings, he and his siblings would walk carefully, trying not to break through. When the ice cracked, they had stomped until it was all crunched—so satisfying. *Funny thought to come to mind right now.*

Olivetan's voice prodded from behind, "Run! Run!"

The path descended, and the parallel ridge of ice—which had begun at the troll's ankles—was now at his neck. Up ahead, the ice ridges narrowed and curved inward. It seemed Callas was going to hit the ridge head-on. Despite the difficult terrain, the troll was not stopping. In fact, his pace increased. Stretching horizontally from one side to the other, a layer of ice divided the cave.

The ice marks the water depth. The tide is out. We are going beneath the ice!

Dropping his left shoulder, Callas tucked his head and launched into the dark space beneath the ice. With each long stride, Wesley's body jerked. He thought for sure his neck would snap. Callas must have realized what was happening, as he reached over to support Wesley's head. Only, now he was being smothered. Back and forth he spun his head, sucking in air and troll slime from between large, knobby fingers.

With clumsy leaps, the troll skidded and slipped over loose rocks. Pangs of anxiety flashed like lightning through Wesley's stomach. He thought for sure that Callas would trip forward and use him to cushion the fall.

They passed a streak of light on the wall. Someone called from behind. With one ear against the troll's chest and the other covered with Callas's hand, it was hard to hear. The shouts came again, "*Thoaian*, Callas! *Thoaian!*"

Easing his pace, Callas landed each step heavier until he finally stopped. A troll-sized heart pounded in Wesley's ear. Callas held him tightly.

"Let me go!" Wesley wriggled, and the troll finally loosened his grip, as if he had just remembered that he was clutching Wesley. Lifting away, Wesley's cheek peeled from the troll's clammy skin. *Disgusting.*

Finally on his own two feet, Wesley pushed his ragged shirt across his face. His right eye winced, burning with troll sweat. Each breath pained his ribs. Wesley stretched and massaged the back of his neck. Callas fell against the wall of the tight space, slid to his bottom, and put his forearms on his knees. The creature hacked and panted, but still he looked as if he were smiling.

A small, white candle burned at Wesley's feet. Flickering light outlined an archway that seemed to be the entrance to oblivion. Behind him, candles trailed off down the riverbed. *Olivetan lit the way.*

An illuminated figure appeared, a candle was extinguished, and it continued over and over again. Wesley could now see that it was two men. As Mahre ran, he stomped each candle out with his foot. *Not leaving the path lit for the enemy.*

Mahre ran up alongside Wesley, out of breath. Olivetan was right behind him.

"I see…you wore out…our…friend here," Mahre spoke with each breath he exhaled. With shaking hands, he reloaded his rifle.

Wesley erupted, "Where are we?"

Olivetan hastily reloaded as well. "From here, we enter into Regael Cave and return the way we came. Simple, really."

Suddenly, Wesley's chin fell to his chest, his legs cramped, and he began to fall.

"Wesley!" Olivetan had taken hold of him. "You listen well. Ninian's soldiers will be along too soon. We need to move."

His mouth was dry, his tongue bitter and metallic. "Can you taste that?" Wesley said, and his head bobbed.

Mahre was right beside him, but his voice was far off. "Callas! *Eistias, na!*" He yelled again, "*Eistias, aderlos!*"

In a blur of movement, the troll lunged forward nose to nose with Mahre. A hearty laugh from deep inside the troll made Wesley's head buzz all the more.

A double vision of Olivetan shuffled to the archway and reached down into the dark. There was a glare of swirling light from circling lanterns. "Off we go, then!" Olivetan leapt through the archway.

Callas turned to pick up Wesley, who immediately raised his hands and backed away.

"No...No, I've...I got this!" Wesley sidestepped through. Another step, and the path dropped beneath him.

His arms swirled at his sides but instinctively came up around his head while he fell forward. He tucked and rolled. Two somersaults, and his legs landed out in front of him. Sliding on his back, he flung his arms out to slow himself. His entire body juddered down the slope of loose rocks. The impact at the bottom pushed his knees into his chest as he splashed into ankle-high water.

The tide was coming in.

Wesley opened his eyes to an eerie, hollow, and dark space. Dense dampness hung in the air, along with a salty, fishy smell. Struggling to gain a sense of direction, his hands floundered, slipping over smooth stones beneath him. Breathless, he spun his head while trying to focus on something—anything. His heart jumped as he desperately fought to gain control. It was then that a pool of light formed around him.

"You all right, Wesley?" Mahre's voice fell from behind him.

Wesley cranked his head around, and a stabbing pain pierced his back between his shoulder blades. He clinched his teeth and let out a groan. Above him, Mahre stood in the archway with his arm stretched forward, holding out a lamp. Its dull light glinted off the rocky slope.

"I'm alright." He moaned and clicked his tongue at the top of his mouth. "Can you taste that? And my head feels like it's being pushed to the ground..."

"That would be the dormire spell." Mahre explained what had taken place. "It's beginning to hang on me, as well."

Wesley staggered to his feet, marveling as he stared aloft. Any warnings that Mahre instilled were immediately replaced with wonder. "Take a look…at that!"

Suspended in the frozen ceiling above them was a ship! Gazing upward, he dawdled across the tidal bed just below the hull. How he wished his siblings could see this. His eyes followed the dark wooden planks across the length of the ship, to a massive hole in the hull lit by a single flickering candle. Several wooden barrels were positioned in a way that one could climb up and in through the hull.

"No time…for the tour now, Wes." Mahre pulled him away and hurried onward, clenching Wesley's tunic.

"Wait…wait…I have…to see this." He pulled against Mahre's hold.

"Callas!" Mahre called.

Wesley had only taken two steps before he was wrenched upward from behind and flopped like a sack over the shoulder of the troll. There was no use resisting. Pushing off the troll's back, Wesley strained to look. "So, you…you brought me down here…" It took more and more effort to breathe. "…below a massive block of ice… where there is b…barely enough…light to see…some spell is re… restrict…ing us…and…and we're move…moving into the tide? I might…have fared better…back…back in my cell."

"Save your breath! Once…once we blow the ship…we…we'll… break the spell…"

"Blow…the ship?"

"Then we'll flee…Regael Cave and…back into the bay, the… way we…we came. And…hopefully stay ahead of the tide."

"Hopefully?"

"Believe me, Wesley, it's…it's the last…place I'd choose to go."
Mahre's voice trailed off as he wobbled ahead.

Wesley gave up and slumped over the troll's shoulder.

The tide slipped just over Callas's ankles as he splashed forward. A
few drops landed on Wesley's lips. Naturally, he licked them, though
he wished he hadn't. Seawater was saltier than he had remembered.

Far beyond the hull of the ship, Callas dropped him back to
his feet. Wesley's legs buckled, and he tottered back, but before
he fell, Callas snatched his shoulders and helped him to stand.
Immediately, the water chilled him, and the tide swished by, raising
the water level to just over his knees. Then it sank away.

Olivetan had lined a row of crates to form a barrier, with a few
lanterns spaced along the top. Thirty to forty metal cylinders were
positioned like cannons between the dim lights, aimed back the
way they had come.

"What…are you doing?" Wesley asked.

"Preparing to engage…our enemies," Olivetan said.

Things just keep getting better. "But the trail of lights…won't it
lead… the soldiers right to us?"

"I hope so."

Olivetan lifted what looked like a thin rope from between the
cylinders and gathered it in his other hand. Mahre stood to the
side, loading rifles and placing them atop broken crates above the
water level.

"What? Why not extinguish the lamps and…and lie in the…
dark? With that gaping hole…in the hull, they'll think…we
escaped through the ship and not…not come this way!"

"Very good reasoning. However, if we hide…or even keep

moving, they may…indeed climb into the ship," Olivetan said, fidgeting with the thin rope in his hand. "The problem…is, they will think that we have escaped through…the tunnels going north."

"And what's…what's wrong with that?" Wesley asked as tide rolled in just above the back of his knees, pushing him forward.

"That would lead them out…of Regael Cave, and the closest… escape route from the cave would be the…the…northern slopes."

"I…I…understand!"

Mahre broke in, "Have Wesley move on ahead…with Callas. At least they will gain some…some ground before the tide gets… too high."

"It is Wesley they'll be…looking for," Olivetan said. "They need to know that…he is with us. It's the only way to guarantee…they… they'll come this way."

"Of course," Wesley said, irritated, his arms now feeling as heavy as his head. "Who else would be dumb enough…to run out into… the incoming tide…below a ceiling of ice?"

"Mahre, send Callas on ahead. Give him a lantern…so he can be our beacon…if things get difficult."

If?

"How long…does it take to get…around into the next bay?"

"That will depend on how…fast you can swim!" Olivetan said and broke open another crate.

"We'll never make it!"

"This is for you." Mahre handed Wesley a rifle. "You get the first shot."

"But—"

"If you miss… no problem. The idea is to…give them a target,"

Mahre said and prepared a lantern for Callas. "It's likely they want to...to take you alive."

What foolish thinking!

"You're making me...the target? The heir...heir of Gaspard?" Wesley shouted but didn't have the strength to lift his arms and cross them in protest.

"We merely...need their attention. By the time they know what happened...you'll be out...out of sight." Olivetan spoke harshly as he draped thin ropes along the row of crates. "Mahre will fire from another direction to confuse them...I'll be ready to ignite the rockets."

Resigning all possibilities of altering the plan, Wesley yielded and sought some clarification. "What will...you do with those ropes?"

Olivetan's chuckle choked him as he inhaled. When he finally got a breath, he said, "These are fuses."

62

Olivetan dimmed his lantern. "We want them to see us… but not kill us." He laughed, but Wesley did not. Unable to hold the rifle up, Wesley had it resting across the top of a barrel. He waited, trembling but languid, up to his thighs in ice-cold seawater.

"It feels as though…as though…something is pressing me down… inside my head." Wesley steadied himself against the rolling current.

"Fight it, keep alert. You…can do this. The spell is only above you. Be glad we…do not have to go *through* it. I will be close by." As Olivetan waded away, he ordered Wesley, "Keep the pan dry."

Wesley swayed ever so slightly as waves pushed against the back of his numb legs. The silent hollow of the cave intensified every sound—droplets of water, gentle wakes of the tide as it crawled over broken crates, Mahre giggling through his nose. Before Callas moved on, he had told a joke in Calbharian, and Mahre was still trying to suppress his laughter.

In a breathy voice, Olivetan called, "Shut it!"

Wesley tried to steady the rifle, keeping his fingers away from the trigger. Olivetan had already drawn back the hammer, and Wesley was not about to fire too soon. Candles flickered from the tops of barrels, lighting a path straight to Wesley. Faint yellow circles expanded and shrank around the base of the lanterns on the crates nearby. A creak moaned through timbers of the ship, as if the death grip of ice clenched tighter around the planking.

Light and shadows extended from the tunnel beyond the hull. Mumbling voices grew louder, then soldiers appeared. Navigating the rocks and leaping from the archway, scores of men splashed into the tide, crept below the hull, and raised their weapons in cautious surveillance.

Wesley fought chills as the tide came in just below his waist. The spell was making him nauseous. His numb fingers had shriveled like prunes. Wet and shaky hands clenched the stock of his rifle. At least when the concussion kicked him back, he would not have far to fall. None of the soldiers seemed to notice him yet, but they were getting closer. *Why does Olivetan delay?*

Part of the regiment took an interest in the hull and began to climb inside. Yet, others were now beyond the ship and making their way closer to Wesley. Several were getting uncomfortably close. The glimmering eyes of the soldiers reflected lantern light.

Olivetan!

The order brushed Wesley's ears in a whisper. "Hold steady."

The incoming tide lifted him to his toes, washing around him. *Keep the pan dry.* Wesley's jaw was tight and sore. *How long have I been grinding my teeth?* He brought his right hand to his mouth, breathing on his fingers in an attempt to warm them.

"Now!" Olivetan called.

Wesley's finger did not move. All his joints had stiffened. Taking his eyes off the soldiers, he stared at his numb hand, attempting to make a fist. *It's no use!*

"There! Look ahead, between the lamps!" one soldier called. With a swift engagement, the regiments refocused, closing in on Wesley. "The boy…There he is! Lower your weapon!"

"Fire, dammit!" Olivetan called again.

Wesley forced his rigid fingers under the barrel of his gun. Switching his right hand for his left, he grabbed the stock. No need to aim—he squeezed the trigger. Kicking back hard, the rifle seemed to attack him, pulverizing his shoulder. The concussive sound rang in his ears for only a moment before the splash. Icy seawater bit his neck and face. He exhaled a gurgle, and bubbles floated away. Muted voices and pops from rifles tapped against his ears. Clasping his throbbing shoulder, he realized that he no longer held his weapon. In a dizzy frenzy, he kicked and pulled himself against the current. Underwater, he swam toward the wall, just as Olivetan had ordered.

It was too far, and Wesley needed air. He feared poking his head out of the water but had no choice. He floated his feet forward, found his footing, and pushed up. Breaking through the surface of the water, he breathed easy. Just enough light shown for him to see the wall ahead. With water up to his chest, he turned to find Olivetan or Mahre.

No one.

Gunfire ripped from the enemy. Unnerved, he sank his head, eyes just above the frigid waters. A fire lance ignited, sending a red flare. Exploding midair, shards of iron scattered over their enemies. An overlapping succession of rockets blasted into flight. Rockets sent metal blades spinning out of control, slashing into and cutting down anyone in their way. Blast after blast lit up the cave. Soldiers scrambled.

In rapid succession, the barrels beneath the hull burst! Flames lunged in every direction, devouring and consuming men like prey. Burning men threw themselves into the water. Fire leapt and spun along the underbelly of the ship, searing every crevice and escaping into the hole in the hull. It was then that the lower aft blew open from the inside. The entire framework ripped apart, and planks tore away, blown into a million pieces.

Wesley's face warmed from the blast, and for a moment, over the water he could see from one side of the cave to the other. The massive glow painted the frozen ceiling in a spattering of reds and yellows. Flaming timbers rained down upon the soldiers. Men screamed and scattered between piles of burning debris. The waters would soon be high enough to extinguish all of it.

"Get to the wall, Wesley!" Olivetan screamed.

Wesley now spotted Olivetan swimming ferociously, a span out ahead and to the left.

An earsplitting explosion echoed into the hollow of the cave. A dull thud thumped Wesley's chest. The ice ceiling cracked and split as the stern of the ship crashed through from above. Large pieces of ice broke away, falling and crashing into the waters. In a buckling commotion, the ship collapsed upon the soldiers, pushing a deluge of water over Wesley. He twisted in underwater feats of courage. After quickly slowing, he was able to push his head out of the water.

The cave was dark again. Only a few voices called, searching for survivors. Floating and flaming timbers sent a mild glow from behind and gave him enough light to gain some direction. After locating the rock wall, he threw his arms wildly, swimming toward it.

"Olivetan!" Wesley called over his manic strokes. It was then he realized his ease of movement. The spell was broken!

"Come along!" Olivetan called.

Mahre yelled, "You've not far to go!"

He followed the voices. Before he knew what was happening, arms pulled him from the water and sat him upon a ledge.

"On your feet! Lean back, slide along the wall, and follow me," Olivetan said.

Wesley didn't respond.

"Are you hearing this, Wesley? We've broken the spell. The ceiling continues to crack and fall. We need to keep moving. When we are clear of the cave, round the corner and swim as hard as you can into the next bay!" Olivetan yelled.

"How will we see?" Wesley sputtered. His stomach tightened, and his body cramped, stiff and trembling.

"Let the rock guide you. Stay close to the cave wall. Focus ahead. Look for the light from Callas!"

Olivetan had already begun to move along the ledge. With his back against the wall, Wesley slid his right foot along the rocky berm. Carefully, he found his footing, then dragged his left foot over. The ledge narrowed. Black waves mocked him, licking like a beast at his feet. Wesley could practically hear the waters taunting. *Let's drag him to the seafloor! Yes, we'll crush his tiny bones! You hold him down, and I will fill his lungs!*

"No!" Wesley raved.

Amused, the rock wall seemed to tip him forward. *Shove him! Thrust him off the ledge!*

His right foot slipped. Heinous waters lapped at his leg—stealing a taste, preparing to snarf him down. Wesley's shriek was immediately squelched by Mahre's woolen coat sleeve, which saved him from being swallowed whole. Mahre held firm until Wesley regained his balance. With his teeth clenched and breaths furious, Wesley moved again, shortening his lateral steps. Soon, the ledge became nothing more than a sliver of black rock.

Olivetan called, "We've exited Regael Cave. We swim from here! Hard left. Stay near the wall, and you cannot get lost! Follow it back into the next bay, and you'll get ahead of the rising tide."

"Jump, Wesley!" Mahre hollered. "Swim hard! I'll follow you!"

Wesley howled, "No, Mahre, I cannot!" To his right and behind, a hazy glow lit the crests of waves. To his left, long echoes of ever-rising waters swirled in a black void.

"Go!" Mahre called, seeming so far away.

Wesley leaned forward and stared down. "I can't do this!"

"Now!"

With a sharp thrust to his side, Wesley slipped. Arms aimlessly pumping, he flopped forward. Waiting patiently, the deadly waters welcomed him.

A thousand needles pricked his face. He hadn't had time to take a breath. Fighting, he climbed for air. Breaking through the waters, Wesley sucked in a breath, but another wave toppled over him. The force pushed him hard and fast against the rocks. Despite the battering, he was consoled in finding the rock wall to follow to the surface. He bobbed up, ready to take another breath when a wave hit him in the face with full force. Then it rose, curling over his head and pushing him under, dragging him away. *Air! No air!*

His arms grasped at nothing—no other chance at a lifesaving breath. He became still, hanging in black waters. *Which way is up? How far was I pulled from the wall? What if I float upward and find only ice?* Unable to surface and with no place to secure his feet, he drifted. Seawater filled his mouth.

Numb.

Silence.

Black.

Peace.

Sinking.

Gliding away.

Ever deeper.

Ever darker.

He surrendered to the abyss.

63

esley hacked into consciousness. Between violent gasps for air, he spewed water and slimy liquid. Intense trembles took over his body. Each cough caused severe tightening around his chest. It was as though someone had cinched a belt to the tightest notch and then cut it loose again and again. With long, dry heaves he whooped and hawed. Fists flying, he struck something solid that gave way.

"Don't fight me, Wesley!" Mahre hollered and pressed against Wesley's shoulders. "Hold still. You're okay, you're okay!"

Kicking his feet, Wesley pushed himself back, sliding over stones. "Take me home. I want to go home!"

Fingers brushed his hair back and cradled his jaw. "Hold still, son."

"Olivetan?"

"Yes, I have you." Olivetan's large face leaned in, forehead to forehead. "You are safe. Breathe slow. *Shhh*. Rest."

Wesley inhaled a shaky breath and released. And again. Against his growing stillness, muscles threw spasms. His constricted throat released bursts of sobs. "Just…take…me home."

"I thought we lost you, Wesley. You're a strong, young man."

Olivetan pushed away a tear and paused. Then, right back to business, he made his way on ahead, saying, "But now's not the time for exploring!"

Wesley pushed himself to a seated position, eyes catching movement to the right. Light spread wider around him. Callas had lifted the lantern next to his own face, head cocked sideways, smiling as always. Callas pulled Wesley to his feet.

"Doaian." Wesley thanked him. "Where are we? Still beneath the ice?"

"Yes, and although we're well within the bay, the tide will soon catch up," Mahre explained. "Can you walk?"

"Well enough."

"Good. We've about three-quarters of an hour to trek through these dreadful icy crannies."

"Let's go!" Olivetan called from somewhere up ahead along his trail of candles.

Ducking under ice slabs and slinking through frozen corridors, Mahre never let go of Wesley's arm. For Wesley, the icy confines had a similar effect to that of the spell. His mind was pressed as the cavern seemed to close in around him, crackling and snapping. *Oh, Mahre, don't let me go.* Just ahead, Callas moaned, struggling through, pinched by sheets of ice. Callas filled every gap of the crevice ahead of them, blocking any possible light by which Wesley could see.

"Seems the crevice has narrowed a bit." Mahre's clasp tightened around Wesley's wrist. "Don't you get wedged in here, or we'll all be stuck."

"Ibdroen uyhthi, terraien," Callas said.

"Yes, I do suppose the slick surface helps."

The water had risen halfway between Wesley's ankles and knee-caps. He was counting off the minutes. A half-hour more.

Coming out of the crevice, they entered a space only about as wide as Wesley was tall, and it was less than three rods deep. Callas had crunched into a corner, allowing Mahre and Wesley to pass. Holding a milky sheen from the candle Olivetan had raised, the wedge above them gradually sloped downward until it met the rising waters. On his knees and bent over, with his other hand, Olivetan seemed to search beneath the tide.

"Drop something?" Mahre quipped as he hunched his back and stirred the water with careful steps toward Olivetan.

Wesley shook off Mahre's hold and said, "Where do we go?" His panicked voice was deadened, absorbed by the thick walls around them, a space that seemed to grow smaller and smaller.

Olivetan shifted upright but remained hunched on his knees, up to his thighs in the rising water. "Take this," Olivetan said, handed his candle to Mahre, and shed his dank cloak.

Mahre was as pale as the ice around them. He reached to float Olivetan's coat out of the way, his candlelight rimming silent ripples.

Wesley snatched Olivetan's arm. "You can't! You can't crawl beneath the ice slab, under the water!" Olivetan resisted Wesley's hold and held him back at an arm's length, but Wesley persisted. "There has to be another way, back the way we came!"

"Mahre," Olivetan said firmly.

With a trembling arm, Mahre reached to leverage Wesley backward.

"No!" Wesley fought the resistance but once again found himself restrained by Callas.

"Follow me through," Olivetan explained, his voice suppressed in the tight enclosure. "Grab my ankle and crawl behind, one after the other."

I can't do this!

Olivetan sank, dark waters whirling in his wake.

Wesley could not get a breath in. Callas let him go, and he stammered in a circle until Mahre grabbed him. Mahre's eyes betrayed his stricken state, sternly and silently telling Wesley to focus.

"Now, go! Look!"

Olivetan had lifted a boot near the surface.

Without another thought, Wesley latched on and dove ahead. Eyes pinched tight, he pulled himself along with one hand, the other grasping Olivetan's boot. With a tug on his own ankle, Wesley knew that Mahre had grabbed hold of him.

Wesley lost his focus, and his right hand slipped from Olivetan's boot. Air escaped him, bubbling past his ears. With his right arm swaying, he floundered, feeling for anything until he finally snagged Olivetan's pant leg.

How much farther?

He floated upward against the slab of ice, suspended only a forearm's length from the seafloor. He pulled himself along, leveraging himself between the bottom of the sea and the monstrous mass of ice above him.

Seconds seemed like minutes. Olivetan's leg pulled swiftly ahead, yet Wesley clung tight. It felt like he was attempting to find the right footing to push ahead. Wesley waited. He needed air, now! No longer were they crawling forward. Olivetan's legs fumbled. Water swirled in Wesley's ears.

Is Olivetan stuck?

A low moan vibrated around Wesley. Olivetan had stopped kicking.

I have to go back! I need a breath.

But how far was back? Wesley shook his leg loose of what he believed was Mahre's hold. The mass above tremored again, nudging him downward. With a firm hold, he thrust himself backwards, out from below the sinking ceiling. In a moment, the last of his breath was forced from his lungs as the block of ice compressed him. From behind, someone pulled again and again on his leg. With each pull, Wesley beat his arms against the seafloor, hoping to assist in propelling himself free. But it was no use! His torso would not budge, and the weight against his back increased as if to flatten him...

Inside him, something released the pressure—not the pressure against his back, but the pressure that filled him with fear. Something shifted in him, moving him to safety and sheltering him from terror, though at any moment he might be crushed.

What were once numbing waters, suddenly entwined him in warmth. Ever so slightly, the inside of his eyelids lightened. And as easy as awakening from sleep, he opened his eyes. The massive slab above him began to glow, the faintest hue of sky blue. Straight out in front of him, warbled and stretched through his liquid lens, were the bottom of Olivetan's boots. What weight had been pressed firmly against his back patiently began to lift. Olivetan was crawling ahead. Water levels sank as the slab of ice lifted away. Wesley pushed upwards, and breaking through the surface of the water, he drew a long, healing breath.

Now on his knees, Wesley shook his head and wiped his face. Ahead, Olivetan stooped, dripping and heaving.

"Take a look at that," Mahre said. His arm extended up alongside Wesley, his shaking finger pointing.

Lifting from the waters, section after section ahead of them, the ceiling formed an arch. Buckled ice rose and reformed itself, creating a tunnel—a pathway! With breaks and cracks, twisting and crunching, a fragmented burrow formed along the seafloor. All the while, a meager blue light began within each slab and increased only enough for them to see the way.

With more than enough room, Wesley stood. The tide was just over his knees.

Still huffing and hunched over, Olivetan turned around, eyes gaping and water dripping from his beard. "Let's go!" Lunging ahead with large steps, he fled.

Wesley sprang forward, chasing behind Olivetan, kicking high with his knees, stumbling, and tripping onward.

A howling sound from somewhere close behind was Callas.

"Aderlos, eistisoev!" called Mahre.

Straight on, they defied the rising tide, the ice splitting and snapping, shaping their path as they forged ahead, stretching upward only as fast as their pace. Stalling the trek, with only minutes left to go, the tide had risen above Wesley's waist. He leaned forward, thrusting his shoulders. His splashes were barely audible over the crackling din of the ice.

"Take this," Olivetan said, handing Wesley a rope, and he pointed upward. "Find your footing, and pull yourself out!"

At the top of the incline, through the hole overhead, stars glimmered in the sky.

Dochart's Glen

64

Plodding upward on the back of his bear, Wesley crouched beneath low-hanging branches. Bristly fur scratched his cheek. Ahead of him, Olivetan lifted a branch, held it high, and handed it back. After taking hold, Wesley stretched an arm behind, offering it to Mahre. He was not sure where Callas had gone but knew he was not far, keeping lookout.

For nearly the entire morning, the four of them had been making their way up the side of a mountain. Though Callas had offered a squirrel leg to eat, Wesley politely declined. His three-course breakfast included pine needles and bark, with a side of warmed black currants. Wesley's stomach moaned. Olivetan had promised bread and salt-cured pork when they reached Arbor Hill—it was all he could think about.

After pushing a couple of feeble tree limbs aside, Wesley emerged from the dense wood, sitting tall upon his mount. Immediately, children ran and surrounded him, clamoring to put a hand on his furry ride. Seeming to enjoy the attention, the bear nuzzled the children, gently pushing them aside while continuing to move forward.

Up ahead, the Underground was gathered in the clearing of Arbor Hill. Olivetan had said they would be awaiting their arrival. *So many of them.* And while dismal clouds hung low, flares of excitement lit the hill. One after another, conversations ceased. Those who were sitting rose to their feet. Some lifted a hand and whispered into a neighbor's ear, while still others pointed and said, "It's the heir of Gaspard."

Derian? But… As quickly as that thought came, it left—they were speaking of him.

"Long live Gaspard!" a little girl called. Others began to echo her.

Then, beside Wesley and directly into his ear, Olivetan said, "Long live Gaspard." He attempted to keep pace as his bear playfully scuffled for some of the children's attention. "You are welcome here, Wesley."

All these years, Wesley had known of his royal bloodline. Yet he now realized he had no idea what would be expected of him as king. By rights, Derian should have sat on the throne. Being the youngest of four boys, Wesley had figured that his part would be quite passive, and he liked that. He gloried in the kingdom, never considering that he might have a role to play. It struck him now how selfish his thoughts had been.

"What do I know of kingship?" Wesley asked.

"It is an honor you will have to learn to receive," Olivetan advised. "All of these people left their homes, rose against Ninian, crossed the wilderness under threat of pirate trolls—for what?" He leaned from his bear toward Wesley and in almost a whisper continued, "A better place, something Gaspard had promised was for all who would come. Your great-grandfather sold everything he had to purchase that field. These people left behind all they've known for the treasure." Olivetan sat upright and gave an approving nod. "They now look to you."

"Me? But they had homes. Th-they had security in Regael…"

"Indeed, which is why some stayed behind, afraid of what

the task would call them to," Olivetan answered. Downcast eyes revealed how broken this made him feel.

Yet, Wesley did not budge. He did not need this obligation. "But, in the least, Ninian did care for his people."

"What?" Olivetan was indignant.

Wesley argued, "I am Gaspard's heir, and Ninian is only after me. No one else must come to any harm. People live at ease in the city and throughout the countryside."

"With all you've been through, *that* is your conclusion?" Shaking his head, seemingly baffled, Olivetan continued, "Are you so dull? What has blinded you?" He seemed to wait, forming his next thought. Finally, he relaxed a bit and said, "The cost is high to do what is right, and these people would pay with their lives."

Wesley was silent. He knew Olivetan was right but was not ready to admit it. He could not continue to argue, hiding what really bothered him. Guilt made him restless. With hushed words, Wesley finally said, "All these years, I have only considered my prominence in the kingdom. I wanted the title without the responsibility. I am ashamed."

Olivetan's gaze grew unexpectedly soft. His demeanor offered courage. Having stopped the bears from moving forward, he looked Wesley directly in the eyes and said, "Then, you are in a good place."

"What?" Wesley asked, astonished.

"But you must not remain there."

"I'm doubting all that I am!"

As casual as a summer day, Olivetan said, "Everyone doubts what is true—more than once in their lives. Don't be fooled, for doubt can work well to clarify our thoughts. You have stared from behind bars in the dungeons of Regael. Does that not tell you something?"

Indeed, Wesley had suffered. His body held the marks. He accepted Olivetan's courage and asked, "What must I do?"

"As you serve, learn to serve well." Olivetan paused, gave a wide smile, and tilted his head, gesturing for Wesley to look.

"Father!"

Wesley kicked his right leg back and swung it down along the bear's torso. In the same motion, he reached out his arms and hugged as much of the bear's neck as he could. He slid through the thick, scratchy fur and let go. The drop was longer than expected. Hitting the ground, he lost his balance. Someone was quick to give him a shove forward.

"Thank you," Wesley called as he ran, not looking to see who it was. He scampered through the crowd, leaping now and then to keep his father in view. "Pardon, sorry," Wesley bumbled. "Excuse me."

Father rushed toward him, shuffling amid the onlookers. Smiling faces nodded at Wesley, stepping aside. With a clear path, Wesley sprinted and was scooped up in his father's arms.

"I've missed you, Father!"

"And I, you!" William's burly arms squeezed tighter.

Wesley buried his face in his father's shoulder, muffling his sobs.

"Let me see you." William took Wesley by the shoulders and studied him from head to toe. "Ah, you look well!"

Wesley dragged his forearm across his face and sniffled, wiping his nose. Father's eyes seemed new, as if he had shed much gloom.

"I am so sorry, son—sorry for how you had to come by the truth." Father tilted his head in a penitent bow.

That was not Wesley's concern at the moment. Despite the joy of reuniting with his father, Wesley began, "I fear for Philor and Aarn. Even Derian—"

"Say no more, I have heard…" William said and pulled his son close.

Suddenly remembering, Wesley again pushed back. "Olivetan said that Mother is alive!"

"Indeed, we have spoken." Father went on to tell him of their meeting at Merchant's Pass. "Now, I must be on my way." His father's tone told him that he must not argue. "You will travel with Olivetan and find refuge."

"You are not coming with us?" Wesley asked.

"No, your mother sent word, told me her route, and said that she would find her way. She said she would meet us at the Glen."

"So, she told you not to come to her."

"I will not have her traveling alone. What kind of husband would I be if I did not go after them and bring them to the Glen?"

"But, Father—"

William raised a hand. "However..." He turned sideways and said, "I've found you a travel companion."

"Philor!" The brothers embraced. "How?"

"I'll explain along the way," Philor said. "I am sorry for what happened at the farm."

"It's good you are here! You need to meet—"

A frightful shrill cut across the clearing. Hysterics erupted among the crowd. Someone screamed, "Run! Pirates have found us! Run!"

Their reunion was scrambled by the interposing panic among the crowd. It was all Wesley could do to resist the mob pushing past him.

"Don't run! He is with us!" Olivetan's thunderous voice resonated over the outcry.

"Father!" Wesley called, lost in the commotion. His head pivoted, searching for his father and Philor. Yanked backward, Wesley found that William had grabbed his arm.

He shouted, "This way!"

"No, wait! Wait, listen!" Wesley insisted.

"Lower your weapons!" Olivetan's voice carried over the din.

Wesley tore away from his father's grasp. Reeling, he sidestepped thrashing arms. Shoved to his knees, he crawled. Shins thumped his head until he managed to drag himself from the scuffle. There was Olivetan, hands raised, ordering the brave few who closed in around him. "He is our friend! He saved us!"

Callas was crouched on the ground, peering between his arms, which were wrapped around his head. Wesley leapt to his feet and ran to him. He threw himself on the pirate, disregarding the slimy skin. Callas whispered something, but his words were mushed together. He spoke too quickly, using words Wesley had yet to learn. Where is Mahre? Wesley thought and scanned the area. Throwing fists, Mahre sprinted across the clearing.

"Mahre!" Wesley called. "Callas is trying to tell me something!"

Olivetan had finally convinced the panicked gunmen to relax their arms.

Speaking between breaths, Mahre asked, "What…is…it?"

Callas repeated what he was attempting to tell Wesley, and Mahre paled as he listened.

Gesturing to reassure the crowd, Olivetan asked, "What's he saying?"

"Pirate trolls are close. We need to move!"

"How many?" Olivetan hollered at Callas.

"Eusecon," he said.

Olivetan's eyes widened. "The fastest way to the plains is through the river basin. We don't have many, but carry only rifles. Leave the rest of our supplies. Mahre, relay the orders."

Still clinging to Callas, Wesley asked, "How many?"

Olivetan frowned. "Thousands."

65

Despite the protest of Habormoss, William said his farewells and with a small group of scouts moved north, following the mountain range west of Coligny. Olivetan refused to get in the middle of the dispute. William knew the paths and the signs with which the Underground communicated. He was resolved to find Sophia and his daughters, and he would personally escort them to Dochart's Glen.

Olivetan led the Underground away from Arbor Hill, south around the village of Coligny, and north into the river basin. That was all he could do. He did not know where exactly he would find the Glen. Once they reached the basin, he placed Habormoss at the helm, with Mahrc and Callas flanking him. Olivetan steered his monstrous brown bear and followed behind the group alongside Quesnel, keeping an eye on Wesley and Philor riding just ahead. With the River Bresle to the right, they trod toward Langloss Falls.

Olivetan could not calculate how far it was to Dochart's Glen. No man had ever followed a map to get there. Those who entered had stumbled upon it, in a way, yet not by accident. The maps were a loose reference. To be sure, there were six safe havens discovered in the charted regions of World Over. In Nantes alone there were three—

one west of the River Proscl and, including Dochart's Glen, two east of the river. Dochart's Glen was closest to them…most likely.

In the writings, Olivetan had read that those who sought the Glen with evil intent could never find it. Those who wanted to simply satisfy their curiosity or look on as an outsider would "never find rest in its denes." This, of course, added much mystery to their journey. Where they *thought* the Glen could be found was one or two hours southeast of Farne. This would set their arrival for sometime late in the afternoon of the next day—which meant they had to stop for the night. This is what Olivetan feared. Could they survive the night?

First, they would need to get out of the basin area that surrounded Coligny, then set up camp in the Plains of Barrow. He would feel a bit safer in wide open spaces, where he could at least see his enemy approaching.

"How will we know when we've reached the Glen?" Wesley asked, more cheerful than he had been in days. "Will we see something?"

"I'm not sure what to look for or what to expect," Olivetan said.

"None of us do," Quesnel added. "For one to get to Dochart's Glen, one must be led."

"Are we to meet someone, then, who will lead us?" Philor asked.

Quesnel answered, "The magic your mother spoke of will lead us. When, where, or how we will arrive is not certain, but somehow, we will get there together."

"You seem overconfident," Philor said brashly.

Quesnel retorted, "You seem…young."

Light came and went through breaks in the clouds. Tree branches like boney fingers lurched above as if to clasp them. They were far too vulnerable south of the falls. Cold wind rushed up the valley through the basin. Olivetan slid on gloves from his satchel and pushed his bear ahead faster. He needed to quicken their pace. If pirates found them here, this would be their grave.

Minutes later, from the forest came the sound of snapping limbs and crunching leaves. Olivetan slowed, nonchalantly offering cover for Wesley and Philor. Then, as if called together, scores of bears began to emerge. In various sizes and multiple shades of brown, they sauntered into the basin from the left, even wading across the stream. The members of the Underground became surrounded by the creatures' gentle escort.

Wesley called, "What's going on?"

"I'm not certain." His voice droned of uneasiness.

"I never imagined I could be so close to a bear and live, let alone ride one," Philor laughed.

"I felt the same way!" Wesley said. "Did Quesnel call for them?"

Olivetan did not answer.

There had to be over two hundred bears among them now, and still more continued to join the Underground. It seemed that somehow, they were keenly aware of the group's need to get out of the basin. Bears prodded people with their snouts to keep them moving. Soon, women lifted their children and climbed on themselves. It wasn't long until nearly the entire gathering was riding.

"Do you think that the bears are communicating with one another?" Wesley asked.

"Yes," Olivetan answered, his eyes exploring the tree line on the other side of the river, ears actively listening for any unusual sounds. "It's as though…they sense something."

"Are we entering the Glen?" Philor asked.

"Maybe something else," Quesnel broke into the conversation. "Perhaps they know our situation best." Quesnel pointed ahead to a pirate flag hanging from a tree. And there was Habs below it, attempting to pull it down. It was the Jolly Roger of Calbha Mor.

"Pirates are closer than we know," Olivetan said and shook his head, cursing.

"Yes," Quesnel spoke. "They are taunting us."

"They've been following us all along," Olivetan said in a sullen tone. "Waiting for the right time."

From the edge of the forest, Habs pointed at Olivetan, waved him over, and pointed again. He repeated the movement several times. Whatever it was he needed, it seemed urgent.

"I can hear Langloss Falls. From there, it's a short trek to the plains." Olivetan turned his bear toward Habormoss. "Philor and Wesley, stay with Quesnel and keep the group moving toward the falls. Mahre, come with me."

Habs succeeded in his task and began to roll up the flag. By then, Olivetan and Mahre had come up behind him.

"That's quite a token," Olivetan quipped.

Habs lowered his chin, pushed his hand through his hair, and jerked his head, motioning beyond the tree. Moving in closer, Olivetan extended his torso to see around Habs. But Mahre had already leapt from his bear and bounded into Olivetan's view.

"No, no...no..." Mahre made quiet rumblings. With his back toward Olivetan, he seemed to be lifting something.

Olivetan clasped his mouth. Two legs came into view on the ground beside the place where Mahre knelt. From his bear, Olivetan dropped and lurched ahead. He took hold of Mahre, who now was quivering. Leaning over Mahre's shoulder, Olivetan saw what he feared—bodies—a group of scouts for the Underground.

"They've all been strangled," Mahre said and mournfully swayed forward and back, lifting one of the men.

"Mahre…" Olivetan said and tried to stop him from moving. "Mahre, we have to go."

Olivetan searched the area. There was more than one group of scouts among the dead.

"We have to go. Mount your bear."

"But—"

"Do it now!"

"We need to get out of this valley," Habs said.

Olivetan jumped to his feet and ordered Habs, "Be sure to have anyone who is left walking mount up. There are plenty of bears to go around."

Habs nodded and hurried away.

66

angloss Falls was wider than it was tall, expanding nearly twenty-five rods with step-like levels. Cascading waters hushed, loud enough to hide any sound of an approaching enemy. Olivetan allowed only a very brief time for rest. Parents stepped into the shallows to wash themselves and their children. Bears drank from the pool before instinctively moving on. Without a word from Olivetan, some bears began to lead small groups of people up the rocky terrain, north of the falls and toward the plains. Habs secured the trunk of writings and maps on the back of Philor's mount. Mahre kept his distance from the group.

Olivetan breathed a bit easier now. *Has the threat of bears kept the pirates from attacking? I do pray it is so.*

In the shallows of the river, Wesley washed his arms and was thrilled to be with Philor.

"Mother found you in the forest? Unbelievable!" Wesley splashed at his brother. "I've longed to see her. So much, I think I'm hearing her voice!"

"When I first saw her, I thought I was seeing a ghost. One of the scouts had to cover my mouth till I stopped screaming."

Quesnel looked to Olivetan and said, "If we are fortunate enough to arrive on the Plains of Barrow, we mustn't stop. We ride through the night."

"But the children—" Habs argued.

"It seems that the bears are here to guide us. Remember, we are the ones being led."

"Very well," Olivetan conceded. He then called, "Philor, Wesley! Be on your way. Callas will catch up to you soon enough. Stay with him, stay with the parchments."

"Has Callas fallen asleep in such a short time?" Habs asked.

One of the bears nudged the side of the troll's head and began to lick his face. Callas stretched and yawned, then he snatched hold of the bear, kissing the snout.

Quesnel laughed heartily, turned his bear with a tug on its mane, and carried on.

Olivetan ordered, "Onto the plains. We must—"

Above the sound of the falls, a percussion hammered Olivetan's soul. A round buzzed past his head and bore into Quesnel's back. Quesnel howled and slumped forward, his head falling against the red-spattered golden coat of his mount.

"Quesnel!" Olivetan blared.

Wesley was frozen, looking back.

"Make for the plains!" Olivetan ordered Wesley.

"Follow me!" Philor yelled.

But Wesley screamed and steered his bear back toward Quesnel.

"No!" Olivetan called. "Get out of here!" Rifles echoed around them.

Wesley jumped mounts, wrapped his arms around Quesnel, and drove the bear into the trees and beyond the falls.

Callas bolted from the ground, and Mahre urged him on, "Eistisa, eidstisa!" Upon his bear, Habs chased behind Mahre, pushing those remaining toward the Plains of Barrow.

Olivetan lifted the rifle from his shoulder as he spun. A wall of pirates charged them—some running, others riding upon bukavac. Strides pounded the earth, rumbling like an avalanche toward them.

With his left eye closed, Olivetan glared down the barrel of his rifle. He squeezed the trigger, delivering a head shot. The pirate troll in the lead jolted back yet clenched his reins. Straining forward, the troll finally collapsed, driving his bukavac into the ground. Its tangled horns dug up clumps of sod in a spattering of dirt. Without a pause, the contingent of pirate trolls raced over their leader, pummeling and twisting his flaccid limbs.

The bears surrounding Olivetan had already begun their counterattack. Some were immediately impaled by the gnarly horns of the six-legged creatures, but they were not so easily tossed aside. The bukavac whipped their heads, attempting to free their horns from the dead weight. With their massive paws, several bears were quick with an uppercut. Their giant teeth pierced thick bukavac skin. Iron jaws clasped and snapped necks, pulling the bukavac to the ground and busting up riders as they fell.

Olivetan fled upon his mount, dashing ahead through the sparse foliage, away from the siege of pirates. Clasping his bear, he kept his head low as rifles burst one after another behind him. Bears rushed against him, flying past him, springing over drumlins, raging, growling. Throughout the scant wood, bears surged back toward the enemy.

Olivetan blazed onward. He would push the group ahead until they were absorbed by the darkness of night. They would escape.

They would make it to the Glen. *O' pray, how far is it to the Glen? Wait, no! No! Keep moving!*

It was only moments before Olivetan rushed into a crowd of people who had stopped as soon as they reached the Plains. Amidst ruction and confusion, a mother ran past him, screaming and crying for her children. Heated words gave way to a brawl among a group of men. Other groups cowered together, seeming to separate themselves from the chaos.

"Where have you led us?" a young boy cried out at Olivetan, throwing his fist.

"Our blood is on your hands!" another man wailed, sheltering a woman and child.

Ahead, Habs lay sprawled out on the ground. "Habs!" Olivetan called as he rushed to his friend's side and leapt from his bear.

With a hand trying to cover a seeping wound in his leg, Habs spoke through clenched teeth. "Took a shot on the way up. Tell me, Olivetan, where is the whiskey?"

"I've hidden it away for the Glen," Olivetan said with a morbid laugh. "Let's get you up."

"Look north!"

"What?"

"Look north!"

Olivetan pushed his way through a crowd that had gathered and gaped. Stretched out across the plains, dust rose to the northwest. Pirate trolls and bukavac were only minutes away.

Suddenly at Olivetan's side, Mahre calmly said, "Rockets."

"What?" Olivetan asked.

"We could use some of those rockets we had back in the cave."

"We need something greater to save us now!"

"Which way?" Mahre called and took to his bear.

Olivetan searched the landscape and shouted orders, "There! We go east, follow the bears going east! Be sure everyone mounts up!"

"But the canyon, the river! We'll be trapped!" Mahre protested.

"We'll debate this another time. Let's get these people moving." Olivetan raced back to Habormoss. "Pirates will soon overrun us. Can you ride, Habs?"

Habs had ripped cloth from his cloak and cinched it around his wound. "Just as well…" He leaned back against his bear and used it for leverage to stand. "Are there other options?"

"Then, off with you."

"You're not coming?"

"I'm going to shield the Underground for as long as I can." Olivetan searched frantically, looking for Wesley and Philor in the crowd. Some spans ahead, Wesley lagged, still clinging to Quesnel. "There! Get to Wesley, find Philor, and keep moving east! Order the others as you ride!"

Olivetan slung his rifle over his shoulder and commanded men into position. Shouting orders in the chaos, he organized a small battalion. Men scoured what little supplies they carried and began loading rifles. Troops aligned in rows, took aim, and awaited orders.

From behind Olivetan and through the rows of men, hundreds of bears rushed ahead, charging northwest, creating a barrier between the Underground and the trolls. Rifles cracked, and fire lances exploded like thunder over the plains. The pirates had armor and weapons enough to take on Ninian's entire army.

Shrills carried across the plains as the bears collided with bukavac. It seemed as if an endless supply of bears raced to create a wall of protection. Some clenched their jaws around the spindly legs of the bukavac, while others threw themselves between the six legs, busting up both beast and troll. The bears could match the strength of the pirates but were defenseless against the weaponry. Bears began to drop, bloodied and torn. The line bulged until the pirates finally blew open a hole and poured through, raging and howling.

"Fire!" Olivetan commanded.

Blasts erupted from rows of soldiers, who rotated—fire, step back, reload, kneel, fire! But it was little use. Olivetan's troops seemed like a mere nuisance against the hoard of pirates. Some of them limped, wounded by gunshots, and very few dropped dead. Most, crazed and frenzied, raced into their meager defense.

Behind him, the Underground was fleeing, rushing to the canyon. Several soldiers had left the line fleeing behind them. *Should we have come this way? They will never get away. Oh, Great King, where is the Glen?*

Olivetan reached for his sabre. Like bricks in mortar, bears steadied themselves among Olivetan and his troops. He braced himself for impact. Sabres clashed, bodies thumped to the ground, bukavac screeched. In a blur of reckless duels, Olivetan swung his sabre, offering what amounted to pitiful resistance. Pirates rode their bukavac over the lines of men and chased toward the canyon, behind the Underground.

Amidst the whirling dust, manic and dizzy, his blade dripping with troll blood and slime, Olivetan staggered over human limbs and bear carcasses. He could hear others screaming, pleading for their lives. He could hear bears growling, biting, dying! He could hear bukavac snarling—behind him. Just then, a weighty blow hammered Olivetan's right shoulder. Before he hit the ground, his left arm was pulled from its socket. Giant fingers crushed his bicep, lifting him from the ground. Olivetan collapsed in the grasp of a pirate troll, shoulder throbbing, his feet now dangling above the earth. Tossed forward, his legs fell up and over his head, crunching his bones as his knees slammed on the hard, dry ground of the plains. A cloud of dirt blinded him.

"Olivetan!" he heard Philor cry.

Through stinging eyes, Olivetan's focus came and went. Philor stood only a few rods away, staring up at a bukavac, its giant head twisting and sneering. The barrel of a gun rested between its horns. The beast was pulling against reins that stretched back to the rider, too small to be a pirate troll…

"I see you have what belongs to me," the young man on the bukavac called out.

Philor yelled, "It belongs to us!"

"You should never have fled."

"It's not too late, brother." Philor thrust aside his sword. "You can end this nonsense."

Aarn called, "Ipabog! No need to rush this. Where will the Underground go? It seems we have what I need, right here. Order the trolls to march them to the ravine. They will either surrender or they will jump to their deaths!"

"You're mad!" Philor yelled.

"You could have reigned beside me!"

"I saw Mother, in the forest—"

"You lie!"

"She'll forgive you!"

"Now, you mock me? I do intend to end this." Between the horns of the bukavac, the rifle barrel exploded—Philor fell backward to the ground.

Aarn dismounted and stepped up to Philor's side, examining him, seeming to make sure he was dead.

"No!"

That was Wesley. Good god, why is he still here?

Olivetan craned his head as Wesley raced past, pummeling his brother to the ground. Wesley threw his fists, striking across Aarn's jaw.

Wesley stopped long enough to cry out, "Aarn, what have you done?"

Clenching his fists, he repeatedly beat at Aarn's chest and face. In no time, Aarn seized Wesley's arms and heaved him aside. He flew to his feet and drove his boot into Wesley's ribs. As Wesley lay moaning, recoiling on the ground, Aarn walked beyond Olivetan and soon turned back, dragging the trunk which held the parchments.

Pirates and bukavac had encircled them. From far off, the screams of those in the Underground afflicted Olivetan. Helplessly he lay, his body broken.

"Wesley!" Olivetan hollered. "Wesley!"

Aarn looked over, sneered at Olivetan, and proceeded on his way. As the trunk slid by Wesley, he kicked at it, and it dropped from Aarn's hand. Rolling over and coddling his ribs, Wesley used the trunk to pull himself up, took hold of the handle, and began to make his way in the other direction.

"And where will you go?" Aarn took his time, following after Wesley before he finally jerked the trunk out of his brother's grasp. "You are as stupid as you are helpless! You should be thankful I have let you live."

Wesley raged and leapt forward, landing on the trunk and tearing it from Aarn's fingers. He lay trembling, jaw locked, eyes fiery.

"You are a bold one. I will spare your life for the sake of our sisters. You know, our sisters will need someone, considering that your friends have murdered Derian." Aarn clutched the back of Wesley's tunic and once again threw him out of his way. Standing tall, he paraded the trunk back toward his bukavac.

Yet after three strides, it slipped from his hand.

Aarn spun in a fury, yelling, "Leave it!" He seemingly expected to see Wesley again.

But Wesley was still in the dirt—aching, watching. He groaned, "Go on! Take it, you fool!"

"Someone has to be the hero…" Aarn picked it up again, and it fell to the ground. He drew up his hands, looked closely, then tried once more to lift his prize. He took three steps with it, and it again fell. His face looked like that of a boy who had lost his way home.

"What have you done to me?" he accused his brother. "Did you find your magic?"

Wesley was silent.

"Oh yes, Philor told me. You thought none of us saw you. He watched you go to the woman with the rings! Have you cast some sort of spell?"

"I wish I had!" Wesley shouted.

One of the trolls had taken notice and lurched up behind Aarn. Aarn pointed to the trunk, ordering the troll to take it away. The pirate troll hoisted it to his shoulder, and now satisfied, Aarn said, "You're pitiful, Wesley." But as he turned to leave, the trunk fell from the pirate's shoulder, hitting Aarn and knocking him to the ground.

By now, Wesley had taken hold of the trunk's handle with two hands.

"You are persistent." Aarn again ordered the troll to help. "But you're not worth my time."

Taking one step, the pirate troll clasped the opposite handle, effortlessly snatching the trunk, dragging it and Wesley along the ground. But over and over, the trunk fell from the troll's hands. Seething, he growled, pounced behind Wesley, and shoved him aside. The troll hoisted the trunk and began strutting away.

Suddenly, it fell through him to the ground. It was as if the troll were a ghost. Infuriated, the pirate tried and tried again to grasp it with no avail. Swinging in anger, its large arms seemed to have no substance. Every few swings, the trunk would lift and fall, until no more. No matter how hard he tried, the troll had no effect on it.

Aarn pulled a dagger and lunged at Wesley, who dodged the thrust and cautiously backed away from his brother.

"You'll not make a fool of me! I guess I will have to kill you to break the spell!" Aarn raged and brought the blade down, slicing across Wesley's neck and chest.

Wesley stumbled back, unharmed. It seemed the blade had never touched him!

Aarn jabbed and thrust at Wesley, unable to make contact. "What? Perhaps it was not you who cast the spell…" Aarn then took notice of Olivetan and ordered the pirate, "Kill him!"

As each of Olivetan's bones cried out, one of which was bent backward, exposed, and pushing through his skin, a shadow fell over him. Gritting his teeth, he allowed his head to fall back into the dust as he stared up at the beast. Maul in hands, the pirate raised his arms. But as he did so, new light outlined the bulging creature and even began to pierce him like a cloud. The troll brought down his pernach with crushing force. Unable to move, Olivetan closed his eyes and awaited the blow.

And waited.

But there was nothing.

Only the sound of…songbirds?

Olivetan opened his eyes. Time and time again, the troll beat down upon him with his maul. Yet, it passed through him without the lightest touch. The troll growled and bellowed in his struggle. Enraged, the pirate launched the maul, and it faded away as it flew. Poised to attack, he clenched his fists and snarled at Olivetan. He desperately thrust forward and fell through Olivetan into nothingness.

Aarn had given up trying to stab Wesley, and he now spent all his attention on taking hold of the trunk. In a frenzy of kicking and swinging, Aarn raged, but just like the troll, he had become ethereal.

With his fists clenched, he screamed at Wesley, "I will find you! I will killlll youuuu!" His voice dissipated along with his substance.

Olivetan pushed up from the ground, feeling no pain. He searched his surroundings. The entire legion of pirate trolls—gone. Everything was crisp and clean. New colors beamed. New sounds soothed him. His arms, though sore and stiff, had healed. The gentle steps of a butterfly on the back of his index finger lit up his nerves. And there was Wesley, running away from him through a green field of wild grasses.

Olivetan looked back as Mahre appeared at his side. With a smile, Olivetan marveled, "We've arrived!"

"Indeed," Mahre said, as amused as he was astonished.

"I've been made whole," Olivetan said. "Somehow, I've been healed!"

Absorbed in the wonder, Mahre's amazement seemed to keep him from speaking.

A trumpet blared from a long way off, welcoming them. In the lush green of the plains, the inhabitants of the Glen approached with royal flags, hailing their arrival. Birds swooped overhead with thin, golden streamers hanging from their beaks. The canyon was gone. There in its place was a stone manor among the trees.

People of the Underground cheered, and the bears roared in delight, welcomed by Dochart's Glen.

"Aderlos!" Callas stood from the ground.

A gasp rose from the citizens of the Glen, then only silence. Olivetan found himself laughing out loud. Likely, they had to be wondering how a pirate troll had ever entered. But in a moment of a moment, in the light of Dochart's Glen, Callas was seen for who he was, and like fog on a sunny morning, the tension seemed to easily lift away.

Olivetan greeted many with a kiss of friendship. He thanked them for his healing, though his hosts were quick to not take any credit.

"We are servants, just as you are," was the reply. Others nodded in agreement. "Always humbled by the incessant magic of these parts."

The crowd began to disperse and make their way to the manor. It was then that Olivetan thought of Wesley. And it wasn't long until he saw the boy, holding Quesnel in his lap. He ran to Wesley and called for Callas. Wesley's bloodied hands trembled as Callas lifted the body.

"Philor is gone! The magic did not save him! Will the magic not save Quesnel?" Tears followed single paths below each of his eyes.

Olivetan guided Wesley to his feet. "It has brought him here," Olivetan answered.

"But what of Philor, why not him?"

"Answers may come later..." Olivetan had no explanation for Wesley. "Come along, now."

Walking behind the celebration, Olivetan held Wesley close, while Callas carried the body of Quesnel. And with heavy steps, the three friends went deeper into the Glen.

A Farewell to Friends

67

esley dragged his feet twenty paces behind the funeral procession. He skirted around puddles that had formed just before dawn. The crowd ahead of him sang a dirge that hung in the air like the mist of the grey day.

A bead of water pelted his skin. Its stony splash shot a quiver through his body. Other heavy drops thudded to the water-saturated ground around him. He looked up to see branches twisted by the wind with dying leaves flicking off droplets high above him.

Even the Glen was exposed to the elements. Or was it? Maybe it sings its own dirge. It seems to be mourning with us.

Wesley had wept for most of that first night. And when he did sleep, his nightmares replayed Philor's murder. Aarn's eyes had held fury like he had never seen. *Will he be waiting for me when I leave the Glen? Will he find a way in and kill me in my sleep? Will he go after Father? Or Mother and our sisters? I'm helpless to save them from here in the Glen!* Olivetan had said that Philor was to be praised for his honorable death. But grief was still suppressing pride in his brother's courage.

Footsteps trod up from behind, and a hand came down on Wesley's shoulder.

"You know what they say about the Glen, Wes?" Mahre asked.

Wesley continued walking, keeping his eyes on the procession far ahead. Then, he remembered—not "what they say about the Glen." Rather, he remembered something that had happened the year his family moved to Navarre."What is it?" Mahre nudged him with an elbow.

"It feels like I've been to a place like this before. Mother told stories—"

"A haven in the hills," Mahre said.

"Yes, that is how Mother referred to it. I remember very little, but the year she disappeared—when Father moved us north—we spent the night in a haven, perhaps several nights."

"Olivetan has told me the story."

Wesley paused. "Of course, since we met, I have had but a shred of memory. He has known me all along, all those years. It's been so long since I've thought about that time. I remember how sad Avlae was when we left."

"Did she long to stay?" asked Mahre.

"I think we all did, but she was upset about leaving something behind…I do not recall what it was…"

Mahre pointed ahead. "They're moving off the path."

Wesley reached out to stop Mahre before he ran on. "What do they say, Mahre? You know, about the Glen?" Wesley pushed his hands deep into his coat pockets to warm them.

Mahre smiled. "They say that if you are buried in the Glen, you will live here forever."

"I don't understand."

"Another time, Wesley. Let's go, the ceremony is about to begin!"

They both ran ahead, splashing down the water-soaked road and then jutting off down a muddy path. Winding back through the trees, they caught up just as the cortege entered the glade. Finally, they toddled to the front of the crowd to see the ritual. Wrapped in white cloth, the body of Quesnel was carried across the glade on a golden bier.

Mahre knelt next to Wesley and whispered, "The bier is made of cedar overlaid with gold."

Wesley had never seen anything like it. He had watched funeral processions in Navarre using old wooden biers with uneven wheels, but nothing as elegant as this. The side rails, high in the middle, curved and tapered off to the front and back. Ornate moldings decorated each end.

Two men ahead and two behind walked single file, carrying the bier by clasping long, golden poles in their hands. The poles slid through gold rings on each side of the body.

Across the glade at the border of the clearing, magistrates of the Glen turned to face the assembly. There were seven in all, four women and three men. Their earthen-brown tunics were layered with rich green and purple cloaks. The men held vertically a long and narrow golden rod, clasped at chest level with their left hands. At the top of the pole, a bronze image of some kind of bird stretched its wings as if in flight. In their right hands, one of the men held a lantern, another a scroll, and the third, closest to the center, held a clay bowl. The women let down their hoods. The one in the center with a golden sash stepped forward.

"That is the dean," Mahre whispered.

Draped around her neck were gold and silver cords with thick tassels. One of her hands grasped thin chains supporting a golden censer. The length of chain looped into her other hand and dangled down.

Those who carried the bier stopped parallel to the crowd but closer to the magistrates. The men kneeled, lowering the bier. The one in front turned and put his arms under Quesnel's shoulders. The one behind reached and placed his hands under the knees. Together, they lifted the body over the side rail and placed it on the grass before the council. The two other bearers stepped over the pole. One straightened the legs of the body, while the other placed Quesnel's hands—one over the other—on his stomach. The men realigned themselves with the bier, lifted it from the ground, and proceeded to the edge of the glade.

The dean lifted the hasp on her censer and slid the lid up. The man with a clay bowl stepped up beside her.

"There is incense in the bowl," Mahre explained.

The man spooned incense over burning coals within the censer. He then bowed and took a step back. The dean put the lid back in place and closed the hasp. Smoke immediately escaped through decorative holes in the cover, and the dean began to swing the censer to-and-fro, left and right over Quesnel's body. The sharp fragrance wisped over the glade and stung Wesley's nostrils. He had smelled this before, but he could not recall where. It was a sacred scent. As strong as it was, the scent was tantalizing, and the breeze carried it up and away.

Another man stepped forward and unrolled his scroll. In a call and response with the other magistrates, he sang. Through the smoke came a chant in cadence with the jangle of the swinging censer. Reverent tones in an ancient dialect resonated through the gathering.

Again, Mahre whispered, "Do you see what is happening to Quesnel? This is his farewell to friends."

Wesley, who had been fixated on the magistrate singing, looked to the body. Bright green sprouts, one after another, leapt from the ground. After the sudden jump into life, the growth slowed, and the plants vined over the body. Stems and leaves grew until the white cloth could no longer be seen.

Upon ceasing his chant, the man rolled up his scroll. Lowering her censer, the dean stepped back in line. The vines tightened against Quesnel's body. He began to sink into the soil—no, his body was being *pulled* into the soil. When the vines no longer stirred, a woman stepped forward from the crowd. She held a flat, woven basket filled with a variety of wildflowers.

The dean lifted a hand, and the woman paused. The ritual continued. More incense was added to the censer. Then came the clinking of chains and a cloud of smoke. To her right, a woman called out, "Servants of the Great King, pilgrims to mystery, the unknown realms greet you. The boundless wayfare begins. We remember our sons and daughters, Derian Delaine, Philor Delaine, Ezra Caen, and Torres Aeches..." The dean continued naming off others who had died on their journey: the scouts, and those who died in battle.

The breeze ceased, but the sacred scent still hung in the air, a sweet sage with the sharpness of ginger. One of the women stepped forward, spread her arms, and silently mouthed words. The man with the lantern lifted it forward, let it go, and it balanced upon nothing.

Wesley felt Mahre's warm breath again on his ear. "The lantern will stay, and the oil will be refilled seven times, lasting seventy days. It is a light for the path into the unknown realms."

The crowd formed a line, and each took a flower from the woman with the basket. They walked to the place where the body was laid. Some simply dropped the flower, whereas others knelt and placed the flower, whispering words Wesley could not hear. When it came to his turn, Wesley took a yellow wood violet and dropped it on all the rest.

When the entire crowd had passed by, the dean gave a dismissal. One by one and some in pairs, the assembly walked out of the glade. No one spoke.

Wesley wept…again.

Long Live
King Gaspard

68

Leaving the lower gardens below Stone Manor, Wesley climbed wide slabs of fieldstone winding upward in a semicircle. Amidst the wild grasses and alongside his path, for every two slabs, an unlit lantern hung upon nothing. Up ahead, a young girl's white tunic seemed to glow in the twilight. She filled the oil and lit the wicks of the lanterns, working her way down.

"Good evening, young king," the girl bowed and immediately returned to her task.

"And to you," Wesley said, wishing that she had not referred to him as *king*. For the first time since he could remember, he was pleased to *not* be of age for the crown. If there was any way to delay his fifteenth birthday, he would find it. Perhaps, the magic could help with that!

He rubbed his forehead, searching through memories. It seemed as if he had seen the young girl before, long ago. "If you don't mind me asking, miss…tell me, how long have you served in the Glen?"

"Our guests seem always to be concerned about time." Her eyes rolled with dissatisfaction, but then upon realizing her inappropriate response, she blushed. After adjusting the flame, she lowered the globe. With a gentle release, the lantern bobbed in midair to a stop. "For your sake, the Glen offers the illusion of passing time. I've been here for decades if we consider the way you measure time."

That's it! If we remain in the Glen, I will never become of age for the crown!

Focused on her task, she spoke while stepping down to the next lantern. "You will check off the days you stay. The sun will rise and set. Your stay is limited to the rest you need." The girl busied herself, adding oil to the next lantern. "But for me..." She paused and smiled at Wesley. "I, simply, am in the Glen." After another humble bow, she added, "Good evening, young king," and she went on her way.

Oh, stop calling me king...

Wesley continued his ascent, passing under one of the many terraces and over a river that swept alongside the manor. Ahead at the entrance to the upper gardens, Olivetan waited beneath an elegant fieldstone archway, right where he had said he would be.

"Patience is the key to relief," Olivetan spoke loudly. He was trying to speak above the roar of the rapids below.

"Yet, what do we wait for?" Wesley said, shrugging his shoulders.

"We have new parchments to examine. We must plan our route to the Dragon Spring and—"

Wesley broke in, "Why not stay here? We are safe from the trolls. Why not lead people to the Glen?" He tried to sound more concerned than hopeful.

"The Glen is but a wayside, and we must not presume upon its graces."

"Yet, the magistrates say it is a foretaste of the treasure."

"And they are correct. The magic that rules the Glen has broken into our world. The treasure will bridge that gap, completing the Fullness of Time."

This only frustrated Wesley more. Havens—if one was lucky

enough to find one—would only provide a limited stay. What kind of magic could lead them out from under the ice, but could not protect Philor? Aarn was protected from the storm, while Quesnel was murdered! *Magic*, it seemed to Wesley, was quite irrational.

Olivetan seemed to ignore Wesley's defiant posture. "Let's move farther in, where we will not have to speak over the rushing waters."

Lagging behind, Wesley followed Olivetan into the first garden. Many tiers held pools, dazzling in the light of floating oil lamps. Moss-covered stone statues adorned the grasses—sirens, sleeping elves, and laughing sylphs.

Maintaining his hardened attitude, Wesley said, "My mother spoke of the *havens in the hills*. From what she did tell us, much of what I have seen here is how I remember her describing it."

"That's right," Olivetan answered. "Gaspard said that in his time of need, he was led to a haven in the hills."

"I thought the things she told us were merely fables. She could have saved us much pain had she spoken plainly."

"What she did was for your safety—your family's safety."

Wesley's stomach churned as if he had swallowed fresh ginger. *Perhaps now was not the time to speak with Olivetan. He would only encourage me in my role as king. "Learn to serve well." Enough! I'd just as soon become a pirate troll. I will wait to speak with Mother and Father.*

Wesley poked at one of the floating lamps. It teetered above the ground as if balancing on a stick. "Is this some kind of spell?" Wesley asked. He pushed the lamp sideways, then as he let go, it rebounded to its original position. "It's quite amazing."

"I wouldn't say a spell," Olivetan said. "Think of it as the essence of the Glen."

"I think I understand," Wesley said. Staring into the sky, he walked a path beside one of the pools. "This essence is what we see as magic in…Wait!" He side-stepped, turning in a circle. "Olivetan, look!"

The dirt path had become a stream. Wesley jumped and splashed but did not sink. His footsteps made ripples in the water, but his feet remained dry. The stream became like steps. Wesley hopped from one step to the next. He kicked and splashed while water flowed under his feet.

From the next tier, Wesley called down to Olivetan, "Mahre told me…something about those who are buried in the Glen, live in the Glen?"

"Mahre says too much," Olivetan called back while making his way closer.

The second garden was dense with thick, tall trees, and stars began to shine through branches far above. Some flittered, but not all of them. Wesley focused. The moving lights were below the branches. With a light coming closer, he lifted an arm to shield its brilliance. Swatting at his nose, Wesley watched the light jump and wisp away with the buzz of a hummingbird. A trail of glitter floated behind, vanishing as it fell.

"What was that?" Wesley exclaimed. "Wait, don't answer. It is the *essence* of the Glen."

Olivetan laughed. "You are beginning to understand! But yes, it is written that if you are buried in the Glen, you will live on in the Glen. Mahre was referring to a passage in one of the writings, wherein Gaspard met with his father, who had died years earlier."

"Gaspard's father was Gilead," Wesley replied.

"You *do* know your lineage!" Olivetan's eyes brightened. "Yes, you see, Gaspard was not the first to be led to one of the havens. Gilead had come before, as well as Junia, Iscah, Jael…the list goes on. You witnessed the burial of Quesnel today. Gilead's burial is written in volume two of the Manor Tomes."

"So, we may meet up with Quesnel again in the Glen someday?" Wesley looked away from his upward trance, grabbing Olivetan's arm.

"It seems possible."

"But why not Philor? Why did his body not enter with us, like Quesnel?"

"That, I cannot say. It is a mystery. Perhaps he chose not to come this way. There are other Havens. There will be much to learn, much for you to work through."

That thought had never crossed Wesley's mind. *There is so much I do not know.*

The two continued their walk, stepping into yet a third garden filled with light and the trilling sound of whatever had landed on his nose earlier.

Olivetan reached inside his coat and pulled out a small piece of parchment. "I was reading this after the funeral service and sharing it with several administrators." Olivetan pointed. "Read from here."

> *Once again, I found myself at Stone Manor. Prior to my arrival, I did not consider myself to be in harm's way. But here I was, so I took my rest. I walked along the river, disillusioned about where I was and what I was to do. Feeling quite alone, it wasn't long until I met an older gentleman sitting on a bench. He joined me on my walk and became my companion for some time. As we talked, the*

man seemed to know me well. We shared stories and
poetry. My weariness lifted. Soon he bid me farewell
and went on with his journey. It was then that I
realized I had been speaking with my father...

"Where is the rest?" Wesley asked.

"We found this parchment torn. It may be that we find another copy among those that Habs has collected."

"Do you think we will see my great-grandfather? He could have been buried in this haven!"

"I simply do not know. This is all—"

"What is that?" Wesley interrupted.

Not far ahead was a single giant tree, unlike all the trees in the previous gardens. Its roots extended from the trunk, seven to eight rods above the ground, creating a dome, a natural pavilion. High above, stretching horizontally, its branches created a leafy ceiling over the garden. Vibrant verdures filled with light revealed a new depth in shades of jade and silver. Endless varieties of songbirds in all the colors of the rainbow swooped and climbed among its branches.

Drawn in deeper, Wesley saw that the notes sang by the birds created the brightness of the garden. For light burst from their beaks, giving color to sound. It was like being able to *see* the notes of a symphony. The deep purple of a C, the brilliant gold of an F, the reds of a G sharp. His hearing acquired a mysterious link to his eyesight. The more intense the sound, the richer and deeper its pigments. Streaks of effervescent colors crossed above them, blending the blues, reds, and yellows, creating a new gamut of festal harmony.

"I know this song," Wesley stated with curiosity and caution. He advanced several paces ahead of Olivetan and stared up at the tree. He cupped his hands together and lifted them up. "This is the tree from my visions, the one that grows from my hands. Only it's much, much larger. What does this mean, Olivetan?" Wesley stood like a statue.

"It is the beginning."

"The beginning?"

Olivetan knelt beside Wesley and pointed upward. "The branches extend beyond where we can see. Look closely."

Lowering his arms, Wesley turned and followed Olivetan's direction. "They look as if they are moving, continuously growing."

"It is the beginning of a reign," Olivetan explained.

"A reign…" *Please, no more talk about me being heir to the throne.*

"An endless reign. The birds sing of the magic that has begun."

"The magic outside the Glen? The magic Mother spoke of?"

"Well, yes. Consider your father. He swears that a flaming arrow pierced his chest, yet he lived. Then he was mysteriously found by Quesnel."

"Indeed. What else?"

"Beneath the streets of Port Regael, Ninian's soldiers fired upon Habs and Mahre. Yet, somehow time itself separated and took two different courses. The Underground made it safely away."

"It reminds me of the boys who found a shelter during the storm."

"Yes, I'd nearly forgotten," Olivetan said. "These are beginnings, glimpses of the treasure."

"But at my mother's cairn…I was in chains, I was drowning."

"And did those—"

"Those were dreadful things." A tangle of thoughts returned, and like briar bushes, they seemed to twist and poke at him beneath his skull. "Is *that* the magic Mother spoke of?"

"There are—"

Wesley jumped right back in, "And why didn't the magic save my brothers? Why couldn't the magic save them like it did the Underground beneath the city? Why did it save me and not them? Had they had visions? Why has Aarn betrayed his family? Will the magic help him? Whose side does the magic take?"

Olivetan waited, then raised his brows as if to ask if Wesley was through. "The magic serves us in ways we may not expect. I cannot say that it will not help Aarn, or even King Ninian may benefit from it. Your mother has helped me understand that."

Wesley did not have the strength to wrestle anymore, trying to comprehend Olivetan's responses. Something brushed by his leg, and he let Olivetan's words hang as creatures came from all around him—bears, badgers, even squirrels.

"Don't tell Callas about the squirrels," Olivetan said. And they laughed together.

Beneath the tree, its roots curved out and down, forming a large dome-like fort beneath. Archways had formed natural entrances, where the animals were entering. More and more people emerged from the wood around them, exchanging an evening greeting with Olivetan and Wesley, people of every color and kingdom.

"Seems like a celebration!"

"Let's have a look," Olivetan replied. "I'm quite interested myself."

The pair made their way with the growing numbers to the entrances. A droning hum of voices grew louder as they approached.

Wesley stopped and peered in. "It's an amphitheater. It doesn't look nearly this big from the outside." The dome tripled in size as they moved from the outside in.

Wesley and Olivetan entered with the rest of the crowd beneath the natural arch. Rows of seats separated by several aisles fanned out from a small platform in the center of the room, where two dignitaries were seated. Dressed in charcoal robes embroidered with golden emblems, their arms exaggerated their conversation as they laughed together.

An older gentleman taller than Olivetan approached. He was slender, wearing a black velvet jacket and dark grey knee-high trousers. A thin white ruff surrounded his neck. Below his wide forehead, his attentive eyes invited them onward.

With a turn of the wrist, he beckoned them ahead. "Gentlemen," he said.

The aisle was clean-swept dirt. The wooden benches looked as if they had grown right out of the ground.

Wesley turned back and looked at Olivetan. "Where will we sit? The rows are full."

Olivetan urged him on, then pointed across the room opposite from where they entered, over the heads of talkative guests. He said, "Look, there's Callas!"

The pirate troll waved. Wesley chuckled, waving back.

The usher stopped just before the platform in front, facing Olivetan and Wesley. In the front row, left of the platform, there was space for two right next to Mahre and Habs. As the two were seated, the dignitaries stood, and the garrulous crowd calmed.

In his ornate black linen robe, one proclaimed, "If one's heart is cold!"

And the crowd responded, "There is no hope!" At that, the crowd stood and hollered and cheered, cawed and yelped. Despite the dignitaries' attempts, they would not be quieted. When finally the crowd was settled back into their seats, the dignitary began again.

"Welcome with me those who have come for respite." Another round of applause tarried on. Callas could be heard hooting from the back. "The treasure is at hand. We look to the Inner Realm—the Province Beyond the River—to claim the field of Gaspard and proclaim its wealth." With that, the man returned to his seat on the platform.

The second dignitary stood. He lifted a silver, silky linen from a table beside him, revealing a crown. With poise, he carried the crown to the front of the platform. "We have a sovereign among us. To him the reign is due. The second throne of Nantes has sat empty for two generations. But no longer. Welcome with me, Wesley Francis Delaine-Gaspard. Let the coronation begin!"

With that, the crowd once again rose to their feet and roared as if claiming a victory. Ovation flooded the room.

Wesley's heart was in his throat. He could not move. He seemed to suffocate. For a moment, he believed another vision had overcome him.

Olivetan reached to him and said, "Go on, son."

"But…I am not ready." Wesley's neck prickled with heat below his tunic. His breaths became short. He clasped his seat to stop himself from shaking.

"You will learn to serve well."

"But I'm not of age! I'm too young to be crowned king!"

"This is merely the ceremony. With all that has happened—"

"No! You said I will have much to work through. This is one of those things. I need time."

"Look, you have some time. When you turn fifteen, your reign will begin, while the formalities will have already been settled. Besides, the magistrates know this, and they'll appoint others to make decisions until you are of age."

Forcing a temperate expression, Wesley said under his breath, "What about Avlae?"

"The law forbids a woman from ruling when there is a male heir. Surely, you must know that."

"Change the law!" Wesley's voice burst over the abrupt silence. "I am not ready! I do not want this!"

A Letter from
Brazenose

Epilogue

Olivetan examined the dressing along the massive double-arched portico. Fairies danced among leaves, ornamenting the voussoir. He had seen the work of master sculptors outside the Glen, but none of their work held such intricacies and attention to detail. It was as if the artist worked with a wider gamut, using tools unknown to World Over. The craftmanship seemed to call for a celebration, a clarion call so that all might take it in and see a thousand new wonders and hear a thousand new songs.

Olivetan sneezed, and his feet hit the ground as if he had fallen from the ceiling. Immediately, he threw his arms out for balance. After a quick glance to see if anyone was looking, he stepped onto the terrace of Stone Manor.

Roaring waters gushed several rods below. Between his index finger and thumb, he pinched the bridge of his nose and wiped away sand-like particles. A quick breeze pushed against his face. He took in the green scent of the forest with a hint of woodsy tobacco from Habs's pipe. Oh how he loved the smell of a pipe. It reminded him of his father. Though it was rare for Olivetan to light one up, he certainly did not mind a good whiff now and then.

To fight the chill, he crossed his arms and rubbed his shoulders.

Across the semicircle slab, Habs stood in a heavy moss-colored cloak, leaning forward against a marble rail. From the shadow of the manor, Olivetan strolled into the morning rays. Itinerant sounds of songbirds enhanced the morning mirth.

"To whom much is given, much will be required," Olivetan stressed.

Habs glanced over, lifted a thick orange eyebrow, removed the pipe from his jaw, and said, "Indeed, that has been my fret for many years. Yet, my role as Chief Agent to the *yet to be kinged* Wesley is only until he comes of age."

"Your word will be sovereign for how long?" Olivetan mused. "Three months?"

"I only speak on behalf of the king. Decisions will be made by his *wise advisors*." Habs chuckled, gesturing toward Olivetan.

"You can put it back on me, but you make it so." Olivetan took a courtly bow. "Wesley only needs time. Three months until he is of age. By then, he'll be ready."

"What if he refuses the throne? He calls to change the law, but he cannot do that unless he takes the throne!" Habs looked away, seemingly to study the waters below.

Olivetan let the silence hang comfortably. It seemed to be the appropriate pace for time in the Glen.

Finally, Habs spoke again. "And do you think that the dignitary acted in haste, appointing us as sovereign council? How do you suppose the magistrates will react?"

"It matters not to me." Olivetan huffed. "You know how I feel about many of them, how they feign authority, exhibiting their theories and intentionally obscuring mystery."

"Would you have them remain silent and offer no explanations?"

"I would have them be truthful."

Habs opened his mouth to counter him again, but he let it go and said, "And what would you advise next?"

Olivetan had been considering that question since they arrived. "Well, when the council of the Glen meets tonight, I will propose that we spread word that an heir of Gaspard lives and will soon be of age for the crown." Olivetan waited for a response. Certainly, Habs had to have given this some thought.

"Dangerous play, my friend." Habs puffed his pipe like a chimney and raised his voice, "Ninian has many on the inside. How will we keep Wesley safe? Let alone, an action like that could lead Nantes to civil war!"

"Do you not think that Ninan will have to conform to the will of the people?"

"*Hmmph*…'Will of the people.' You seek to force his hand. He will attack like a wounded animal. The council will not send Wesley back to Port Regael. Ninian has too many on his side within the castle walls."

"I'm not suggesting we send him back into—"

"Just what *are* you suggesting?"

Now was not the time for this. "There is much to consider," Olivetan conceded and changed the subject. "How did Callas take the news?"

"He understands that we need Sophia to reverse the spell."

"And he'll continue on the journey with us?"

"Yes, yes," Habormoss grumbled. "I do pray that William and his men find passage to Sophia and the girls."

"William seems strong again," Olivetan spoke confidently. "We'll trust he finds his way."

"Yes, we shall trust he is kept well."

Olivetan stepped away and walked parallel to the railing. He pulled his cloak a bit tighter around him. Dull red leaves floated down into the rapids. A gust of wind swirled up the river valley. Crisp leaves scraped the marble floor, scattering across the terrace.

"And what of the shipment? Did you receive what you were promised?" Olivetan called back toward Habs.

"And more." Pipe in mouth, Habs marked an invisible point with one hand and stretched the other to highlight the extent. "We have caves mapped from the Dragon Spring all the way to Coragaes Pass. *Safest* way to travel."

Realizing where this conversation was headed, Olivetan continued, "Fortitude is not molded by a soft pillow."

"Our journey to the Glen was not so comfortable. Never mind the loss of Quesnel and others. We'll find peril soon enough; no need to go looking for it." Habs's face wrinkled, and he lifted a hand as if Olivetan would disregard anything he had to say.

Seeing that Habs was not up for a little banter, Olivetan raised his arms in a tender gesture. "I sail to Telos Isle for my brother's sake."

"The Underground has no use for your brother!" Habs huffed, his voice as sour as the look on his face. He continued, "He has failed us twice before. Few trust him, if any. It seems you would divide the Underground."

Olivetan searched the cloudless skies, giving thought to his next words. "You do not know my brother like I do. He may have different convictions, but bring out the bread and wine, and we will all sit at the same table."

Speaking with his pipe clenched in his teeth, Habs asked, "Will this be another consideration of the council?"

"I do not seek their permission. The council may disagree, but I do not intend to leave my brother behind."

"Be certain you do not speak out of pride."

Olivetan understood Habs's concern. Yet, he figured that this conversation would come up later. "We shall meet at Brazenose, nonetheless. For that is where both our paths will lead us."

Habs muttered something, but Olivetan let it go and did not attempt to decipher it. The two remained quiet for a while. This time, the silence was uncomfortable. Olivetan was already dreading the evening meeting.

"Pardon me, sirs."

Thankful for the interruption, Olivetan was glad to see the girl who had been lighting lanterns the night before. Her midnight hair contrasted the same white linens. The maiden hurried across the terrace and handed Olivetan an envelope.

"This arrived in the night from Brazenose," she reported.

"Thank you," Olivetan said, and the girl dismissed herself. He then spoke aloud, mostly to himself, "How do we receive mail in the Glen?"

"The albatross," Habs stated. "At least, that's what the tales say."

Olivetan laughed as he said, "Like a carrier pigeon?"

"In the writings of Gaspard…" Habs cleared his throat. "'As men, we stumbled upon the Glen, but the albatross can view it from above. Some call it a myth. I say men don't see because they do not want to see.'" His tone was gruff again.

While the albatross story held some of his attention, Olivetan mostly kept his focus on the letter. "I am not sure I'm ready to read about where we'll be off to next. I'd like to appreciate being in a safe place for a while," Olivetan admitted.

"But certainly, you do long to hear from friends," Habs tempted, and his mood lightened.

It had been months since Olivetan had spoken to anyone in

Brazenose. He turned the envelope over in his hands. The maroon wax seal looked authentic. Retrieving his glasses from his inside pocket, he examined it closely.

"This *is* from Brazenose," he noted.

Olivetan often imagined what the treasure would be like. He had only fragments of peace and wisdom, made up of incomplete sentences. He'd had glimpses of the treasure, but the edges were rough, and some of the pieces did not fit together quite right. Although those things bothered him, the things that were clear kept him busy enough.

No more duplicity. While there were certainly many who suspected him of working with the Underground, it was now plain for all to see. There was no turning back, but he knew that from the beginning. Olivetan and Habs stood now at the helm of the Underground's movement south to the Province Beyond the River—the Inner Realm. Outside of the Glen, nowhere would be safe.

"How did we ever get here, Habs?" Olivetan asked. The immensity of it all sought to crush him.

Habs curled the corners of his lips and gestured to the letter. "Are you going to open it?"

Olivetan broke the seal and removed the letter. After a breath, he unfolded the note and read aloud to Habs:

> *Gavell and Soren, servants of the Great King to those in Port Regael, Navarre, and Northern Nantes—peace to you and the hope of Gaspard. We trust you are kept well, and we eagerly look forward to your arrival.*

Word has reached us concerning the breach at Beggar's Bay. The tales of your perseverance through the storm have comforted us most dearly. The icy curse has not come to Brazenose, and for this we are grateful. But threats of pirates and dark spells remain.

Virulent forces of pirate trolls were stopped at Fehrael, but rumors tell of the fiends outside the village of Breda and as close as Coragaes Pass. Brazenose has fortified its walls, doubling its sentries and its weaponry. Citizens are afraid—afraid to leave, afraid to stay. They fear the pirates will come here to invade the Inner Realm, and their fear is not misplaced. It is the shortest distance to cross the deep waters of the river. Is it not for this reason that you come, as well?

Ninian has sent his latest weaponry, along with the promise of a visit within the month. He, too, protects the treasure, though it continues to elude him. He does not allow passage into the Realm. With news of the trolls, the last bridge was destroyed. We will be grateful, for whether the treasure is protected out of reverence or out of greed, it is protected nonetheless, and for that we are content. Yet, we know you must cross. Therefore, we trust that a way will be given.

A final warning—we learned that Medici

has cursed the river. It has been reported that a ferry
comes and goes, traveling the river at night. People
board but never disembark. Witnesses refuse
to even touch the water. Villagers now refer to it as
"the River of Doubt." We will be vigilant.

  Be of good comfort, for your labors avail
much. Send our greeting to the others. May
the Great King go with you on your journey to
Brazenose.

Olivetan closed the letter and slipped it back into the envelope. He then nodded toward Habs and turned to leave.

He had only taken a step when Habs spoke up. "We have much to do. Have you thought about when we will leave?"

Olivetan turned back and answered, "Enjoy some respite, friend. A good rest is half the work."

The End

Pronunciations

Characters

Aarn: ARN

Aphrosyna: a-FRŎ-sə-nay

Avlae: AHV-lay

Callas: KAL-lus

Cid Mei: sid MY

Derian: DEAR-ee-an

Esvara: es-VAR-ə

Habormoss: HA-bor-moss

Ipabog: IP-ə-bäg

Mahre: MAW-ree

Medici: med-EE-see

Ninian: NIN-yun

Olivetan: AH-liv-tan

Philor: fə-LORE

Quesnel: QUEZ-nel

Ragnar: RAG-nar

Languages

Calbharian: cal-bee-YAR-ee-an

Creatures

Bukavac: BOO-kə-vak

Places

Calbha's Curse: KAL-BEE-əs kərs

Diachrieno River: dee-ä-CREE-nō RI-ver

Fehrael: FAIR-el

Nantes: nan-TES

Navarre: nä-VAR

Orhe Mireth: OR-yə mer-ETH

Palanquin: PAL-ən-quin

Port Regael: port rə-GAL

Timaru Desert: ti-MAR-oo DEZ-ert

Tumbrel: TUM-brel

About the Author

J. Ellis Blaise hails from Lake Geneva, Wisconsin. At an early age, he descended into dungeons with pen and paper in hand. Enchanted by spells and sipping bitter tea warmed by dragon fire, he wrote tales of magical places. He gained an audience among his peers as his elementary school teachers read his stories to the class.

For nearly two decades, J. Ellis Blaise has served as a pastor, spiritual director, counselor, and chaplain. His debut novel, *The Fullness of Time*, began as a bedtime story for his four children. His wife—a creative genius with the flare and grace of a goddess—granted him frequent passage to the kingdom of Nantes, where he completed the first book in the trilogy.

Through myth and mire, the *Treasure in a Field* trilogy silhouettes the order, disorder, and reorder pattern of life.

www.ingramcontent.com/pod-product-compliance
Lightning Source LLC
Chambersburg PA
CBHW011654010726
47499CB00011B/3260